The Last Dance

By A. Foster
Aka Annette Foster

1 The Fountain

Dorothy died. It was plain as that. Her whole life had been that way. She was born, like all kids, grew-up on a farm in the middle of the flatlands, got married a little past sixteen years old, sadly never had kids, grew old and then died. Martin was standing in the middle of the Peaceful Saints Hospital entry way. After the doors tried to shut and spring back a couple of times, he finally noticed and moved just a little more. His feet carried him a bit further to the outside garden area. There was a fountain. It was noisy, yet pleasant. How can a thing be good and bad all at the same time? It had three lovely tiers, and fell slowly but methodically. Small birds played around the edges of the yard. It was a nice place. A hidden garden, built for calm. It was the first area you came to when you arrived at the huge white, sterile building, and the last thing before you left. It was protected, by yet another set of doors to the outside world. It was a place that felt welcoming…to the spirit.

Martin Cleaver wanted to shout at the inanimate object. That being the noisy, fountain. What would he shout? He had nothing to say. Words, caught in his throat. He was never a man of many words, but a part of him wanted to belt out, everything he had every uttered, in one breath, … but instead it would not come. Instead, he felt light-headed and lost.

The old man had been married just over forty six years. He was six foot high and still in fairly good shape, except for mornings. He had a hard time with mornings. Dorothy knew that and had ways of making it better. Some of it was because of the war. But everyone faced that kind of stuff, so Martin really did not put stock in depression or other mental maladies. Besides it would be okay. He would have to just muddle through. He had served his time, he knew how to get by in life. Yet, how was that going to work? Oh, and some nights. His legs would ache unbearably; Dorothy would rub them at times like that. Dorothy was gone. A wave of sadness like cold syrup washed over his heart and clung to his soul. Not sweet like on buttermilk pancakes made on Sundays after church when she finally got home, waiting for an expectant first bite, no. Not like that at all.

A sad thought further consumed his memories, no more pancakes. No more waiting for her to get home. No more shouting that she was late! Did he do that? Yes. He did. He remembered. He did not want to, but it happened more often than it should have. Why? Well. It would pass, so it never hurt anyone. Well, maybe his wife, but she knew he never meant any of the stuff he said. But some how standing by the cheerful water, he wanted to cry. He was a grown man, but he wanted to bawl.

"Get a hold of yourself. Go home." The words echoed in his head. They were distant. Like some one talking across the room. The statement was at him, rather that by him. Odd.

In total indecision he stood… waiting…

That part of him that he had refused to give. It was that small part, that one piece he always held back, he would not believe in her god. He would do anything for her, but nonsense was simply empty air. She was gone, and the world was upside down. It would never be better. He also, firmly did not want to believe directly because he was already in heaven. He was married to an angel. At times, well… he just forgot and took it for granted. It was not always like that, only at times. They both knew he loved her. "Faith", it had been a soar point between them for their whole life together. She prayed and he was a "good man". That was enough for him. That had always been enough for his family. They went to church. They never needed to be born again, whatever nonsense that was about. She would go on so; from time to time, Dorothy that is. Then one day she stopped. Why had she stopped? It was about the time she received the first stage diagnosis. It had never been clear to him why he did not want her prayers, now they were gone, some other piece of him was missing also.

"Mr. Cleaver, are you okay?" The nurse from inside had noticed him standing in the same place for a very long time. He had been back and forth for weeks, so she recognized him. In fact she would never forget his face or his wife's. The nurse had them all memorized, all those that came to fight evil of one kind or another. Their names were written in her bible at home. It was a habit she picked up from her grandmother. While in church she penciled in the names of all those she loved and prayed for… sometimes, many times… more than once if the need was great.

Nancy's grandmother had taken to writing just the names alone, as she told Nancy when she was a little girl, the needs were too many. So the old woman simply wrote the most important part, and let God handle the rest, with His hands, and His mighty glory. Nancy liked to remember her grandmother most. She had become a nurse directly because of the woman. An on-fire evangelist that believed in equal rights for all, especially women. That is how she ended up with a career. Grandma had seen to the price of her instruction and school, to give Nancy a life, she herself never had. That was okay too, as grandma preached by raising one, we all raise together. Just another reason she was so loved and missed by her granddaughter today and forever.

Nurse Barns was a professional and could tell from her experience "matters" were not okay. This specific matter, whatever "this was" had not been good for the big man, lost at the fountain. Dorothy's name was on the list, and Nancy knew the answer.

The old adage the bigger they fall…etc… well the words had clear truth in this place. Time and again, she had watched. Basically, he was not the first she had startled, by calling out; back into the present. They had to keep moving. That is what she told herself, as she prayed quietly, as to make sure no one else heard her. Some became offended at times. So sad…"The caretaker" knew that people that stop… die. That is what Nancy had become. The guardian of the fountain in a way. It was a lovely place for a reason; to help those who are sick feel better, to help those lost, find comfort, but for those ready to die, a dangerous calm. Not to be dwelt on, in case it lasts to long and the effects do not diminish quickly.

This man's name was on her memo board. Mr. Martin Cleaver, it was written. In case of death notify, next of kin followed by; Dorothy's full name and date of birth. Their affiliation; connection, married. Nothing personal or dear to their heart, just words, that made since to strangers. The names typed fresh and updated, the list that goes out to the whole staff after midnight each night, was already in her hand. "They" count the living and the dead. It is all numbers to the shadows that run hospitals. Those that make sure the lights come on and stay on. Yet, the names, well the men and women that work with the real people, the lives that are saved and lost, they never forget. Maybe some can, but they are not many. Nancy Barns had seen Dorothy's name, when she came in. She had seen it constantly since. Now she would see it disappear. It was a great loss. She was a bright smile, up until the last.

Martin refocused his eyes and glanced back at the pretty nurse. The woman wore a crisp white uniform, and a bright cheerful name tag, he could simply not read at the moment. She could not have been more then twenty. Maybe she was older? Can you be a nurse and be so young?

Where had all the years gone? Where is my Dorothy? To many thoughts came charging in all at once and the weak man felt overwhelmed. Yet he was a military man. Or at least he had been. This load would just have to be adjusted and repacked. Then it would have to be carried. How far? The distance you may ask?, the answer, "the rest of his life."

"I am okay, thank you ma'am." A lie, but one he was unaware of telling. Martin moved on out the double doors, leaving the protected garden behind. He tried to avoid looking back at her as he left. That might lead to having to speak further, which was not going to happen.

Martin Cleaver made himself go outside. It was cold. It was also dark, clouds were black and menacing as far as he could see in every direction. what time was it? Early, the hour of the wolf maybe... a little passed two. He really had no idea. There was a light snow on the ground. He could not remember when it fell, or what day of the week it might even be. He made himself step into the parking lot to find his car. That was not as easy task. Normally, you might think…, no problem. Well, this was not one of those "kinds of days" or nights, or early mornings. This was nothing like any time, marked on the calendar he could ever remember or relate to. It was never going to be easy again.

*A short note to say
Thank you for supporting a true dreamer.*

God Bless!

Death is Liar

My name is "C",
Don't say it out loud.
If you label me,
You reveal me.
I will deny I exist.
I hide.
I have power,
I change your life,
I kill…
And all those you love.
I touch their lives,
With, evil and unclean hands…
I take hope away,
And dash faith to the ground.
My name is "C"
And the truth is I lie.
That is the real source, of my deceit.
That is how I win.
Listen to my song.

Poems

Death is a Liar
End
Pancakes
Keeping Still
The Burden is Light
A Blanket from the Bin
Lord
Tricks in the Dark
Just Strands of Straw
Loss
Safe Havens
Unseen Color
(to see you)
Forever Dance

The Legal Stuff

This is a work of fiction.
Names, characters, places, and incidents
are the products of the author's imagination only.

All rights reserved.
Copy write A. Foster, Ann Foster, Annette Foster.
c/o BooksbyAFoster.com.

Again…"This is a work of fiction.
Names, characters, places, and incidents
are the products of the author's imagination or are used "fictitiously".
Any resemblance to actual events, locales, or persons,
living, dead, mistaken for dead, or undead,
is
entirely
coincidental."

Thank you.

Oh and because this is a fiction everything in it is a lie,
or based on the truth of people I know.
Which is again fiction!

Do you understand?
Okay.

A special thank you;

Pastor Dave.
He taught me…to read the bible, really read it.
The magic of the words, a gift to be shared.
A living, gift.

A note to;

Cowboy, I know this is not a western as promised, but I
will write that one next. :)

The angels I remember,
have too many names to be listed, but that does not
mean they are not written here,
in every word.

Don Quixote, and sweet Dulcinea,
ever a song of heaven,
sang to friends, claimed.

Table of Contents

1 The Fountain	2
2 End	15
3 The House	16
4 The Road	21
5 Morning has broken...	40
6 What Happens?	54
7 Lisa	70
8 Angels Fly, Men Walk, We all Dream	76
9 The Church on Sunday	86
10 The Madness of Death	114
11 Loose Ends and New Beginnings	122
12 Well Intentioned Intruders	127
13 Tedra, God's gift	138
13 Pink is the Color of Real Roses	152
13 AGAIN	160
14 The Morning	167
15 The Bank, the Cost of Living	177
16 History Means Everything	186
17 The Fires of Loss	201
18 Cakewalk	213
19 Bad Luck?	216
20 All Plans Need a "B"	232
21 The Ride to Heaven	235
22 The Point of Friends	244
23 The Flight of Angels	249
24 It was getting later...	259
25 A Promotion, A Raise, Hope	269
26 A Bridge Too Far	279
27 Passing the Flame	287
28 Divide and Conquer	295
29 Another Bad Penny	303
30 Someone, Call the Police?	209

31 Dorothy, a fragrance... a perfume.	313
32 What you bring with you...	316
33 Grateful Hearts and Ever Friends	327
34 Insurance Pay and Life Returns to Normal	330
35 It's not a waltz!	335
Notes and Acknowledgments	350
International Poet	351
Jesus Loves You	352
More Books	353
God Bless Flag	355

Thank you...

God!

Beginning with the...

(2)End

The coldest place in the hospital is not the patience room.
It is not where they perform surgery,
although it is very cold there... as well.
It is downstairs in the laboratory.
That is where brain-y-act people put things in jars.
They have no hearts so it makes things very easy.
They color outside the lines to help people,
In a different way,
everyone is a number.
you understand...

But it does not always work.
Sometimes it even turns out wrong,
badly!

No magic cure.
Some times no hope at all.
A big white building that hands out
death,
that we have to pay for...
It seems unfair at best.
at worst it is a mindful plan
to strip us of our weak souls.

The old man went home to an empty house.
Dorothy had died.
Hope had died.
There was no place else to go,
but home.

(3) The House

Martin did not remember the drive at all, up until things went wrong yet again in the same 24 hours. Vaguely there were lights, he stopped when he had to and went when it was necessary. That was automatic. He had been going home to the same place for so long, that to go anywhere else was simply unclear. It was late January. The weather was cold and the ice on the roads played tricks. It took some effort, but still in the end it was all reflex. Martin just went through the motions. That was the only thing he was sure of at this point. Well that had got him at least most of the way home.

The lights that passed him from the oncoming side were very bright. They gave him a headache. Maybe it was not the lights at all. When had he eaten last? Martin could not remember. He was not hungry. Perhaps he thought to stop, but it was late or really too early, and most things were closed. He hated fast food anyway. It all tasted the same and Dorothy would be angry. She said it was bad for him, bad for his heart. It was going to kill him. That was ironically not funny at all. Mostly because Martin had no sense of humor and the very idea of irony escaped him. The subject would make him mad at times. Dorothy had been quiet and rarely laughed. She did not want to upset him. He could be that way for days. When was that? Time was funny, at least at the moment. Or rather ever since earlier when the man in white from the hospital told him, he had to let go. What ever that meant?

"Let go." Two small words. Five letters from the alphabet. Hardly a sentence really, much less a direction, a command, an action.

Martin tried to remember what Dorothy had said the very last time… "Sweetheart, please talk to Doctor Macsen. He is a good friend." That was also the very final and last thing he wanted to do, air his past in front of strangers. Yeah they had known each other for years, him and the Doc., but associates and getting your cold checked out is not the same, as telling someone you see things, or people are hiding in the barn.

A small voice in his head, a bad voice with an ugly tone reminded him. Dorothy can not be mad anymore, she is dead. He had to let that mull a bit. What had the woman said? Cancer? Why had Dorothy not told him sooner? That was only one of about fifty thousand questions he wanted to ask, someone, anyone. No one had any answers that he could understand. They all kept saying the word dead. That was at the end of every conversation to the point, there was nothing left, nothing at all.

A deer jumped out, from no where. He was only a few miles or so from home, and he should have been watching better. No, he did not hit it. Thankfully, but the little truck did swerve hard and raced sideways on the old road for several feet, ending up in the ditch. A large knot was now forming on Martin's head and the pain he already had, simply doubled. This was getting harder, was it ever going to end? The pit in the man's stomach was his answer. Dorothy's god must be really happy? He gained the most beautiful woman in the world and left…, what? Martin. That was the answer. That was the whole answer, and he did not like it. They were only in their sixties. It was too soon to go. It was not fair and if there was a god, he was not kind. That is the way Martin felt. Strongly, fiercely, passionately, his mood was consumed with a sad, ugly darkness.

With his left hand he felt along the door panel and opened the door. It was hard to do. The bushes pressed in from the exterior. Martin shoved with all his force and it gave way. The cold air outside, woke him from his stupor. It was like a growing haze since he left his sweet wife's side. What were they going to do with her now? What happens next? Why is she not in the truck yelling at him for bad driving? He wished with his whole heart that he could hear her scream at him. She never did that, no not once. Yet, at the moment, it would sound like music to his ears. Instead, there was only silence. He got out, turned and reached back in for his jacket. It can be cool here at night, even cold. His hand grabbed the thick coat, but not before brushing softly against her white wool sweater she wore to church. It had ended up behind the seat. Tears sprang to his eyes, but he squinted hard and forced them back. She left him and that was not fair. He refused; he simply refused to think more about it at the moment. His head pounded.

The next thing happened. Martin was looking at Dorothy. She was smiling and laughing. It was like sweet music. Something he remember strongly, forgotten so long ago, that it only now re-presented all that was missed, a vision, a dream, a hallucination from the blow to his head? The sparkle in her eye and the tiny dimples in her cheeks, a real angel. When had he forgotten to look at her like that? He could not tell how old she was before him. The visage in his mind and memory was so perfect. She was just Dorothy, beautiful, lovely and the underappreciated wife of Martin Cleaver.

"You need to hurry." The countenance of his kind love had turned serious. "Quickly now. You need to get home. Walk with me…" the woman seemed to fade slowly and then vanish before him. She seemed first to turn toward home and then simply slip away.

The street in both directions was empty. The truck was in the ditch and Dorothy was dead. Martin felt his brow. There was blood trickling down from the wound. Not a lot maybe, he could not tell, but it was wet. He was a little giddy. It was probably because he had not taken time to eat. He kept coming back to that. He should have stopped back at "Big Burgers" regardless of the consequences. Eating nothing had penalties of a different kind. His stomach was full of acid, and he had no chalk pills to stop the burn. Well, that was just part of the long list of things going wrong, that had no end at all.

It was just a few hours before dawn, maybe so Martin did not concern himself with checking for a flash light before leaving the car. The house was not more than another five or six miles up the road. He would just walk, and come back later for the truck. A spark of anger consumed his heart. Martin turned with one, fluid if somewhat erratic motion and kicked the drivers door. "Bang!" The dent was about ten inches. A waive of dizziness almost knocked him down as he considered how stupid that action was by any accounting. It had damaged his perfect truck, it had hurt his foot, his leg, his knee, and the world spinning was going to have to stop, if he was going to walk the distance. Martin waited. Gradually everything slowed and then returned to normal again. Vengeance against a piece of inanimate mental might be mentally satisfying but physically the vehicle wins. Even if damaged it could never feel the pain Martin had wished to impart.

The tired man closed the door and struggled up the small incline. It was a bit more difficult than expected but the whole day had gone that way, why should this be different.? Finally the man achieved the road, the tarmac, the black. He stood, if a little unsteadily and looked back at the vehicle in the ditch. It was getting later with every breath, but he needed to look. The front end was banged in bad. The passenger door had a log sticking through the window and the back window was busted clean out. How had he thought it was only a bump? He should not be standing on the black at all. He should be dead. Wow, luck was a great thing. Then he had mixed thought. If he had died, would he see Dorothy? Could he see Dorothy? Would he ever see her again? Tears clouded his vision.

"Luck", Martin spoke the word out loud to no one. He sure could use a little, the good kind. His truck was totaled. He would have to call the insurance man and tell him what happened. First, he had better get home. Martin was so tired and there had not been even one car down the avenue in hours. Only his! Martin turned and left the crash. The truck was not going anywhere, anytime soon.

The sky above was cloudy still, even thicker than before. But, still...here and there openings to the heavens, bright stars beyond could be seen, sparkling. The temperature was probably only 34 or 35 degrees. That was brisk, at least for Martin Cleaver. He liked it. He had always liked the cold. Well, maybe that was not true really. He liked the quiet life and living way out, provided that. Not so many people around to get into your business and try to tell you how to handle your life. He liked the freedom to do as he wanted to do. Dorothy and Martin kept to their selves, mostly. Now, it was just going to be…Martin.

Pancakes

My wife, I remember makes the very best, or she did.
I have to get that through my head.
She is back at the hospital, laying there, not moving.
How did that happen,
I don't know.

We were at breakfast talking, just talking.
No. She was talking, I never did. I listened.
I wish that I could hear her talk now.
I wish that she would nag at me.
Tell me to do something, anything...
That I do not want to do,
Just so that I can say...
I have done it,
for you.

For you my wife, of many years, numbers illusive with time.
Passing us by faster than we know, that they go.
The ones we love.
They leave us here.
They go where we can not follow.
To their God. To their place.
They depart.

A place called heaven... sounds far...

I want to go.
I want to be with her.
She said He loves everyone,
even me.

She was beautiful, I miss her.
She was everything, God give her back.
Please, ... hear me.

(4) The Road

The avenue was a two lane road that went from the off ramp at highway six just out of town, to the small lake up at Rock Mountain. The lake's name was Potato. Martin had always thought that funny. He had never been out there, maybe because of the name. He never really liked comedy stuff or too much laughing, but that has already been said. It was just…it was loud, too loud at times and made him angry. Dorothy and her family went for a picnic, a retreat thing, once. He remembered it suddenly, as he passed the small sign by the road. It was just a sign, but it made him feel, even more empty than before. Memories were like that, powerful and unexpected, surfacing when least wanted at times.

They, her relations, came to visit, for a few days. There was a religious meeting of some kind and they talked her into going. Even if he was not happy with the idea, Dorothy had still gone with them. Martin hated visitors. That was the other time he had been by himself. They, the whole group had camped at Potato Lake for a few days. Oh sure, he was invited, but really. That was never going to happen. He hated camping or being outside ever since his return from overseas. He wanted to be at home. That is where he belonged. That is where Dorothy belonged.

Why?
The revival thing?

That was not important, and he could not figure out why it was paramount to her then, or important to him now. She had given him that sorrowful look, until he went to his room that day. That was his only way, of letting her go. He did not want to watch her leave, even then.

Nothing Martin wanted anything to do with really. Not a good reason to go to the lake for the first time anyway, and since then, he had never found another reason to go at all, either. That did not seem important to the man until this moment. Some very, very small part wished he had gone, if only to have been with Dorothy. He noted the sign as he passed, but continued on. A heavy feeling of loss, a wave of regret came and then receded, put aside by exhaustion. Even so…

Martin wondered now what Potato Lake looked like? Was it blue or green? Big or small? Dorothy's hair bright and lovely like honey, how would it have looked, so pretty against that back ground? That and the trees, his mind quickly colored in the pines he knew would be all around the place. It was a cheerful thought, if a sad one, as he never went when he could have gone. The wave again came and retreated a little slower this time then the last.

Along the Avenue, there were only a handful of homes, lots off the main-way that filled the area. Each had several acres to its ownership, so neighbors were not really close at all. This was a quiet place and people tended to keep to themselves, yet they still knew each other. Many went to church, if not all those Dorothy knew. They would come and pick her up, every Sunday. His wife had stopped driving a few years ago. It was about the same time she started getting sick. That was annoying at times. She would be sick all week and do nothing, no cooking or cleaning or other things, then go to church. She would go even if she was terribly bad off toward the end. Martin could not understand, but she did seem somewhat better, on those days. That is when they dropped her back at the house, then she started downward again. He hated that.

How could she be "up" for God, and down about coming home? Even now, Martin Cleaver was at a loss, it made no sense.

How come Dorothy would do that? Why would she leave him? He loathed being left. Ever since he got back from the service, things had been, well not right. He only wanted her around, everyone else in the whole world could die, as far as he really cared. He just wanted to be home with her. Martin wanted… he wanted…

Martin walked on into the darkness. It seemed to deepen, if black could ever get blacker? There were no street lamps along the edges at all. This was rural, the way he liked it. Close to the country, the animals, and things that mattered. Well, not anymore. It was more like, things that were left. He was left. He was among the things that were left behind. The man continued walking very slowly. One foot was dragging, just a little. His gate was more like a shuffle, but there was no one to notice, no one human anyway.

Where to?
Home.
No.
A house with four walls,
windows, doors, and floors…
All empty.
A house, a dwelling, a structure.
Now vacant.

Ever so slowly the few clouds above that commanded the sky, lost ferocity. The offered bad weather cleared reluctantly, to present a thousand, thousand, thousand stars. Brightly they sparkled in the heavens, like a chorus of angels. Their lovely and timeless brilliance a picture painted only by the hand of God. No other artist born could have brushed the stokes across the heaven and left such beauty to capture the breath from the heart, before it is or was... taken.

Martin was deaf, and continued to walk with purpose. He did not want to look up. In fact it was all he could do to walk forward. Not having eaten, a car accident, and "all the rest" which he could not stop returning to, had taken an extreme toll on Martin Cleaver.

Violently.

"I HATE YOU!" The man screamed out without prior notice, without realizing he was going to say a thing. He yelled it from his heart. He pulled it from his soul and made words from feelings, he had no other way to express. "I Hate You!" He never stated the "who", as it was implied by his fist clenched toward heaven's gate. Tears filled his eyes till he could no longer squint, them back. They fell. They fell until he was blind, and his knees became weak. He fell as well, forward onto the black.

A wave of dizziness clutched him, like a giant doll and through his insides against himself. "It", nauseous waves kept coming and coming, his head pounded and he could not lift himself back up at all. Martin lay there in the darkness beneath the stars crying for the first time, in his entire life. He felt small. He also knew, exactly how tiny he really was, without hope, and the universe...laughing right at him was just too much. Heartless creator, wishful thinking, was all he could consider, Martin felt there was nothing left.

"Dorothy, please… don't go, where I can not follow." Wet, salty, warm tears of heartache rolled down his cheeks. Loss, grief and forever combine to overcome even the toughest warriors. They are fierce opponents, when faced alone. Martin was alone. That is how he felt and that is how he was going to have to get used too feeling. The weight of it was greater than he dared to consider, even now. A sense of terror was forming. The kind that makes you feel you are on the ocean, far out beyond the land, and know you can not swim. You are safe, but not. The boat is still afloat, but the waves, they grow larger in size by the moment. There is a sense of direction, but no compass to show the path. There is only the motion of movement.

The darkness of the night grew, reclaiming the thought of mornings arrival. A deepening whirl, a black hole gathering power with emotions combined together careless of the outcome. "It" liked how things were going. It wanted too wrap itself tightly around the man and make him part of itself, its very being, the fabric of its existence.

"Yes, be still, be mine…" hissing, softly, an echo, the real sound; black crickets on a lonely road, otherwise unheard by the living. Still green leaves fell early from several of the trees near by, for no reason…at all. Or at least none that would make any sense. Leaving the limbs bare. The surroundings extremely cold, and yet colder still by forces beyond nature. A drop of several points on the thermometer, would have been true, had there been one on hand to read. Instead, Martin Cleaver could see his breath come before him in clouds of white, and then drift to nothing.

Fear breeds,
in places...
where we give it rest.
Give it no respite.
Allow it no ease.

Growing further, stronger still, doubling and reemerging...seeing that It was gaining a hold. Joyously It relished and savored the moment. The demise of the weak, the goal a sweet cascade of ugly and evil married into depression and loss. If it had hands it would have rubbed them together, symbolically back and forth as if passing a great treasure between It's palms and fingers. A soul is a high valued commodity. A believer is worth much, but unbelievers, are still a steady diet, to minions fed on the "black".

A light, a single light in the far distance shown ever brightly in the forefront of Martin's spinning vision. It was coming right at him. Not slowly, not quickly, just steadily. He blinked and tried to focus, to see. It was painful, and basically useless. Fear, gut fear grew. Was he heard? Was "HE" coming to take him to a bad place? Was "HE" real? The man could barely swallow. His tears, dried upon his face, cold traces of scars yet unhealed. Breathing was getting harder with the passing of every moment…

What was death like? Would it hurt less than now? or more?
Martin fought the deeper inner desire to scream out, even as it filled his spirit.

Closer and closer the light came. It grew larger and somehow more powerful as it approached. The brilliance was otherworldly. A horror in the pit of Martin's stomach came up like a burning from bad food. This was the end. He was already dead? The roaring was terrible. There was a hell and he was going there now. Dorothy, his sweet wife, begged him to believe, begged him to be a good man, but…he never did. He did not want to. He had seen bad things in bad places, and God was never there. He looked. Well at least that is what he felt, swirling in his gut. A bad awful empty kind of emotion, of loss, is all he had. It was all he had for a long time, before even this night.

Martin Cleaver had killed people. He had taken the lives of twenty-eight men. They were the enemy and he did it for his country. Yet, that was not the end of the story. It was only the tip, leading into the first paragraph. Martin had been married only a year, when he went in. But he was good at everything and advancement was sure. But not the usual kind. The important kind that changes lives, in places where the law is unclear, or gray, or made up as it goes. Coming home after that, well... home had and has new meaning, when you believe yourself already a survivor of hell. His nightmares had been bad for a while, Dorothy had been steady the whole way. She was a great lady, and never fell short on anything. That is why he had been drawn to her, and why he married her. She was a prize worth wining.

The only bright spot in Martin's life, was Dorothy. Now that was forever taken. Martin's mouth was dry and his tongue was stuck to the roof tight. He could not speak at all. He wanted to scream, but simply… could not. His body made a noise, but unheard over the metal sound(s) that followed.

The resonance of bad noise(s) coupled with the timbre of their meaning; brakes squealing filled the air, branches splitting from limbs, gravel and rock, snow and dirt... mixing and colliding and recreating norm into disaster. Strong metal and old rubber on the black-hard road, wrestled to see who would win? The struggle was both mechanical, and somehow spiritual, with the later prevailing in a higher sense. Perhaps otherworldly in the way that physics did not play fair. The road was iced, and refused traction, but the force of determination was met with destiny. The dawn had been subdued by the darkness, thinking it had won, yet the war was not over, not even begun. The horrific moment was coming to an end, and nothing would be the same.

Martin lay still. Afraid beyond belief. He shook. Every part of his body from his toes to his nose, he hurt, with cold and pain in-specific to, and not part of how he found himself on the ground at all.

How had he come to be here, in the middle of nowhere? He was nearly home, but not. Instead he was lost, damaged and waiting for the next thing to happen, in his life.

"In the valley, when we are lost,
ever does He walk beside us."
Angels sing...a beautiful thing!

"Dorothy, sweet Dorothy, I will never see you again." The man spoke low as if in prayer, but not. "I am…" he could not voice the word. He fought his dry mouth, arid as a desert in mid summer. "I am…" he tried again. Nothing would come forth. Pain, loss, and now deep fear reigned in his heart.

The chaotic noise drew to a low rumble. The smell of rubber burned on black top, mixed with dirt and road debris was an intoxicating combination. The noise, an engine maybe?

If "they" were from hell
and come to take him,
they were not
traveling first class.

Then, from nowhere, or perhaps directly from heaven?, a lovely face came within Martin's view. She was like a sprite, a fairy flower from some silly book. Angelic and beautiful beyond mere words, her visage hovered over him. She had bright green eyes, light brown hair similar to spun gold, and a look that would bring joy to even cut flowers. The beautiful other-worldly, young woman then spoke. Her lips moved, and soft sounds came out. Martin could not quite understand what she said. He wanted to. He just could not.

Finally, he struggled out, "Are you an angel?" His words mumbled, the very best he could. They felt thick in his mouth and he could not remember when he had last drank anything?

She gave him a bright smile, but did not answer. Instead she was just as suddenly gone. She had turned back to the truck, waiting near by and waved to her father. She then ran back and opened the door. "It is Mr. Cleaver, Dad. He is hurt." The teen looked expectantly at her father. She held the door open waiting. The hot air from the cab escaping into the night.

"Okay. Let me get my bag." Sheldon Farman was a veterinarian. He lived just up the road from Mr. and Mrs. Cleaver. They had not really been friends ever, but Mr. Farman knew Dor from church. That is how he had been introduced. A couple of years back at a social pot luck, Dorothy Cleaver had helped arrange the party for some friends, leaving to another state. She was like that, always helping others, making them feel wanted, needed and missed. Well that was his first meeting and his first impression of her anyway, and everything he had heard since or saw by a distance, reflected the same.

The Vet thought first to go for a phone and call for help, but that would take precious time. So he dismissed it. The nearest place was Dor's or past that his own home. Or take Mr. Cleaver back to town? That was a bit farther for sure. This was a bad spot in general, hard to get help out here...easy that is... anyway. Life was a struggle. Better to act quickly do what he could and get the man, his neighbor into the truck. Then he could get him some real help at the emergency center near the firehouse, maybe. That would still be a long drive, so better to rely on his own hard learned skills first, then make a plan.

Lisa closed the door and waited for her father beside the truck.

Sheldon opened his door, stepped out, pulled the side lever to the seat and grabbed his bag. He was as close to a human doctor as anyone was going to get at this hour and in this place, with any speed at all. Mr. Farman had also served over seas as a medic… so this was second nature to the man regardless. Move quickly, efficiently and handle what was needed, that was his training. That is how he approached everything in life. This was going to be no different at all.

He left the truck lights on, and also pressed the flashers. He left the engine running. The lights would help to see things clearly and the motor would continue to make the cab warm. Sheldon then moved with purpose to the victim's side. He, the man on the ground, was about twenty feet out from the front of the truck. As he moved toward Mr. Cleaver, his daughter followed in his tracks. Ever at hand if he needed anything, she was prepared. Sick animal or sick human, all the same.

It was very cold, bitterly so. Sheldon knew he had to move fast.

Martin's eyes were filled with light. A devastating kind of emotion grew like a wild storm, like the seed of a giant tree sprang from a lifetime held back. He could hear the engine, and his heart knew things were happening, even if he could not comprehend all of it. Moments later, there was figure. It had hands on him…, it had put strange hands on him. They were firm, not unfriendly, but insistent. They checked him from head to foot.

Someone was talking to him, but they were just words, sounds, tumbled together and sent back and forth, from no one he could see first hand.

There were the other sounds also. The bugs, the crickets... not so loud as before, but still present in the background of the moment. How could their be bugs of any kind in this cold? It seemed like a fair question if he had not been so lost in a whirl of thoughts that would not hold still. The answer was common sense, they could not be real. The uncommon sound plagued him, even still.

"Am I dead?" He chocked the syllables out. "Is this hell?" Either no one heard him, his breathing labored, or there was no one willing to answer. It did not help to calm him. His heart beat faster, and his dread began to mount. He took a few breaths.

Some how it passed. The bad feeling was reseeding and the safe, peaceful one, he felt around Dorothy was returning. It was because of the hands. They would not stop. They were kind, but thorough. They were not angry, or threatening, but helping hands. They moved all over again, re-confirming, making sure things were okay, assessing what was going on. What had happened?

The fact,
the younger man did not hear Martin's words.
Only God heard them.
He hears and knows everything,
before it is every said or known.

No broken bones, that was good. There was a big gash on Martin's brow over his left eye. Also, Sheldon found a large bump, higher up. Perhaps a concussion? Perhaps not. Hard to tell, on the road, in the darkness, late at night or in this case early in the morning. Sheldon glanced at his watch. "How did this man get here?"

Blood had clotted and made things look worse surely, but all of it was easily serious enough to take down any man of Martin's size and weight. That was not even inclusive of his age. It was a testament to his stamina that he was out here now still alive… on the road at this hour.

"Mr. Cleaver. Can you hear me?" Sheldon tried to make sure it was not worse than it looked. "Mr. Cleaver. What happened?" He waited for some sign of clear response.

"You need to come with me now. I will take you to the hospital." The last word hung there in the air. It was an evil word, a wicked, malevolent declaration of an action Martin would rather die than take. It represented everything that had happened since Dorothy first got sick. All in one eight letter word, defined by pain, medication that had side effects, loss of dreams, grief unbearable, and hope forever taken. Just like his wife… gone.

Martin heard it like a yell. A mortal calling to the last word you ever want to hear again, echoing all things raw. "Please no. Please do not take me there. I am begging. Please. They killed her. They killed me. They kill everyone." He began to ramble.

The response was heart wrenching. What to do?

"You are hurt, Mr. Cleaver. We need to go and get you fixed up." Sheldon figured the man was in shock obviously. He slowly tried to help the aged victim back to his feet. Soothing sounds of comfort that he used on horses, cows, and other wild animals came out of Sheldon. Second nature to him, as that is how he calmed the worst patient's back down. They needed a steady hand. His grandfather who had raised Sheldon since his parents died in an accident, had taught him that. He had been a veterinarian too, that is or was Mr. Farman Senior. The big man had taught his grandson all about animals, and more about people, than he was aware of. The ways to sing them to sleep when they are in pain, without fear, or to fix something quickly, before it is noticed worse than first expected, were skills. The old man, blessed Sheldon with a quiet spirit, taught by long, lonely hours holding sick creatures with every number of legs. That coupled with his sincere love of God, made a perfect combination. Sheldon had received all of it, in one form or another, by heredity or his faith in is Grandfather, which only gave him stronger faith in God as well.

Sheldon's grandfather was a wise man. Gone now, lost to cancer, but his wisdom no less sharp. He told his grandson before he passed, that people often misunderstand their own emotions. They get confused. So treat them softly, like God' treats his smallest creature. Kindness and gentleness; were the secrets of the veterinarian trade, but above all comfort every man's soul was the lesson of his Senior, that was as God expected. Sheldon could hear him even now, quietly in the back of his mind, somewhere in his heart, cheering him forward. Helping him, to be strong for this stranger, this man in need that Sheldon could not and would not fail. That was his first and only intent. Sheldon's grandfather's honored memory and God's hand, were ever present to the situation now unfolding. Sheldon knew that and was sure with his whole spirit.

The young man was God fearing. He did not believe he had come across Mr. Cleaver by accident. That was to easy. More than once he had seen things happen in his life. He knew right off that this was important, not just because he was human and it was the decent thing to do. He knew from Mr. Cleaver's response that the darkness on the road this night, was deeper than he could see. Sheldon dared to glance around. Only for a moment, as time was passing… all wrong. Like when you feel it should be earlier, but is is… far later than you know. The echo of the crickets was still ever present. It was not a comforting sound as it usually would be. Crickets in the forest, early morning...or late at night. But it was cold? It felt ominous and tight, like something waiting to reach out…but held back. There was a creepy feeling of being watched as well. Eyes, unseen but close by, that were absolutely unfriendly on any scale, were all around.

"It will be okay, Mr. Cleaver." Sheldon called back to his daughter Lisa, over his shoulder. She had remained waiting, not far. She was about half way between the truck and the man on the ground. "Bring me a blanket from the back of the truck. They are in the camper. Hurry please!" His voice was strong and had the right tone. The one that would tell both Mr. Cleaver and Lisa, that everything was going to be okay, without actually saying those words. That by the simple sound of his voice, and a command, Lisa already knew to expect, he had set the stage for everything that followed. In fact, she kind of kicked herself for not thinking ahead, taking things for granted and getting at least a blanket right away. That is along with whatever else she could carry her father's way... but she wanted to be on hand first. Sometimes Lisa had been needed to hold things, help with bleeding or other procedures that took more than just Sheldon Farman, veterinarian, first class. She was being groomed to be her father's partner in the business. Well it was a family business anyway, so partner was a funny word. She just wanted to be a vet like him and work with her dad the rest of her life. Her father was a great man, and would do all the right things, he always did, so she watched carefully, listened intently, and moved with speed as necessary.

*One step at a time.
Assurance of the fact
that all was well, was important.
It kept wild creatures from bolting,
and helped small scared ones
be a little less flighty.*

    Lisa who had been standing at the edge of the light beam on the road, still within its brightness, ever watchful, waited. She started to step a little closer, and it felt like twenty degrees would drop, just beyond the edge of the brilliance. It was not true, maybe a trick of the excitement, Lisa thought. But cold was cold, and she hated the cold. Hearing her father's request she responded immediately. She had been intent on her father's every move and every action, doing what he did best as best that he could. In response to his instruction, she ran around the side of the truck to the back, and threw open the camper door. She jumped right in and rustled though the boxes. Grabbed the first thick blanket she came to. It was wool and smelled like warm horse. Lisa loved that smell. It made her feel closer to memories of rides in the fields and happy things. Maybe it would help make this lost soul feel a little better? A passing thought from a young girl, a prayer on her lips, all the while, doing as she was told. Not speaking of the physical, but her own sweet thoughts of rides and quiet times, put her own remembrances closer to Him. So maybe somehow, those same feelings, would help here and now? That is what she wished to convey with the simple cloth; a horse blanket, and unspoken prayer. "The Lord" always beside her… listening…

*Ever that I speak to you…
Ever that I dance for you…
Ever let me sing…
Saved, daughter of the King!*

    When she climbed back out of the camper, onto the pavement and came around to the light, she could see it was the blue one. Perfect. That was the wool blanket with the big star. She liked it best. It was extra soft, but very strong. From where she stood at the moment, Lisa could see the old man on the ground even in the deeper darkness this far from the truck. He looked dead. Laying still, there on the black surface. Swiftly she went to her father's side with the bundle.

Unexpectedly… Martin Cleaver made a small noise. It was not understood as words, but more an utterance of feeling. It was the very sound of a spirit, lost in the dark, waiting for the process of movement, the direction "north by northwest", a piece from his past. It made perfect sense and nonsense to everyone and no one. Neither Lisa or her father responded. It was not for them. It was something different altogether. Yet, the world between death and life, is a precarious place, that few ever get the chance to view or hear the echo of…

Now standing beside her father, "Will he be okay?" Lisa stood quite still, holding it out. She was scared for the old man, it was so cold out here. He must surely be half frozen. The blue blanket was all she could offer, but her heart wished it was more. She did not speak very loudly. The whole area felt thick. There were no clouds in the sky, but the pressure was like a heavy storm, had come up from the south unexpected. If she closed her eyes, she could really feel it. It was like a building of electricity that told you to go inside, all without a word. Her hair felt funny, like it lifted and stood out, ever so… Prickly bumps rose as well. Not goose, not any foul, just bumps… scary response to something…not even seen… indeed.

Lonely roads of life, we travel…
making decisions in the dark,
that take us to another level, of thought…

Sheldon, answered, "I think he will be okay. I don't know what happened, but we need to get him into the truck." The girl's father tried harder to lift Martin. He had done this before unsuccessfully, but he knuckled down and pulled again. The older man was at least forty, okay maybe fifty pounds overweight. Sheldon was not a wimp, but Martin was not helping at all.

Martin was awake again. He seemed to have come to. He was definitely not asleep or passed out, but sort of still out of it. He was not combative as much as simply hard to handle. Like a drunk that had lost control of his arms and legs, given over to the alcohol. In this case, there was no smell. What ever happened to Mr. Cleaver had much the same effect, but obviously was not self induced. Or at least from what Sheldon could ascertain so far.

"Please, don't take me back. Don't ever take me back. She is there. She is still there. She is supposed to be at home waiting." A chocking sound for a few moments followed. Sheldon stayed still, hoping he would learn from the muttered words, something that would help.

"What are they going to do? What is going to happen?" Martin mumbled more. Most of the words uttered, too low for anyone to catch. The only part that was extremely clear is that he did not want to go anywhere but home. That was crystal, to Sheldon and his daughter. To do anything else, would be difficult at best, even if it was in his own best interest.

That was dilemma.

A moment of recognition passed Lisa's features. "We can take him to his house, it is close. He is Mrs. Dorothy's husband, father. I know him. I am sure it is him. Well, I have seen him once or twice." She recognized him in the brightness of the truck lights. It was just as she first thought. How had he come to be here?

"Yes, I thought I knew him as well. He looked familiar from pictures I have seen a time or two. Dor must be at home? She will be worried sick. We will take him there."

Lisa watched as her Dad struggled, offering what assistance she could. In one expert motion, he had retrieved the blanket and wrapped it across the old man's shoulders. Lisa stepped forward immediately and lent her own shoulder as well to help balance things out. Now they were all three staggering together back to the open cab. The heater was doing a great job, filling the space with waiting comfort, despite the openness of the cab door, left ajar by accident.

> *The comfort of God…*
> *Can be felt, physically, and emotionally.*
> *It is a gift, paid for in blood.*

After several minutes they had managed to stuff Mr. Cleaver into the center. Lisa's father climbed back into the driver's seat and his daughter took her place, shotgun. They all had bright red faces from the cold and the warm cab was a welcome sanctuary. It seemed to also wake Mr. Cleaver out of his shock if just a little. His eyes flickered and opened. He did not seem drunk, but dazed. Sheldon would have to wait to get the whole story. First things first, get the man to a safe place and see to his needs.

"Thank you." Realizing all that was going on. Martin was stunned that he was still moving at all. "Thank you both." He went on to explain haltingly. He had been walking from a crash…the crash, trying to get home. Then the storm came up, and he could not remember a lot after that. He mumbled a bit more and then went silent. His eyes closed. He seemed to kind of fall asleep, which was not good at this point.

Sheldon checked his wrist. He had passed out maybe, but his breathing was easy and pulse okay. The small town veterinarian kept driving. Better to be home, then missing from everywhere that anyone would know to look, on the road at this hour, in any case. Besides, his own heart had felt lighter since they had returned to the truck. The gloom that seemed to cling to everything, slipped away now…forgotten, unimportant. Getting Mr. Cleaver home, that was everything.

Sheldon and Lisa both looked at each other but said nothing. The sky above was completely clear. All storms had been passed for nearly a whole day from the area. There had been a few clouds maybe, but storm? None they knew of. They did not want to upset him. But his words were confusing, especially about the weather. However, they said nothing. They passed a "glance" between themselves over the matter, but that was all.

    Mr. Cleaver had already had a rough day. The strange part is, or, was that he never mentioned Dorothy. Not while they were in the stranger's truck, driving toward home. He wanted to. He found, he had no words, and could find none as the vehicle traveled on. He felt like a cow had sat down on top of his chest, and breathing was difficult. If that noise would just quit? That flat sound, far in the back ground…, he could think. Then again, maybe he did not want to do that, as that brought him back to his wife, every time. However, the pain eased, just thinking of her. He missed her, everything about her.

    "Dorothy…" he mumbled low.

    Once everyone was in the truck, the younger man, put it into gear and drove on immediately. The old metal horse was doing a great job, for being over twenty five years old…pouring out hot air from both the main dash vents and lower ones. Sheldon drove on. He went straight to Mr. Cleaver's house. It turned out that was another twelve miles or so, still up ahead. That decision, the one to take him home… was the best thing to do at this point. Well at least to the young man. He would want to go home, if he'd gotten hurt. He had been, hurt that is… a long while ago, but that was a different road on a different night. The one he had lost his own parents, and his life that would have been…and was not… in one scoop. Sheldon deterred back from his own mental edge and kept his mind on the moment, and the black top ahead.

    Any talk of turning around however this night, to go back to the emergency room, made the old man unsteady. The best idea, Sheldon could think was stay on task. Besides, as his daughter had said it was close. Then he could call for help, after he was able to assess Mr. Cleaver better in real light. Trying to make a decision on the side of the road, when you have an extreme situation can usually lead the wrong direction. Better to find the least resistant path to getting Mr. Cleaver the help that he needed. Even if he did not think he needed it.

Sheldon drove on in silence a while. The heater blasted the cab. Lisa hummed under her breath. It was a song that Dorothy also hummed from time to time. Martin did not know the words. Dorothy never sang them right out, she just made soft sounds from time to time. They were always pleasant. He thought to ask the girl now, the name of the tune, but his heart held him back. He felt comforted, rocked and told to be quiet; like when grandma tells you in her garden, shh…so you can wait and watch as the hummingbirds sit and not fly off.

Martin's eyes were closed awhile. A few times he opened them and watched the trees pass by along the road. Then he would close them again. The way was much further than he remembered. What was he thinking, walking into the night? He was not thinking. That should concern him more, but it did not. Going home… even if it was only an echo, was better than not having one at all.

Tears long overdue their right to fall, silently won the battle of exhaustion and grief. The old man fell asleep. The girl kept singing.

Somewhere in Martin's memory, nearly forgotten was Dorothy…there on their wedding night. He prayed if he was dreaming, never to wake. Then he realized he prayed, and was disturbed.

>How odd to be at peace,
>and at war…
>at the same time…
>inside…

Remembrances of a good time...

Keeping Still

The fire has burned low my love.
I dare not move to fix it.
You have fallen asleep against my chest.
I feel you breathing.
I hear air, moving... in and out...
as you slumber.

Your hair is a wave of brown,
like a warm blanket,
the only comparison,
a treasure my grandmother,
would have made by hand.

You smell of the earth.
The trees and the outside,
have come inside with you.
We hiked all morning,
and now...
they are a pleasant memory,
swaying my senses
as I sit holding you close,
in my arms.

The fire has burned low my love.
I dare not move to fix it.

(5) Morning has broken...

The sun came in the front window, bright and beautiful. It was an announcement of all things grand and miraculous. That is if the world still possessed hope. Mr. Cleaver woke to the smell of bacon and eggs. Even, if he was not happy, he was hungry. The last time he had eaten anything at all, he could not remember. Vaguely he smelled pancakes. The memory of Dorothy, the love of his life, flooded in, all around him, like the very air. He closed his eyes again tightly. Moving from this place, this bed, was no longer anything he wanted anything to do with. Death in the dark?, that may have been preferable to living in the light as he now had a chance to think about it. How could he do it? How could he move on?

"Dorothy." Martin softly spoke her name. She was not beside him. She would never be there again. The very word, her name, hung there in the air. He wished he could make it real and tangible and hold on to it with both hands and never let it go.

Knock, knock. The door sounded in compliance, has if in direct answer. It was an echo of the actions made by Lisa on the other side. "Are you up?" Knock, knock, slightly louder.

"No." Martin replied. The tone was by far harsher than he had intended, but he did not have the desire or energy to apologize or change anything about it. Parts of last night came to him, flooded in from holes in his consciousness, crippled by a head ache the size of Nebraska.

Knock, knock. "You need to come out and eat. If you do not, father will..." she hesitated, "take you to the place." The girl was very careful about not using the word hospital. The mere mention had sent the man into hysterics half the night. Her father had sat and prayed, and kept close. He was only outside a few moments now, for a break. Lisa had heard Mr. Cleaver and knew he was in fact awake. She needed him to respond, or her father would have to do, something. From all accounts it would not be what Mr. Cleaver wanted. So, his response was more than a little important.

"You need to eat. You need to come out and have breakfast." Lisa was very insistent. She had learned to handle wild animals from her father in his veterinary business. People were often similar, or seemed so at least in her short years of experience.
They often needed a firm hand, and you could not take no for an answer. Small creatures seldom knew what was best for them. People well… even less often.

Martin Cleaver…thought about it. The only way to get these people out of his life, was to comply. He moved slowly and sat up. His slippers were on the floor, beside his bed, waiting. Someone had also laid out his robe. Peering down at himself, he had "his" dinosaur jammies on. How had that happened? They were in his drawer sure, but he would never have worn them in a million years. They were too silly, and generally too stupid. Dorothy had ordered them through a catalogue, by accident. That is what she had said. She should have returned them, but told him it was impossible. Funny, they fit really well and were quite warm. Dorothy would have laughed…

Well anyway, when he seemed upset about them, the silliness of it all, as a gift that was her answer. They could not be returned and that was the end of it. That is how they ended up in the drawer. She put them there, even so, as in this house nothing went to waste. She never varied after that to buy him the "plain blue" he was use to, and refused to change.

No doubt the young man had been helpful in this area as well. Changing his clothes, putting him into his own bed, all of it had been done. How embarrassing. He had let himself fall so flat, as strangers were now in his house. This was uncomfortable, and yet comforting?

"Are you coming out?" the young girl was insistent. "I am going to go stir and turn the bacon. My father will be in, shortly. Breakfast is ready in five." She knocked on the door again twice for good measure, then turned and headed back to the kitchen. There was no sense in standing there. It would only take her time away from cooking and let things burn. Besides, she was not getting very far, really… no where. Lisa thought it might just have to take her father to get him out. It had taken both of them last night, to drag him in, but Martin was more out at that time. Today, had better be a different story, or her father would not take "no" for answer. Her father had taken on bigger than Mr. Cleaver by twice, but it was not his favorite thing to do by any means. Better to have a compliant, happy patient whenever possible. Dad was a doctor not a wrestler…unless pressed.

Martin fumbled with the shoes. The floor was cold so shoes were a good thing. He stood slowly and tried to put his robe on. His body ached in places he did not remember hurting. Slowly, he succeeded. Memories of the crash came in bits at first, then as a solid gulp. Memories of the big white building… they were ever present. A bitter, foul taste was in his mouth. Martin smacked his lips a couple of times then headed to the small bathroom. He dared not glance even once to the far side of the bed. He knew what would be there. Nothing! It was empty.

The mirror was waiting. The image was not a good one. The man looking back was a wreck. The semblance appeared to have been beaten to a pulp. There was a gash about two inches long at the brow line. It had been neatly, expertly cleaned and sewn. You could barely see the threads they were so perfect, so uniform and so small. There were bruises on bruises all over the rest. Black eyes, as if he had donned a mask, belonging to a bandit.

Tiny blue dinosaurs were printed in funny back and forth design at his collar. They stuck up as if on parade, just over his robe at the neck line. The dino jammies from his wife, ordered by mistake had finally been worn.

Odd and even still funny, that is what she had said. The order had been an accident. But she had smiled? He remembered. How come he did not remember that until now? He felt like a kid for half a heartbeat. It passed. There was a terrible story unwritten, now or ever, that came and went on Martin's features.

How deep do the scars of our life reach?
Only God can take away sin.
Only God can forgive.
Jesus is the truth and the light!

Suddenly, a gripping feeling of anger took his heart to a bad place. Martin wanted to yell, but remained quiet. He wanted to yell at them, the strangers. He desired to tell them "Leave his house!" He was the master of this place. It was his home. The image looked back, sadly. He did not believe he would have made it home at all, if they had not come by. A calm... came back over his visage. The heat of the moment drained away, and with it most of his strength, or what he had left.

What was he going to say when he went out?
What could he say?
Thank you?
How come that was hard to say?
How come it was thick to speak kind things to people that deserved them?

Martin washed his hands and face, the best that he could. He tried to hold his toothbrush, but his hand was injured still. Broken? No. He moved each digit carefully. All flexed, if not well, they would… soon enough. Fingers okay, wrist? It was sprained maybe. The man switched hands. He could just work around it. So…

Martin Cleaver could take care of himself, despite the fact that he had apparently challenged death last night. First the accident, then the crazy walk in the cold proved he could live on despite his best efforts. Yet, no matter how Martin turned it over in his mind, he was not sorry he had walked. He really had wished he had died. He would not say that out loud, as Dorothy would surely come back from heaven just to slap him. It would not be a good reunion, she was not a Shakespeare fan. They had even discussed that, when they were kids, in class. Wow, where did that come from? Dorothy had been in the play at school, Romeo and Juliet, when they were children. She loved the part, but explained even then, that suicide was wrong.

At this point, that may be the only thing, that prevented Martin from ever considering it directly. Her words still echoed, even from so far gone, years past. They were the same, yesterday, today and tomorrow. He believed what she said, and held it close, out of respect maybe, but more likely...fear.

The lonely man pushed the thought to the deeper end of the pool, located somewhere imagined. He hoped that it would stay there a while, and not plague him the rest of the day. He got the message then, and she was clear.

In a hurry and generally disgusted he jabbed his jaw with the plastic brush. A wave of unwarranted anger blossomed. He would not be hurt if she had not left. Why was she dead? Obviously no one could control what happened. That was not the point at all. It was just that it happened. If he had gone first, none of this would even be important. It would not be at all. However, it was. So it had to be dealt with and could not be avoided.

Martin finished up the best he could. He did his morning business, just like every day since he left the service and came to live here in this house. That at least had not changed. What else? That so far was a short list. The man kept moving. That was best. He went out of the bathroom, took a long breath and stepped out of the bedroom as well. He moved slow, but with purpose down the hall and out into the small living room. No one was around. The light of morning came in every window, inviting the new day to come inside with open arms. Someone had pulled back all the curtains. Not one was left closed.

Flowers were the main design everywhere. Every vase, every tchotchke, every knick-knack, every where, Dorothy loved flowers. It was easy to tell. He just had not noticed quite as clearly, until this moment. It was wall to wall, daisies, and carnations. Soft colored, humming birds lined the wallpaper to offset the tiny butterflies at the edges. The carpet was a gentle brown, with a light green mix, like walking in a garden outside, except you were inside the whole time. The couch, the chair, the rocker even, were all lovely, and a mirror of his wife's heart and soul. Beautiful! How had he not noticed until…just now?

The reason was probably simple. The man usually did not like the curtains open. It was very bright. He had not wanted them open for years. He started to close them all back up, but it crossed his mind that may be trouble. It might show that he was in the wrong frame of mind, and then they would never let him alone. He moved on toward the kitchen. Might as well get things over quick, tell them he was okay, and they could go. That was the plan. It was a good plan. A man with a plan was hard to stop, or at least that was his belief, held to… his whole life.

The sound of bacon cooking, sizzling and singing all on its own could be heard from where Martin was at. It, the smell drew him on, like invisible hands caressing his nose, taunting him. His stomach made a loud, if rather obnoxious grumble. Complaint?, maybe, or even probably.

Your presence is a blessing.
We need to remember…
and… give thanks.

The kitchen was bright and cheerful, like the rest of the house. Everywhere that is but his bedroom or rather their bedroom, which was still significantly dark. He could run back and hide if he had to. That had crossed his mind more than once in the space from his entry way, to the end of the hall. It was dissipating now. Courage, a warm comforting feeling surrounded his soul, being home. It was a façade maybe; a moments respite, because the facts had not changed. Dorothy was gone. It was a quiet instance, but the reality of the burden, only pushed away, not vanished.

God gave me an angel, a wife, a helpmate.
I had no idea the worth of that gift,
bestowed upon my unworthy life.
Regret has nothing to do
with the sister of joy.
Loss is the little brother,
of the spoiled.

    The new angel he had seen last night, briefly… reappeared at the stove. She was a girl, about sixteen or maybe seventeen. Somehow she was familiar. Dorothy had gone to the same church for a long time. Perhaps that is how he knew her at all, the young girl I mean. Maybe some picture his wife had shared? That had been rare too. Funny? Another thing that had come to a halt, long before Dorothy had left for real, forever. She had stopped doing "things" that meant "stuff" to her. She had stopped going places and running errands outside the house other than church. She stopped attending meetings and gatherings from friends she knew from there. He was glad of that, as he was lonely when she was gone. But her mood hand changed also.

    As Martin thought more about it now, he wished that she had never stopped going. It had made her lose interest in most everything. Not that they had a lot going on, but her spirit, became subdued, almost withering away... for lack of water, in nearly all areas, while blossoming in a sacred or cherished few.

    Dorothy had stopped working in her garden. She had stopped filling the bird feeder outside the kitchen window. She had stopped nonsensically talking to him about all subjects. She had stopped, and then she died. Now that he thought about it, he missed it. He missed that the most. Her speaking. Her voice... He had grown angry sometimes, as it sounded like evil whining, giant bees buzzing in his ears. That was why Dorothy wanted him to see the doctor too. He just did not want her to talk when it was noisy like that. He did not really want her to stop altogether. At the moment, right here right now, he missed it. He would probably miss it every day for the rest of his life, only worse so, as it would become more solid, that she was never coming back.

"I am glad you are feeling well enough to come to the table. Father was going to take you," she stopped herself. "Father will return in a moment." The girl turned back to the stove to finish cooking. She was wearing Dorothy's apron. It fit her well. He wanted to be mad at that too, but he was not. He was too tired to really be mad at anything. He also hurt too much to care.

Martin slowly walked to the table. He pulled out the chair carefully. His wrist hurt quite a bit, but he did not want to make a big deal out of anything. They would stay if he did. He knew that. He was sure of it. Martin sat down. He made a noise, he could not help. It said volumes about the truth of his condition. Lisa was a smart girl and had worked with her father for years. She watched now with an eagle eye, listening for every tell tail clue that would reveal all, while stirring breakfast.

Poof, a cup of hot coffee appeared. Moments later a large plate with eggs, bacon and toast followed. No pancakes in sight anywhere. They must have been only in his wishful dreams, as they were missing. They would remain missing, probably forever at this point. Why was that important? It made Martin a little sick to his stomach. Everything looked so delicious. He said nothing at the moment and swallowed hard. He needed to get a handle on things quickly. If he was not in control, then someone else would be soon enough. That would not be okay.

With a renewed effort of will, Martin worked up his best mood. He could do this easy. Or, at least that is what he tried to convince himself of...

Martin starred down at the lace table cloth. It was lovely. The old man found he had never really looked at it before. There were flowers in the design, similar to those on the curtains. Dorothy had made both by hand. She had made everything. She was good at everything. Or… had been good. Tears slowly filled the man's eyes. His vision blurred but cleared quickly. He sniffled slightly, and picked up his coffee cup. The warm liquid was refreshing. It made him feel much more normal. Well, better anyway.

The kitchen door opened and Sheldon Farman stepped inside. "Good-morning." He smiled wide noticing that Mr. Cleaver was at the table first thing. "It's great to see you up." The younger man came right on in like he owned the place. In fact, he did feel pretty much at home. He had known Dor from church long enough to feel they were not strangers. No he had never been to her home before now, but he knew her, by her fruits. She had ever been a ready helper, a kind heart; a sweet light, to honor Jesus. However, Sheldon never remembered seeing Mr. Cleaver in church during that time, even once. He was not judging. He was simply accepting of the situation. The truth, the reality was yet to unfold as to why Sheldon had found the man on the road…lost. As a follower of the Lord, he was not the kind to fill in the blanks him self. Sheldon would wait and let God unveil things to him in His time. The young man just accepted his place in the scheme of things and moved forward.

"How are you feeling?" Sheldon had turned very serious. If things were not okay, he would take the man one way or the other to the hospital. He did not want to do that. If necessary he would call others to help. Some part of his heart, would not force things, if he could find another choice. Sheldon was just a veterinarian. Yes he had plenty of experience in the army…on humans as a medic, but still. Better to be safe then sorry.

The old man liked the younger one well enough. Perhaps he would be dead if it were not for him and his daughter, stopping and helping. Yet, maybe he could have been with… No! Again, Dorothy would come untied at the seams… if she were here, to know he even thought that for a moment. So, Mr. Martin Cleaver was going to have to step out of his comfort zone, or end up out of his own, control. Martin figured there would be some kind of fiasco, if he did not show marked improvement from being a lunatic, walking in the night. He quickly gathered up his wits, and silently asked Dorothy for the right words. Even gone, she was still supporting him in ways he was yet to understand or be aware of…

"Thank you." There. He said it. That should be enough, but more than likely it was not. Martin knew from his wife, and her kind, that all "do-gooder" types liked to hang and help, far passed the "thank you…" This was not going to go any other way. He could handle it. He was okay. Really! Well, maybe.

The younger man came right over to the table. He pulled out the kitchen chair casually, Dorothy's chair, and sat right down. His daughter moved like a gazelle, swift and sure. A cup on the table, coffee in the cup, cream and sugar fresh and waiting, it happened fast. Lovely Lisa was going to make someone a wonderful wife, a helpmate worth having.

Martin glanced at her, and for only a heartbeat, he could see his own wife, wearing the apron. The smile was reassuring but somewhat serious. Then the image was gone and the pretty girl's face beamed back at him instead.

It was just like he remembered in his dream… Martin's from last night. He had it when he finally fell asleep which had been hard at times, fitful at best. In the other world, Dorothy was pouring his coffee, and telling him it was going to be okay, she had talked to God and He was sending angels. Then he woke up in a cold sweat. The room had been so dark. Dorothy's smell had been very strong, and comforting. He had cried, and buried his head into her pillow, to keep from the embarrassment of sound, itself. He was a grown man. This was all stupid. Everybody lived and everybody died, he just wanted to go first.

Martin looked straight across at the young fellow. "I am okay." His voice came out in a stutter. It was not nearly as strong as he had meant it to be. With his right hand he grasped the handle of his own cup of coffee. It gave him a tangible anchor to reality. He moved the cup to his lips. The black liquid was hot, just right, and gave the perfect wake up to his stiff, slow thoughts. He let his senses enjoy the moment. Then he gathered his courage back up, and tried again.

"Really!" He said with a bit more vigor.

"Breakfast, is ready father." Lisa sat a plate down on to the table for her father that matched Mr. Cleaver's perfectly. It looked like a feast. A warm welcome feeling seemed to permeate the kitchen. There was a pleasant buzzing sound in the back ground. Not like the bees that made noises and made Martin's head hurt, this was different. More like a lullaby, that you could just not make out the words to, somehow. Then before you could say them, or write them down they were gone again, kind of like a dream, like last night even. Then she followed with silverware and the bottle of ketchup. There was no question they were having breakfast together. The strangers were not leaving, at least any time soon. That was pretty easy to gather.

"Sir, I am glad to see you up and around. Obviously you are better." The young veterinarian recognized uneasy, anxiety without difficulty enough. Scared animals telegraph their moods and intentions, if you watch carefully. The man knew that well, and knew animals well, that included the two legged kind. People, they were not so different. Time and again he had found that to be a truth in his line of work.

"Yes." Martin replied. His words felt thick. His head hurt, dull and hard to follow thoughts raced back and forth from time to time. Yet over all, he was okay. He hurt yes, no doubt. That was not going to get better in five minutes. He had gone through an accident, but he was not an invalid. He had been knocked flat, but he was still standing… well not at the moment, but it was metaphorically the same.

"Where is your wife? Where is Dor?" that was the one question Sheldon wanted to ask upfront. He wanted Martin Cleaver to answer when he was not delirious, and had some sense of his actual words. That might spook the scared old guy, but it was necessary to make the proper decisions in this matter. He knew from bits and pieces in the night, that she had died. That was why the poor man was so afraid of returning to the big white building. He was obviously in shock at the very least. In addition, Sheldon also made out the facts about Martin's truck. It was surely still in the ditch, not to far from where they found Mr. Cleaver. At least Sheldon figured that. He was after all an old man. It was cold and late, last night when they came across Martin, how far could he have walked?

The unclear question that needed an answer…was that an accident? The truck? Mr. Cleaver had said things. He was very depressed and his wife's death had left him badly shocked. He clearly wanted to die, and had made that apparent to Sheldon more than once. That is exactly why there was no way, the younger man was ready to leave the old man on his own. None of Martin's extensive array of injuries, were life threatening, but painful surely, but still did not add up to death on the road. The cold would have done that. It was way below freezing last night, and even this morning, things were not that much better. Frost on all the glass windows, and mist before your face when you breathed outside, were sure signs of a bitter winter, still holding tight to the land. So, the summation of the situation is that Martin was blessed to be alive. Sheldon wanted to keep him that way.

There was ice on the road last night too, surely. It must have been that which caused a perfect storm. Sheldon did not like to think otherwise. There was no reason to dwell on the other pieces of things, the old man had brought to the surface. Martin did not know God. Sheldon prayed, that could be changed. Yet, for the moment he was focused only on helping as he knew how. The rest would be up to the All Mighty.

"I have a lot to do today. I am going to leave my daughter." Sheldon stared directly at the man. He took a long breath, "I can come back this afternoon and pick her up…if things are still just as fine…as you say they are." he drifted to silence. Scooped up more food on his fork and shoved it hungrily into his mouth. His daughter was a great cook.

Stating a thing right out like that was the best way to go. That way there was no discussion. Rightly so, there should be none. Sheldon readied himself, with a few rebuttals to nonsense, if there was any forthcoming.

The vet's words were strong. He tried to sound matter of fact. That way his words would not be questioned at all. Sheldon actually had a gift. He was very good at his job. He could speak all subliminal languages, body, nuances, utterances, facial expressions, eye rolls and the like… It was kind of the way you talk to all animals all the time, your tone level and patient. A measured gate that took years of experience by others, Sheldon Farman was a natural at. His gift was exactly what was needed. He treated everyone, with the same intensity, but they were by necessity, mostly real animals. Sheldon seldom practiced his trade on humans. But that did not make it less affective, then or now.

Martin thought to tell him "no". He wanted to say it. He formed the words in his head. He sent them to his mouth, but it remained shut. Why? Open! Say something… Say anything… He could not. He did not.

Since there was no response that Sheldon deemed worth hearing anyway, by way of language or otherwise, he powered on.

"I will be back." Sheldon picked up his fork and shoveled the last of his breakfast down his throat, loving every bite. "Eat up Sir, you need your strength. Lisa makes the best breakfast around, or at least that I know of." The man smiled across his plate. Then he picked up his cup and took a big swig. There was a lot to do today.

"My truck…" the words fell out…barely audible. Martin's voice was still hoarse, even to his own ears.

"I will take care of it. I will be back." It was funny he did not mention Dorothy at all? It crossed his mind to be direct, but something held him back. It was odd, but Sheldon had learned to trust his inner senses. All the real information Sheldon had gathered he had obtained in tiny pieces. She had been sick a long time. Dorothy had faced a great burden by herself, as she had not shared things very often, or at least of that kind of depth, Sheldon was now aware of.

A while back, Sheldon remembered something about it at church. Cancer... That had been months back, or further still?
It was only a guess that time had passed by and stolen her away, while life went by every day in Sheldon's own world. It made him a little sad. He knew a lot about her indirectly, but never really knew her

personally. Now she was at the hospital. The big white building that brought fear to the point of panic to her loving husband. So sad. It broke Sheldon in two to watch Martin Cleaver suffer. A man without God is truly alone, even in a room full of people.

Perhaps it was better to let time work on that a bit? Sheldon thought to himself. He did not need any more details directly from Martin, he could find out the facts for himself. A ride to town was a necessity anyway. Sheldon got up, pushed his chair back in, under the lace table cloth. He walked over to the sink where his daughter stood washing a few things. She stopped and looked up. He hugged her without a word for a moment or two. He was ever grateful she had been with him. Her mother would have been so proud. Lisa handled situations often better, where adults fell apart. The girl was rock solid.

Sheldon smiled and said his goodbyes. Without further pomp, he left. Just like that. Martin was still at the table. His breakfast not finished for the moment. He wanted to get up and say, "get out..." but instead... he picked his fork back up. Martin returned to the task at hand, if for no other reason than starvation was only just slightly more important at the moment than exhaustion. Fighting on any level would have taken energy, he simply did not have.

Lisa turned back to the items in the sink and the soapy water. She began singing softly. It was beautiful. Martin found he could not move from the table… for a long time. He lingered, willingly and unwillingly, fighting an inner battle. He felt peaceful, and guilty for feeling anything good at all. After a long while, the man finished his coffee and then rose slowly. He turned and went back to the bedroom.

The girl cleaned the breakfast dishes and then just started cleaning the house. It was a second nature thing to do. She enjoyed being useful and taking care of things. that included small animals, large animals and lost... sad... souls found on the side of the road in the dark.

Prey for the "black", saved by the Light.

(6)
What Happens?

  Mr. Cleaver finally returned to his room. He went back in. It was dark there. It was safe. He found the bed. He lay down. Martin closed his eyes. If he could just sleep!

  Her smell, it climbed inside his head. It came from everywhere and no where. The bed, the bedding, the clothes in the closet, only the beginning. The book she was reading, the water glass she had not yet taken to the kitchen; still on her bed stand, yet...more of the same. The carpet, the curtains, things she touched and loved, were all around him. All important, and worth nothing now, as the one piece... gone. Dorothy, the essence of something sweet...no longer a part of the fabric of his very existence, now and forever changed.

"Dorothy" he called. No one answered. No one would ever answer again. He fell asleep. Seconds past, minutes, hours, days… another knock at the door. Martin did not hear it. There was a second knock.

Lisa peeked in. She could see Mr. Cleaver on the bed. She held her breath and listed a moment or two. He was sleeping. That was a good sign. She closed the door softly and returned cleaning. It was busy work, but important.

The Burden is Light

I go to your house,
and make tea.
Talk to me.

I clean your dishes.
I mop the floor.
I start dinner.
I am here.

My life,
it has things wrong.
Yet, it is you,
you that is suffering.

I see that.
So I lift the weight…
all of it…
as I can carry,
to share what it is,
that I can.

There is nothing more,
I can do…
to shift my load.
I am tired.
Yet I can see,
that by helping you,
I am helping me.

Together,
the load…
has no weight,
at all.

In the big "white" building;

The cold room at the hospital was silent. It was located on the lowest level. The morgue, a place were references, facts, and fear of the unknown gathered together, and waited for the next step to happen. What ever that may be? The woman in the sharp, pressed-perfect, white coat looked down at the pretty face of the old woman. Her still body lay prone on the table. She seemed happy to the onlooker. Or perhaps at least at peace, or maybe something similar to that, some how? The worker wondered briefly if the old person had a good life or a bad one? It did not matter now; it was just a thing that kept Surame from being too bored, late at night.

Surame Kelly was in her mid fifties. She ran the bottom floor of the hospital few cared to loiter in, or spend any more time then they dared. Like death could some how reach them, from the other side, grab them and drag them back to the dark...even while they were alive? While the hallway and main corridor echoed, and seemed most uninviting to the new or seldom seen, it was a welcome quiet to others.

"Silly people", that is what Surame said often, maybe not out loud, but to herself. "They have no idea, none of them. Bodies are just dust…" That is what the good book said, and that is what she believed with her whole heart. But that does not mean they should be handled badly, or wrongly... by those with fear in their soul(s)... She focused, "Better to know we will all take the same path in the end, unless the Light comes." That always made her smile, even in this solemn place. Speaking to no one.

A cricket chirped,
out of place.

Ms. Surame Ann Kelly had been raised without a god, but had been blessed. In her time here among the bodies waiting to be processed, the forgotten, or the truly lost or thrown away, Surame had learned the value of life, through death. By accident she had found a New American Standard, in the lower right hand drawer of the previous morgue manager's desk. The name inscribed, "friend". It was the best day of her life or really night, as she worked the last shift. But the truth and fact like the name of the owner of the bound tome, the bounty of the blessings held within, made everything else worth living for.

In the words between the pages, she had established a connection far more than a friend, but a God to worship and love. One that would bring her heart peace, which she had lost, since before she could remember. Surame had truly needed one... a friend the day she got here, to the huge white building. It was daunting. Not so much by its size, but a combination of its aged-old-blocks, bleached-white, not painted and the overly large columns outside, made it very impressive, for an otherwise small, obscure town. The founders put a lot into the construction foundations of the structure, and there was a feel to it. Not exactly like a church, but in Surame's way of thinking, it was almost as close for a number of reasons. God was always near to those in need, as that is when most see Him clearest. In a way it was sad, but true. She liked to think... He, her Mighty Lord was with her all the time, not just when she was hurting most. As she looked back, before she was saved, in her very being, she could see his hand. Always beside her, closest when she felt furthest from all others.

How she came to be here, working in the big white building in the first place? The woman had been hired via a posted ad in the paper, two states away. Only by accident she saw it, on a table at a friends house. He had received a newspaper from the town because he liked to follow the news there. Something about a Christmas box? Something about being in the military... but she was not really listening. She was reading. It appeared to be perfect. The job that is. What a funny reason? Odd to want a paper from a town you don't even live in? Next day she applied. The day after that a letter came, she had been fully accepted. It had been postmarked the same date she had sent her application to them. The two letters would have had to have passed in the mail. How would the manager of the hospital even know of her a request for employment? The speed of it was amazing, but overlooked. Coincidence was something Surame would have deemed the likely hood of all things workings as they did, but now was different. She did not believe anything at all, was chance.

Regardless, the joy of the message she received for the job, was huge. Surame needed work, and no further questions were asked? Well directly...and exactly...

   Only thing mentioned, typed as if non-cha-lant-ly, but relevant to everything, at the end of the short but professionally written acceptance was a caveat. A codicil, or in this case a disclosure that her resume was not disputed or checked. It was held to be accurate and would hold up under any review. Surame hated that part, as she had perhaps expanded a little on her abilities. Yet variance at all would be cause for dismissal. It was not in her nature to lien over in any way, across a line that might be questioned, but a strong sense of urgency pushed her... forward. It had remained with her, since leaving the big city, and kept her sharp still. No she had not lied, by any means, but details of gray were not the same. Surame prayed for forgiveness of all her sins, as no one is without them.

   Regardless, a letter of response that the post, the position... was hers and when to show up was listed. It was immediate. Surame had moved to town and went to work within twenty-four hours. It was and had been a miracle... she knew that now, if not then.

   The book, the Holy Bible, had and has been... "One" ever since, a friend to her. The word was powerful, and potent to reach into the darkness of a place so cold in the heart of the white building, that even space itself, would be a welcome retreat. That is why the halls echoed. The orderlies that brought the bodies down, never stayed any longer than necessary. They would sometimes just leave the dead even unattended, and go back up. Surame felt that was disrespectful. Even if there was no one on duty, they could bring them in... they were supposed too. They knew what the minimum was to be done. At least for the waiting part. But she would find lost souls... the left ones... every now and then. Surame said nothing to anyone, as it was better that way.

*The walls were not scary
to the attendant,
but ears...
listeners...
maybe...*

When she received a notice from upstairs, she preferred to go herself. But, she could not work twenty for seven.

Basically, the whole downstairs floor was run by Surame now, and the day man. His name was Jacob Blane. They had finally met for a few moments after she had worked the first week. After that they barely ever saw each other. That was great with Surame. It left her basically her own boss, during her time on the clock. Maybe she was not "in charge", but she could do a great job, while she was in control of her small world. So as long as either or neither said anything or God willing...nothing at all, everything remained the same...quiet. That was good. They rarely saw one another, herself and the other man. They worked opposing shifts, which was fine with her.

The morgue was technically closed or at least unmanned...for six hours each cycle. That was primarily for cleaning. It was at that time the bodies would have to be brought in directly by the attending and placed in the cold drawer, then signed off on the main sheet. Usually they, every one that is from the above... did not follow policy. It was hard to say why? Again, Surame had her own ideas, fear being a big one. She had also noticed a huge difference between those that "believed" and those that were living day to day. It was well reflected in their responses, to visits down here.

As for the "white house" cleaning crew, they were seldom seen. Shadows that would come through, and make sure everything was in order. It always was... Surame would never leave for home, unless it was. Some times they even skipped things, because she had already done what was needed. Gradually, they came less and less, and finally would even... just leave her supplies. As for the other co-worker, he gave her no trouble.

They barely talked, one or twice in passing again from time to time, but rare. There was no connection at all. They just worked at the same place. He was technically the supervisor, and got paid more of course. But he never flaunted it, or made her uncomfortable. He just did his own thing.

Surame Kelly was a good attendant. Her actual title was Morgue-tech. It was part of her job to read the files, Make sure everything was in order and ready for pick up or disposal. That may mean a nice burial, or cremation... or.. The fact was that not everyone could afford to be buried. So that was just the way it was in life. It was the last... "or"... that even she felt a bit uncomfortable with at times. Bodies were useful in medicine and schools. She understood that well enough, but it seemed that many of the bodies went that way, especially true for poor families. The social worker, Tedra was her name... The doctor's daughter, had been down last week and asked for a list. Surame was surprised anyone cared to check on anything, and said nothing about her own discord with the situation. They were not friends, and Surame trusted no one, even still. It was best to keep herself centered on her own duties. However, she assembled the requested inventory list; names, dates and COD's(cause of death cert.), then sent it over to Ms. Macsen's office. Surame had also put a copy of it in her own desk drawer in case she needed to refer to it later, concerning Ms. Macsen. That is if she should call again or come by. Then lastly Surame made a second copy for herself. Why? She still did not know. It was even now safely put... away... at home.

Sometimes there is no safe place.
So... we must stand and hold the ground.
(Blane routinely went though the office, keeping track of things...)

In reviewing the sheer number of files Surame had seen in the last two years, patterns simply presented themselves. Still, even hard to find parallels and mirrored deaths seen from a distance, that did not, could not and would not match ages, or gender for the proper numbers to be statistically correct...appeared, presented repeatedly and provided with mismatched data on purpose or mistake...maybe, was not direct proof of anything. But just being off by numbers... that was not so outstanding at all, it happens. It was something else. A nagging in the back of her mind..., a subtle off beat to the rhythm of her heart, how else could she explain the discourse she felt about the details. If particulars transposed, or entered wrong continued... the reality of their being ultimately intentional... solidified. Even if Surame fought against it. She did not want trouble. That did not mean that it was not going to find her, even down here.

The morgue technician found to her amazement their were things written that kept her attention, in nearly every file. Not at first, but slowly, building to a plot against everything good. The idea was funny, and did not seem real in any tangible way that she could put down in writing, say to someone, or even pray to God about, except in noises... alone and to Him only. Utterances of despair... and prayers for the Light to win, over all things dark. Yet a conspiracy was growing, getting stronger and being given space... She could not even share her thoughts with anyone but God. He always gave her comfort to continue, but she was watchful. The shadows seemed deeper than before.

Surame had to be a good girl.
Her brother, was watching... from heaven...
but that was both a prayer and nightmare,
"it"... trying to win,
by finding a small rip in the fabric.

How could she tell someone else, anyone else, that she felt funny about nothing? It was the bodies, the number of them, especially with cancer. Not all but some, that did not always "feel" correct by the remains they left. How do you explain "feel" without sounding crazy to a doctor here in the white house? Especially by the way, in the same sentence as "dead". You don't. You lose your job. You don't make any noise, or run any extra tests or anything, that make you stand out. Things that get noticed, get looked at closer. That made her think again about Ms. Tedra. She was in a far better position to see if there were any real basis to anything. She worked for social services, not the hospital directly. That meant she could not be fired.

The idea of being looked at closely, gave a chill to Surame that would not leave right away. It was unnerving. It could very well be unsafe, to her position to be too friendly or think too much about Ms. Macsen. Prayers came to her lips. Then, best, to keep away from the main stream, or at least that is what she had learned so far. Others, had met with resistance for not going along... and then...moved or left. She had heard rumors.

> *No one...*
> *ever asked*
> *about the turn over*
> *in staff.*

Surame preferred to think it was just anxiety, and late night thoughts, but her inner spirit warned there was more. A long while back, she had begun taking notes in a small journal for her own comfort shortly after receiving the Lord. It had happened here in the cold. These notes, these symbols of pain and sadness, loss and despair, drawn and placed with each goodbye, she did not share..., with Ms. Macsen. Yes the names and causes were listed, exactly alike... but more notes on the sides...along with obscure pieces of thoughts, no one would understand above gibberish, and all of it written in a made up shorthand, only her brother could read. She wanted to prove to herself she was wrong. But in the months that passed, the figures... held true. No "real" proof, just things she wrote... not actually connected to any one file... Not useable by anyone that did not clearly understand what she was trying to tract exactly.

> *Shadows don't leave traces,*
> *most people can follow,*
> *but a few...*
> *the remnant that pray.*

Her hand shook a little...Thinking about the notes in her pocket even now. No one could read them, but her and God, and; she wanted to say her brother's name out loud but did not. ... ? She pushed the notion aside and continued her work quietly.

63

Slowly, over the time Surame had been employed at the big white building, she found the true meaning for living after all. "Jesus." She had read the bible twice from beginning to end, but when done... simply returned to the underlined passages for comfort, or to worship in earnest, backed by scripture.

That was even now her reason to be hopeful, as she stared into the lifeless eyes of the aged angel. Then ever so gently, she took her right hand, kissed the tips of her fingers and touched Dorothy. Lightly she closed the old woman's eyes... Odd how they were still open at all? Dorothy Cleaver had been listed over two hours ago, but no one had done much to prepare her since that time. That was an oversight that did not sit well with Surame. The dead must be respected, as life must be respected. A beginning and an end were equally important. But there was more to it. There was a forever, and that meant that what she did here, and at this time, was only a pre-curser for the next. It was to be given every solemn tribute.

There was some notes in the file, she saw them earlier. Something about cancer. Just another name on a long list. Yet, there was a sadness too... attached, a sentiment that something else, was going unnoticed, yet important. Surame looked harder. Yet, saw nothing different than what she was to expect from the body. But her sense of left footed, or missing the obvious,... just would not let go.

"I can tell my friend. You have seen better days, by the first appearance of all the facts... but the ones ahead, they will be beyond description. Heaven is a real place." Surame talked as she worked, often. She herself and had come to a point that death had a totally different meaning. In her heart, she knew, all were just passing... and time was indeed short to the distance of forever.

Ms. Kelly was good at her job. The reason, she respected the passing of life and the very miraculous gift of birth itself, due to her first hand experiences with both. In her country of origin, few bothered to bury the dead at all, they just cut them up. That was especially true if they were hated…which most that stood for freedom fit that description well. If they were buried it was in a mass grave, without a marker. That was far from here. That was then and this is and was the now. Ms. Kelly was thankful to live in America. She quickly chased the evil memories from the forefront of her mind.

The woman's hair was dark black, held back with pins in a large bun. Surame had come to this country from a bad place, where death was somewhat more meaningless. She had seen tragic killings for senseless reasons, that had no actual base. Religions that took life at will, from the weak and used their "cause" to control and devastate whole populaces. She had immigrated to America. Thank God and the angels that had a hand in getting her to it's incredible, beautiful... shores.

> *God Bless the place that gave her a home,*
> *from all that was…*
> *to a place where hope still existed*
> *and exists!*

Because her licenses were not from this country, she could not be a doctor…, yet. That would soon be changed. She had been going to school during the day part of the time. Nothing would hold her back. America was everything that she had hoped for and more. Once she had made good, then she would save. She would get enough money some how to bring her brother to America too. He would be alive… still. He had to be. God did not let prayers go unanswered.

The woman's memory filled in the gaps immediately in her softened mood. She could not help it. She remembered; Masaro had forced Surame onto the waiting truck. There had been tears and promises, but they had not been heard by either, over the den of yelling and screaming people. The chill in her heart was real. Not because of death. If her brother was one of their victims, he would go to heaven surely, all heroes did. It was the passing of his life that concerned Surame. They took special notices of the ones that spoke out when they found them.

Again, she pushed it all harder away. She looked down into Dorothy's face and smiled. "Sweet old lady, I pray you say hello to my brother if you would? Tell him, if he is there with you… I am sorry." The woman placed her warm hand on the dead woman's cold brow. She let it linger only a moment. "God give you peace." Surame spoke out loud, as no one else was around. She dared to be herself, when that happened. Otherwise fear kept her silent. That is what had happened. Her life, had been modified by her experiences. Finding God, had helped her make it through the rough parts, but that did not end the battles she faced daily. She pulled the white cloth up and placed it gently over the body.

Being saved...
Being born-again...
Did not make you perfect.
It made you His!

Surame moved away slowly and went back to her desk. She sat down in the old rolling chair, that should have been replaced long ago. She did not care. It still worked, mostly. It was only a little broke, and if you did not lean too far back it did not throw you forward unexpectedly. Besides, she was not the kind to squawk over every little thing. Laughing to herself ironically, like that would ever happen in a million years. Besides, she would have to go and ask someone in another department, like "supplies", for a replacement. That was out of the question. Surame preferred the morgue. It was a good place. The rest, was too cold and she was not thinking of or considering physical temperature. Instead, she was pondering the overall unfriendliness of a few, and rudeness of others.

The woman then picked up the clip board. The time of death… date… place… reason…or actually, cause, and a few other important facts were listed. Cancer was prominent on the page. Not an uncommon story at all. Surame had seen so many go down that road, it left her empty inside. Somehow…if they could put a metaphorical toll booth in just too slow things down, they would create enough time to find a cure, sooner than later. Maybe?

There was a number on the right of the page. Next of kin listed as Martin Andrew Cleaver. She would have to give him a call. This was a small place, and part of her job, was moving the body to the next level. Either the carcass needed to be cremated or prepared by a mortuary for burial. She hated that part of her work, the calling part. It was the worst. People just did not understand the process. Sometimes she was matter of fact, sometimes she was much softer in her conversations, but it did not matter. None of them were ever ready, for the "what next" part.

> *Why does death haunt the living*
> *who know there is eternal life?*
> *It is not a weakness, it is a truth.*
> *His word shines!*

She took a drink of her cold coffee and sat the cup aside. She picked up the manila folder. With a huge sigh, she looked over the paperwork she had so far on Mrs. Cleaver. It was a good idea to prepare in advance just a moment for calls. It helped, some times. Not always.

Surame prayed, while no one saw, a private moment. Then she picked up the phone and dialed. It rang several times. No answer.

This was repeated… not once, but many times. Surame did not like ending her shift without having at least left a message. It did not happen.

The woman put the papers back in the file, shifted it to the stand on her desk. "Dorothy Cleaver, no one wants to answer. We will have to take this up again tomorrow when I come back, or Mr. Blane will handle it later…when he comes in." She felt bad. It was unsettling there was no one to claim the body. No one to answer the phone. Mr. Blane was also just not as nice with the old people as Surame. It all bothered her.

Dorothy was cold, at least what was left of her. The warm, friendly, beating heart was now still, forever. The loss would be felt in many ways, most importantly, and unpredictably by the ones least expecting it. Back at the beginning, the first day of church, Dorothy

Cleaver had kneeled and prayed, for this moment. It finally came. Sadly so, in a way she could never have dreamed. Regardless, in heaven, the angels always sing. That was, and is not a surprise, ever.

     More things happened from that point on. Basically routine however. That is except; for the tests, that Surame just could not help but run. It was like a splinter under her skin, and she was not able to stop her self. From that point on, it was only a matter of time, before the clarity of all her fears were written in blood before her eyes.

A Blanket from the Bin

The cold hospital is not an evil place, on purpose.
It is frozen to slow down the progress of death.
It is harder to attack that way, ("demise") it moves sluggishly...
Allows doctors, nurses, caretakers and loved ones,
a chance to do skirmishes, that offer a tomorrow, at times.

Angels, they move gracefully.
They are outside the realm of hot and cold,
and live between the lines of love and hate.
They fight battles unseen, with dark foes...
ever trying to bring down the innocent and beautiful.

Prayer warriors, go willingly into the artic night.
Daring to come against the heat of ice too cold,
to be just "cold" any longer... burning like hell itself.
They bring their words, of their King.
They bring His Light, to shine.
They are not afraid.

The place... is given warmth
by all those that make a difference.
It is given peace,
by the patience of perseverance.
It is given,
True Hope,
by the Son of God,
Jesus.

(7) Lisa

Lisa was nearly seventeen. She had worked hard all of her life. That was just the way of things. She was raised out in the country, not near any big city, so doing things that needed doing, was just second nature. Because of her father, she could stop bleeding, stitch up a wound, take down a cow by herself and knew exactly how to handle wolf pups. Not a job for just anyone. Taking care of Mr. Cleaver was easy-peasy. Not near as difficult as the three miniature Nigerian goats, Mr. Walker bought from out of town, that all came down with some kind of cold, at the same time. Now that was hard. The thought of it made Lisa cringe just a little. Who knew some thing, or in this case… some things, so small could make such a big mess. Ick!

She started with breakfast dishes and kept going from there. Then, cabinets were next, then the floor. She pulled out the sweeper and cleared the dust from ten years with out slowing down even once. Dorothy had been sick a long time, and it was not her fault things had fallen into disorder. That just came with cancer. It ate up every part of a person's life, slowly and methodically, unless stopped. That was a longer thought. Lisa was in a light mood. She moved swiftly. The only regret, that she did not know just how bad things were with Ms. Dorothy until too late.

Next the windows, opened and washed followed by the laundry. Splish, splash the water went, and all the time Lisa sang, just under her breath. Amazing Grace, "how sweet the sound". It was her favorite. Occasionally she would sing something else, but would soon come back to the same hymn. It was so sweet and seemed to drive the residue of darkness back completely. Anything that thought to have followed them home from that dark road, was now running back down it. You could not be near Lisa, and not feel the Light of God. His spirit was ever around her.

Today was much better then last night. It had been a combined effort between her and her father to get Mr. Cleaver inside. He was a bit out of it for sure. Sometimes he was clear as day, or seemed so, then he would talk to her… his wife… and she was not in the room. Kind of sad, and unsettling, the girl felt bad for the old, lonely man. It made Lisa's heart hurt so she started praying. She did not stop that night until they had him settled in bed. After a few hours of sleep on the couch herself, the day was much brighter. Prayer was still her first and best response to all things.

Her father had sewn up Mr. Cleaver's head gash, like the pro he was… but held back on the "woof" treat at the end. That thought made Lisa smile. Every dog in the county that had been operated on, knew there was a happy ending in the black bag. In this case, just being home and safe, was happy ending enough for all concerned.

The day passed. The shadows grew long. They were not however as deep as they were last night, not by far. The whole feeling she had endured before on the road, had dwindled with the light of day. The girl looked out the kitchen window from time to time. She watched the sunlight hours, pass, lovely but cold. No storm in sight, just temperatures that made you run for the inside.

Lisa hoped her father got everything he wanted done. There was a list. A couple of patients needed to be seen. That was now last... on the list... really. Finding out about Mr. Cleaver had pushed the whole world into a funny place. Time was different. Important things that were at the top moments before, were now far from anything. Lisa continued to pray. It gave her peace.

Shadows of pain, sorrow and weakness,
clung tightly as they could,
but not tight enough.
Lisa was good at her work.
All were swept away,
vacuumed up,
placed in a bag,
disposed of,
or drained down the sink.

An angel watched from the window
Took care of the house.
Sheldon Farman was safe also.
He had not left alone.
They were armed.
They would follow him,
and bring him home.

Dor had died. That hurt Lisa. She remembered the old lady from church. They had not talked often, but Dor was well known. Always happy to help a neighbor, always something nice to say, that was Dorothy Cleaver.

"Wow", Lisa thought it would be hard or even devastating for many. All around town, the old woman had made friends, if distantly. She was like an angel that came and went, without moving the candle flame, even a little. That was from a story Lisa had heard as a child. She thought a moment, the name of it... "Angel Fire". A child's story to bring comfort, nearly forgotten. It made her smile. That also had to do with her own mother, now gown. Some memories were hard to examine too closely, so she moved on. She just worked harder.

Lisa's father talked about angels all the time when Lisa was growing up.

Dorothy, the woman… the sister among the ladies, the ever ready friend to just about everyone, had touched people again and again. Not directly so much, but all knew her. Her loss would be felt… deeply.

Funny, she had never seen Mr. Cleaver in church? That was not so unusual really. Not every one went, Lisa knew that. She was not judging. It came to her. She kind of remembered his name on a prayer request for salvation once or twice. The whole church knew the name, if not the face. They would know his face soon. They would come. They always did. The ladies and the gents, with their baskets and such, would arrive to help a neighbor, in a time of troubles. She had seen it many times in her church. They loved on each other. They took their faith very seriously.

Lisa continued her tasks, ever looking for the next thing to do. She cleared out the refrigerator. Left' over's; there were a few. Laying everything directly on the table, she figured out what to keep and dump. Then, she decided to start dinner. It was already half past 4:00. Mr. Cleaver had not come out of his room even once. He would be hungry. Her father would also be back, hungry too. So she started right away, placing the cast iron skillet on the burner.

It struck her funny suddenly. Her father had not called to check in at all. She slid the big pan aside and went to phone on the table. She lifted the receiver. No dial tone at all. She looked at the back. It had been switched off. Why? Why would anyone turn it off? She puzzled for a moment and then turned the dial switch back to the on position. A second later the phone rang in her hand. She placed it down and picked up just the receiver. "Hello?"

"Hello, is this the Cleaver residents?" A strong woman's voice on the other end asked ominously.

"Yes Sir. It is." Lisa found that her throat had gone a bit dry. "They are not..., can I take a message?" The girl finally responded to the sound of dead air.

A few crackles…

"This is the Hospital. Mrs. Dorothy Cleaver is here," the sound of a voice coughing low followed. Then, someone clearing their throat just a bit, a sad tone, but still strong, "Mrs. Cleaver's body needs to be viewed and arranged for…Please have Mr. Cleaver call or come down as soon as possible. If he can not, we will need next of kin, or whomever Mr. Cleaver sends, that knows her. We need a valid witness for paperwork. You understand?" The man was silent for a moment or two, then resumed; the number for Mr. Cleaver's reference is; followed by numbers that Mr.

Cleaver would never dial. Lisa took them down on the pad anyway, having no idea of the future.

"Thank you, Sir." Lisa replied, writing everything clearly the best that she could. Her hand was shaking. What did the man mean arrangements? It sounded like a great responsibility she was very glad not to have to carry herself. So sad to lose someone you love, and then have to face so much, was more than she could think about at just seventeen. Lisa thought it was more than she ever wanted to have to think about at all.

Lisa hung up the phone. She left the note on the table, exactly where it should be, next to the phone. She moved on, toward fixing dinner. All around the kitchen there were little do-dads of funny things. Heart shaped salt and pepper shakers on the table, bird shakers in the window, hummingbird mix in a jar next to the coffee, and friendly atmosphere all around. Mrs. Dorothy was so very busy, spreading hope all the time, Lisa felt extra cheerless, she had never bothered to get to know her better. That left tears in Lisa's eyes. Her own mother had passed a few years back. She would have given much, to spend even a few minutes more… with her. That part of her own heart never healed. That wounded feeling, that un-granted wish still laid on her heavy, at times. She imagined that the old man felt the same.

Loss

How can I express,
something that can not be written down,
unless you can grasp lightening,
harness thunder, shush a whisper…
or ask your self if you should?

Loved ones go to heaven.
A few of us, will go to hell.
The eye of the needle is small,
and things of worth are in question.
The value of life,
precious.
The value of forever,
The price of blood,
paid.

On behalf of the unworthy,
whose only chance…
is Grace.

(8)
Angels Fly, Men Walk, We All Dream

Sheldon got into his truck and turned the key. It was old but reliable. That is the way of most farm trucks. They never get the best mileage, regardless of when you buy them, new or used, but that is not why you purchase them. Ask any man that has been behind their wheel, pulling something or needing to carry something, unexpected, with no time to mess around... knows. He waited just a few minutes to warm it up, before pulling out of the long drive. Sheldon turned back south as he got onto the actual road, barely above dirt out here, this far. That was the way he liked it however. The country life was the best life. He had seen other places, while serving his beloved America. But regardless of where he had gone, nothing was ever as beautiful as here. Home, was here and it always would be. There was nothing like it anywhere... at least that Sheldon had been to.

The man drove slowly. He tried to remember exactly where he and his daughter had picked up Mr. Cleaver. The man was old, so he could not have walked too far. Well, one mile, then another passed. It was still about thirty or a little more to the main highway, but surely, he had driven passed the wreck already. His dash board meter read ten miles from the spot he was sure. The man could not have exceeded that far? Walking in the cold, out here? How long had he walked? Sheldon felt he had to have missed the truck. He thought about turning around.

Then to his surprise he saw it. A small red truck, at least the tail gate and back end, barely sticking above the rise were just ahead. He pulled up, stopped his own vehicle and got out. He walked slowly over to the edge. The whole area felt strange. The sun was out, but it felt muted here. The black of shadow seemed to try to reach across the line, and gray out the colors. It felt wrong, and made his upper teeth hurt. They always did that when a storm was coming. But there was none. The sky above was ice cold, clear and sharp. From where Sheldon stood, if he looked back at his truck, it seemed further away than it should be. Like a tunnel, that appeared from and within the air around him. It was disorienting. He shook his head from side to side slowly. It had been a rough night with Mr. Cleaver, he figured he was way more tired, than usual.

    He looked straight up again at the sharp clear blue sky, and the feelings of "ick" receded. The man moved closer to the edge of the road. Somewhere inside he was reciting a prayer, from his childhood. It was the same one he had used his whole life, when fear came. It was the only thing he remember about grandma. She had not lived long after he had arrived to live in their house. Cancer had bad timing, if there ever was a time to be okay, as there was not. Yet still, the prayer was echoing and growing stronger in his head.

Lord,

The darkness
"it" has come,
for me.
Your shield, I beg...
Your shield for me,
and my family.
You Jesus,
King of All.
You are the Light,
the Candle
 that casts no shadow,
the Beam
that burns the unseen.
I am safe,
as
You
 are
 with
 me.

Amen.

Sheldon could see everything. It was not a good site. The vehicle was damaged pretty bad. Sheldon tried to be positive. Perhaps he could do it? He could pull it out, if his rope held. But that was a pretty big maybe. He was half a mind to try it, because he wanted to help Mr. Cleaver. The old man was in such a bad way. But it could easily go way wrong. There were other things more pressing than a wrecked truck anyway. Mr. Cleaver was alive and doing okay, well at least physically. That was a blessing. Time and prayer were going to have to help with the other things that he was going through. Sheldon felt so bad. "To go through so much, and not have God?" That would be hell indeed here on earth, with only worse to follow.

"Better to call Jack over at the station." Sheldon mumbled to himself. He could handle everything with expert skill. His thoughts now silent and kept only inside, the odd sensation of being listened to, eerie and unsettling. Bad feelings pervaded the general surrounds. "Might cost a little bit, but sadly there was not a lot of choice."

The young veterinarian did not feel he could get the vehicle out of the weeds and brush, much less, back up the incline and onto the road. Well, at least by himself, especially without trouble, maybe the kind he was not able to handle? Being honest about his skills had kept Sheldon out of a lot of difficulty in the past. Give him a cow in labor, breach even, and he was on it. But this type of thing, well, it was a different hero altogether that was needed. Sheldon knew his own limitations, and that was okay by him. There were thankfully alternatives. If that was not true it would be a different matter, but it was.

As he stood there looking over the mess, he was more that shocked at the condition. The whole front end was bashed flat. The front window was broken and half out. The axle was twisted in the front, as both tires were facing the wrong direction. It was going to have to be pulled, by force from its resting place. How did Martin Cleaver ever live through that? He wanted to ask someone, but he was all by himself, standing in the cold.

A shiver ran up and down his back. The evil feeling was returning ten fold. From where, or what caused it, he could not tell. Suddenly without any real reason he could place his thoughts on, he ran to his own truck and jumped back in. He hit the fan on the heater button and warm air blew out twice as hard. Sheldon was thankful he had kept the truck running. He put the old girl into gear and moved on down the road toward the urban world and safety? What an odd thought? He pushed it away. He had several stops to make. But they seemed distant. He could not focus clearly. He prayed under his breath… for several miles. The darkness, the weird atmosphere, retreated, grudgingly.

The taste of innocence is sweet,
and the taint of evil's passing,
reflective of emotions poorly spent.

In the bushes near by, eyes watched...
They were not friendly...
They were not kind...

It was going to take him half a day to drive back to town, get a hold of Jack and return. He also had two other stops to make. Charlie Burk had a cow going to drop anytime. Sheldon needed to check on her. That was on the list. That was important. It had to happen today, at least some time, as soon as he could. If Charlie lost the animal or rather if Mr. Burk's family lost it, it would go bad for them. They had small ones still at home. Their eldest daughter had also moved back and brought her brood. Milk was not a "want" it was a "necessity". That was the same story all around. Times were tough and getting harder, not better.

Normally, the next place would have to be John Folder's house. That could be passed by if he had to. John would understand. This was the day Sheldon always came by to check on Mary, the crippled man's prize turkey. He was working to enter the Tom at the upcoming fair. One day, one way or another, would not make a whole lot of difference. The fair was still a month away, and things were going well. If he did not show, John would know something came up. Getting Mr. Cleaver all fixed up and back on track; that was important. That was paramount.

He should probably head back over to the hospital before anything else. That errand was priority before any of the rest. He knew just about everyone there. He would find out for himself what happened. This was not the biggest town. News traveled really fast, amazingly fast. Dorothy Cleaver dying was a big deal. She had touched many in the community. The list of people that were going to miss her was going to be long.

Sheldon kind of felt funny… Why had he never thought to ask Dor about her husband? He remembered seeing his name on the prayer list, perhaps twice. Maybe it was three times? He had never thought to keep praying. Just because she had not listed it again and again on the sheet at church, perhaps he should have kept Martin's name handy. Prayed on his own? Kept praying…Maybe he should put this funny idea to work, and start some kind of prayer list? Helping others, holding them up, always made Sheldon feel better. He had learned that from his grandfather as well. He was a very smart man, well respected by all who knew him.

Last night Mr. Cleaver went through hell. Well at least the kind found here on earth. Not near like the real thing, but close enough that Sheldon never wanted to take part himself. After they got Mr. Cleaver home and in bed, he went in to check several times. He hated to leave the man alone, but he also hated to intrude. All the way up until midnight, he thought to take him to the hospital, but the poor old man would just cry. So Sheldon made promises he did not mean to make, and did not push the older man back out the door.

Sheldon had known God his whole life. His grandfather had seen to his prayers first thing. There was no question to be had… Jesus was the savior of the world… It was a fact. To witness someone so afraid, so shaken by shadows, death seemingly watching, like a morbid cartoon? It was terrible, and heart wrenching, loved ones left behind. It took a while… but Mr. Cleaver then slept. Fitfully, but probably exhaustion and grief were the masters of his body, not himself at all.

As Sheldon drove on in silence down the empty road, going over everything he knew so far, he continued to pray. He had to leave the truck in the ditch. There was no way around it. But, if Sheldon could do anything to help Mr. Cleaver from his personal suffering, that would be way more important. Trucks can be replaced. Usually they were even insured. Not like hearts and souls at all. They were much harder to console and heal. The morning sun made the world new again. It helped with the vet's mood on several levels. He needed that.

One sure thing, Dorothy was in heaven. How did he know that…? Sheldon smiled. He knew it because he had seen her. He had seen her heart time and again in action over the years, at church events. Her name was often mentioned in connection to being right where she needed to be at the right time, helping others and talking about her savior. It was personal to the woman. She had been a giant piece of something important and shared by many. She never hesitated at or in that task. You could see Jesus in her eyes.

Even now, Sheldon knew the angels were singing, to have her voice join the choir of the King. Sad for those left behind, but a celebration in heaven.

"The arrival of a daughter, a daughter of the King… has come."

Tricks in the Dark

Evil does not need to be,
ever in the shadow.
In fact, it likes to walk,
among us… best.

It hides and tries to pretend,
In plain sight!
To be a friend,
a lover with trusting arms,
a kind person,
that has a plan.

If you do not see,
all that is before you,
you have not asked
to be saved…

If you do not know,
what is before you,
you will still,
account…
for your stupidity,
your pride,
and your…
naivety.

It is not the same as,
unknowing.
It is denial.
The favorite joke,
told among dark-lings
that follow us home,
if we do not cut…
the string,
of sin
and
deceit.

Something
 we can not
 do…
Alone.

(9)
The Church On Sunday

The parking lot was more than full. There were no spaces left in the open field next door, the lot across the street at the market, and all public ways in both directions. People walked along the side walks, across the well kept, somewhat green grass, now only slightly hidden under a blanket of snow... containing holes. Lawns and garden parkways a hit and miss of weather conditions, a mixture of mottled color, a combination of growing things and ice.

They... the people, talked in hushed voices and wore their Sunday best. This was not however Sunday. This was the first Wednesday, of January. The bite in the air was real, but it did not stop anyone. Most would have come, even if there had been a blizzard. Some had reasons, some did not need any.

Lee Marion was at the front of the line, near the church entrance. The inside was already nearly full. There was an old organ playing some ancient hymn. The artist, making the antique play out, nearly beyond its limits... yet perfection. It was lovely. The promise of hope still to come, not just a season, but a splendid reality. It helped Lee get a hold of herself and the moment. She unconsciously shifted her bright purple hat to the left, a little lower than she meant too. The tiny birds on the side, clinked, but did not fall off. Thoughts of fixing "it" or in this case them later superseded what she wanted to avoid, which was everything that was going on. Controlled chaos, was the best description. Everything that was taking place, planned and unplanned;... was beautiful, exquisite and sad...

White flowers, as far as the eye could see in every direction filled the view. Where they came by so many, at this time of the year was a wonder. Lee, loved it. The church was breathtaking for being small and old. It was not run down however, but showed great care. Yet, "age" pure age was the feeling, the emotion that held the walls plumb square and the roof high and leak free.

If there was standing room only, Lee was going to stand. Her kids were fighting back and forth, like kids do. She wanted to go home, but remembered. Dorothy had come in the worst weather to bring dinner and even extra food when she was sick. Not once but a few times. She had often stayed and taken care of both Lee's sons, until way late in the night. That had been a couple of years ago. She had always meant to come over and say hi, and thanks to the old lady. It, just never happened. Lee got better and life went on… as usual.

Lee had no idea Dorothy was even sick. She never said. Truth was they were not close. She had seen her once or twice more since being ill, but that was all. That had been a rough time on a personal level. However, Dorothy Cleaver was just "a" lady from the church. One, just one… Lee Marion did not even attend very often. Not since her husband had left her. He went off to a better life without responsibility. Well, that is what he said anyway, one that did not involve children and a whiny wife. But now Dorothy Cleaver was gone. She had not left of her own accord. Lee felt angry. She felt regret. She felt loss. All three much greater than the night he, the scum bag, left. This was deeper and far more real.

Her husband was so much less important now. The divorce was finalized long ago, and he skipped town not to pay any support. No surprise. That happens more than not, in most cases. Lee had had stand in food stamp lines and grovel. It hurt some part of her, that she soon let go of. As whatever, "it" was, was holding her back from helping her kids, get what they needed. So, slowly… she had pieced her life back together.

Lee wished with her whole heart that she had remembered in time to say something to the old woman. Perhaps she would not have made it through that darkness, if Dorothy Cleaver had not come. With her simple food, and needed things? She had made a difference that could not be measured even now, as it was still returning on the investment of her deposit. Dorothy Cleaver had not judged, just helped.

In retrospect, Lee realized, it was clear Dorothy never would have said anything to Lee. It would have taken Lee's efforts. Dorothy was a giver, and taking back, was not in her nature. Lee would have liked to have at least, given her the due, of gratitude. Yet, that was the kind of person Dorothy Cleaver was. Now, all Lee could do was wait her turn to get inside, with her brood in tow. Regardless of how long it took, she would make sure she paid her respects.

While the crowd gathered;

*Angel ladies, ever,
crocheting hats for the homeless,
blankets for the sick
and items of value for service....
gathered in earnest together,
in the church kitchen for prayer.
They... were one less now.
May... put the cookies on the tray.
Anna, tried to make the coffee,
Sarah had to help.
Sharon, she just would not stop crying.
No one was angry at her.*

*They kept moving forward.
The ladies of the church,
cheerfully
accepting
their loss
with grace.
Knowing their sister,
was with their
Lord!*

Other attendees;

Mike Fallo stood near his own car. It was a deep forest green, 1968 Chevy, Malibu. His "baby" and she looked gorgeous. He had washed her, and waxed her. He had come in style. He was outfitted in his finest dress uniform as well. Mike had arrived very early and had a great parking space. He had watched since before dawn as people arrived. There were all kinds. Some with kids, some without, but all of different walks, not connected clearly, but by an unseen thread. He knew, he held one of the ends himself.

Funny, Mike had fully decided he was not going to go in at all, the church that is. He was just going to wait here. He had no plans to do anything else. He could go, or rather would go to the grave site later. When no one else was around, that felt better. He had only parked so close, to get to see, whatever there was to see, without getting too close. That was better for him. He had a lot of trouble in crowds. The sheer number of individuals... strangers and families coming from all directions, would have once made him have an attack. But not anymore. Not ever again.

Dorothy was kind of a stranger to him anyway. Mike Fallo was not from around the town, or even from the closest city. They did not even share the same state. He had received the news of Dorothy Cleaver's death in a paper, a newspaper. It was one he had some how been subscribed to for a long while now. Ever since he had received the package at Christmas so long ago, he had followed events in the town. This one had drew him here in person. When you get a chance...; those kinds of chances in life that rarely come along, to pay your respects, you just want too. Maybe even... you just need too or even have too.

Dorothy Cleaver had sent some items in a box at Christmas. Not recently, it was from...before. The package arrived at Mike's camp, when Mike was in service over seas. There had been a kind note. It had been in long hand, like his teacher in third grade used to write. It was beautiful. It had also changed his life. It had empowered him in ways he had never dreamed. It had taken him to his knees, dashed him on rocks, protected him from fire, and stood with him in hell, at least the kind found among the evil here on Earth. Humbly he stood watching now. He was trying to decide if he "did" want to go in after all? No one knew him, but that was okay. She did not know him either.

> *The voice of the saints call to the fallen,*
> *the lost, the misplaced, the forgotten,*
> *and those in the deserts far from home, missing snow,*
> *but not black ice.*

Mike thought again about the church box and the funny stuff that had been inside. Trinkets and toys and such, along with her long letter, which he still kept in his study bible back home, the one he used for church on Sundays. Back then, in the box... there had been a new testament and psalms, with pictures. It was small enough he could take it with him, and yet, weighed nothing. It was old, not the casual one you buy at the five and dime. It was pretty, well more like a piece of art. The small pictures inside were exquisite. He found he spent time looking at them. Daniel and a Lion, Noah and a side view of the great ark, Mary, Joseph and Jesus, together in the barn at his birth. He wondered where she had found it? Dorothy I mean. Where did she come across the little book? Or perhaps how she had acquired it? Was it a treasure passed down? It sure felt like that when he held it and read it's pages at night. The kind of thing you only got from like…your mom. ? Well, just saying.

Mike was an orphan. He had been tossed aside and cast off. The system had not been better, once it found him in the first place, in a drug hotel, at a crime scene. Mike was just another statistic, by most accounts and most people. That is how he had come into the world and lived... up until the box.

From that point, he had been fostered out...which was the last he ever knew of any kind of family connection, until he was let go at 18, he had been shuffled around lots of government facilities and "foster" homes. He had been to the proverbial there and back, many times. But he knew what a real mom was supposed to be like. He dreamed about it enough, he had a list. A real list, well not anymore. But when he was a kid, he wrote one out. It had been a kind of joke at first, then later... a kind of prayer from a child that never knew how to pray. The old woman... somehow... she must have found a copy, which was of course not possible. That was also a joke; kind of like an odd thing, that makes you wonder. It, the list... had been tossed long before, at one house or another, in an entirely different city far from here by an angry person. That happened lots too. A series of angry people... but that was a different matter then, and life had changed a lot since.

Yet, Dorothy had hit every bullet point on it. She had basically covered everything on that crayoned colored page in one small, boxed container sent to a stranger. It made Mike feel funny, just a little, in a way that could never be expressed, it had to be experienced.

He remembered, there were comic book clippings, a few drawings, important articles, other news posts; tiny things of interest. A set of jacks, a yoyo, and a hard caramel sucker, large enough to last at least a week. Also, candy cigarettes that you blew on and they puffed out powdered sugar. (a stop smoking pamphlet from the surgeon general, given to the public, if written for which in this case Dorothy Cleaver had done…in case the person getting the box smoked). The boxes were not specific, or at least they were not supposed to be. But in Mike's mind, you could not now convince him that it was not personal. God assured him as much as he stood looking on at the growing line in the distance. Dorothy was not a typical saint... that was obvious by the fruits he could see, from his vantage point, in all directions.

More stuff was still...there, the Christmas miracle, a box of caramel corn, with a prize and a second surprise taped to the outside, from another box, not included. A cross, not made of silver but solid steel was also in the container. It had a really tough chain to match. It was the kind of thing that would never break, for any reason. Not a typical size to be warn around the neck, no. It was like three inches long. It made him smile a little, thinking of comic scenes as a kid watching a vampire movie. It worked much the same way now, only the evil he was facing in the deep desert while in service, was real and not a fairy tale. Instead the enemy tried to shoot you or blow you up with real bullets and bombs. Crosses did not stop such things, but they gave the owner , the knower of all things Jesus... peace, when there was none to be had, anywhere.

Michael Fallo was six foot four inches. Dressed his very best, out of respect. The loved and cherished, steel cross was hidden. Even large, he wore it around his neck today, close to his heart, under his shirt. This time in honor of her. Dorothy Cleaver had written... God would be close to him always, if he prayed. He still did not understand how the box came to him at the right time? The exact right time, as only God's timing can be. But he believed her words, every one of them, even if he had never heard her say a one. Her fine long hand was a painted picture of Jesus's face, between the lines, lovingly imprinted. Every time he took it out, he found it the same. The visage of the Lord, still gazed directly at him, with a kind face, and a forgiving heart. Mike could not explain it.

At the cross, Jesus forgave.
He forgives still.
All that needs be done,
repent, accept,
believe.

After that had happened, the packages arrival had come, Michael felt his life change. He was not so fearful, or unsettled. His general performance went up, and a new found sense of honor and pride had taken over. It had propelled him into a better life. Michael Fallo had been born again. Fully accepting Jesus as his living savior. Some part of him, wished he could have talked to the old woman, now gone. If just to tell her, that he had changed. It would have to wait now, until he too got to heaven, God willing. There he was sure, they would laugh together and be true friends.

A few months later...after the box had arrived... Service Man Fallo was released from duty. Mike had always meant to look her up then. Not a love affair, it was gratitude. He had thought to kill himself. That was still a sharp idea to think about in his head. He was not judging himself, but holding himself accountable. God had a plan for Michael Fallo, and whatever it was, he was going to be ready. In the mean time, he was on the path. That had led him right here, this day.

Mike had killed people. In the line of duty yes, but dead is still dead. That was hard, but it was deeper than that. Mike had seen a couple of friends die badly, and just could not figure out how he had been spared? Dorothy Cleaver had made that very clear. She had sent him a second chance, a new beginning in a box of "stuff".

Since then he had worked hard to help others with similar situations as well. Mike Fallo was now a hot-line manager for suicide, mostly dealing with vets. That was the last thing he ever thought he would be working on with in his life. It was the very night her package came, and her kind words on paper about a Savior…that had made a difference, changed his whole thought pattern. He went on to make it out of that bad place, and to put his life together. He had a wife now. He, well really, they were expecting a kid. If it was a girl, he was voting to name her Dorothy. His loving wife would totally get that. She was such a softy.

Mr. Benjamin Chanan had been contacted by Mr. Fallow. It had taken a while, but Mike had found the bread crumb path... back to the beginning. Months before Dorothy had passed away, he had sent a letter to Mr. Chanan. Mike had found out that he had helped in the ministry... the Christmas Treasure Boxes. Mike had asked about the way the boxes had been chosen, and how he could know more? After that letter had been sent... Mike Fallow had received the weekly newspaper right along. Mr. Chanan figured that was the best way to keep up with the small things of this small place. So Benjamin simply called a good friend and put Mike Fallow on the list... of the out-of-towners. The ones that had found their lives different somehow..., in some way unexpectedly... and wanted more. Benjamin knew it was the Holy Ghost moving.

Even then... at that time, Mike had meant to come and meet Dorothy Cleaver. He wanted to perhaps attend church and tell her that she had made a difference. The paper had been delivered with sad words of her death. The news had been profound. Windows in our life are so very short some times. Putting off what we mean to do... has consequences. Then life changes and it is just simply too late.

The question of the boxes...; Well Benjamin Chanan was a quiet angel. No he did not wear a rose pin... but he owned one. It was his mothers. He was proud of it. Benjamin had helped both at the hospital while on his job there in maintenance, and indirectly and yet at the same time... at the same church Dorothy attended. He had done so for nearly twenty years on both accounts. They Benjamin, Dorothy and two others, cheerful volunteers; had put the long list of military men and women together. It had been the names of all those to receive boxes. They were the names of those in a hot zone. Benjamin always worked to put things together and keep them running. He had a soft spot for all things military, as he had a son, now gone. Having lost his wife early on, God had used him, and filled him with a sense of purpose. The letter from Mr. Fallow had made Mr. Chanan cry. But he would never have admitted it to a soul. Well, maybe Dorothy, but that was because she got it. She always "got it".

It was Mr. Chanan that had arranged to have all the boxes sent overseas… It was those same boxes that had arrived at just the right time, the very one given to Mike, among them. That one container made of simple cardboard would and did ultimately bring Mike to this place now. Many would say that alone was a miracle, but others…

<u>Yeah</u>
<u>Yeah...</u>
<u>I'm a Christian. I go to church.</u>
<u>high pitched chirping sounds...</u>
<u>low,</u>
<u>far away...</u>
<u>and yet, close...</u>
The sound stopped abruptly,
a man in a black suit walked by.
He said nothing to Michael Fallow,
but he also cast no shadow,
but no one noticed.
He went toward the church,
but did not go in, but walked on by instead.

Mike found unwanted wetness, at the edges of his eyes… He prayed… he prayed she had no pain. He prayed for her family, and that angels would help all that needed a hand, or would need one. Mike was also, so sorry he had never met Dorothy Cleaver in person. He judged by the number of vehicles and the shortage of space available to park any more, that she had been truly blessed. She had touched the waters of life and the ripples were everywhere, seen visually as those that now came.

After thinking in through... he stayed at his car. It was enough he was here. There were so many, but somehow he still had to come. It was comforting to see, even elating to his heart. God's hand was clearly visible everywhere... and that was just one woman. It cheered him and made her memory all the brighter. His right hand strayed to his chest where he touched the cross beneath. It was not a crucifix. "He" was not there. He had been lifted, and raised to heaven. God was, is and always will be...real.

Linda Childs sat in the front pew of the small sanctuary. She was silent and stoic. Last year, Dorothy Cleaver had helped her walk through her first cancer treatment. They had laughed and cried a lot since that first time they met. It happened by accident near the big fountain at the hospital. Benjamin Chanan had left a flat of flowers on the bench. Dorothy had taken upon herself, to just start putting them in. Linda thought she was part of the hospital staff at first, but that idea was given no time to take form.

Dorothy had seen Linda come in. She had known the terror in her eyes, first hand, so it was easy to spot. Dor was not going to let that be the way things went. So she looked right up and smiled. God had gotten her this far, herself. She was not going to let him down, by being weak.

"Hello. You are such a nice young woman. I am old." Dorothy had just started up the conversation, like they had been friends forever. "these nice flowers could sure use planting…" as she had motioned to the remaining bright colors laying out in the small plastic container. "the man that works here, is very nice. I like to help as I can. You don't mind do you? Helping out an old woman? Helping out…" again her smile. It was both disarming and comforting. Like someone had brought the sun inside.

Before Linda had known what was happening, she was beside Dorothy, getting her hands dirty. She had half an hour before her appointment. Linda had come early. She wanted to make sure she was not late. She wanted to skip it, but the tests were clear. She could not. Things however were changing, right there at that very moment. All the sickness she had been feeling, the anxiety of coming to the… hospital… was ever so slowly drained as the two women worked. When the clock grudgingly stole away the saved space, the early minutes only available because of her own fear, now missed and even cherished forever, it left Linda sad. "It" was a small miracle both women had found together.

Burdens carried by two, are shared,
and have the power, of gathered prayer,
if the knees are bent
He…listens…always.

Linda had glanced at her watch. She had to go. She had gotten up to leave, but that was not the end. Dorothy had just gotten up with her.

"First time?" A hushed question. Dorothy already knew the answer.

"Y…es…" a tear ran down her face. She could barely feel it still. As if that same tiny salted drop, had left a permanent trace. No one could see, but it was there.

"I have time, I am going that way. Lets just go have a little sit, a bit, then we can talk… a bit… and then…we can be friends forever." Dorothy hugged Linda. Right there in front of the fountain. It was not a cheerful hug shallow, but deeper, a loving one. It expressed comfort, hope, and faith all in one motion. "forever friends, sisters…daughters of the King."

Linda was floored. But said nothing. Her voice had left. Dorothy Cleaver just interlaced her arm together with her new friend. "let's go."…

Chemo, bad days and good. Hair on the floor, wanting to die all of it part of the bigger picture. Dorothy never wavered. They soon shared things that few dared dwell upon. Linda's last test had come back good. Better than expected. That had been the news of the day.

Dorothy however, already knew she was passed the point of no return, even back then has they had placed the first flower into the fine black dirt at their first meeting. They never slowed down after that day. Hope made each moment special. That was the old ladies lesson. Linda Childs had learned it well. She had a plan. She was going to live. Her heart was only broken as it felt like a part of her had gone with her friend. With her very will... she tried to hold onto every memory, going over things again and again in her head. It was so hard to lose a sister. But she would see her in heaven. Linda felt changed, and knew God now, personally. Dorothy had seen to that… Not like she had not "known" him before. But he was never alive, until Dorothy told her the truth. But that, was another day, in a long collections of days, that Linda wished were years instead. She did not get enough of her friend and never would.

Now Linda planted flowers at the front, in the garden at the big white building. She did it twice a month. The shovel had been passed, and it was a honor to take on the responsibility. No one exactly promoted her, or made it her job. Mr. Chanan would just leave them there, and she would come and put them in. Linda smiled at that. She also watched as she gardened. She sang and kept vigilant in case another "sister" walked in... and she knew it would happen. Just as Dorothy knew it would happen when it did for her.

The garden...It had been that pretty place, in that bad place, the hospital, that had made a world of difference to Linda. Garden angel took on a whole new meaning for her, as it brought up visions of Dorothy leaned over a petunia with flowered gloves having fun. The area, before you leave, where the water makes nice sounds, and welcomes the suffering, that was their favorite spot together. After treatments, the one that first day for Linda, and all those that followed after, they would share something to drink, if they could keep it down, there, near the blooms. Most times, only a moment or two toward the end. Things were not okay for Dor. That was obvious, but not to her, or those that loved her. They preferred to remain blind. Heartache was better digested slowly, rather than all at once, at least in Ms. Child's experience.

Linda Childs wore a hat today. It was soft blue, with tiny flowers at the edges. Dorothy had helped her pick it out. They both knew their hair was a lost cause, but hats… that made it worth while at least. Fashion Zebras… that is what Dorothy called them both, as they wore new bonnets during Easter. New sun hats with big brims in fall and every different and vividly colored baseball cap for both short and long walks. Winters were hand made beanies, of wool yarn and especially Mo-Hair. Just because it sounded so exotic. Who knew it was just another type of goat, unless they looked it up. Well, it really is a pretty goat, anyway. Instead it seemed like a wild animal from the north, hard to find, by its name.

Linda cried inside, but kept ever silent. If she let go now, she would never, ever stop. That can not happen. One other thing she learned from Dor, not by voice, but by action, "Don't let them see you flinch. Keep your head high, and walk on." That is the message Dor spread. Jesus loves you and the rest, well; they can work that part out or not. It was all the same to her. She was a down home gal, from the roots of her family to the roots of her uncolored hair. That made Linda smile, ever so at the edges of her mouth. Hair was always a funny subject, if you had the right frame of mind to brush it in. Dor always put Linda in that structure, that imaginary land where what you wanted made a difference. She was going to miss that beyond words.

Just Strands of Straw

I look into the mirror,
my hair has dropped to the sink.
It is a trail of tears,
years of taking care of split ends,
fluffing and drying,
tying it up,
leaving it down…
now, just gone.
My crown of glory
it is…
gone.
Maybe
and
more than likely,
forever…

Yet the Glory of My Lord,
is ever upon me,
shinning brightly,
in all
of…
His Light!

Yes, my hair has fallen,
to the floor.
I have not.
I am loved
and
cherished.
He sees,
"me".

A tear unleashed ran down her cheek, dropped to her blouse and made a small wet mark. That was not supposed to happen. Linda quickly tried to rub it with the tissue, without making too much commotion, or draw too much attention to her self. She bit her lip, quit what she was doing and returned to staring at the front podium. Emotions were for later, not now, was the best course of action she decided.

The flowers were lovely. Linda focused on them. She glanced from one arrangement to the next. Surprisingly, there were many, although several did not appear to be too expensive. There were even hand picked winter offerings, and dried petals in baskets. This was a poor community in general. A couple however, stood out. One was pink roses, long stem… They were set in a vase of milk white glass. It looked very old. Linda smiled a funny, knowing kind of look, she often shared with Dorothy on the few special occasions, ever sweet moments they both felt good. It was in response to a thought, whomever sent them, the lovely roses in a mix; truly expressed it well. It was not a bouquet of love so much, but ringed in white daises, and babies breath, cheerfully speaking volumes about depth.

Linda, pulled her bag just a little closer, took out another tissue and dotted the edges of her eyes. She no longer felt like balling until she could not make another noise, it had passed. She had won this battle, this round. She had held back the tide. She had to make it through this ceremony, and then that would be enough. Linda could go home, and talk to her bird for a while. They would make up songs about Dorothy and play the piano softly in her honor. That was later. She just kept telling herself. That was later and it would wait. This was important. Showing your support for someone… Showing those that matter, left behind, that they are not alone in their suffering. Dorothy was surely in heaven. That gave Linda the ever so small feeling of strength, deep inside. She could do this, all of this, whatever this was for Dor. Linda Childs…garden angel… hardened her reserve and waited for the pastor to begin.

The ladies from the church had done everything that was needed to be done. Colleen Hines and her girls were veterans at funerals. Not something to brag about really, but if you were to do such a thing, Mrs. Hines name would be at the top of the list. She was old school all the way.

She thought that was the right way and it was necessary to give the proper impression. Sanctity and grace were not to be taken lightly. Colleen was white napkins, bleached brilliant linens, and satin in all the right places. Silk flowers, some of which could be used again and again, and the best plastic ware, as not to appear cheap.

This was to be a funeral without a body, as Dorothy Cleaver had been cremated. That was still unsettling to some, but it mattered not at all to others. The difference clearly in the idea of keeping what we are, and not who we are, chained to something that has no use, any longer to anyone. Dorothy's remains, now in a box, a nice box, brought over earlier by a friend. That very nice Sheldon Farman. It had been hand made, ordered ... A carpenter with special talents had seen to its design. An artist had painted fine small flowers on the outside. There had also been a handle on top, as if she... Dorothy Cleaver that is... was going places, but she was not even there. Her spirit, her soul. Colleen knew that as she knew that Dorothy Cleaver was born again. Or had been. Or ... Well... in heaven now anyway!

The handle on top of the beautiful box... the woman thought; an odd addition to the norm, but considered part of the art of the container, not deeper than paint on canvas to a master artisan. There was also a small latch and lock. The key... not present.

Colleen had watched carefully when "she", Dorothy that is, had been brought in. Her container had been kept in the back... placed their earlier... waiting to be presented. Only moments before it had been moved to the decorated front table. Dorothy Cleaver was to always be handled with respect. That was important.

Miss Hines worked downtown at the records office. She was methodical and precise. It reflected in everything she did. At this point this day, it was a tree, rooted in her subconscious. Her ever steady faith in God, planted years and years before, that made her walk straight, and fill in the lines for others, to be as complete and perfect as possible. The tree, was how she pictured HIM. Something solid to hang on to, when the whole world was upside down and backwards. Not a small one, but a King

Redwood, with roots to the center of the earth and branches to reach space. Falling apart ever, was not an option for the woman. Today would be no different from the rest. Well, at least in public.

Dorothy's loss was very specific to Miss Hines. She had been church friends with her for so long, that her vacant seat would be a vacuum indeed, to all. Dor had known things...How? Colleen could never find out. But she was always three steps ahead to someone's door that needed something than was typical or really possible. That had only slowed with Dorothy's illness but not by a lot. Colleen felt insecure inside. There were be a greater burden to make sure, nothing was missed. Prayer lists would have to be updated, more often. She had slowly taken the duties on, as her friend... lost the battle. But the heaviness of them, was not full, until now.

Colleen pulled herself away from the flowers she was staring at. The pink was hard to miss. Lovely, and expensive. Who sent them...?, there had been no card. The color was enough. Pink. Colleen knew that was Dor's favorite. She always picked it over any other when life presented choices. The younger woman had watched some things, and vowed to carefully try to watch all now. The reason; people truly in trouble, seldom saw it in themselves until too late. That very thought relating to Dor's cancer. She could have...maybe... worked on it harder, found out somehow sooner? Colleen did not like to dwell. If she had just let them prayer sooner, or more or? Tears welled up in her eyes and she stopped all of it. The line of thinking, was not helping in her duties this day. So Colleen Hines, straighten her belt and skirt, pressed her hands down their length for wrinkles and stood even straighter.

"This will go well Dor, I promise." She whispered low under her breath to no one.

The clock was still ten minutes until the hour, for things to begin. There would be a nice speaking…by the pastor. Then there would be... always a few words by those that knew the deceased. Followed there after at the house for food and talking. That would be at the home today of Ms. Cleaver. In this case it was going to be at Dorothy's house. That was the first time anyone was, or would be invited by her, without her actually sending notices. It had been arranged. Normally, no one ever went there, for any reason. It was not noticed by anyone either, until she died.

Lisa had already cleaned up and made things ready. She had left a message for Colleen. That was great. The other women not on hand yet, would be headed that way. They would set up tables and put things out as needed, if there was more to do. They were a unit, working as one, for His Glory.

Food, drinks… a time to talk and chat. That was the best way. It helped people to heal, if just a bit. Dorothy Cleaver was well loved. But that really did not matter, Colleen Hines always did her best for all funerals, this was not going to be any different. She secretly hoped it would be her finest however. Her friend deserved that.

Ms. Hines had worked behind the scenes for a solid week. Preparations from flowers to food, among other things were not new to her. She had made all the calls, and spoke with everyone. There had been reactions… that still puzzled her. Yet, they did not surprise her.

The first on the list had been to the florist on 5th and Main. The lady there took the call right away, and knew exactly what was expected. However, when Colleen asked for the price at the end of the call, the young woman said, "Paid". After several tries, Colleen gave up. The woman meant exactly what she said. There would be no cost, no charge at all for the flowers delivered to Dorothy's service. Let me say also there were not just a few…, but many. That was mighty nice, at least Colleen thought as much. Then to her continued astonishment, she ordered items from both the bakery and the deli, and found the same answer when the ticket was due. "Paid." No one said by who, nor would they say more.

The largest bill, the one to turn her kind friend to dust… That had been in Dorothy Cleaver's will. She wanted to be cremated. It was not to be changed, and it had been notarized, not once but twice on the same day, by two different people. Clearly… there was a reason.

Thankfully they had found her papers in at the bank, in the safety deposit box. That nice Sheldon Farman and again Lisa his daughter had helped the old man, with the "hard stuff". The paperwork that had to be handled, concerning death. That is how Colleen had found out about Dor's passing. The day they the man and his daughter brought items into her office at records. She had held it together then also, but not by much. Names come and go, but when it is someone you really know... and they are just departed like that... well it hits like bricks.

Together, in their search for information... The veterinarian and the rest found Dorothy had left things remarkably in order. There had been a short will, which said basically everything went to her husband. It was very simple, as Dor was not rich by any means. She really did not have anything to pass on, of great worth and value. The house would go to Martin, as they were joint tenants with full right of survivorship. It was also very old and very run down.

They had no children. The place, the home... well it had only a small mortgage left. It would have been paid for completely, but Mr. Cleaver had never gone back to work. Upon returning form service, he could not hold a job. He tried for a while, it just did not happen. So he stopped looking. Dorothy worked for the district up until she could not. Money was tight, but now a new time had come. That was still changing from moment to moment to keep too close a tract. In the end something would have to be worked out.

Loved ones left...
unable to care for themselves,
in some way or another...
never matters the ultimate reason,
only that they were still here.

Colleen had worked years at her post. She had seen her share of legal documents. She felt sadly odd however holding the papers that early Monday morning, as Mrs. Cleaver's will was written in long hand. It was very personal, extremely so. There were tear stains on the paper. Colleen knew what they looked like. She had seen them before. It leaves a particular kind of water mark. Dor…must have been in a lot of pain. She had processed everything quickly, efficiently and completely. There had been witnesses. It had been in order.

Back... among the items in the box according to Sheldon, a letter had been found. It was sealed tight, and had her husband's name written on the outside. It had been taken back to the house... had been passed, from hand to hand, until it was now sitting on Dor's dresser. It lay there on the white doily even now. Unopened.

The words inside:

>*My dearest love,*
>*You will be okay.*
>*I have prayed for you.*
>*He has listened.*
>*My prayers are strong,*
>*and will not return void.*
>*I leave you in the care...*
>*Of my Lord.*
>*Love,*
>*Dorothy*

Collen Hines continued her business. The arrangements that she had to make to pull off the best goodbye; she called the number. Her hand shook slightly as she dialed. Then she waited for the other end to answer. Ring, ring.

"I knew you would be calling." The man's voice was very flat. He was the only one around that handled cremation. Not everyone agreed to this type of final rest. It had always been a touchy subject between Colleen Hines and Edward Dego. They had gone to school together. As a boy he had scared Colleen at a funeral, his father had arranged. Having a friend hide inside a casket to jump out at just the right time, left memories perhaps stronger than meant, for a joke.

Edward had spent all summer after that washing every "public use" car in town, from the sheriff to the fire' chief's own blue truck. In addition he had to do the pastors as well for both the Baptist and the Methodist, equally. That even included the two buses they shared between them. It was the only thing his father could come up with. That and a trip to the wood shed, that broke a paddle on a tourist, if you know what I mean. That was besides all his usual duties. He had also had to learn to work the oven that same summer. He never made jokes again, about the passing of anyone. The look on her face, twelve year old Colleen…that day, was still etched on his heart. He had thought her so pretty, but never would he have the guts to say a word again, expect in business when and as expected.

    Colleen had only gotten more beautiful over the years. Edward's fear of further invoking her hate, kept him from ever daring to cross the line again. Even all grown up, a single look from her, reduced him to a kid again. He became awkward, and stupid, and even fumbled when he spoke… so he wrote out things to say. Even for business, which he knew well, he depended on his pen and paper notes. It was just a way she had, that could turn him to jelly.

    "Everything is handled. Dorothy Cleaver's remains will be at the church, as you instructed, at the right place and the right time." A few very long moments of silence followed again. The man wanted to make Colleen hear every word, to make sure she missed nothing, as that would make her upset later. She took things very seriously. He knew that. Extremely well indeed, and would never make another mistake around her or that had anything to do with her again, if he could help it. He never wanted to fall short AGAIN in her eyes.

You are beautiful, to me.

    The caller still remained completely silent. The man, a little more impassioned, "I know you don't like cremation. I understand. It is okay. It will be okay." The man finished. He tried to put a lot of emotion, and yet none at all in every word. It was confusing and his stomach hurt. He could not remember if he had breakfast, or if the lack of it was making him feel faint. He waited just a few more moments. A rumble of ugly tremors made noises in his office from his stomach and lower region. His hand quickly covered the phone for fear something wrong would be heard.

Then finally, he blurted out, "No charge. The bill was paid in full." He hung up. She had no time to respond to the last part. Yet, somehow she was not surprised, it had been the answer the whole morning. Every person she needed, every person she called, echoed; paid in full. None would make further comment.

Colleen Hines now stood at the front. It was the right day and the right time, and things were going to go off well. She gazed out from the curtain area, checking seats. The music would be Mrs. Wendel's son on the big organ. He was pretty good. It needed tuning but that could not be helped. The music would cheer things up just a bit. From the look of the group that was a good idea. Not that there was anything bad happening, but there was certainly nothing uplifting going on. She took a moment to say a prayer. Then left her spot on guard. She walked out the kitchen area, and down the side hall and then up the main aisle. She headed straight for Jessie. She walked with purpose... right over... and touched him lightly on the arm. It had been a sudden feeling and impulse as if Dor had asked herself.

"Amazing Grace, please. If you get to the end, and we are not ready, just start again. Do it until the pastor gives you the high-sign." She smiled. He nodded. Great she picked one he knew well. Thankful, he smiled.

Jess Wendel complied immediately. He was a little unsteady at first, as this was his first time as the prime entertainment. But he soon fell right to his work.

Angel's gathered in the rafters.
They watched as the people came in slowly.
The music started, and they grew still.
They did not want to miss a note.
Songs to the King...
Amen.

109

Wendy Farnsworth glanced up, just in time to see two angels trading places between the beams. They were seeking a better vantage point, in which to take in all things that were happening.

"Mommy, look." The little girl put her hands to heaven.

"Hush sweetheart. We need to be quiet in church. They are starting soon." The only reply. Mom reaching into her purse to find a sucker, one was always there. Quickly offering it up, the child accepted. Now sucking on a cherry charm, Wendy just smiled and watched, as the visitors played in the rafters. They laughed quietly, smiled and made funny faces at her, to keep her busy. They so loved children.

The pastor, Marcus Pinwheel Sr. had been the leader here for nearly fifty years. He knew every one of his people. He knew there families and their kids. This was by far one of the harder ceremonies he had ever had to give. She was a pillar, ever holding up the very roof of the place. Dorothy Cleaver was some one that was always there, in the front row, rain or shine. On days he had rushed, Dorothy was a cheerleader. She always knew and kept him honest.

There was a new man coming to town. He was to take Marcus's place. Soon. Pastor Pinwheel was getting old, and felt it was time. In fact he, Dorothy, Mrs. Wix and a handful of others had made plans. A celebration would be arranged. Set on the calendar by Colleen Hines. She was such an angel.

Roses in the garden of forever,
are the saints that stepped up and to and not away,
holding up hope when there was none to be found,
with faith...
blind.

In preparing for his retirement, they had all agreed on one man for his replacement. It was to be a boy, now a man... that had once attended the church as a child, and was not far off in the big city. He had not yet answered the call. They, the small group of believers had prayed for God's hand to move. To hold up their small church high and give them what they needed when they needed it most. In the mean time, retirement was still in the plan, but today it was all on him. Well Pastor Pinwheel and God. This was HIS house, and he served humbly and faithfully.

Dor was his angel, now missing...or rather moved on. That was okay in every way he knew of. His soul told him, she was safe and well cared for, even now singing and celebrating would be happening in her honor. Glorious to be home with God.

It made Pastor Pinwheel smile, and his wrinkled eyes were suddenly extra bright. It was a glaze of tears. Dorothy would be sorely missed indeed. She was trouble. "Work hard on your sermon fellow", she would taunt. The pressure she would bring, as there were at least a few taking notes. "Be sharp." That is what she would say, to him. She loved to rib and tease... to make him work harder. He would miss that. Pastor Marcus Pinwheel Sr. had grown accustomed to Mrs. Dorothy Ann Cleaver keeping him on his toes. Who was going to do that now? His own heart ached. He looked in the mirror, the one in his tiny office. He combed his thinning hair and tried to smile. He was old yes, and should retire.

The face in the surface, the reflection in the mirror looked back, and appeared joyful. The question haunted him however, "How can you retire from serving God?" He could almost hear her sweet words somewhere echoing, "You can't." Of course it was not real or true, but the message, the wisdom, gave his spirit comfort.

"You got this." Dorothy's voice again somewhere, but not anywhere…heard and unheard.

The aged man closed his eyes. "See you in heaven my friend. You are sorely missed here. It will be tough going, but I believe you, as always." Marcus smiled. A big deep and real grin. His heart ached. She had cancer, and it had eaten her up, like a starving wolf. She was not the first, and certainly was not going to be the last. She was just for him, the most painfully missed. Dorothy Cleaver helped everyone, had the nicest things to say, and never knew the word "no" existed. Now, others would have to step up. How would that go?

      Marcus Pinwheel Sr. bowed his head in prayer. Keeping eyes closed tight;
a thousand past sermons filled his head, then left quietly. He found he was just alone, with God. That was enough. It gave him exactly what he needed when he needed it.

Amen.

*Dear Lord…Mighty King,
I come to you, as a child!*

Now I lay me down to …

*When I was small, Grandma told me to pray.
When I was older I did it because…
I found, "He" answered,
every time.*

Loss

*How can I express,
something that can not be written down,
unless you can grasp lightning,
harness thunder, shush a whisper…
or ask your self if you should?*

*Loved ones go to heaven.
A few of us, will go to hell.
The eye of the needle is small,
and things of worth are in question.
The value of life,
precious.
The value of forever,
The price of blood,
paid.*

*On behalf of the unworthy,
whose only chance…
is Grace.*

(10)
The Madness of Death
The Insanity of the Living

Martin Cleaver was not going to go to the church. He had no intention at all. But he knew that was not how it was going to go.

"They" had called so many times. "They" had also shown up at his house... since the news had spread. "They" had made him sign papers and talked to him. Endlessly, "They" spoke to him. "They" made noises that seemed coherent to everyone except him, in the room. Question upon question, about things Martin had no answers to at all.

That was who "they" were. Everyone one of them. The doctor, the lawyer, the banker, the church people, the kind strangers that called, that Ms. Hines and her again and again, and the cremator worst of all. How could they take his Dorothy and do all the things they were doing and then burn her up? How could "They"? That man Sheldon and his daughter Lisa, what words could express...love and hate in the same sentence? If they had let him die, none of this would have been, it would just not "be" at all. The confusion of gratitude, not to be left, to the darkness, which threatened him daily, in ways he prayed could not be seen, if pray it was called, at all? Martin was not saved, but the shield of those present, encompassed his being, without his consent or approval. To try to remove it forcibly might cause reactions he was not ready to face. So instead, he went along.

Bewilderment had to be learned to be lived with, as it was not leaving quickly. He tried to remain quiet. It was just a repercussion of grief, or so he told himself. That way no one could see, exactly what was happening. Martin could wait them out, and then they would be gone. It was the best idea, or thought... he could come up with, that would keep him from losing his temper, and maybe a lot more. The man drew on his military training, patience. He had sat for hours waiting for the enemy, to shoot them from a hidden place. Marksman, top rank. That had been part of his life, back then anyway. He still had the skills, at least of waiting. This was not the same, but yet... hiding was part of the parameter plan in either case. Staying from the view of all that was real and accountable too, was a choice.

Lisa Farman let "them" in. It started with the phone, ringing and ringing and it never stopped. She had turned it on. Martin had not realized it had been turned off. Dorothy had done it ages ago and it had always been left that way.

Martin wanted to be mad, but dread kept him silent. The young girl had not asked about the phone, she assumed. Martin could not now turn it back off, there would be even more questions. It was a gut kind of thing, where you find you are locked onto a ride at a fair, that never lets you off. That is how it was, having her here, having them here. Lisa and Sheldon had moved in. Not intentionally, but on a limited basis. The doctor had set it up, and even received his own approval, when Martin was weakest. It had happened that first night, or rather the first day when he woke up from the awful crash. Now he regretted it... or at least he thought he did. The doctor would think it a bad sign if he did not keep moving toward "getting better". So Martin was now on a mission to regain his own control, of his own life. It struck him, somewhere deep, that Dorothy had been protecting him. He had not readily noticed until now. The whole world was slowly untying. Sheldon, Lisa, the doctor Dorothy wanted him to see, which now he had no choice... All of them... and there were more each day since.

The whole arrangement was temporary. Well that was what Doctor Macsen had said. That is probably why he agreed, although he still did not really remember doing so. It would only be until Martin was up and around and feeling more like himself. The fact that he would never be okay, was not something Martin wanted to share with nosy helpful souls. So he had to go along. Today, was the worst. Today, was the church gathering. It made his stomach roll. He had made great strides from leaving the hospital, and crashing. Yet, it was mostly a facade. Could they tell? Martin did not believe so. He just had to keep moving ahead and he would be free. Or at least rid of interfering strangers.

"They" had repeatedly asked him things, and made decisions for him, when his answers were vague. Now he was stuck with some of those. Those feeble moments of acceptance. They would come in, and press him, if he did not comply. It would not go well. Maybe it was in his head, maybe not.

The questions; Did he know account numbers, bank numbers, bills to be paid and handled, things to be taken care of? Did he have a key to the bank box?

Even worse, the hospital called and called. "Could he come down and see her?" They wanted him to come back to the big white building and look again at her precious face. But it would not be her. It would just be a cold shell. That made him crumble inside all over again. He hugged her pillow every time he went to his room, with an embrace that would break bones. Desperate to feel her back in his arms. Nothing. Just fabric and stuffing, but there was her smell. Sometimes, he could just... but then it too was gone. Or at least not as strong as it once was before, and losing potency daily.

When was she last sick? Do you have her diary? Martin did not even know if she had one... He did not think so, but there was a lot, he did not know about Dorothy. He had lost touch somehow, surrounded by his own daily demons. She just made everything okay. She made everything work out, and go along smoothly. Now, nothing did. It almost made him angry at her, but that was fruitless as well. The bigger part, is that she left him early, and he could not follow.

When can we come out and see you? His answer NEVER! But he dared not actually say that. Why? Out of fear. He had to get a hold of things, or things would get away from him...

They just kept talking at him. Sometimes they would come in person. If he was upset, Lisa or Sheldon or both would make them leave. They were excellent watch dogs, oddly, vet and his daughter. Then there was the phone again. It would rang and Martin would answer. Then, he would hang up on one of "them" and then another would call. Some man said Dorothy ordered a bible with her name engraved on it. Martin owed him 250.00 for it, and oh since she is or more correctly was dead...would I as the spouse like to pay by credit card? Was there money in the bank? Who had asked him that? All of it a mass of perplexity.

Martin wanted to hear; Dorothy is better and will be right home. She is making pancakes in the kitchen. Her sweet voice, singing that song... the one Lisa sings now. Only Dorothy sang it better, even if not really as well. His heart hurt like it was stabbed in either case. Some days he walked slower than others, but all days the pain just remained. It did not feel better, but he tried to make it appear that way the best that he could.

Martin had retreated to his room in the early days. He barely could think the noise in his head was louder than ever. It might have been the second day, the third, the fourth or a week or more. How long had that young girl been in the house? Weeks surely. She just kept making him get up every day. Lisa was always nice. She would not leave. He had to be reminded some times, that he had agreed, as his memory was not okay. that is to the "live in" thing... Everything was sliding together sometimes, and Dorothy was in and out of his waking and sleeping dreams and thoughts equally. Sometimes she would talk to him, while others did. She helped him with answers, or pieces of them. No one else saw her or heard her. Martin dared not act as if she were real, as something told him, she was not. That too, would be a bad sign.

The pills the doctor gave him at their first meeting, had helped. Even if he would deny it to the doctor's face, as he did not want them. He wanted nothing to do with crutches metaphorically in bottles, doled out to make you "feel" better. But the reality was, they had worked some. Lisa had taken possession of them, and made sure he was on time. The knowing smile she continued to give him, every time one was left at his plate, before a meal, told him... "or else" without a word. So he complied. Secretly he was thankful.

Well, Martin could change his mind about Sheldon and Lisa. He thought to do so a couple of times, then thought better of it. Yet, well...

Lisa, the girl… should just leave. Can't she see he was fine? They had done enough that first night. Then there was the second and third and he lost count. Well, yeah he could and did need the help. But then the days became a chain, ever longer. What day and or how long? Martin really no longer had any idea.

Lisa and knocked on his door. It was church day. Today, Dorothy Cleaver was to be laid to rest. How long exactly between the beginning of this nightmare until now, was easily counted on a calendar by any normal person, but eternity or five minutes are the same, when you are in hell. Martin was in the dark, trying to see out.

Would she be at rest? Martin did not know what to think beyond tying his own shoes. If the noise in his head would just stop being so loud all the time, he would not have to yell. He tried to keep his tone level, but his answers sometimes came out on their own, even if nonsense. Martin fought for control today of all days, as there would be many eyes watching. This was a major test, he was sure of it.

They, they … who were they. The doctor was coming by, not for the first time, or last. The stupid doctor that his wife had wanted him to see, was now invading his house on a regular basis. A handful of tests, the man had said were needed, and taken. Martin was fine. Well, not really. After that, is when Doctor Macsen gave Martin pills. Martin would have thrown them out when he first received them, but did not get the chance. In fact he had tried to do just that and been caught. Then he remember words… lots of them… and angry voices. It had not gone at all. Lisa was left in charge. Martin was no longer the last word in his own house. It had been a turning point, in that he realized just how precarious his position was at the moment. Freedom was in the balance. Maybe they would come and take him? Where?

Lisa was there, or had been at the first meeting. Martin only had pieces of that time in his memory. The girl had become the warden of the bottle. She gave him one tablet when it was time, and a knowing look. The rest she took with her into the kitchen, and never let him see where it was kept. Lisa was worse than Dorothy. You did not even dare ask her…

about… anything…she could figure out herself ahead of you. Well as to say, she kind of already knew the pills were heading to the trash, or the toilet. How? Hum?

Now, he was resting. The days had come and gone, together and as one. Martin felt better. Well, better than he had in a long time. The pills made things a bit clearer. They made his stomach hurt at times, but the world was less loud. Things were less black and white and gray was possible again. What did that even mean? That he stopped yelling at Lisa. Maybe if he had the pills before, he would not have screamed so often at his wife? If that were true, he felt a real pang of sadness. He did not want it to be...

Martin sat at the end of the bed now. Lisa had just knocked again and walked away. He heard her go. He slowly bent and put on his shoes.

Today, Dorothy Cleaver was being honored at church. They were going to gather and say good-be. Afterward they were all due to show up at the house. That was the plan. It did not matter what Martin wanted at this point, as he had let most of the wheels of motion, run him down. He would be thrilled just to make it through the day. It was easier to be around people, but not okay… He still preferred to stay home, but that was not happening. So he would settle for coming back as quickly as he could. After that he would never leave again.

Safe Havens

*The house is quiet.
It is past the hour of dawn,
and before the hour of noon.
Yet, nothing is moving.
The world here...
is upside down.*

*The Light walks in places,
yet full of shadows,
to run them back to the edge.
He always guards the gate,
and makes sure,
the dogs,
are aware of all who come,
and go...
The motion of air swirling,
slowly changing colors,
the passing of feathers,
angel wings...
and shiny weapons,
of ice and flame.
Equally deadly,
and oddly beautiful,
at the same time.*

The lightning sometimes strikes,
in the middle of the day,
while few sleep,
and many listen, but do not see.
It is painful, but numbing.
Until you are no longer aware,
that you have been attacked.

A force beyond the water's edge,
playing in the muck and middle.
To kill and drag back for later...
eating.

Swim strongly,
the center of the river is deep.
Float along if you must,
but do not give up.

(11)
Loose Ends and New Beginnings

Sheldon had come back to the house that night. He had found out all that he needed to know in town. Dorothy had passed away. She had been declared dead yesterday evening. Nancy Barnes, the nurse normally would have said nothing to him. He was not family and that would have been breaking the rules. But they knew each other. This town was small and word was going to get out no matter what. The fact that Mr. Cleaver was in bad shape, well that was important. Sheldon made sure she knew everything. Nancy was a great person. She was great at her job and it fit her personality perfectly. When she asked are you okay, or can I help? It was true to the bone and back.

Sheldon went on too explain that his own daughter was back at the house. Mr. Cleaver was not doing all that well, and he was going to need someone to go out there and check on him directly. The man was not coming in on his own. That was obvious enough. Well, at least not without a strong discussion on the matter.

Nancy Barnes wrote down everything Sheldon told her. Nancy Barnes wanted to kick herself. She knew it. She knew it when he left. When Mr. Cleaver was in the front garden by the fountain, he had shown bad signs. She should have stopped him. Something about the way he was acting warned her, and she did not press him, when maybe she should have. It has just been such a long day. Nancy had thought to say a word or two, but maybe if she…

Nancy pushed all that aside. She needed to do something now. The nurse picked up the phone and started the chain. Nancy would go from one person to another, until she achieved her goal. In the mean time, others those that were connected to her were brought up to date on Mrs. Cleaver's passing. She needed to get to Mrs. Cleaver's doctor and explain, what had happened. They, the hospital social worker would arrange for someone to go right out to the house. Nancy Barnes new Sheldon Farman

122

really well, as they went to school together as kids. If he said that he could not "just bring Mr. Cleaver in" then she believed the man. Old people could fight. She had been in a tussle or two herself, with an elder, not willing to be treated. The situation had to be handled right. Loss and grief were powerful and difficult no matter how old the surviving spouse was, but after 30-40 or even 50 plus years, they never did well.

    Sheldon had left Nancy Barnes there, dialing away, and handling things. He liked that about Nancy. All their lives she had been there, at the right time, well almost. He had never asked her to marry him. He had doted on another woman, and fell. That was not the best story, or line of thinking. So, he prayed under his breath, that he had done all that was needed, and moved on.

    From there the veterinarian drove over to the gas station. It was the one at the edge of town, this side. It was not far really. It was owned by his friend. Jack Lindel. Once there, the station man was great. He met Sheldon at the front. Together, they went into the back mechanics bay area. Jack was more than glad to go help Mr. Cleaver, but he had to finish changing Old Lady Wix's Cadillac tire. She had picked up a spark plug, pretty as you please in the center of the tread. It was impossible to repair. It tore up a brand new tire. That was sure going to cost, but Lady Wix, she could afford it. She was rich, well the richest woman around. Maybe the richest in the whole state? Maybe?

    Jack Lindel had also checked her brakes and a few other things this morning. In the middle of his work... Mr. Seedtree... the bank manager... had been by. With the "bad" bank papers in his hand the whole time, "they" had talked. Mr. Seedtree had long since gone, but that interaction had slowed Jack down a little. He was working hard now. He had made a decision. His friend showing up had startled him a bit. It had instantly made his stomach kind of turn, as if his intentions were easy to see, or hear or feel? But they were not. So Jack kept moving forward.

    Jack and Sheldon spent about half and hour talking, while Jack worked on and then the job was all done. He went inside and called Mrs. Wix's house. No one answered, so he left a message. Then Jack came back out and was ready. He closed up shop, put a sign out, back in two hours, and shut the front. He did not bother to lock up, as no one would probably be by at all. If they were to stop, they could wait if they liked, and get a soda out of the refrigerator in the back. That was okay with Jack.

Sheldon followed the station man's big tow truck back down the road to Martin Cleaver's wrecked vehicle. It took a little over an hour, but only due to the angle. Mr. Cleavers small truck had wedged itself tight, and even the heavy chains of Jack's station truck, were strained to succeed. But in the end, the red vehicle came loose, and pulled easily up the bank and onto the road. From there Jack made short work of hooking things up.

All the time Jack Lindel worked, he never realized how cold he was getting. It was nippy yes, but since he had left his truck, and drew near Mr. Cleaver's vehicle, the man found his breath, came in mist before him. He worked quickly and things went okay. Odd however, Jack could hear crickets?. Lots of them, but really low sounding and maybe a bit far way? It made him feel creepy. He shrugged it off. Too cold for summer bugs?

Jack Lindel was a tank. Six foot two inches, army vet for eight years. He had to get out, due to an accident with his right leg. Not in combat mind you. That was the stupid part. It was on ice at a radio station in Alaska that had done him under. Changed his whole career path. But being home, back at the station was okay. He had adjusted well. Besides, his mom was getting older. She would need him around a bit more anyway. So things always worked out.

He was a big man. He could take the cold, he could take the heat. That is... or was his claim to fame in the service. It was the only thing now, that kept him from the assault… as that is what it was.

The sounds, lessened.
Angels stood near the man, on the road.
Swords draw.
Uneasy.
The bad… was gone,
it was just echoes,
but there was always,
new danger near.

Hell is not always hot over cold,
It is exactly what is needed,
to cause the most…
pain.

Not really knowing what to do, Sheldon told Jack to take Mr. Cleaver's truck back to his shop. It was going to have to be fixed, or it was useless anyway. At this point it was probably totaled. Sheldon was no expert, in fact he knew almost nothing about such things, but the metal frame was a giant pretzel, by any standard. He did not want to make decisions for the old man, but in Mr. Cleaver's condition, it was necessary. Sheldon was trying to do his best anyway.

The dark feeling Sheldon had before when he stopped earlier, while standing on the edge, looking out… was gone. Or at least it was so dissipated as not to be felt, unless helped by night, and the "pure" lack of light. Sheldon prayed anyway. He had a basic personal relationship with Jesus. He called it prayer, but really it was just going over things, all day with God. Trying to make sure he was guided and not making it up for him self alone. Sheldon also believed with his whole heart that he received answers constantly. Not always voiced as you might hear someone speak, but heard, felt and experienced just the same.

Prayers were different. They were the kind of thing he saved for special quiet. Sundays…, and… or the kind when he was home, or especially when he was kneeling, or at the bedside of a friend. There were just times kneeling was not possible, so talking all the time, seemed a bit more effective in Sheldon's life.

After the hospital and the truck, Sheldon went on about his daily business. He had to keep working and keep making enough money to put food on the table. Finally, Sheldon drove back to the Cleaver's home. It was late, but his daughter had saved him dinner. It was just sandwiches and soup, but it tasted like steak, salad and a roll. He was so starved. The man had been so busy he had forgotten to eat all day. Maybe that is why he had such funny feelings on the road. Well, mostly around the accident area. It was creepy. The vet did not care to dwell on such things. He prayed and ate. The morning would come early, and he still had so much to do.

Back at the hospital, Nancy kept working forward all morning. She called the social worker, and all the others on the list. The one she kept in the top drawer of her desk was well used. All the people that do what needs to be done next, were on it. The names of most of them that could help anyway. Tedra Macsen was the one in charge and Doctor Macsen's own daughter. Again, this town was small indeed. Her cheerful voice answered immediately. After a few minutes the young woman responded with all the right things to say. She would get right out to the house. So Nancy, hung up the phone. Her day had gone from bad to better. The wheels were turning.

(12)
Well Intentioned Intruders

"My wife died yesterday." There was a big, silent empty place in the chain of conversation. Finally, " I had an accident."

Doctor Macsen had come right out. He knew the address by heart. Not because he had been there, he never intruded. But, Dorothy's file had shown up often on his desk. She had been sick a very long time. Dorothy was a fighter. Doc was sorry to see her lose, her battle. But he was sure, heaven had gained and the world had lost something truly special. Something unique had been taken from the very fabric of life. She was different than just about anyone he had ever known. Taking being sick, as just one more thing on the list, to get by, one way or the other that was her attitude. She never let it have more than its due, or more specifically as little as she could. If Dorothy Cleaver could not do it, make it through the day… metaphorically then she would push others forward. "That" described her clearly, through and through.

Doctor Macsen had known Dorothy her whole life. He separated that in his own head as doctors try to keep patient and friend… apart. To do anything else would court danger. Telling loved ones and close ones their family and close kin were going to die was way too hard. No one could do that and keep doing that their whole career, even if it were sprinkled with miracles of a cure now and again. So a nice wall, built of faith and trust, held back the tide of pain, he saw, or most any doctor saw daily. That is if they lived in the wrong place, where death took a heavy toll more often than not. Although even if it visited only occasionally, the overall feeling was the same.

The Doctor knew Martin, pretty much all of his life as well. If not directly as friends, then as a patient for the flu or a shot over the long years, but nothing more. Yet he was also the husband of Dorothy Williams-Cleaver, which in an odd way, made him ever so slightly more than... on the list, because of her. It was hard to watch people you know suffer. They were not patients like those that come and go and change with the wind. They, most of the people of this town, were all family. Or pretty close to it, in the right way. They cared about each other. They wanted things to go the right direction. There were always one or two bad apples of course, but not many. Pretty much; you could ask for a cup of sugar, help with a tire change, a few extra bucks to pay for groceries, or to build a big red barn and you would find the remnant ready.

"Can you tell me what happened?" Doc spoke low and calm. He did not immediately turn on the light. In fact, by choice he left if off and would leave it off unless there was no other choice. His own eyes were adjusting just fine for the moment. He was glad enough that Martin had let him in at all. Lisa, pretty Lisa, smart girl, had done a fine job of caretaking. However even when she had tried to get Mr. Cleaver to come out, out of his room…she had been told get out…a few times. Of course she had not listened. To her credit, she had handled a lot of sick animals, and treated Mr. Cleaver with the same grace and dignity as Marcus Plums aged horse. Better to talk to him sweetly, he was already on the ground.

"I was just walking home and got caught in the cold." He mumbled a little. He did not move at all. He just lay there in their bed. Dorothy's pillow was fluffed, waiting.

The tone of things, were not going well. Dorothy had made Doctor Macsen promise to look in on Martin. They had discussed it at length on two different occasions in his office. That was a long while back. Dorothy did not really have to do that. He would have done it anyway, the looking in part. But she was dying, even then, and knew it. She needed to hear him say it. Doc never let his patients down, well at least on anything he could do to help them. So he said, exactly what she wanted to hear. He would stand by it also.

As he pulled the chair from the side table, closer to the bed to sit down, his own thoughts wandered. He had made plans to come here yes, but in a few days. Looking in on Martin was no longer a request, this was an emergency. What he did and said next, in the few minutes that followed would determine much. The top of the list, and most tragically… the sharpest point; was Martin Cleaver okay? Was he well enough or should something else happen?

This part of the job, was even worse then watching your patient drift away, wasting into nothing. This was the chaos of the wreck, left behind by sickness, the foul essence of death, lapping at the last remains of the loved ones, that dare not face the future… alone. They need to be given hope… Doctor Macsen knew that well. Without it, was the abyss. He had looked into its gapping maw himself. Not so long ago, he had buried his own beloved wife. His heart was full of compassion for Mr. Cleaver.

The man continued to ask important questions. That was his job. The doctor wrote a few things down, but he was careful. Just the basics, this is a casual visit. Do not alarm anyone, like the social worker too quickly, to overreact to depression. He would keep a personal eye on this. He had not only said it out loud, to Dorothy, he felt it... connected, as he had experienced it… first hand.

"Do you know what day it is?" The questions continued, in a calm way. Not to appear to intense or too intrusive. The determination as to if Martin would then be allowed to stay, alone, was just between Doc and his patient. However, freedom if given no other choice for safety was at stake.

Deep in his gut Martin knew what was happening. He had better hold up. Pull it back together, or…what? What would happen? "Dor…" he started to say… and stopped. If he acted like he was talking directly to her, the doctor would just write it down and he would be done. He could not let that happen. He was in hell yes, but there were always deeper levels, yet to be felt…and experienced.

"Doc. I know she died. I am not stupid. I am not even out of it. I am just missing her." It was a clear answer. It was the right answer.

"Okay. I get that. We need to do stuff, concerning … things. But it can wait." He paused a moment and cleared his throat. "I want you to remain here. No driving." The doctor started putting his medical tools back in the bag." The exam had been brief but thorough enough to pass from emergency, to stable in the doctor's medical book. At least the physical part. The mental part that was a different issue. It was not a totally new one either.

Doctor Macsen moved a bit slower than necessary. He had been here a bit more than one hour by his wrist watch, but it felt like only a few minutes. However, as long as he appeared "busy" he would not be rushed from the room, out of hand. Doctor Macsen had gained a lot today, even if it were slightly random or disconnected information, he had the basics. He knew about the accident clear enough... but Martin had mentioned other things, or at least talked around them. Not the crickets, not the sounds, not the nightmares about shadows under the door... but there were pauses in the conversation, that doc just knew... However that evil... was the one thing, Martin meant too, but felt he could not. Martin thought that if he spoke any of it out loud, it would be real, and be in this world, instead of his head.

"Lisa can stay, a few days. I spoke with her father." Doctor continued calmly. "She will make meals for you." He snapped his black bag shut. It made a final kind of noise. Like a "pinch" in the air. Like an "I dare you" kind of sound… "You will do what she says…okay?" It really was not a question. There was no response other than yes that was going to be accepted.

Martin was quiet.

"I am leaving these. We have talked before…about this, not directly but through your wife. You know that. I believe more than ever, you need to listen to my words. Dorothy wanted you to be okay, hear me. That is going to take time." He put the pills on the table. They were for depression. Martin had refused the idea that anything was ever wrong with him. The very thought had made him crazy mad. But he found, he had no response now. None at all. He just watched from the bed. Trying not to appear as if he were hiding, even if he felt that was the right reaction.

Martin remained quiet.

There was a knock at the door. The doctor answered, "Come in."

Lisa opened it immediately and entered. "Sir," ...

"Yes, thank you. I want you and your father to stay as we discussed. Mr. Cleaver here is in agreement." and then he set the pills on the table beside the bed. He turned his attention back to Martin. "I will send my daughter over. She can make… arrangements and go over your needs." Doctor Macsen got up from the chair. He took the back side of it in one hand and moved it to the original place where it was before the man came in. Then he slowly, with purpose moved to the door. Casually, he looked back toward the bed. He could barely make out the figure from here, but with his eyes adjusted as they were, Martin was outlined well enough. "Do not remain in this room, past today. Do you hear me. If you do, Lisa will let me know." The last part was a kind of threat. He was a tough love kind of doctor. No gentle easy words from him, he was all business. He believed in a little lee-way, but not for long, for any reason. Codling a wound, especially of the heart, led to disaster. It led to infection that would have to be cut away. That process was never pretty, and better to be avoided at all costs.

Doctor Macsen stepped beside Lisa, and smiled directly at her. "You are doing a great job young lady. Keep it up." Then he re-opened the bedroom door and stepped out into the hall. Lisa walked with purpose to the bed table and picked up the bottle as if it were a prize. Then she slipped it into her apron. She turned abruptly and left, the same way as the doctor.

Martin again wanted to throw out the bottle. He thought he did. He dreamed he did. He also remembered her taking it right in front of him. And then… it was not even there. He did not want to go along. He, he, he… it was like a record, stuck in a single position. The room returned to darkness. Martin felt confused and very alone, after the door closed.

Doctor Macsen was as near to anyone was ever going to come by… to being a country doctor. House calls… people would think in these days and times, that just would never happen. Maybe not, but the small town charm that kept the families here, and not moved away, was exactly why Macsen, made the effort. Not just this time, but every time. It had led his own kid into the social work field. She witnessed first hand, how empathy and compassion could be used as weapons against hunger, sickness and even death. That made him kind of proud. He was thrilled she had come back from the big city and now chose to make a difference, here among the people that needed her skills. Tedra, that was her name. It meant "God's gift" and she had been just that... not just to him and his wife, but to just about everyone else she helped. She had made a great social worker, just like he knew she would.

Forty plus years in the doctoring business, left Macsen fairly sure that he had made the right choice. Mr. Cleaver was beat up sure enough. The accident had been a bad one. Macsen had stopped at the side of the road for a moment and spoke with Jack from the station, on his way over. Jack had been there, pulling out the truck. It had not been an easy job that was for sure. Both men were shocked that Mr. Cleaver walked away at all.

Back at the house, when Doc examined Mr. Cleaver, he had been more than pleased with what he found. The veterinarian had done a fine job of stitching Martin Cleaver's brow. There would be little or no scar, if things healed as they should. the wound was pretty big. Nearly two inches. Not deep, from what Sheldon had said, but head wounds always bled, a lot... even shallow ones.

Good man that… Sheldon Farman. He was fantastic with animals and people… Macsen had laughed lightly to himself..., better make a note to tease the younger man later, about taking his patients. That made him smile even now. He liked Sheldon a lot. He had been very good friend's with Sheldon's grandfather. The man was a solid rock to the community. Just like Dorothy, his passing five years ago, was still felt from time to time. Hers would echo in that same manner. Doctor Macsen held back an unwanted tear at the edge of his own eye. No time for such things. He had too many obligations.

*We that can remember
keep alive those that have been forgotten,
in the small room,
the place in our hearts,
where God plants the best flowers,
and no tears…fall.*

As for the rest of the wounds and damages on Mr. Cleaver, the worst was grief. Mr. Cleaver was recovering from shock, that would be the easy part. It was less painful, when your mind let you out… of the moment. When you, finally woke up and the reality set in, you would soon pray to be oblivious all over again… or at least numb if possible.

Doc continued on out, down the short hall, through the "indoor garden" living room and into the small kitchen. Lisa was right behind him. He went over to the table and sat his magic bag down on the surface. The miracles he was able to dole out, nearly spent for the day. He had been here a long while really, but he wanted to make sure all was well.

Lisa passed him quickly and went straight to the coffee pot. She poured him a nice hot cup and brought it back to the table. "Can I fix you anything else?" She smiled. What she wanted to know was how Mr. Cleaver was doing, but it was not polite to ask. She figured okay at least, as the doctor had not called for an ambulance or other service to take the old man away.

"Thank you for staying. No, I am fine. I will take the coffee." He grinned and accepted the cup. It had just the right cream and sugar amount. How she knew, he had no idea. He said nothing as he was busy thinking about Martin. "Please have your father call me. Otherwise, yes, Mr. Cleaver is okay for now. The pills…" he motioned to her apron.

"Yes. I know. I will." She smiled.

"My daughter will be by later. Tedra. Let her know if you need anything also..."

"Thank you sir, I will. I will also make sure my father gets the message." Lisa replied with confidence.

He smiled and drank the rest of his coffee in a couple of gulps. Sat the cup back down gently and picked up his bag. "Okay, I will let you get back to things here." and he smiled. The craziness of earlier still fresh in his mind. He would never forget the flour all over... It was quite a sight. Then he turned toward the living room. "I will let myself out." The Doctor called back over his shoulder as he was already on the move.

That was fine with Lisa, she was behind. Last night had brought little rest, she needed to clean up here still, and last, but once first on the list... Lisa promised to bake a cake for a friend. That had gone wrong, but could now be righted. So she smiled and quickly returned to her earlier task.

She became very focused on making the cake once again. It was for a party. She had promised a friend, and it did not matter if it was Dorothy's stove or the one at home, Lisa was going to succeed. In fact she was doing it from scratch. Well, making it. It seemed easy enough in the beginning, when she first got the idea. But it soon became a bit more complicated. That had passed and Lisa was closely looking at the recipe trying to make sure, of where she left off, and what still needed to be added. Or in this case, added again.

When Doctor Macsen first came in, earlier this morning... he had been just in time to see a poof of flour and other dry ingredients expand like a miniature fourth of July and then float harmlessly, like ashes of gray and bright white to the floor. The mixing bowl somehow flew off the small stand, having not been set just right. It was a shocker. Dorothy had always held the tab down, until the container clicked into place. She had never passed that little important fact on to anyone. She had just kept using it as it was, until she no longer needed it. She made things work,

134

mostly because she could not afford to replace them. If it still worked, it did not matter. In the end, it lasted long enough for her use.

Lisa, had turned from the refrigerator, just in time to see the bowl soar of its own accord across the small space and land upside down in front of the sink. Unbroken, but with the ingredients tossed precociously in all directions, now worthless and causing grief in the process. A bummer really, but Lisa was not the failure kind. She grabbed the towel, made a small noise in her throat and got to work with clean up duty.

"Looks like arrived just in time for the show." Doctor Macsen had teased. "Wow, that is going to take you a while. Speaking of which, you can stay right?" The man watched, waiting for her answer.

"Yes Sir. I already spoke about this to my father. He said it would be fine. He is going to stay as well, as Mr. Cleaver… well, he gets scared." She said the last part a little lower than the first.

"That is really nice of you and your dad." He returned with a grin.

That had been their first moments. Doctor had not said a whole lot more then, he just went right into Mr. Cleaver's room. Before he disappeared, he asked her to follow him and help, in about an hour. She had smiled over the monster mess at that time, and shook her head yes. It had taken the whole sixty minutes by the clock to get back to "go" on the game board concerning her cake adventure. But Lisa was tenacious.

Now as the Doctor was leaving, she called after him as an afterthought, "When you get back to the hospital, could you say hi to Nancy at the front?" The girl looked across the kitchen. She caught the man's eye for a moment, just a few feet inside the main room. "I like her. I think my dad does too. Do you think she likes him?" Her bright eyes smiled brighter than words could say out loud. "I think he gets lonely now and then. Well, you know… what I mean. Just saying. Don't forget now. Say hi… from me…" She beamed brightly and continued mixing ingredients.

The doctor understood that what was not said, was concern. Lisa had survived a car accident. It had killed her mom. Her father had survived a car accident. It had killed both his parents. How does the same thing keep happening to the same family? It was not a good train of thought. It made you feel like they were being directly attacked, when there was no possible way, the two incidents were connected. Well, none that anyone could ever come up with anyway. There had been rumors and gossip, but that was not unusual... when things were not clearly explained.

In church, as you draw nearer to HIM,
"they" will seek you out.
"they" will hurt you if they can.
Who are "they"?
You tell me,
after "they" come for you, and yours.
Then you will know.
If you are not silent.

"Sure thing. I will do that." The doctor answered. "Your dad, ... he is a hero. You too girl. Mr. Cleaver sure needed a couple of angels last night. Oh and tell your dad, nice stitch work." He beamed at the girl. The Doc really meant it too.

"You bet… I helped…" She smiled again. "I am going to be just like him." Her voices hesitated… "I am saving."

The cost of school, expensive beyond belief. Truth was, Lisa may or may not get her chance, depended a lot on the economy, and what programs she could apply for. He would write letters to a few friends on her behalf. If he could, Macsen would help make it happen. It was tough all over, but if they all helped each other, then "anything was possible". That made him feel a lot better. That was Dorothy Cleaver's saying. "Anything was possible, or is or would be…" She would be so missed.

"You will make a fine vet. Okay then. Mr. Cleaver is in the best of hands." He turned and continued out. She returned to cleaning up the crazy mess and baking. Lisa was not sad. Things just happen. She would start over, and mix things by hand. She could do that easy-peas-y.

      The day moved forward. Mr. Clever remained in his room. Lisa cooked and cleaned… and sang. "Amazing Grace…

(13)
Tedra, God's Gift
Not a Lucky Number... a Blessing!

The day was nearly over, by the time the social worker showed up. That also happened to be the Doctor's own daughter. She had made four other stops before Mr. Cleaver, but that could not have been helped. Life was going wrong all around.

At 4:30 pm, the sky was already growing full of clouds. The storms were back... to stay for a little while. Winter was not over and the temperature was dropping. According to the news from earlier, Tedra heard it was going to snow, maybe an inch. She could handle that easy enough. Besides it was not going to even start, until much later this evening, or maybe even early tomorrow morning. Here in this little valley, sometimes... or even most times... "unpredictable" described everything, but especially the weather.

When she got to the house, Lisa had already finished a cake and was pulling together a dinner. Tedra went into the bedroom. Stayed about five minutes and came right back out. She said very little... and walked right through, back to the kitchen. For only a moment, she glanced at Lisa, made a sign to kiss her fingers and then crossed her chest. It disturbed the younger girl. But she said nothing and smiled as brightly as she could. The circumstances were still very dire, even now. Grief did not disappear quickly, it lingered like the bad smell of burned food in a skillet, left for a few days, without washing.

"I know..." Lisa whispered.

"It will be okay. Your father will be here." Tedra responded. "Be safe." and then she continued back out to the living room and out the front door. She got in her lime green, VW bug and it roared to life. Tedra felt sick, and needed to go home. So she did.

Thankfully, earlier in the day... she had done everything right.

There had been a wife beater across town, that would not stop taking out his gambling losses on his wife. How much is a pound of flesh worth? If she, his weak willed, trodden down "slave" continued taking him back, Tedra knew one day the woman would just end up dead. That was horrific enough, but they had two little girls. They were often witnesses to the insanity. There was a lot of talk, the children should be taken, but Tedra felt hard pressed in either direction. A wrong decision, a mistake, was forever. It would make a new path, not of God's original design, "family". It was only to be taken, when there were no other choices. To a child, even bad parents are still parents, and separation was a terrible rendering of any family into ruins.

However, and more directly... Tedra Macsen was a prize fighter, when it came to protecting innocent children. She had yelled more than once at their father directly to his face, not in front of the kids. But there were witnesses. Tedra did not care, call her boss. Julius Faber was a fair man and knew the ropes of every file. He would add his voice to hers... Besides Tedra had learned long ago fear was of the devil. The Lord gave her no such spirit.

Besides, Tedra did not really care if she lost her job. She was good at everything, kind of a pretender type. She could read a book, and do just about anything if the instructions were clear. But funny, the weak, cowardly... imp never did, call I mean. He never spoke to her regional boss, Mr. Faber, not once. In a small town things usually get around, this particular... incident... she was remembering...did not. He was, is and always would be too embarrassed to turn her in. He was afraid of her. He was a sheep and Tedra was a wolf. He was six foot going on two, and she was five going on seven. The social worker saw him very clearly after that. Wife beater, file number six-four-three, code seven... go to heaven; that had made Tedra smile. He should be afraid. He better be. He had no idea really… how dangerous a rogue worker could get in her free time. Tedra wished Mr. Six-four-three was a afraid of his own wife. Then her job would be easier, maybe.

> *Fleeting thoughts came and went,*
> *of gardens,*
> *dug in the night,*
> *by the light of stars alone.*

There was still time to consider the problem. Prayer was the best way to handle it Surely that was always true. But if things did not go as they should, there were other ways of moving things along. Yet that was not a pleasant consideration, and Tedra preferred not to go there. Besides, "prayer"...would have been the answer she got at church, at her Dad's table over a meal, or on her knees. But sometimes, she wanted to do so much more, and take matters… well, never mind. That had not happened… … well... at least in case number six-four-three. Tedra had lots of files and put them away herself in the cabinets. No one helped her, and Jules liked to stay up in Flag at the main building. No one came out this far unless they really had to.

The next stop had been a single mom. Tedra had arranged for her to stay with friends, at least until the baby came. That would give Tedra at least some time to find a family. It was better than abortion. Perhaps, if she prayed and things went right, the young woman would keep her son or daughter. That would be difficult of course. Raising a child was hard enough, but doing it on your own, well, not for everyone. All things worth having; take effort and sacrifice, too much for a few. If that was not the outcome, well, Tedra had more friends. They had friends. Someone along the giant chain of people with more heart than the normal share would get back to her with a name. A family would then be made possible, that had no hope before. Either way was better than the alternative. Abortion was murder, the death of a child. The perpetrator or criminal the mother, the accomplice all the imps and minions that readily helped... the remaining crime scene leavings... a hull, an empty shell of loss, a different kind of wounded sprit for life. Abortion was heinous to Tedra, and left her mouth tasting bad like metal. You know, when you have to have a filling re-drilled, and the tiny bits of debris fly all over your mouth. The hygienist gives you a rinse, but it really never works. You end up swallowing tiny chunks of... ick.

> *Regret is the little sister of death.*
> *She comes and stays forever,*
> *and runs her fingers through your hair,*
> *until it drops to the floor.*

What happened to the father? Well, that was a long story, that was still being written. The girl either had no idea, or was afraid to say. So the choice would be hers alone. She had no family of any consequence. Her pregnancy had severed all ties, there had been, which were extremely small to begin with. So, "alone" really meant "her and her kid to be" by definition. The young girl did not know Jesus either. So there was even a great depth of sorrow to the whole picture. If you have no foundation the house of your life rarely stays defined and sure. Instead chaos often if not always reigns.

So far, the girl's decisions had been the right ones. At least that is the way Tedra felt and it made her want to work even harder. Life over death was always a preference, at least to Tedra Macsen. That had become her mantra, her life song. Dorothy would be so happy. The old woman had worked with the younger woman before she died of cancer. Not for long, but for long enough, as God's timing was, is and always will be perfect.

The story was not unusual. Just another ripple in the water from the many splashes Dorothy Cleaver made regularly. The girl had been at the town clinic. She had been waiting her turn to speak to the "right people". That really depended on perspective.

She had not decided for sure to keep it? Her baby... By that, she was thinking of having "it" removed. Quite by accident or perhaps by unrevealed design, Dorothy sat down next to her that very day. There was no knowing if she did it on purpose with intent, or simply right place and right time. The old woman thought the two ideas basically the same when doing God's business. She volunteered all over, or did stuff unasked… but often it was at the direction of angels flying about that shifted the breeze of "need" to match the available "help" and "assistance".

As for anyone else that watched the way of things…it is or rather was always how it appeared to happen where Dorothy was concerned. But that old woman always had plans. Tedra was sure of it, every time. Dorothy watched and calculated and made a difference in people's lives, because she wanted what God wanted. It always made her, "show up" at the right place. It was uncanny really. Tedra had seen it happen first hand more than once. Oddly and as she considered it now, she herself had started the habit too. At least a few times, Tedra had been able to intervene in her career; not to save a baby as yet, but at least to stop one or two angry men, from completing harsh offenses against weaklings. As yet that was a different side of the story, not yet unfolded and full of levels to explore, at least that is how Tedra felt. There was so much to be done. She wanted to mimic Dorothy at least in her path, if not in every instance

She did that, make a difference… when she was alive. Dorothy volunteered… a lot. That is until she could not. By necessity Tedra's father, Doctor Macsen had told her the situation regarding Dorothy's own health. Out of respect, Tedra had said nothing, but tried to make things ever easier on her friend, as she could. They were sisters in the Lord. That is before the end, which happened way too quickly for too many people. In this case, the young woman who was going to kill the small baby she carried, and had barely changed her mind. Why? Because of Dorothy. Persistent, kind, ever watchful, ever thoughtful, now missing from the equation... It was up to Tedra to continue to support Breana Maylin. Tedra prayed under her breath that she would not let her friend Dorothy down in the task. It was a huge responsibility.

Tedra Macsen was good at all kinds of things. But the emotion part was a little complex. She often believed there were far less gray in the world than others would want you to believe. But that side of her, was often tempered by seeing real suffering in her line of work, every day.

Dorothy Cleaver was or had been a volunteer over at the clinic. Boosting the morale of the lost, like unwed mothers was right up the kind, aged woman's alley. She could talk and talk and never stop. Tedra had seen it, or rather heard it... in action loads of times. Some girls said yes and put off their ill decisions for days then they just stopped altogether, under Dorothy's relentless "praise of life". They slowly realized that she would not give up, and neither should they.

Jesus is your savior.
He will never leave you
or forsake you.

The third stop she had made was Henry Farnsworth's house. They had more than their share of troubles, like all the rest. Mr. Farnsworth had fallen from the roof two years back. He had tried to return to work, but just could not. Mrs. Farnsworth was crippled from birth. She walked with a limp and it gave her trouble often. Nothing could really be done. Between them there was no income and one little girl, named Wendy. She had to eat. All of them needed to eat, regularly.

Sadly Mr. Farnsworth was old school. He did not want to apply for assistance of any kind. So her stop at their house never went well. That is until they got it down to a system. After a while Tedra worked out a well orchestrated plan. Since she knew before she ever got to their door, what to expect, Tedra just changed her approach. It had made every thing better or at least okay.

The social worker had a big box in the back of her car, full of food. There was always enough groceries in it to last for a least a month. They were a gift courtesy of a combination of the Baptist church ladies, and the restaurant on Main and 5th. They boxed up and froze everything left over, that was still worth eating. No one said a word, that worked there, as they all supplemented their own lives from Tex Marz's refrigerator. He was a farming man… turned restaurant owner, turned super cook. He was a big jovial man in his late 60's. It was his pleasure to bring his farm goods directly to his own tables and to share their bounty with others.

Tex Marz was one of a kind. His family had worked the land for four generations. They knew everyone and everyone knew them. The Marz's family that is. Good people from their deep roots in the community to the top limbs of grateful generosity, no slouches anywhere.

It took five minutes at the door, as Mr. Farnsworth was asleep. That was ideal. Tedra had gotten out of the car, retrieved the box and stood ready. Mrs. Farnsworth was up, and in the kitchen. She motioned Tedra on in from the window. The social worker did not hesitate. It all went off flawlessly.

Tedra had turned the knob and took her box quickly forward. She nearly raced to the kitchen, pantry door already swung wide, she stowed her bounty. A cup was waiting, already hot, but not burning on the table. Tedra grasped the handle took a long swig and smiled. She made a shhh… with her finger to her mouth and half smiled, then headed right back out. Mrs. Farnsworth smiled back, a sheepish grin. The woman was appreciative, and would be completely silent about the visit. No one would know. There would just be food in the house. He would not ask, she would not say.

That stop had gone so well, that Tedra nearly sang, leaving the drive. "Amazing Grace…" was on her lips, but forced away, by her last chore. Well, the next to last, as Mr. Cleaver would take the prestigious spot of final stop. That way if it took a long time, she would not be rushed. He was important. Not that the rest were not, but it was...personal...because it was...Dorothy. Tedra would be slow and methodical as was needed, to make sure that nothing was missed.

Marci Samuels. That was the name followed by an address on the paper. It was just off the ramp, two exits from Mr. Cleaver's. That was okay. Make things a bit smoother on the time table. Good planning or at least it seemed so. She had already been out there a time or two. This was mostly follow up, but Tedra had to stay on top of the situation. That is if she… file number four-eight-three was going to be out there by herself, still… In case things went wrong suddenly, there would be help when needed.

145

Marci was an 86 year old farm gal, said so in her file. She did not look it in person. Marci was four foot, two inches all spunk and glory as Uncle Ray would say. That was Tedra's father's brother, long gone now. He had sayings for everything.
Tedra wished she had paid a bit more attention when he was still alive. She could have written a book, he was so funny at times. He was also serious… and this was a serious matter. Freedom to live the life you want to, or time to be told you have been tagged and bagged. That is what Tedra imagined it felt like; to be mummified, no longer to have any choices left to make. They would be made for you. What to eat, when to sleep, where to go, what to do… measuring how often you did all of that on paper, by strangers, paid to keep track of you. Not love you, just make sure you stayed alive, until you died.

Marci Samuels had a bad memory. Well that was probably true her whole life, but she never cared until now. Alzheimer's was the word, if the facts were necessary. It was the early stages. She was already old, so slipping a little bit more than usual, not unusual at all. Her father, Doctor Macsen wanted to let the woman stay free, until it became a safety risk. He had spoken to his daughter at length concerning the matter. Putting Marci in a hospital too early would be a death sentence, same as cancer. She was a sharp shooting, go getting, hell raising, crazy lady. She was not going to let much get ahead of her, if she could help it and that was clear.

Marci Samuels had six cows, a small heard for one old person. She had two dozen chickens, all prized white, and picture perfect. Well… a few checkered ones were about the place also, but that was "country colors" after all. The speckle ones were kind of part of the scenery, not really counted with the rest. Or at least if you asked her about it that is exactly what Marci would say. The man that came out from animal control, tried to press her a little too often. He counted things a bit differently, but she was a tough old bird and the animal man, never won. That was likely to remain the status quo, until she left one day. Then it would be different. The animal man would come and take her perfect white chickens and her six cows. Tedra thought it odd, perhaps comical to wonder, if he would remember to bother with the checkered ones(?), as they were really only scenery. She agreed completely. Beautiful picturesque foul… that came to visit the cages at night with the rest, but roamed further than most, every day for longer.

Unseen Color

There is a small flower,
that often grows everywhere.
It is tiny and hard to see.
Often, considered or thought,
a
weed.

This is a little,
special and unique
flower,
from an even smaller seed.

Faith.
It…
is the promise of spring
to every butterfly.

However, and by the way, that was the answer. If you asked her how many? As Doc Macsen knew from prior discussions and received responses. He had asked. That had made him aware of just how crucial her way of life was to her. Without it, she would slip away, sure as if cancer took her or any other severe illness. Alzheimer's was nasty, and brutal… but she did not have anyone, no family. So when she forgot things, at least there would not be any direct damage. Doctor Macsen thought to himself, it somewhat shielded her from a kind of sadness. Or so he liked to think, or even tried to believe. The truth was, it was not. The weight, all of it grew heavier every year for him, with every new face, and with every old face…lost. Marcus Tyrus Macsen felt each and every one, and remembered them at every age… their whole lives recorded and kept close to his heart.

Tedra had arrived and checked on the old lady. She had been found sitting on a bail of hay in the big barn. How long she had been there was hard to say. Probably not for an extended time, as she was holding a basket of gathered eggs. Perfectly placed in her lap, over a dozen resting and waiting to be brought back to the house, each one a golden treasure.

Sadly, the doctor's daughter had made the calls, to all the places that already knew the story, and were only waiting for the word, to go. That is why... she had arrived so late later on… at the Cleaver's house. She had stayed instead with Mrs... Marci... and combed her hair. She kissed her brow as the men from the medical ambulance placed her on the gurney and loaded her into the vehicle. No, Tedra had not known this one long, this file number, this individual; as her father had been out here mostly. Just the same, the whole loneliness of it all, weighed on her, like a rock.

The social worker wanted to change jobs. But if she did, she would have to give up gardening. How were the two connected? Well, full moons often provided the answer to bad planting issues. Tedra liked to feel the dirt between her fingers, and the power of a shovel had such finality.

So instead of dwelling, Tedra closed up the house, fed the animals and wrote notes in a file. She would discuss it all with her father over dinner later at home. She would go to his house. She had her own small apartment, but home was better. She had grown up at the small ranch, "Two Wolves" and only recently acquired the townhome to be closer to the hospital. She hated it and planned to move back. That is if her father was okay with it? Funny, that lightened her mood. She knew he would be happy. Well about the moving part. However, he would cry tonight, when he was given the news. Marci did not suffer. Tedra was sure. There would have been a bad feeling about it, and there was not. Poor old woman, just ran to the end of her time.

In a way it was merciful. Marci Samuels was already losing her world here, better to move on to the next. God even now…surely loving and accepting her in his arms. Soon Marci would be minding plump chickens and feeding gentle cows in a better place.

Cry, yes. That is what her father would do. But not in front of her, Tedra just knew. His heart too, was getting tired. He was getting weary. He took each death very directly. There would be a great loss coming when he joined Dorothy and the others. "They" the angels would surely sing in heaven, long and loudly Tedra just knew and was sure of it, when that happened. Yet here... not at all. Instead it would be the beginning of and the end; for her in too many ways. She rather not consider any of it. But that is or would be for another day, not today. It was still in the distance, looming and scary but not here and now.

Marci Samuels would be mourned, at least by both Tedra and would be by her father.

Tedra left her last stop, Martin and Dorothy Cleavers home. She had not stayed as planned. Only the basics, enough to complete the report, but she would make sure she had enough, if she had to go back again and again. From the Cleaver's house Tedra headed straight for the ranch. It was about a half an hour drive. The sky was getting darker... because of the clouds.

The sound of darkness?
Silent...
Sometimes.
Chaotic and unsettled whispers,
At the edges of thought.
Unheard.

(13)
Take a Number Still Pink is the Color of Real Roses

Jack came back to the station. Nancy Barns was waiting out front in her car. She watched as he pulled into the back area, and drove the big tow truck around just right, and then lined it up for unloading. Nancy got out of her own vehicle and walked. She followed him on around as it all took place. She watched as he moved with skill and speed. He was good at this. He was good at lots of things. She hoped he was good at getting her car to stop dying at lights. It was not okay, and she had nearly gotten hit yesterday. Ever since she got gas at the new place, far side of town, her pinto would not stop puttering out. It was aggravating.

Jack was in his mid fifties. He had never been married and really never cared to be. He still lived with his mother, but not because he had to. She needed him, and he understood the arrangement just fine. She had been a widow early in life and struggled to always be there for him. To provide him with safety and security when there was none. Now, it was reversed.

Jack, her son... did not make her wait on him, but she did cook and clean. She wanted too. Until she could not, then it was okay. Jack just changed the way things were, and became the caretaker... in one instance. She had a stroke. He would not let her go to a home. So he worked a lot and paid Mary Francis to watch her every day, until he got home. Life was okay, just the way he liked it.

Nancy looked on. She had been there when his mother came in two years back. The hospital that is, because that is where she worked. In fact she worked a lot of hours, and knew a lot of people due to that fact alone. It was a good and bad thing. It gave her an insight to the whole town. She saw bad things happen close up, quick and slow. Everything from a broken bone to the all too common, "C". (cancer) Nancy hated even thinking about it out loud. She had her own history and was not willing to look back.

As for Jack's mom, the night she came in, was awful. Pretty much the same as all the rest, except it hit home for Nancy. She liked Jack. If not for a romantic interest, he was always friendly and fair. She would never forget the odd, lost look he had at the fountain. Kind of the same as Mr. Cleaver, but perhaps one layer less of the onion, or something like that? That was part of a crazy saying her Aunt would spout out. Onions were layered on purpose, they all had strong taste, but the deeper ones, well, they were deeper. No more explanation was ever given Nancy about the remark. Yet, as she grew up, got older and went to work at the hospital that changed. Victims of life tried to pass the fountain unscathed and failed, she was sure now... she understood onions well enough.

It was bad for Katherine Lindel, but she had made a lot of progress. Mary Francis was a good person, but if Nancy did not have to work, she would have volunteered to help out. She just had to work. It made her a little upset, for no reason she could place her open thoughts on. Jack was kind of a hero in her book. Thinking about him, made her feel funny at times. But it was clear, he had no thoughts in her direction. So she brushed it all aside and kept things on target. Nancy stood close and waited for him to finish. He sure was handsome. He never saw her however, at least never that Nancy noticed. But he was nice, and they were friendly if not friends, that was better than not friends at all.

(to see you)

You don't see me.
I see you, everyday.
I am afraid to say hello.
You may say good-bye.
I just want to ask,
if you like dinner,
have you eaten?
Do you eat?
Of course you have…
or will..
or might…
I believe I will bite my lip,
until it bleeds.
I wanted to know,
what color is your favorite?
Do you like your coffee black?
If there is cracker jacks in-the-box,
do we,
should we,
fight over the peanuts,
and split the prize,
or…
I have no courage.
I am lost,
the map…
blew out the cab window.
The ship sailed,
and left the baggage,
on the peer.
I am craving
chocolate…
It is my solution…
to the mathematical problem
I Came By…
of fear?
If it only added up!

Jack finished unloading the twisted red truck. He was still amazed that Sheldon had told him Mr. Cleaver had made it… like… twenty miles on foot in the middle of the night, or that was the story anyway. It hit freezing every night now in these parts. Mr. Cleavers was truly blessed to be alive. He sure hoped the old man was going to be okay. In the mean time he would do his best to help as he could. It was just the right thing to do.

Jack unhooked the chain that held it fast, and it whipped back free. That should not have happened. It narrowly missed hitting him in the face. If he had not moved his hand in time, it would have severed his wrist. He was more than a little surprised.

The sound of crickets,
maybe two
or even three
could be heard.
Jack listened,
and thought it odd,
it was too cold for them.
Then they were gone.
No sound at all,
for the space of a long breath.

The man glanced up from his work and looked around, uneasily. He felt colder than he did moments before. The air was stale, and his breath came out in a mist. Then it passed. All of "it", whatever "it" was. What the heck happened? Jack was floored. He felt a little sick and remembered he had not eaten. So he made a mental note to get some food. He could run over to the restaurant and grab a burger before getting on with things here at the station. Jack was not a terribly deep man, so he quickly moved right along, the event over, never really thinking much of it, or giving it a second thought.

Then, the best part, well the good part anyway. That is when Jack Lindel noticed Nancy Barnes waiting near the side of the big bay garage door. She had a nice smile. For only a moment, he let himself think about that. But not long. Just like the previous thought, he could not dwell on things that he could do little or nothing about. He kept to the current moment, and made decisions quick. That left him little second guessing time at all. In the case of Nancy Barnes that was a good thing. Part of him would have rather lingered.

"Sorry, I was a bit busy. Can I help you?" He smiled. With his right hand he finished hooking the chain back into place, vaguely thinking of how it had snapped on him moments before. It could have taken his hand. It was a close call. One he did not want to consider. So, his job done; for the moment as concerned the red truck. The heap was not going anywhere for a while, and not likely to be more than a solid hunk of junk without hours and hours of labor and more money than it was worth to fix. So until the insurance was called, and the man was sent out, to make the final determination about things, it could just sit right there. It was safe enough. He had plenty of space, and he was after all…the boss. If anyone had anything to say, he would just take it up with… himself.

Jack thought he rambled a little. It was her. He headed toward the office, where she now stood. Closer in proximity to her perfume.

"That belong to Mr. Cleaver?" Nancy's voice shook just a little. "I heard he had a bad accident." She could not help but stare. It was a mound of metal and hard to tell where the cab was exactly supposed to be as compared to the rear bed. What a mess! There was a large hole in the windshield. It was exactly where Mr. Cleaver's head was, or should have been… or… Mrs. Barnes was guilty. She had felt wrong that night, especially after Mr. Cleaver had left for home. She maybe should have tried harder. But if she did that with every one that lingered near the sad fountain, none would ever leave.

"Yeah. Sheldon Farman took me back to pick it up earlier. I don't know how he got out and walked over ten miles. It was really cold last night. The water on the big tanks, at the house, were iced over. I had to break everything loose for the animals to have better access. It was bad." Jack droned on. He caught himself and stopped. It was not like him to be so wordy around, women. Well, Nancy, now… talking to her had never seemed real hard to begin with. But he could not let that go anywhere. He had chosen and kept to his path.

"I spoke with Sheldon, earlier at work my self. He told me," The woman glanced away. "the whole story." There was no way you could see it, but she carried a burden self made. It was growing. She was kicking herself about and regarding the fountain mentally if not physically. She had been pretty good for months, knowing and intervening from time to time. Mr. Cleaver… he just got passed her. He said he was okay, and she believed him. She should not have.

Nancy swallowed hard and pulled herself together. "I am having trouble with my car. It does not want to seem to stay started… at stop lights. It dies." The last word… hung there. Oddly… Then … the air moved again. It was like a blip… their eyes met directly, by accident. They both felt it, but could not voice it. So they silently agreed to ignore it.

"Give me a moment, and so I can clean up. I want to wash my hands." He was suddenly extremely aware of the grease and stains, on his hands and clothes. He felt awkward and unnatural. Not a good emotion at all. Quickly he stepped past Nancy and went on inside. She followed, to the interior office and waited. He continued on to the back bathroom. There he looked into the mirror. He felt older than he looked. He felt kind of lost, and empty. He washed his hands with the orange stuff in the plastic container. The heavy duty soap the kind that "gets it out" all kinds of stuff.

With his right hand he smeared it slowly onto his left. Then he looked down. He was covered in grease every where. What happened? It was not like that? He had spilled oil over his whole uniform? How had that happened? The man continued to rub his hands harder and harder together. Somewhere... he heard birds... he kept rubbing. The birds got louder...not angry, more like spooked, and the wrestle of wings filled the air all around.

Jack bowed his head. "I am lost." The feeling cleared just a bit. He stopped. He dried his hands. There was a good and a bad thing going on, along the shadows at the edges, unseen. Beautiful Nancy was waiting. The red truck was in the back. He had unloaded it from the tow truck. The work part was done. He felt heavy, and wondered if the insurance man would come this week, or even how long "it" would have to stay? The truck. It was like a splinter in your hand, that was nothing at first, and then festered... not noticed in the beginning, but then too late.

Why he had suddenly concerned himself with insurance people, was way beyond his imaginings. Jack took the towel from the bar and wiped his hands dry slowly and methodically. There was no grease. Yet he kept wiping. It was all gone. Yet he kept moving through the motions. How had he thought it was all over his body? That was not true at all. Finally he stopped. Jack rubbed his eyes and looked at himself in the mirror. He needed to get some rest. He had been working too many hours. Even still, Jack was behind on payments. It was mostly because, he had to pay Ms. Francis something for helping with his mom, and it had slowly drained him. Finances were always an issue. So far Jack had always done what was necessary to pay and keep up, but the fight was going all wrong.

Mr. Seedtree always had answers. That is what Jack had heard. That is what he feared and wanted all at the same time. Answers!

He flexed his hand. The one that he still had. The chain almost took it off. That had never happened before. It felt oddly unsettling to consider, the "what if" factor. Jack Lindel brushed it away. He was not usually so deep. His stomach hurt. When had he last ate anything again?

Jack finished and went out the bathroom door. He walked back into the front office. Nancy was still there, standing near the magazine rack. She was beautiful, and her smile lit the room. "I can check it out now." He pulled a smile out from somewhere unexpected. Looking at her, always made him feel better.

"Thank you. I know you have your hands full around here." Together they stepped back outside. They walked across the lot, to her small blue car.

"Get in and release the hood. Then start it and wait till I say…" He liked things better, talking about cars. That was clear to him. Funny feelings about red trucks, giddy ideas about girls and all of it… "stuff"… were the wrong road. He needed to remain alert. Helping Nancy with something tactile and relevant, were perfect to capture and keep his attention.

There was a since of safety in familiar things.
Sadly, it is not really true.

Nancy opened the door and got right in. She was very good at following directions. The key turned and the engine…

(13 AGAIN)
It is not a bad number!

      Emily Franks was at the market, the general store. She was not happy about the price of tomatoes. They had gone up since yesterday. She should have bought them then. Worse yet, the yams were outrageous. How could she make healthy meals for her charges at this rate? She had worked her whole life for a decent pension. It might have been that too, "decent", if it were not for the economy taking a dump. Politicians all over the nation should be made to live on pennies a month. That is exactly what they expected of the peasants that put them in office. Funny, how that worked? Emily was not a big political person by any means, but she did vote. It just never seemed to help in her life.

> *The people gather and cast,*
> *hopeful votes for a better tomorrow,*
> *while they watch,*
> *friends and loved ones starve.*

      Regardless of cost, Emily placed the items in her cart and moved on. The list was a little long, but many items were hopeful, not always "buy-ful". That meant that if they were on sale they had a chance of making it home. If they were not, then something else would be bought and made "do" with. In home economics the teacher would tell Emily as a young girl, always have a list, so you don't over buy. That was not likely to happen ever, then or now. But Emily had modified the idea, and it worked out okay. Instead of overbuying for the sake of spending, it was simply buying what she could afford, for the least. A collection of coupons, special offers and tandem buys… helped sometimes. Not always. More and more they were going to tech. stuff and stores that demanded you were a member, not just by signing in, but continued use of everything they offered. You have to join this, or be a part of that or no deal for you. There were the big stores that you paid for entry once a year, but that cost was about the same as a single bill of groceries to a poor houseful. So not the best idea for just everyone, I guess. Besides, there were no warehouses nearby. This was too small a town.

Emily was a loyal customer of the local small... family run store and that helped some time. They gave a little discount here or there for regulars. Basically necessities were always the same price, too expensive, for her wallet today or at least on most days sadly.

Emily pushed on.

She had to feed herself, her daughter that was disabled, and her father. He had a bad heart attack a couple of years back. So Emily had to have him move in. Now she spent her days trying to figure out what happened? She wanted to know what her own life should have been and never would be. Instead Emily found she never lived at all, at least since her daughter was born. Now even what was left was gone too. It was a sad fact and could not be helped. There was no one but her to be the caregiver. If she ran off, well, it was unclear what would happen.

Emily dared to think of it now and then, running off... But she never dwelt on it. She would just be homeless somewhere else, starving slowly and her family here would be put out. They would be on the streets. As long as she could keep things together, that was not going to happen.

In the morning she took care and prepared all things needed, from lunches to bags of extra clothes for various reasons, incontinence and such. Then she took one to one center, one to another. Just enough time to run a few errands, pick everyone back up and go home to take care of everyone still…until she fell asleep… around 2:00 am. All of it an endless cycle of rinse and repeat, that was comforting and scary to the woman. How could she keep up doing everything for everyone forever?

    The cost of adult diapers was outrageous. It could not be helped. She had tried doing without them. It had not gone well. So other things had to be dumped, or pulled back on, to afford necessities. Funny, a few were in the "food or die" category. What she could not get here, she could and would stand for... in the line over at the church. They had boxes once a month. You did not even have to leave your name, or look anyone directly in the face, unless you wanted to. They were kind. They actually cared.

Boxed LOVE
All members of the Church,
please spread the word
to those in need,
Food pantry will be open,
Available the first Saturday
of every month,
Until God comes!

    Dorothy Cleaver, she was the one, she was the one to go to. From the very start, a sniff of smoke on the wind, to a full blown forest fire, Dorothy was ever the firefighter for human rights, dignity and loving strangers. How crazy their first meeting had been. They had ran into each other over a pile of bananas just in from the islands. They had talked for an hour about life, and the price of potatoes. Soon they had even traded recipes, phone numbers, addresses, and celebrations for birthdays and Christmas. Wow. A friend from no where that was Dorothy in every way possible. She was like one of God's own angels, come to earth, to make bread, and be joyful.

Emily felt sick. She had just received the news, from a friend of a friend. Dor was gone. In fact she had been gone nearly a month now. Emily had missed the funeral. She had missed everything. Keeping up with her own responsibilities had robbed her of the only joy she hung tightly too, seeing her friend. Now that was gone.

While holding the tomatoes, contemplating the shinning red surface, Emily Franks found herself crying. Silently, relentlessly… she placed the red fruit back down gently. Pushed her cart slowly, away, and moved on. Two aisles over she picked out a nice box of tissues. For the first time in her life, she opened it before paying. She put the rest in her cart, and immediately, tried to stop the torrent, that just would not end. Stifling her sobs, she gathered herself back up.

Macy Bicks was watching. She was just standing near by and just watching. "Dorothy?"… the woman's chocked words came out low, nearly a whisper.

The two ladies eyes met briefly… there was a quiet moment. No reason to go into long detail. In the back ground, music played, softly. It felt like holiday music maybe? Or old church hymns with organs possibly. Comforting instrumental compositions low and far away somehow, yet close and personal... that made every one feel better.

The color of fruit, the texture of rainbows…
The dull but sharp and peppery taste,
of vegetables, cooked and uncooked,
by newbie's, babies learning
to make play dough.
Angels, ever laughing like lemonade,
with raspberries at the bottom.

Two basic strangers, barely aware of each other, only by chance and living close, knew they had connected. God had bridged gaps that were unseen, in ways, undeniably miraculous. They shared another short moment, smiled the best they could and passed on by. There was a mumble from each, low like an utterance… barely heard.
"God Bless…"…

Emily Franks sniffed hard, blew into the white soft paper, and grabbed another. Then she stuck the used ones in her purse, in a small plastic bag, she kept for such things. She also had others; one bag for seeds for long walks to feed birds, one for leftover's if you went out, as if she was ever lucky enough to do so… and one for … . That covered just about everything. Except the one on how to collect your thoughts and emotions about a loved one or friend, gone too soon?

Mrs. Franks continued pushing her cart. She gathered what she could, on sale and not, waited in the line, said nothing more to anyone and headed back out to the car. It was a four door, station wagon from the late 60's. Not much left of it, but it still ran, well enough. She opened the back, put everything inside and paused… just long enough to see… "Macy…" the name popped in her head. No last, but the first was clear as a bell. Dorothy knew everyone in town, and everyone knew her, even if they did not know they did sometime. That was hard to explain, but ripples in life are very similar to ripples in a pond. One kind gesture moves across the face of the Earth, touching and retouching souls with His Grace. Dorothy had passed this wisdom on to her friend. Connections were valuable, to the heart.

Emily made a note to herself to find some time, even a few moments, to run into her again. Her name was Macy, Emily was sure of it. How she remembered or even knew, she could not actually recall…

When she was not so rushed, or feeling so displaced about events, Emily would find her new friend. Dorothy would have liked that plan. Then she returned to the task at hand and half slammed the big door. It was a little off, so it never closed easy. Then she went on around, got in and headed off, back to the cycle of her life. Somehow however, running into Macy, had amplified her mood, both good and bad. She felt more alone then ever, as Dorothy was so very dear to her. She understood all the things going wrong in her life, but never judged. Yet, the hope of a new friend, just whirled passed, lifting her heart like a bird on wing. That was the echo of Dorothy, passing one friend to another in her life, spreading Jesus, as if His good news was the first and best, and none that came after was worth talking about.

Emily Franks smiled. The day just got so much brighter, even as the true and real clouds gathered over head.

A handful of Angels,
were hanging around the 5 and dime,
watching for the shadows that were seen earlier,
Now gone, perhaps afraid they had been found?
Perhaps not there at all?
But the Light of God sure and real...
spreading hope and peace.

(14)
The Morning

It "truly" started first, with Martin's shoes

      Martin knew the dawn had arrived. He did not have to look out the window. The man could just tell. He felt his right hand wander to Dorothy's side of the bed, a twinge of "lonely" hit him. It was like a stake being twisted in his heart, that could never be pulled out. Maybe that was exactly how it was going to remain? Maybe that is how Martin felt it should be; painful. Not just because of her loss, but all of it. Everything from the first day to the last, a long emptiness of "life" that still felt too heavy to allow him to move too quickly. Physically as well has mentally all things were okay or getting that way, on the outside, but not in truth at all.

Gray roaches...
scurry to the sides of the room,
running beneath the baseboards,
under the drywall and deeper into the barrier.
There they wait, for the night.

      He woke up slowly and methodically. All other people or "things" were still quiet. That was not unusual. He pulled back the covers and sat upright on the side of the bed. Mornings were hard and easy. Hard because there were no pancakes anymore. Well, not "Dorothy" pancakes anyway. Easy, well that was more difficult to explain. The light of day seemed to bring calm to Martin the most. It had just never occurred to him, he only "knew". If he believed, which he did not, he found himself thinking it was the best time; the first light. A newness to a day, every day, brought by the sun (son) had undeniable magic. No, the right word..."hope"! Some part of Martin longed to be happy, but found no value in it at all, yesterday, today or tomorrow. They were all gray.

    As for this date, it was especially important. At least compared to all the rest and most relevant to all too come. It was different because Martin had to go out. He had been weeks hidden away; a while for sure and he had even lost count. This was a test maybe? He had no proof of it, but in case it were he was and would be determined to succeed. He yawned and stretched longer with purpose and intent. Martin was working toward getting his life back together. Well, not really as that was not going to happen. It was a facade. Martin had a plan and he was sticking to it vigilantly.

    Lisa had stayed at the house off and on, mostly on. She was a great help with the every day stuff. But, that was not the problem, or concern. The issue; "it" was difficult or really impossible to keep from her... the moments, that he wanted hidden from the world. The times, the episodes... when his dreams, his nightmares, all of them; became real, and the world shifted, to the other place. The hidden hole he fell in and had to be dragged back up from... !

    Martin would be covered in sweat and screaming in the night, it was hard to say for how long at a time; yet, somehow in the other room, he could hear Lisa. That had to be impossible as he had been losing his hearing to the point of deafness for a few years now. Yet, the girl... her soft voice...praying far off. For him? It was like a small light that grew steadily brighter and drove off the darkness in all directions... until he found peace and restful sleep again.

    It had happened a few times, but the young woman never spoke of it directly to Martin. When he had come out of his room, in the light of day...after. Lisa always treated him, like it had never occurred. Odd, they never even talked of it. No questions were asked or answered. Martin worried a bit that she was telling the doctor. About?, how severe?, and the rest of the details of ugliness. Yet he did not think so in the end. It was like, her gentle words far away... just made the room, his room stop spinning.

Her voice ever the song of prayer... ? for him... That is how he remembered it. Until he went back to a quiet sleep. The last image... "flowers" in a garden that has no boundaries and never ends.

Martin closed his eyes. Movement...soft footsteps, pleasant, missed sounds ... Lisa in the kitchen, early. He now could hear her for real in his waking hours, from the bedroom. He could also hear the birds outside the window, just a few. The whole world was coming alive. Everything was so diverse. "Delight" had returned to the ordinary in a new song. Martin had received hearing aids. Sheldon had given them to him. They were Sheldon's grandfather's. He had brought them yesterday evening, after speaking with his daughter Lisa. Again, Martin did not think she shared anything more than his deafness, with her father... which was fairly obvious. Well, at least to everyone. Why he denied it to his own wife while she still lived, was a question that demanded an answer, but at the same time resigned itself to be lost without one.

They were one of the best presents Martin could ever remember getting. Funny, they fit as if made for him? They were old style and slightly large, but the weight of them felt pleasantly reassuring. They seemed to ground him... stabilize his actions and subsequently allow the old man a personal and unexpected serenity. Martin found himself listening more and talking less simply because he was "hearing". He never wanted to take them off. He could not now come up with a single reason he had not purchased them earlier. Dorothy had tried to speak with him over the matter, but he had always refused.

Then like a flash, as if cold water had been thrown in his face... Martin remembered the reason. He could not voice it. He could not and would not give it due again, if he could help it. That was especially true in the light of day. The dark night terrors were bad, and to taunt "them" in the daylight hours was never good. However... "It" the bad feeling he had carried and carried, seemed ever lighter. The pills were working maybe? Martin did not believe that. Well, he did not want to believe that. He was not worthy of getting better. Martin felt he was not important anymore to anyone or to anything. All he had left was his past, and "it" was trying hard to recapture his present day life and consume him if it could. The last weeks "it" had become more erratic. Not stronger, but more desperate...

Whatever the underlying sickness, taken shape in this world or more precisely in the one Martin walked through still... was on the run since Lisa arrived. She had made it her mission to clear out every corner of the house, from dust... truly the equivalent of lack of living. Opening the drapes and giving darkness no space... Day after day, peeling away the skin of shadows that clung as they could, now fearing their own discovery.

Last night, after dinner when he had received the gift, the true kindness of hearing... Not a healing physically, as it was something far less tangible but in the end far more relevant... touched and felt deeply. At that very point, something, had changed, maybe not entirely, but profoundly. Something more than the young woman's homemaking skills, driving off virtual rats and roaches... by soap and water, splashed on with song. Ever pleasing to the Lord above, it was more than that. Bigger than Sheldon's engaging generosity making sure someone in need received what was required. The young man's faith ever strong in knowing doing the right thing made a difference, even if Martin was unaware of it himself.

It was an inner change in Martin. It was a stronger ability to accept what was happening, and to not be a victim, but maybe, just maybe face his life.

It was morning. Martin stood slowly and walked to the foot of the bed, the center of the room. It happened there... standing in the middle. No one around, no human witnesses save himself...

Martin drew in air and filled his lungs ever so slowly and then exhaled as if expunging something. Maybe a memory he wished he could erase? Maybe something... else? His eyes closed and he felt sick. A piece of life had changed. This action was an acknowledgement of that. He could hear, the good things. Words, utterances, laughter and even the fall of tears. Those especially echoing louder in his memories than ever. The ones for joy and for pain equally. The bad may come back, but he could pay attention to the best and make an effort. This was a beginning.

> *In the garden of heaven,*
> *where the children gather to sing,*
> *there is and was much celebrating this day.*

The morning light dim at first, now getting brighter all around, slowly yet powerfully lit the room. It drove back the remainder of the night, leaving no trace. Martin felt more confident with every moment that passed. His eyes found the floral box on the table. The one, the container... holding the remains of his dear wife. The one with the stupid handle, as if he was going to carry her around somewhere? It was hard or rather impossible to think she was inside it. Dust now. She knew. She knew about the noises. She knew about everything, and she had protected him. She was gone and there was no defense left after.

> *No security that he could see...*
> *no walls, nor fortifications,*
> *that he could believe in.*

It was the malevolence of "it". Sounds, inside his head?, that became louder than those around him. Not words at all. It had started long ago and grew. Being deaf, or partially so, gave him the vague idea of safety. It was not true.

The sounds were not bugs. They sounded like them, all kinds...and different. Well not real insects, but that was not clear even at this point. But not knowing that one way or the other, Martin subconsciously just wanted to be left in peace. So "it" had prevented his progress forward. The hearing aids, had removed doubt created by his own imaging's. They had made clear, there was a war between the light and the dark, at the very boundaries of our senses. A hidden war, Dorothy spoke of it. Martin hated it when she did that. But he still heard the words and remembered them even now.

Dorothy was afraid of this day. She knew that the Lord would call her home, and life would be bigger and harder than it should be for her beloved husband. He was a hero, and the world was too big to remember him among many. So she would make sure, he was always okay. Through prayer and daily worship she had forged ahead. It also took planning, but she was very good at that. Calendars and coupons, saving money and cutting corners to make sure tomorrow was assured. Friendships in cement and stone... all around, guided by the hand of God and his very angels..

"We... are not alone. And those we love... are also His!"
Words worth remembering, spoken at the first service of the new pastor.
The first day of spring, after Dorothy left for heaven.

How come he had always been so angry at Dorothy, even about this?, he had no idea. It was a pang of regret, deeply felt. Just another of so many burdens he carried like the baggage of a world traveler, put on one man who never went anywhere, only added too never taken from.

He had started to refuse the gift, the hearing aids. But, the look on Lisa's face was not accepting to that Martin was sure. He could almost hear Dorothy beside him... telling him to be nice, be kind, "they mean well". He then wanted to buy them after he had opened the small package and looked inside...to "pay his way" but Sheldon would not hear of it. He said they were just in the drawer. So Martin had finally accepted. Now, the very morning coming to life, hearing things missed, like water running in the kitchen sink, even more birds gathering outside near the feeder for breakfast and soft laughter...somewhere, not far off. He could not help but feel humbled.

Yesterday's miracle,
new now,
and...
never again old.

That bad feeling, the one that kept him in silence... had not as yet returned. In fact, the whole world felt different. Lisa was even singing that song in the kitchen. He could just hear the words now, "Amazing...grace...how sweet...". Lovely. The miracle; Martin could hear the words. A part of him long to listen even harder. "saved a wretch like me..." A pain crossed his heart. He had been a wretched man for a long time. Somehow that needed to change. He was not yet ready to go so far as say "God Bless" or anything like it. But maybe, just maybe there was still good in the world after all?

It broke the spell that was gathering to change his mood. A feeling left at the edges of the walls where the baseboard met the floor. A fleeting thought of sweeping out the room came to Martin. Why? He had no idea. It had been the only one he would not let Lisa in. Maybe he should reconsider? It would have to wait. He had to get moving. Martin quickly changed from his pajamas into day clothes. Then socks and... nothing. No shoes, or at least no boots. His every day "go to" was gone. His back up dress shoes were all missing.

No matter where he looked, he could not find either pair. The work boots were not in the closet. Opening the door, he looked up at the top shelf. No dress shoes were there. Yet instead... a single box containing a pair of shoes sat on the ledge. Dorothy had bought them from a church sale a long while back. She had paid $3.00. The tag was still on the side. It made him smile reflexively. Dorothy loved rummage sales and yard sales and thrift shops and, and, and... She always came home with the cast offs of others, but sometimes something cool would show up. Not these shoes. They were terrible, bright green, tennis-shoe style with steel toes, hideous. He hated the color and thought them to be "clown shoes". He also thought she had dumped them the very day she bought them. He had made such a fuss. They had even had a roux over the stupid things. Now, Martin was without choice... so he pulled them down. He went to the bed and opened the box. Funny, they were rather nice actually. Perhaps a bit better than he remembered?

Green alright, like the Irish flag. Wow, a leprechaun would be proud for sure. Yet, it was this or nothing. What had happened to his work shoes he had no idea, and he had not seen his dress shoes since the funeral. Time was short and Lisa would get impatient. She was driving them to town... it was imperative. His truck was still at the station. He was not probably going to get it back at all. The insurance man had made it clear it was totaled, when he called on the phone. Martin Cleaver still had not seen the wreckage personally, but he did not remember it being so bad. Probably some way for the insurance man to get a kick back or a "take" somehow. Martin Cleaver was a suspicious man by nature. There was always an agenda. No one just did things. Well, maybe not everyone was like that? Lisa and her father sure were not. That made Martin pause a moment. Had he lumped in "all people" together?, because he hated so many, or at least had such bad feelings all the time that he had presumed.

    A flash of the celebration, his wife's beautiful gathering at the church had brought a new level of awareness. Dorothy was loved by many and for some crazy reason "many" were loving on him now? How that was connected still confused Martin. It made him uncomfortable mostly. Like a man that has been invited to dinner at a strangers house, only to be treated not as a guest but as a member of the family. The clumsiness of it all, is how to react?

    That day, his wife's remembrance... most had given him some space, but a few invaded. They were shaking his hand slowly, saying words, he could not hear mentally or physically most of the time; hugging him and crying. Then... coming back to his own home to further impose their good natured respects; even leaving more food at the house than an army could eat at the end. Images flashed quickly, in and out. Martin could only focus on the box containing Dorothy's remains. Everything else was a blur. Similar to the episodes of darkness, it was just a depressive moment... and it passed.

    That box was even now on the dresser, on her side of the large "empty" bed. Mostly he tried to avoid looking at it, as it confused him. Then other times he could not look away.

    Martin sat back down on the edge of the big queen size four poster and slipped one shoe on and then the other. They fit like they had been hand made just for Martin. Tiny elves must be dancing happily in some cobblers shop somewhere, as they felt great. He smiled for no apparent reason. That was unusual.

Now ready for the day, Martin went out of the bedroom, down the short all, across the small living room and headed for the kitchen. His feet felt firmer on the ground some how.

Martin went into the kitchen and the pleasant site he had grown use too was before him. Lisa was finishing up a few things at the sink, and basically ready to leave. She smiled immediately when she saw him.

"Good morning Mr. Cleaver. I am glad you are up and ready. I have to do one or two errands myself, so I will drop you at the bank." Her cheerful mood lifted his spirit. It was like a fresh breeze through a dark cavern, promising light and freedom on the other end. His spirit was renewed.

Lisa looked at the old man, and prayed in her heart. He had seen some rough days surely. The nightmares had been real enough. She had prayed outside his door the first time she heard him. She had stayed there for nearly four hours, before she was sure, all had passed. How had Dorothy taken all this on herself? She should have asked for help. Funny, she could think of a dozen things she should ask help for, for her own father. It is hard to ask for prayer sometimes, as it makes people vulnerable and afraid. Maybe even partly anxious, that they might be judged by the very people they are asking to intercede on their behalf. What if they reveal their heart, their very core, and they are rejected or betrayed. Worse, what if stepping forward and asking was not the worst? What if your answer was NO? There is terror in receiving the answer, your heart knows is most probable. It alone has the power to hold back many, perhaps even "all" at times. Thankfully, that is not our burden. Lisa was aware, but the thoughts in all aspects came and went from time to time, in her heart, to touch her soul, for reassurance.

Lisa was going to do the driving. It was her car this time. To those that watched the house, watched them leave... it did not seem to matter.

They just continued at their posts. Martin thought he heard whispers, funny far away sounds, representative of gossip or unfounded threats by bullies in school yards, never challenged? All of it just out of range, the clarity distorted. A very slight breeze, but it carried a bad smell.

Crickets follow you home.
They find their way in.
They sing at the wrong time to keep you up.
Then while you sleep,
they eat,
like a plague.

The clouds above were a little dark, but clearing. Not the same at all as the night Dorothy died. It was a funny, chilly, bizarre day, with higher temperatures, but... still made you layer your clothes. Not sure if it was going to ever be warm enough to take the first sweater or coat off, but best to be ready. Wind chill also made everything more severe. If you have ever been out at the wrong time ill prepared, you know the damage that can happen quickly. If you are unaware, you need to ask questions of those that can help you...

(15)
The Bank, the Cost of Living

Mr. Cleaver was never late on any payment in his life. Dorothy was good at the books. She handled things. That is probably why, Mr. Cleaver was never late on bills. It was, or at least had been, a perfect circle. He now stood at the window, the teller window of the 1st Bank in town, also the only bank. He had not been out and about for weeks, other than the "Celebration of Life" at the church... until today in fact. He felt a little unsteady still. That will have to be covered later, as he could not yet think clear enough currently, to fix his head around the idea, they wanted a lot of money for two days. He had received a note that said a payment was due. It was past in fact by two days now and the cost was too high. Wow? There was also a long... attached note about buying his home and property. That is if it were for sale, which it was not. That part made Martin angry for no reason at all, and got his stomach all tight and knotted; just to have received the offer.

Today, he was going to handle things. He was better.

The trip to town was fairly uneventful. There was not a lot of chit chat, and he was glad of it. Martin was trying to go over what he wanted to get done, the reason he was going at all. Lisa did not slow down even a little at the spot where Mr. Cleaver was found that first night, nor where she knew the truck had been crashed. She kept a steady pace, even after they reached the main highway. They were quickly in town.

They pulled into the bank lot. It was the most important reason they had come. Lisa Farman offered to come with him inside, but Martin refused her help. She had done enough around the house, for over a month. He wanted to pay her, but she refused. Lisa was a good girl, actually a young woman. Nearly grown any way? On the one hand he was a cheapskate and that was great; finding people that went way passed good you could take advantage... but then on the other, it was like an itch he could not scratch. The pressure of being indebted, to "nice" was uncomfortable. His wife was the superior one, he was not. She was an angel that walked beside him, now gone. That made his heart ache to think about, so he set it aside. Why they kept insisting there was more to the picture of his life, left him exhausted emotionally.

     Regardless, Lisa had brought him to the parking lot and left him off. She was going to meet him down the street at the market. It was not a long walk, and the end of winter was in sight or at least the feel of it. The temperature for the day's high was supposed to be in the low 50's. Yet, maybe that was a little too hopeful, dwelling mentally already on spring. There was still snow due in next week. At the present... there was only a few inches here and there even now still hanging on in patches from days before. Otherwise, the sky was clearing or at least as of 11:00 am this morning. Later, was anyone's guess, as the newsman on the box was rarely even close in his forecasts. It was often better to just look up and guess, then depend on the anchor. But..., the other reason Mr. Cleaver's mood was better... "and I mean maybe"... the pills were helping him. The reoccurring feeling of wanting to fold and hide so much, at least was not as bad as before. He hated to admit it, so he did not.

Dorothy had tried everything,
as her love was deep for her husband,
but sadly found you can not help...
someone, anyone
that will not be helped.

The song of angels,
can not be heard by those
intent on being deaf.

Martin Cleaver asked; Why? Why were so many well-meaning people; they all liked his wife sure enough, but why help him? He was just, well, he had not been the most pleasant man over the years, to anyone, much less to Dorothy. That was just the honest truth. He had no ideas of entertaining that his image; that his dark reflection was any different to anyone else. Dorothy probably told everyone exactly what he had put her through. He hated to admit it, and it killed him now. The weight of guilt was growing, even as he was healing in other ways. The abuse, the yelling, okay and sometimes the hitting, had been wrong. He knew it then, but could not stop it. He knew it and it constantly dragged at him daily as if "he" was reliving it from or even by her perspective, her loving martyr like view.

Dorothy wanted so bad to make Martin Cleaver safe and well, she refused to consider there was any other path. She would often take on so much more than any knew, to feel she was gaining against an evil, she had no hope of stopping. A monster that only bided it's time, until her death.

Why had it not been so important then, it was hard to figure? But "now", every word, every unkind gesture he had done, or said over the last few years, seemed to echo. Not all together at the same time, but often. Like an ocean tide, coming and going over the sand; his raw emotions, beating him up in cycles.

Places like the store, the post office, the bank, were now all on him. He would have to deal with the responsibility of life. Martin hated every minute and wanted to avoid all of it. He was not sure, but Martin also still believed he was being watched, and maybe even tested. If that proved to be true, he would make it. He would double his efforts to put together, all the pieces.

Dorothy had made life in general trouble-free on him, and had done all the paperwork. Checking, savings, insurances... whatever, it was; she was the go to person. Martin was misplaced somehow on the real road of life. In fact at the time, it all made him uneasy, or nervous to the point of anger. He had no reason, except it all brought up the noise again in his head and that went bad every time. Martin remembered he had taken out his emotions on his wife often in this area of their marriage. That was the way of it. Actually that was how it had been for a long time.

Abuse from the ones we love closest,
is the deepest and sharpest wound,
it never heals,
but feels
reflexive to the bone,
and perpetually cyclical.

The specific event or instance was illusive, Martin had a harder time, remembering when it had started at all; the sounds..., as he truly loved her,... now gone. What was left...just living. Not the same at all as being alive. Really, as he considered... he had not lived for a long time. Dorothy had kept him moving, but the real Martin was far away and sick often. Even now it was all about going through the motions, so "they" would finally leave him be.

Today... Martin could hear. Maybe that was a new path. He did not dare to even consider it. Just one step in front of the next. There was also... noise. Not the same as before, the bad stuff. But there were new things all around to hear, as he walked toward the front door of the building. He grabbed the handle with strength and pulled. Martin stepped inside. It was not a big building, but then again, it was in a small town. So it was probably big enough.

There were no other customers. Just one teller at the window. Again no one else in view. There were a few offices and a hallway to somewhere, beyond the main area. He started to rush straight up to the service window, but instead went around through the empty line. It just seemed right some how to do so. He looked over at the young lady and waited. Soon she glanced up and motioned him to approach.

"May I help you?" She smiled.

"I, am" He started.

"You are Mr. Cleaver? I was told to expect you. Could you please wait a moment?" She became very serious. A kind of numbing silence seemed to fall on everything. Like being in a fog, suddenly. It was strange and made him want to go back and catch Lisa... to come inside with him. But that was stupid...? Right? So he nodded at the woman.

Martin did not like how this was going. The young woman just starred back at him. Did she not get it? Where was he going to go? What else could he say? No? "okay..." he stumbled out. All of his motivation and acceptance of responsibilities, all his fine personal speeches were dwindling into powder, to be blown away at the slightest wrong breath.

Faith is believing...
in the face of doubt; and uncleanness,
regardless of the outcome,
to accept forgiveness and to be truly thankful.

A flicker of loss like an ember that would not be spent; made his right hand go to his chest and cover his heart instinctively. It lingered there a moment. Then returned to his side. No one noticed. As before, there was just him and the young teller that he could see. She... turned and disappeared toward the back. Martin continued to stand and wait.

Time was dragging. Was she gone one minute or ten? Martin Cleaver looked at his wrist. He had not put on his watch. He had no idea. Martin glanced around. There was no clock in the main area at all.

Those that believe by choice,
there is no forever,
will never live to regret it,
as they still draw breath.
The darkness can wait, "It" has plenty of time.

Martin Cleaver had bent over backwards to be nice to Lisa and her father. Maybe not for all the right reasons, but he had done it anyway. Some part of him wished he could have been or even, maybe could be... more positive, but he could barely think straight at times. That was not all new, but the added tasks and every day needs had to be handled. Martin Cleaver had to make sure he was capable, to the point of proving it at every turn. If not, well that was not a consideration. That was hard to explain to anyone. Even if he wanted to, and he did not. Only Dorothy had understood. Only she had known everything about everything. Again, the pills the doctor gave him might be making things better, it was hard to tell.

Lisa made sure he took them, one way or the other. There had been a few discussions about it, but all one sided. His side. Her answer was already given and surprisingly for a kid, she was harsher than an adult. So at her pressing, he caved and had taken them, on time and regularly. A part of him hated to admit, his days had become... more stable.

The last month, a lot had happen. His whole life had changed. It was a pivotal time, when deciding just to breathe had become an issue. Dorothy had created a perfect bubble. Her love had surrounded him. It had been heaven and he had not taken notice, until it was too late. He had been slammed into hell overnight. It had taken a while, just to be back outside the house, their home. Everything was so different.

Dorothy had cooked the meals, cleaned up, did laundry, arranged appointments, paid bills, and kept things simple. All that was gone now, as Dorothy had passed away and was never coming back. Martin was far from any path. The one just about everyone walks… that "one"... the one forward... was illusive for him. He had tried to keep moving, but his mind kept returning to the big white building. His heart was still stuck in the garden, just at the door. He dared not speak of it... to anyone.

Martin glanced around, and could not see the young lady that was supposed to be helping him. She had left her station to go and speak to the manager maybe? How long was this going to take? He wanted to make sure he did not keep Lisa too long waiting for him. She would probably come looking for him, if time slipped by in the wrong direction.

On the way here this morning, Lisa... by intuition or simply watchful intent had made a special effort to "not" take Main Street near where it was, the white edifice. The bank was close but not next to it's unpleasant face. Instead she had made a detour, and went around on 2nd. Even she understood how pain could echo. As for herself she never went down highway 181 in winter. She never crossed the bridge there... over the river. Even though it had been rebuilt perfectly. That is where her mother had died. It had been an accident... or at least that is what they wrote on the papers. It happened in February...not recently of course, but it was the time, that time...of year. From the beginning to the end of that month, it was a dark space on the calendar for the girl. After that green grass and flowers filled her memories and life continued. Lisa called it the month of turning. Winter let go, and spring came at the edges of her world during that time. So she longed for March to come.

      Strangely so, it was also the same place that had claimed her father's parents. Highway 181. It was a dangerous area, everyone knew that. The road was prone to rocks falling in areas, and worse. The bridge over the river was up to code and declared perfectly safe by the highway crews. That did not matter to Lisa. It was a vigilant watch, not consciously perhaps, but deeper... for shades of patterns. They were like puzzles all around her and she could see them, clearer at times than others. Once she tried to explain the "seeing" to her father, the colors and shifting lines... but he was busy and wrapped in work. He did not notice, or worse... hear. So she never tried again. Only... somehow she knew it was a gift. Why, because it had always helped her and those around her, sometimes directly but mostly in some round about way.

      Lisa was kind of odd according to some. Really smart like her dad, and lovely like her mom, or at least that is what she heard since she could remember. There was also the other things. Lisa could guess numbers in jars of beans at the yearly contest in town, to within three beans every time. She could add numbers nearly as fast or faster than a person could use a calculator. Then lastly and perhaps most profoundly important she had the "knowing" like her father. One might ask what that was and it would be a fair question. The answer however was a bit on the tougher side of the meat. When to attack, defend or flee from a confrontation. Animals and people could be unpredictable, especially at the very worst of times. Lisa could calm an animal like no one's business. It would help her go far as a vet.

As for the crossing... the bridge... after her own history hit the city news, an echo of her father's past record... his own parent's deaths...people went around that area mostly. Well at least when it was snowing. They took the slightly longer route 180. Yet still 181 remained open. Highway 181, the new bridge over the old bridge, built from the pillars of yesterday. When Lisa had first been old enough to fully understand what death was all about, she had gone to that place, that evil spot. The place her mother had left the earth. It had made a difference because it was there, she had been released of guilt. The overwhelming punishment for surviving... That is where she found God. In his great forgiveness and embrace, she knew peace.

We believe we can do all things,
and do not need help with the darkness...
until it is all around,
and up has no down...

(16)
History Means Everything

Today was a good day. Well, at least in some ways. Mr. Cleaver had finally gotten out of the house. He had to do business in town. Doctor Macsen said he should not drive as yet, so Lisa was his chauffeur. She had her license almost a whole year already. They had to use her car, which was a rusted out 1968 Chevy. Not the best condition on the outside, but her engine was strong and it got Lisa every where she needed to go. It had been a gift for good grades her last birthday. So transportation was no problem. Also Mr. Cleaver's color in his face was bright and his tone stronger all around. The sad part was the letter. It had come from the bank, on Saturday and could not be handled until today, which was Monday. Mr. Cleaver had been terribly upset. He had stormed for an hour. Then Lisa had told him they would go... Monday. That had helped.

Lisa had not bothered to call her father, as she had seen this before among the "wild ones" when caged or worse... in wounded animals. They needed time to spend out and exhaust the emotions that were too hard to carry, and let the healing come back to square one. Lisa knew with her whole heart that patients that remained calm and focused got better faster. So the ranting was useless and better used up and discarded as quickly as possible. It was like a mental, "cutting away" of the infection, to get back to a stable footing.

As for Martin... his time in the military service, had taken away his ability to rebound. What had happened to him overseas... had been horrific. Even now he could barely think of it. Dorothy had made working at getting better, not necessary. In fact what ever happened he carried "it" and "it" grew. In a way in loving him so much she had kept him from dealing with his life. Then the memories and such began to cloud and other things happened. Sometimes Dorothy would talk about Dr. Macsen, even inviting him to dinner once. That had made Martin really mad when he found out, but somehow a piece of him, knew she had sacrificed much to bring a stranger into their inner circle. Martin was just not ready, and maybe he never would be. So she cancelled the doctor back then. Or at least he had thought so. Later after receiving the pills exactly on their first meeting, the first interaction, Martin and Doctor Macsen... at the house after Dorothy's death; said a great deal about how much Martin did not know... about much of anything.

Things were all changed. Now, it was different. He had no choice. The passing of his wife, the accident and more, beyond his awareness, left things unsettled. Worse still, things buried had found new life. Easy was never going to be part of anything again, when it came to the existence of Martin Cleaver. He knew that deep in his core.

The last truly lovely day... he cared to dwell upon was Dorothy's goodbye. The church services had been beautiful. He was not even going to go at all that day. He could barely think. Sheldon, that crazy vet, would not leave him alone. He even threatened that if Martin did not attend then "he", Martin that is; was unable to take care of himself. He would not be permitted to be left at his own home alone. Maybe forever? It was a veiled threat, from friendly well intentioned noisy people, but real enough. The state often if not always put the lost in hidden drawers to be forgotten. He had no family to stand up for him. He was as alone as it can be or ever gets to be surrounded by a crowd of hopeful helpers. Yet, Martin would cling to being home with all his will. Dorothy, or what was left of her still, was there, in the very walls of the place.

That made Martin smile. Home. It was a garden of colors. He had no idea until recently. Perhaps he had forgotten or the darkness of shut windows cheated him of their memory. Lisa had opened up the whole world. Every curtain in the place, every day... wide and not allowed closed again, until the stars were seen outside in the sky above. Lisa had made sure of the cycle, every day from the time Doctor Macsen left, up to and including today. Oh, and it would continue or else... if she were to remain around or not, or so the girl had strongly implied with looks and actions. Not too be questioned, much the same as to wither he was going to take his medication or not. Martin knew he would not have a choice. She would not have it any other way. The result had been "Light" everywhere; flower gardens on the sofa, the chairs the walls, the kitchen backsplash the table cloth, the curtains. Dorothy loved floral "stuff" and the garden theme was nothing less than magical.

It led him suddenly to a remembrance; Dorothy always wanted to go the park, the one at the base of the Liberty Statue. The one that you had to take a boat to get out to. The one in New York City harbor, New York. He smiled... as he had forgotten until just now, this very moment. Maybe that was a good sign about today? He was looking back and it was not hurting so much.

The time? The memory of her as a young girl... It had been during their first years together. Just before he had gone into the service. Dorothy was supposed to take a trip to several important America sights. The nations capital, Boston Harbor, the Liberty Bell, they were all on the list. But Dorothy's favorite was the woman with the torch. She longed to see her for real, not in a book. The Statue of Liberty was to be the highlight after several stops on a student, "patriotic" fieldtrip. She had earned her way to go, over the prior summer season. But their marriage, well... Life happens and that was just a "silly thing". ... that is what she had said. Dorothy just let that dream drift away, with small hopeful words, that maybe they would go together one day?

Somehow Martin felt the floor drop ever so slowly away, not exactly physically, but more than emotionally. His stomach hurt. Martin Cleaver looked around. The bank lobby, it was basically empty. No one had come or gone for several minutes. Still he stood... waiting for the teller to return.

"Not able to take care of himself?" What that could lead to? It was hard to figure out, as it had never been stated in exactly that manner in his own home. Oh and by a punk. Even if he was a well meaning punk. "Taking him somewhere else"? If it were not the echo of Dorothy's presence Martin would have throttled the boy... Sheldon. He found he wanted to sneer and scoff but the truth however, it felt like a "false wind". That is what his own father would have called it. A lie stated before it was given breath. It was not a threat, as nothing about Sheldon was threatening, but more a warning of possibilities all too real. Besides, Martin knew the man was right. He should be at the funeral. Well, not really as there was no body. They had burned her up, and put her in a small case. It had a handle. How odd? How did he know this? Sheldon had shown him a picture in advance... It was in a magazine, of "boxes". Angrily he had pointed at the blue one with white and pink flowers. They were roses. That had been the choice, as putting her in the ground for the worms, was not okay either. What did Martin feel was right...? None of it. She was an angel, and God coming down himself to escort her up, was the only thing he would accept. Funny...? He did not believe in her God. Why did that image play out in his head...now... at the bank. More of the same fleeting thoughts of disconnected ideas raced by. Then nothing.

Martin needed to attend the services of his own wife. If he did not, it would appear he never loved her, even if it were not true at all. People on the whole always judge others. They all cast stones first and asked questions later, or often never bother with the last half.

Martin Cleaver could barely wrap his heart around her being gone, meeting people and taking part in ceremonies was just too much. Yet, he did it... thanks to that funny young man, so annoying. So he put all of himself in a small box that same day, metaphorically similar to Dorothy's... all of his emotions... the ones he was really afraid of, and then he hid them at the house. No one would be able to find the package he put them in, the container. He would have to be strong and muddle through without .his angel beside him. It was her turn to need him, and he would have to rise to the occasion, or hand off his very freedom, maybe?

After a rather short argument, Sheldon had slammed the door, and went out to his truck. There he had waited.

Martin had gathered himself and dressed. His uniform, it was the best he could do. His suit smelled bad, and needed to go to the cleaners. His wife would have laid it out and aired it out. But that was not going to happen. So he brushed it the best he could and put it on. His fine uniform was perfectly kept, even if it smelled... musty, not from age, but the essence of dust, a place best forgotten. Only Martin could even detect the odor. No one else would. Dorothy was a proud military wife. As much as she hated all that it had taken from her husband, she was just has honored and prideful, that his sacrifices...their sacrifices... had been made for a greater good... the good of the country.

It took him a little while, to dress that day. Longer than normal perhaps. But it felt good to put on his uniform. It was tight, but not too bad really. That was a small surprise. There were even ribbons. That was a long story, he dared not tell, even now. His hand shook slightly as he adjusted them in the mirror. So many dead, and he was alive...He would go to his grave with the words of many soldiers, brothers... in his heart, and only echoes of their bravery to show in the waving of every flag.

Perfect that day, as if pressed and dressed by the best, Martin had walked out. Sheldon had been more than surprised, but tried hard to hide it. Better not to spook anyone... that was the way of vet's. They could handle the roughest situations, by patiently waiting their worst patients out. A suppressed smile, and the young man threw the truck into gear leaving no doubt he had succeeded. Together, Sheldon and Martin Cleaver had gone off down the road...

At the church, the lot was full. The street out front was the same. The one around the corner and down around the next block. Every person in a hundred miles had come...

The bank however... was not at all the same. Martin felt lifted by his thoughts of that day. He did not want to go at all. He was threatened and bullied, and grateful for it, at least in the end. A peace came over him now. Something he had not had before. A feeling, from everywhere, and nowhere at all. Martin did not feel, "alone".

Outside in the snow,
a flower pushed up through the soil.
Tiny leaves of promise.

"Mr. Cleaver." A new young woman from behind the clerk counter opposite the teller windows had walked out across the small space, to where Martin stood. "Mr. Seedtree will see you now." The girl was maybe in her mid twenties. "May I offer you a water, or cup of coffee?" Her smile was genuine.
    He was startled for a moment, far from the bank in his head and heart. Abruptly brought back to the point, of why he had come. He wondered how she just seemed to appear? Martin answered, "No ma'am. I don't want to be any more trouble than necessary. Thank you." Martin mumbled back. She took him by the arm as if they were best friends. It felt

as if a warm wind had entered the cold building. They moved toward the big door of the managers office.

In a casual low-voice she spoke. "Sir... He likes fish...ing..." The last part drifting away as if barely spoken at all. She stopped just outside the oak door entrance. She then released his arm. "He is expecting you." Without further hesitation she turned and went back the way they had come.

The word kept repeating in his head. Fishing?

Mr. Cleaver knocked lightly on the door, and heard, "Come in." So he did. Martin walked right in. Well, at least as far as the doorway. Not all the way... It was a large office, seemed even larger than it should be from the outside, if that were possible? There was a long fish tank on the far side. It must have been at least a hundred gallons, maybe two. It was a tall show tank; styled so you could clearly see the fish from anywhere in the room. Martin had never seen such a tank, in all his travels, except maybe at a sea or maritime museum perhaps or maybe a public aquarium. Other than that, the room was fairly empty. Just the usual... well mostly.

chirp...

A big fat man sat behind the desk at the far end of the room. There were two chairs in front of it. Oddly they seemed smaller than they should be, as if to amplify the importance of the main chair. The man had a tube running from the side of his huge nose, down somewhere beyond the desk and untimely to an air tank. Or since there was a repetitive sound, an air maker maybe. Martin could hear the machine ever so softly, working. It was fairly small and compact. Must have been expensive. How did he know that? Something Dorothy said about a friend trying to get one. They had been turned down. Why was that suddenly important?

The machine's tube was strapped to his jacket and went down behind the desk. The obvious use, it was helping him to breathe. It was not polite to stair, but Martin couldn't help but feel a little sorry for the man. What would life be like having to drag that around every day? Martin was ever so glad, he could walk, and was still generally medically sound.

"Hello friend. My name is Frederick Nadler Seedtree. I run this bank." He cleared his throat. It took a couple of tries. "I am the new bank manager, so you and I have never met, Mr. Cleaver. Right? That is your name?" Mr. Seedtree looked down at a file, then shuffled a few papers on his desk absently, "I understand you are a little late." Then he looked up sharply at Martin. Their was disrespect written there, as clearly as if he held up a sign.

Well the first part was a deceptive lie. the Word "friend" meant nothing here. It was a pleasantry at best. Martin felt his military training kick right in. This was another dangerous moment, presenting possibilities of an outcome unpleasant right on it's face. Not like a hidden trap, but one a predator would use to push the quarry into a tortured position.

Mr. Seedtree, did not move from his desk. He spoke rather abruptly and not very kindly. In fact he had a rather rude tone to his words. Martin could feel his own anger growing. He had promised Dorothy, at least in his head before he came in, that he would not(!) get mad! He could feel his grip slipping. Somewhere inside he found himself quietly speaking... to God? He was going to blow it. Martin felt that this test was or at least could be harmful, perhaps in ways he did not want to consider.

Then... and suddenly, strongly, Martin felt ashamed.

chirp, chirp...

    He had never been measured less before. A little late, was still late. He was thinking that he needed a better way to stay ahead of things. How many other tasks was he missing, or was late on, because he never knew they were there at all. Dorothy was so great, but he had grown weak and dependant. He had never realized just how much, until now. He needed to gather himself back together. Life required him to be strong and the hero that his wife once knew. Where was he going to get that, that power... that self knowledge of inner awareness, to right what was wrong. What had been incorrect for a very long time. He felt so alone. Like a tire deflating he stood their waiting to hear Mr. Seedtree speak again.

> *The sounds grow in the background,*
> *rarely heard in the foreground,*
> *but felt in the near-ground,*
> *and seen in the far-ground.*
> *Chirping.*

    A giant fish swam across from one side to the other, and gobbled a huge second fish down in one bite. It was incredible and deeply disturbing. If Martin had blinked he would have missed it completely. Martin felt suddenly a little sicker to his stomach than even before and more unsure of himself than a moment or two since.

    "Sit down." The man ordered. "Oh... you can close the door first." The man looked up just long enough to meet Martin's gaze. Then as if dismissed, he glanced back down as he continued... shuffling papers back and forth... again. Seemingly he was looking for the right file, which was wholly out of place for someone in his position. He presented perfection, all things lined up from his black handled stapler to the multi lined business phone, his legal black pens and overly sharpened #2 quality pencils; to the tiny square "bank" award, in the semblance of the world globe. That was the center piece of everything really. It was all glass and very "fine".

The file, the one containing everything that was important about Martin and Dorothy Cleaver was not where it belonged. The paperwork... Mr. Cleaver's, was just not on the desk as it should be. Mr. Seedtree was getting angry. Martin watched mesmerized by the growing redness of the man's face. The blood vessel at his neck, visibly pulsed a bit larger than pretty much anyone... would consider normal. Or at least by Martin's reckoning. Vaguely Martin wondered if he looked like that when he lost his own temper? It had never occurred to him until this moment.

A single chirp. Then another. A moment or two later... a few more. Bugs? Here in the bank. Here in the office of the bank manager? No! Martin looked around cautiously.

Yet... worse, a feeling was growing. It was the same as the night he had tried to drive home. It came back clearly to him now. The night his whole life hit the rocks. The night he wished he had died, so he could have gone also. Where? To heaven. Dorothy was going to heaven. Well, she went to heaven that is... That is what she always told him was going to happen, since he could remember. She described it directly a few times, that is until he made her stop. Yet, he could not now remember her words as much as the face she wore speaking of its beauty. She had made it clear, even if it made him angry. God was real.

Why mad? He was not sure...

After a few rough battles... Dorothy did not "do" that so much directly, but at every turn... she took advantage to mention or talk about, all things "Jesus" if there was a window. He, was-is and will be... the savior of the world. It was annoying. This was life, and death was just death. But he still wanted to follow her. How did that make sense?

A black thought, a picture in his head, a memory... of his sweet wife, just there on the gurney, all cold. It was back in that place, that evil place "the white building"... He had gone down to the basement, to where they take... the .... well... He had no voice inside to say. He had not stayed long, or maybe he had? Martin could not remember clearly. There had been a woman. He had nearly forgotten. A foreign woman... had he imagined it? She had been lovely, and so kind... it was hard to picture that she was real. Too nice. She had been the one, working to move things forward for Dorothy. What did that all mean?

That was all there was. He had blackness from that point, until walking down the road, and being found my Sheldon and his daughter. The memory was hard to re-live, and Martin did not know how to make it go away.

There was also that odor. Martin could never stop smelling it. The same strong scent was here in this room. The one that had been in the morgue. The one that had begun at the house, and then followed her to the hospital. Their it grew until it consumed and drained and took, all that it could... before she died. Even now, all over again... the fragrance was growing, like an unseen fire.

"No that's not her!" referring to the empty body on the gurney... in his mind. He felt a strong voice in his head bring him back from panic. It felt like being talked down off a ledge. "Heaven." Just the word an echo in his mind, the voice... Dorothy's. It could not have been. She was an angel, and God took her. If there was ever a reason to be sure, it was that. Only God could take an angel home to a real place called heaven. A kingdom without pain, to be allowed to be... happy, singing and laughing forever. Now that is an eternity, Martin could believe in... well if he believed. It was a great fantasy. But if that is all it was, then Dorothy was dust... That left him very hollow. That was the physical reflection of his simple and complete lack of hope.

The sound, the chirping of crickets... was louder this time. It had been small, and now... not. Not all at once or in a specific sequence, but raising in tempo. The bugs, were here. They just were. How could that be possible? The room was feeling heavy, like the air pressure was increasing. Mr. Seedtree was mumbling a little... and not pleased. He was even making an "ugly" face. That is the only way that Martin could think to describe it. It was getting worse, all of it. Martin stood still, barely in the doorway. He did not move forward to the chair, or bother following any direction. He just tried to think clearly. Everything had become, unsettled, and he felt like he had just got here? But knew he had really been here for some time.

Finally, "Alison." The bank man punched the intercom on the phone and nearly yelled into the receiver. "Where is the file?" a spasm of coughing followed.

"Mr. Seedtree, that death certificate just came over. Linda Evans has already looked at it in the insurance department. "Mrs. Cleaver died of congestive heart failure. Not cancer at all." There was a happy note in the secretaries or in this case, "assistant to New Account's" voice. Not because of any shallowness of heart at the severity of things, but cancer had taken so many. It was not often to find it not the case. Then she continued, "The loan clause, is correct and the loan is paid in full." I will bring everything in to your office in a moment. Sorry, Sir. For the delay." The small voice on the receiving end chimed. She almost sang.

The words were crystal clear to Martin Cleaver. At least the part where he had heard "paid in full". The rest was packed with heavier questions, but not for this time and this place. The whirling sensation of going straight up in an elevator took him by surprise. Martin was careful and waited; but only because he wanted to out stay the enemy from its goal on the field of battle. Training kicked in full, and the basics had returned.

Martin set aside his immediate questions. Things like; What life insurance? Cancer... yes. That is what the doctor said. Not once, but repeatedly and far too often, especially toward the end. Well, that is when his wife could no longer keep her illness hidden. But the woman on the com... had said, no. No to cancer? What is or in this case was... congestive... failure? Martin felt overcome by the desire to go back to the white building for information, and yet the sickness of the idea threaten to make him vomit.

Mr. Seedtree set the phone receiver down carefully. He looked up at Mr. Cleaver directly. There was at least a dozen steps between them. That is from the desk to the door. It was still halfway ajar, basically still open to the lobby. Outside were voices. It seemed like someone had left "the gate open" sort of say, and a couple of dozen people had come in to do business. All the people talking and working and being very busy out in the other room, seemed to change the climate of the situation. It was like two storms, colliding and yet no one at all taking notice, except Martin himself. He felt a flood of mixed emotions.

The manager's eyes looked somewhat like those of a giant praying mantis... set directly on Martin. Working on how to consume him as a victim? Maybe. Mr. Seedtree cleared his throat quietly before he began. "Sir, I apologize for the inconvenience." His tone radically different. "It appears that their has been a mistake." The smile that shown clearly now, was strangely distorted...and left his features appearing melted? It ...was not pleasing or pleasant in any tense. It was criminally deceptive. Sickly sweet had taken over, where rotten breath and foul ideas had flourished only a short time ago.

"I would like to make you an offer for your house. It will be a very good offer." His eyes seemed to close, blink... but take too long to open. Then, finally... "You should take it. I will prepare the paperwork." A funny twisted look appeared, more violent, more insidious than before... on the disabled man's visage. Only for a moment, then it was gone.

"I..." Martin Cleaver found he wanted to say a whole lot of things all at once. The chirping sound had grown so loud, and yet, the clear voice on the phone said, "paid in full." It had been like ice water to a drunk. Not drank internally, but splashed directly over his head. Martin moved back a pace, still in the room...barely, but the exit ever closer.

Squish.

Martin looked down. He saw his green shoes. Funny, odd, crazy-emerald-colored, ... tennis shoes. Oh yeah, with steel toes. Who would ever need to have "steel toed" every day shoes. They were not work boots by any means. So just a fashion statement. Well, maybe not. He moved his shoe. His right shoe. He lifted it and moved it over. There on the bright white linoleum floor was the body of a small, black bug. To be specific it was a cricket. Must have come in to get out of the cold? Some people think them to be lucky, but for some reason, he could not quite understand, Martin was glad it was dead.

The room felt different. The man behind the desk was smaller. He did not seem so "bigger than life" after all.

"No." Martin finally found his voice. "The house is not for sale." He turned like a prisoner who had been set free from a chain gang. He walked briskly out the way he had came, passed both the lady that told him about "fish" and the other one... the one he had overheard from the call he was sure... She did not even glance at him, as he left. The were both occupied helping customers.

Mr. Seedtree... was not happy. The plan had not worked and changes were going to have to be made quickly, or everything was going to fall apart. That was not going to happen, if he could help it. The man punched his phone. "Alison", she did not respond right away. He hit the button again, harder, "Alison!" a heart beat or two later.

"Yes, Sir?" The small voice responded.

"Bring me the file on that old ladies property. The one the preacher man is supposed to get in her will." He hit the button to mute. It would take her a few minutes, but she was fairly capable. She would know exactly who he was talking about...

"Maybe he will sell? We can work around the issue for now" Seedtree spoke to no one anyone could see. "We can still get what we need." The last part, only to himself, or so he thought.

(17)
The Fires of Loss

Jack was "settled" that he would take care of his mother for the rest of his life. He was a good man. Okay, maybe a bit of a mama's boy, but she had earned it. Not in a bad way. In a good way. Yet, or perhaps but... there was another connection to his servitude, the "guilt".

Nancy Barns was beautiful, but that was only trouble. Probably. Besides, he had lost all interest in women, since he had seen Mary die. Mary, Mary... sweet, sweet Mary... his heart beat. They had been together, well..., she had been out drinking with him. They had been having a "good" time. Both, under aged and stupid. It happened a lifetime ago. But that was no excuse. So long before, but still just like yesterday, even now. Repeatedly, the haunting memory surfaced to remind him of his poor choices just often enough to keep him in line.

Seeing Nancy and fixing her car, that had been nice. They were friends all the way back since high school. Jack hoped they always would be. Same for Mary. Mary Francis was a neighbor for years, moved in next door to Mom's small place, ages past. They had met and become great friends too, as kind close people change from strangers to those you know. Mary had stepped in when Jack's mom became real bad... She helped before that too, but more especially since then. A stroke can sure change the picture of everyone's life. But romantic thoughts were dangerous. So Jack Lindel tried to keep clear of them as he could.

Today was not a good day. It started with the phone call from the insurance man about that stupid red truck. He hated it. Ever since he picked it up, he had the creeps. That was the only description he could come up with which adequately captured the emotion. The man on the phone told him he was not coming out right away. That happened nearly a month back. Today he simply called again to say the same thing. Today was supposed to be the final awaited appointment, well the last one the insurance man set... since the last call. Their had been six others. Seven should be the lucky one, right? Well it was not. At least for the insurance man's schedule it was okay, he could just come another day. That had already proved to be true, and unchanging. As for Jack... it just ruined everything. Again.

    Jack Lindel did not feel "lucky" for himself. Instead...he felt like he had the flu. No one had come to the station all morning thankfully, so he had not had to work very hard at all. That was a blessing. Yet, he rather be out picking up something or on call somewhere else, than stay even one more minute at the station? He could not really say why... That was even worse. It was just a... "feeling"... that made him hate the day. Like being out of step and forgetting something important, combined but way worse.

    The man glanced out the front window. The clouds were getting thick again. He really just needed to try to be in a better mood. It was just... impossible.

> *bugs, not the ones you think, no.*
> *the other ones.*
> *they come in,*
> *on things.*
> *that is why we wash stuff,*
> *and take care of each other...*

    A brief notion of pulling the "red" wreck outside ran through his head. "red... red like blood... the color of flame, and scorn... and heartbreak..." the small, barely voiced utterance of a broken man. "... what color would forgiveness be...?" Mr. Cleaver didn't care, as wrecked was wrecked surly. Taking up space is what "it" was doing. In Jack's mind, it had been sitting "there" far too long using up valuable room. A flash of it now in the forefront of his mind, mingled together with everything he ever knew that made him... unsettled. While he still watched the clouds in the distance, the pull was great to focus on the bad. It tried hard to overshadow anything that would sway Jack Lindel from the here... and the now.

Jack continued to think more specifically on the red truck. It was slowing his ability to make use of the bay area. It was in the way. Like a thorn in his hand, he could not pull out. Or... maybe in his side... at first like an ache and then a stabbing wound, taking his breath away and preventing him from calling out. It was a small thing, that was just a thing, then a bigger thing, and now, it was everything!

Black spiders hanging upside down,
to the see the world the right way,
waiting for crickets,
that don't belong.

Jack had an odd thought. Other than Mrs. Wix's Caddy, and then Nancy after that, he had been completely flat. No business at all. Why had that not been clear to him until this moment. A whole month and the place had the feel of abandonment. The red truck was bad for Mr. Cleaver and bad for Jack Lindel. Some part of him suspiciously thought, who else was it bad for? Odd...

Over the last few weeks Jack also found in all honesty, that he had become more sullen. About ten days or so back, Jack had come across a picture of Mary in his glove box. The one in his work truck. It was old. She was beautiful. Perfect, just like the one he kept in his heart... He did not know how the real one got there, the paper picture I mean. He did not remember doing it. But it took him two hours to move from the vehicle, that day. Jack Lindel was just stuck. The feeling had just hung on... since. Like a dead weight strapped to his back. It was all his fault and the blame he carried was so heavy, it would soon become to much to move at all. Unless he just ended it. That would be okay? That would be better! That would also leave his poor mother with no one. That was a greater debt. What he owed to her. Jack was pinned. Living in the gray between the lines of black and white, until he did not even care what day it really was... then or now.

The one sure and tangible thought... get rid of the red truck.

The picture of Mary. Jack had placed it prominently in the top section of his tool box. He had not put it in the tow truck originally, which still concerned him, but he had chosen once he found it... to sit it there. Not because he wanted to continue looking at it for the wrong reasons, but because he felt it, no she... needed to be respected. She had lost her life, from a stupid action. He should have been more responsible. That is what he was doing now. Being responsible. To his mom, to his customers, to anyone he could, to make up for something he could never fix.

chirp!

Well, if he took the time to just pull the red truck out of the bay, it would be a good thing. So Jack got up from his small business desk, more like a counter that served as dinning table, puzzle table, card table on the right night... or used as... other necessary flat space. He walked slowly over... and stepped into the door that led to the bays. A strange kind of embrace met him there. A sweet sickness brought on by broken pipes, unnoticed as yet. A spirit of evil, a cloud of misfortune... seeking victims of any and all ages, close enough to be grabbed and taken back like prizes.

hissing softly, like snakes...
let loose in the dark, as to not make anyone afraid,
and running not an option.

Jack's flu like symptoms seemed to increase. The thought of taking a handful of aspirins occupied his every move. His legs felt thick and heavy. He wanted to laugh out loud, and could not remember; at what joke? His birthday was not for several weeks, but it occurred to him that he needed to buy new socks. His feet were too big? His shoes seemed loose? Black dots were at the edges of his vision... like sparkles of nothingness, waiting to fill in what was left still holding on.

Just down the road a car was coming. It was not a big car. It was a plain four door six cylinder, cheap... barely running... "make it on a prayer", white vehicle. Oh and it had four doors, but only three worked. The driver, a younger man in his early thirties named Joseph Malachi Lamb, or Pastor Lamb. Why would that be of importance, is like asking why people pray for things, but then don't really expect an answer. Especially one that relates to them... specifically. While others fluff it all off as consequence, repeatedly, until there is no statistical value in it anymore. "They" are the walking blind.

The white car was on "E", but that was true eighty miles back. Thankfully, he was sure there was a station up ahead. At least according to the maps he had reviewed before his trip. Yet, Joseph was sure the angels were pushing him now. The distances were too far, and his car was sucking down too much juice. However that was not as important as all the other things. To those that have not been listening for bugs, and grasping that we are not alone, but pieces on a board... there were. More than before and growing with each day... left to fester.

As for the angels... There were three of them. Two; flying low to the ground, parallel to the blacktop... one on each side, hands extended and touching... the cars rear lights. Helping... as was their favorite thing to do. The wind in their hair and feathers... sweetly making no sound. Quieter than even a well experienced owl. The last, smaller one... in size, was sitting shotgun inside. He had his own map in his hands and a bad look on his face. Alarm...

The small sign on the side of the road, posted in pleasant green and white,
"Last Stop." The painted words, prophetic to more people than were aware at first viewing. Over a long space of time... some became captured while only a few escaped, while others, had to deal with what they had brought with them. That is; before they could focus on living again.

An explosion... a leak ... found a source of ignition. Lots of things in a station are explosive. Lots of things go wrong. Jack felt the "black", grab him like a full grown gorilla. It took him by his legs and used him like a rag doll; to beat out frustrations at being ignored. "It" had waited too long. Time to have a little fun...

After the initial deafening blow... fire danced out in all directions. It ran along the floor in every available route like molten water, up the walls and across the ceiling. The red truck was framed in it, appearing to be untouched... but no. Only lastly displayed in the celebration of chaos. Up close and personal, Jack Lindel watched the whole station, his entire world disintegrate. The small picture of Mary... burning from the bottom to the top into ashes. Yet that... that was a mistake. That woke Jack up... He started screaming. He was on fire for real.

The back glass doors of the building blew out in a thousand pieces, leaving only the frames that had held them. The windows, the ones in the front... shook. The side door to the building, the mental one... super heated and became a slab, no longer an entrance or exit, but part of the wall itself. Melted into oneness. The lights remained on, half of them, brightly lighting the mixture of hell and beauty of every color... evil jumping up and down with delight at the expense of life itself. Hungry for souls!

The cloud went up high in the sky. Like a volume of expended vomit from a great beast: a gaseous visual show, presenting to the world... "its" power. The clouds above, dark already, waiting for more rain to come... mirrored everything. Yet, those further off, would not have readily noticed, as the two joined. The storm and the black of death. It was only the pastor that saw the face. It was in the midst of everything. High up in the sky above the building. Hideous, like some kind of formed being. The white car pulled into the lot, and Joseph wasted no time. His braked squealed. He left precious and expensive tire rubber on the black top in his rush. He slammed the car into park. The two angels let go and flew straight passed the vehicle... directly toward the burning building. Joseph opened his door and jumped out. He ignored all that was dire and trying to keep him from the most important thing, what his heart was praying, "life... Lord... Here to do as you want me to do. Here to be who you want me to be!" The pastor mumbled below his breath as he headed to the front entrance.

The whole building was consumed. Smoke plumed out the bay doors. It tried to escape and be free. But inside, it was growing still and making the air, completely un-breathable. The gorilla let go. Jack found himself laying on the floor, unable to move. His lungs hurt, his body felt broken everywhere. He knew he had to get out. He knew he was in danger of dying right there on the ground. The hard cement of the bay floor, felt harder still, then anything he had ever known. Some part of him watched... in his tool tray at the top...the picture... the last of Mary... turned to dust.

Maybe this was better? If he were dead, then he could stop living in a good way. Not like taking his own life... no. He could be free of all that sadness. A hissing sound in the back of his mind, was turning more... into laughter... at him... and then gross, overwhelming joy... at his expense. He found he could no longer take air in at all. It was too thick with heat, chemicals, and d e a t h . . .

Joseph pulled open the front door, or what was left of it. Only the top had glass, not the bottom at all. It had burst outward, with the explosion. The rest of the office appeared somewhat in tack, as if in defiance of everything. Black smoked filled Joseph's vision. He rubbed his eyes... turned and looked down. A book on the floor... a large yellow phone book. He picked it up and propped open the exit with it's weight. The billows of shadows, waiting to take what was theirs... drifted harmlessly outside. That is until they were met by resistance. The sound of swords, cutting things... shredding things... grew quickly. It was a battle in this world and the next, but seen by none.

The pastor was too busy to concern himself with anything... but the moment. He felt pulled and led... and led and pulled. After the phone book, he turned as if on a mission sent by God himself. The man could feel a surge, of energy, and adrenalin. The billows of black assaulted him, to no avail. He moved further inside. Fire danced everywhere. Time was short, or even run out. The fact that he was still moving at all, a miracle. No gear, no breather, no mask... just the ever stronger desire to follow his heart, to serve God and do all that he could.

The entrance to the back bay area, the frame, the doorway... was like the very entrance to hell. At least it was a fair comparison, as no human could of or should of been alive at this point. Joseph took in the whole room in an instant from his vantage point. There on the ground, a man. A single man. A few steps inside the inferno. He appeared to be dead possibly, but the pastor was not going to stop. He felt that he was following a road, preset. Immediately... he went to Jack's side. He bent down and checked. A pulse greeted the pastor, only it was fluttery and faint.

Joseph Malachi Lamb was never a really big man. He was kind of on the skinny side actually. The pastor stood 5'2" in his stocking feet. He had few if any muscles, even as he had tried over the years to stay in shape. Joseph did not ask how he was going to get this man out, he was just going to do it. Like David and Goliath, doubt was not an option. Jack was a much larger man and his weight alone would have given two grown fireman a bit of trouble. Make no mistake, this was a massive problem, that had to be dealt with now, or the time... held in place for the moment... would be gone, forever.

Joseph felt tears spring to his eyes. It was a mixture of the onslaught of burning black and the lack of air, which had been consumed by the evil all around. Short of breath, Joseph gasped out, "God... I am here... Help me... please!!!"

The room... the bays, the whole work place behind the office... instantly became silent. Like the moment before something explodes, that has no other way to get out, but pent up power released at the end of a barrel. Not this time outward, but inward. The far doors, the ones that still held the metal frames now empty, the glass spewn all over the parking lot outside. It hit there. An answer...

A bright, lime green VW bug catapulted through the barrier. It was as if the very hand of God had picked it up and threw it through. The face behind the wheel bright and intent. Tedra...

Landing with a crash it was like a giant hammer striking the head of a nail. The force was incredible. The driver then throwing the "lime" quickly into reverse, the big door getting caught on the windshield and the side door of the small vehicle, the result, the main larger door pulled and then ripped away. Leaving a giant gapping hole, where there had been none before. There the smoke found a new escape. "It" knew time was short and it had to be fast, if it was going to take... all that it could and keep... all that was ... still there... for the taking... and keeping.

Tedra threw open her car door, stepped out and immediately ran into the evil black. Smoke and fire everywhere... Her eyes ever falcon-sharp, picked out the stranger first, there beside the station owner. It must be him. He was lying flat on the cement. The first sight of them both was rippled. By that, "it", the scene before her seemed to be changing and shifting... oddly. Maybe from the heat? Yet there was more, something else. Tedra was sure of it. She saw "Him" also. The magnificent being, standing beside the man on the ground, and Jack. He was dressed all in white... like snow. There was a moment, she wanted to sit down and just stop. Her spirit was lifted, by the very visage of the power and might so plain before her.

Then, as if waken from a sudden but sweet slumber, she looked away. Instead her heart went to the victims on the floor. Obviously there was one, but their would be two or even three, if she did not move.

Death... watching...waiting...
a shadow at the edges.
Unseen as it was at one with the black oil on the floor,
even as it danced in colors of red and yellow and hot white...
as only black can.

Tedra was sure... like seeing rain fall, while still in the air, before it hits the ground. Magical, and surreal... an angel. Her mother had gone with them. She had seen not one but many of them before. At least from a child's eyes. Now a grown woman, again? She would have to consider the whole instance at a later time. Part of her was elated... her dreams were real. The other part was all serious and time was out.

No moments for whimsy childhood memories if she were going to help herself now, as she was in the thick of it, or them. Yet, she had been given "hope" directly. It was tangible and material to her soul.

Tedra brushed all thoughts aside, except escape. She ran over, to where Joseph was kneeling on the ground. Jack was prone and quiet. His eyes were closed.

Death is always silent...
when it is winning.

"Grab his arm..." she directed. Joseph instantly followed her words. They were so calm. Together... they lifted Jack to stand between them. With a bit of effort, they stumbled together out the opening, left by her vehicle. Outside, they kept moving until they were several feet away from the burning station. It was still on fire. In fact it was consumed. Now the clouds that filled the sky were hard to discern from weather versus... black fire.

The welcome sounds of a fire truck... approaching, grew louder. It was like the music at the end of a long movie. A hopeful ending, to a dramatic event. This time, at least, did not claim anyone, only property. That could not always be easily replaced, but life, that was never possible, and far more damaging.

(18)
Cakewalk

The statue of liberty stands overlooking the harbor in New York. It is on a small island all by itself. People come from all over to visit. Regardless of who you or they are... there is a moment that all understand the word, freedom. Those for and against. It comes on like a quiet storm. Once tasted, it can never be forgotten. The knowledge can never be unlearned. Like a lesson, taught by a bad parent, twisted later by a saved child to see the truth clearly.

A better focus would be on a greater idea. A true way of living and being alive. A freedom that has no bounds, except the ones willingly taken on or even begged for. To be re-born. To know God. His glory so much more than the here and now. What was, and is, and is to come, they sing. Time is short and "He" touches all lives.

Neta Selah walked among the tourists. She had worked all morning and the catch was pretty good. Three wallets, two watches, some jewelry. Morgan would be pleased. Maybe he would even be in a good mood? That would be the best part. That meant she could just be left alone. She hated it when he was in a bad mood. So if she paid her price, the one for her "keep", then the focus would move on. How long had it been? Months for sure. Maybe a year or more. Time just did not matter any more. At least she was not on the street. She had a place to sleep. Well, sometimes.

Anyway, none of that mattered. She had at least four more hours left to work, that is before thinking about heading back. The apartment was on the far side, so it was not an easy trip. But the park here... it always had the best pickings. People on vacation were often in the best of moods, and rarely noticed when they had been clipped.

Neta as that is how she preferred to be called; moved back to the line where the tour boat was coming in. She would ride back to the mainland and hit the ones getting off, as they headed home. That way, they would not know if they were robbed on the island, or on the boat. Dividing the possibilities made laying the blame anywhere, especially on her... harder if not impossible.

The girls stomach rolled. It had been doing that for a while. She tried eating earlier. She bought a hot dog from the vender. But now as the thought of taking the floating bus back was evident and before her, she just wanted to puke up her guts. So she moved out of the line, down to the walk way. There she leaned over the rail and fed the fish. Not once or twice but repeatedly.

"Are you okay?" The voice of the nice old woman, a sweet country drawl reflecting the unmistakable tones of somewhere out west; came from nowhere. Neta could not remember hearing anyone walk near.

She glanced up. A white haired woman of about sixty or maybe seventy years, looked on at her. She was pretty, smiling... with edges of concern at the corners of her mouth. Not mean at all. Just worrying over a complete stranger? Neta was instantly wary. In her back pack she was carrying this woman's wallet. She had taken it hours earlier... If found on her, on Neta Selah for any reason, it would be the third time. Panic was taking over...

"I'm okay... " The girl uttered the best she could. Trying to sound stronger than she felt. "Just bad food and a little sea sick." Putting every once of energy into her response, to make it acceptable. "I'm going back...

214

but thank you." Smiling slowly, even though she did not feel like doing so at all.

"When I was pregnant, I had the same thing happen to me. Often. You should eat some crackers Dear-y." The knowing grin on her features expressed a world of true wisdom. "Happens to all us girls. It will get better." The woman gave her a pleasant reassuring look. "You are so young. It will all be so easy for you." She grinned. "I have grandkids now, but I still remember." She chuckled. Then she turned away and joined her small group of women, waiting near by.

There were a few voices, explanations from the old woman to her friends and back about nothing important... details about their trip and the places they were still going...

Neta Selah stood there. Watching the woman retreat. Breathing was more labored than before... just a bit. She no longer felt like heaving up her guts. She felt like bawling. She felt like screaming.

She felt stunned.

"Pregnant?"

(19)
Bad Luck?...

<small>Another crash. Has anyone bothered to keep count?</small>

Martin Cleaver had no idea what just happened, only that for some reason, he needed to get out of there. So he did. He walked right out of the front doors, like a bird set free from a small, cramped cage. The diminutive town bank left behind, and the sky was dark... yes, but limitless. That whole encounter was momentary, fleeting and scary as measured and compared to a lifetime of nightmares. He had learned a lot and a little of what he still needed to know; but only the tip of so much that was going to get filled in, one way or the other. The questions he now wanted to ask, came right to mind. Then got all mixed together, and threatened to overwhelm him.

Dorothy's loss was a giant sore that was mending. It had been going along "well" even. Martin had shown great signs of progress, until now. Steadily he powered on across the parkway to the sidewalk, that would lead him in the right direction of the grocery store. Lisa was there or she said she would be. He did not slow his step at all, until the bank was no longer within view. Then and only then he paused. Martin found himself slightly faint so he leaned against the building. It was a brick storefront. The bookshop. "Fill Your Cup" was painted on the picture style window in large lovely green and gold colors. There were also decorations of pink roses at the edges, and bees... zigzagged here and there with an artist's brush. It was a very welcoming mural.

Dorothy did not die of cancer? How could that be? He saw her do the treatments. He saw her struggle. Martin watched her dwindle

216

away... He had held her hand, up and until the end. Until her flesh was so cold, ice... was warmer.

    Martin's wife had friends at the hospital. They all showed up at her "celebration of life" ceremony. Many there that day had come wearing wigs or hats... and little, just-alike-kind of pins, showing support and healing. Dorothy had a "pin", a flower pin... at home on the dresser. Martin could see it clearly if he closed his eyes. He use to like it. Martin had even commented on it when she first came home wearing it. That is until he found out the symbolic sadness of it's design. Well, all the cancer ladies had one, so it had to be "cancer" related right?

    It was already half passed noon, and the sky had changed. Big clouds had moved in quickly. There was an electrical, unsettling... feeling to the air. Maybe not for an hour or so, but soon. The sky, the big black... was going to try hard to make life difficult for everyone it could reach. That would be especially true for travelers. The last remaining piles of snow, left over... from days before, were about to be packed down again. Unexpectedly, even perhaps, unnaturally, life was moving the wrong way. Not for everyone, but all "it" could touch or take with it.

    Dorothy had not been at the church for the celebration. Even now she was not at home really either. But that was a different idea, or conviction entirely. Speaking of the ceremony, that day... that everyone said "goodbye".... it was, truly beautiful and memorable.

    The fact(s); it was just the container, that had arrived in time. But, not everything else. The old pastor knew what happened, but was not going to cloud the day and spoil the commemoration. Everything went forward as planned. Sheldon was informed, but did not tell Martin Cleaver until later. After. The truth; the pretty box with the forever flowers, had been empty. It ended up being just a show piece to help others get through a bad time. All the well wishers, strangers and just "people" went through the motions, believing she was inside. Instead... Dorothy's body had somehow, not been handled, processed and "taken care of" in time, so it was just the blue, handcrafted wood... with roses, and a shiny bright handle... that day.

Dust to dust
Who is it that we should trust?
Jesus, the only Truth and Light!

All those people showed up to say words over a container? Martin had such a hard time going in the first place, he was secretly glad Sheldon had left him in the dark for a time. If he had known it was all a show... what would that have been like? The reality was Dorothy's ashes came days later. The non-reality was that for Martin, his wife was still back at the morgue. She would be there forever, in his mind. The memory just would not change.

Sheldon and Lisa put "her" in it...after. Dorothy that is. When her remains came back from the cremator. Until then, the box had just sat empty... waiting. Now... it was... not, there was dust. Sure. Her remains were there, inside. But Martin could not make the connection between leaving her at the hospital and the container with the flowers and the handle...they gave him. To do what with? It was even now in his bedroom, on the table. What else? Or? It was really not the moment to consider the options for sure, but they were still swirling around anyway. Thinking was difficult.

It had been huge. It had been overwhelming to come to terms with who Dorothy really was, to people outside of himself. He knew how special she was, but had no idea, others did as well. It made him happy, yet sad, as he did not want to share even the smallest part with others. She

218

was precious in his heart. Only, by keeping her so pinned down to his every need, she had not been free. Her spirit was so beautiful or had been, but his mind fought about the tenses of his dreams. Martin thought... Dorothy should have been allowed to soar to the mountains and back. The uncovered selfishness of his own personality became apparent even to him, and it was stifling. Like loving a wild bird so much as to keep it in a cage, yet that alone not enough. Then to smother and suffocate it further with demanding "need", to provide happiness. What a terrible burden?

    A tiny bell rang, the door to the business opened and a young lady half stepped out. She looked straight at him, as if she had called him over intentionally, out of a crowd. But, Martin and the lady were the only ones around?

    "Can I help you, Sir." The voice ever pleasant and calm. "It is a very cold day today. Why don't you come inside. I have the fire place going." Her hand reached across the short space and touched his shoulder. It felt like a Coast Guard Hero, pulling him from deep, thrashing waters, to the safety of a life boat.

    "I..am..." Martin tried to reply.

> *God is always with us.*
> *When we are asked our name...*
> *we say; "I am" first and then...*
> *followed by the definition only, of who we think we are,*
> *not who the Lord truly is...*

    "Yes, I know. That is okay." The young woman just smiled and pulled him gently, toward the door and then on inside. Like frostbitten flesh, warming up gradually, at first... okay. Then the real pain sets in as life is confronted with the blood of a pulse. She walked him passed the wall of books near the front, passed several more and then to a center area, around a large stone fireplace... built to allow readers to gather, and discuss dreams. Maybe and perhaps, share their faith, without being persecuted.

It was large indeed, a giant raw-stone hearth about six or maybe seven feet in diameter at the base. Each stone unique in some way, from the one next to the one before or the one that followed. The whole creation a useful, work of art. Oddly for a business to succeed you would think there would be more books, and less space set aside for... huh? Maybe for enjoying reading? Sharing ideas? That would be like putting people first over money...? But as Martin dared to look from wall to wall, there seemed to be racks and racks of books still. Plenty of merchandise regardless. Around the warm inviting blaze were several chairs and a long overstuffed, comfy couch, for readers to relax. To take their time and remember what it was or is like just to breathe. It was a welcoming area that invited strangers to become friends by its simple design.

"Sit here. I will make tea." He followed her with his eyes, but then moved slowly forward and complied. Martin sat in one of the big earth-brown chairs. It was one of five others... none, small. He had never been here before. It was a book shop of course, which he seldom cared about. Not really his thing,... reading. But he could not ever remember one being in town. Was it new? It did not appear new at all. The huge, aged-creation by an artisan, that felt seriously inspired showed staid use. Then again, other than going to Dorothy's funeral at the church... Martin had not been this way in ages. If it had not been for all that happened at the bank earlier, he would still never have come this direction.

A flash of remembrance,
Martin listening to his mother, read him bedtime stories....
It lifted his mood considerably.
Then gone, as that is the very definition of a flash.
It burns so brightly there are few if ever any...
embers.

    As he looked slowly around, it occurred to him that his sweet wife would have fallen in love with this place. She thrived on "this and that" type shops, and the yearly rummage sales, for "things" that made you feel, "better". How he suddenly knew that, he felt unsure. But he could nearly, if not clearly even now hear her laugh, as she would speak of a find or treasure?... It made him homesick, for yesterday. Tears filled the corners of his eyes, unbidden and unwanted. A funny feeling like butterflies floated in his stomach uninvited, then turned to bats and then... it passed. Martin pulled himself back together, well, as best he could. Things had already gone way passed, falling apart a few times, but that had to stop. It had to!

    He hoped she had been here, Dorothy. But when? It left him sad to consider. Martin had come to terms that he was very stingy with his "Dorothy". But that did not fill him with regret, well not exactly. It was more like having a beautiful bird that should fly free, stay with you. They are fed and kept well, so what is the difference? That depends Martin had come to realize as to whose perspective.

    The room was not large or really very small. It was medium. There were shelves everywhere and Martin Cleaver now had a great view...or at least a unique angle. Books of every size lined them. Some were on their sides, some straight. Some tilted, and not well in order by any normal standard. One important point, there was no dust, so the place, the business was well cared for and the owner had pride. That was not to say, it was "orderly". No. In fact it would better be described as a mess. The local news might even report; "What happened here?" after showing pictures of a major tornado strike. Even so, everything... was still on a "shelf". Martin felt oddly lifted by that thought.

The young lady had disappeared in the back. He lost sight of her among the rows and rows of books. There seemed to be so many of them, as to rival the library considering the size of the shop.

A rather large green animal jumped out and back behind two baskets of yarn. They were sitting beside another chair slightly across from him, but still within view. The contents of the baskets; supplies and crochet instruction books. "How to..." volumes and titles everywhere near by. He looked hard and read the titles within view on the shelves to either side; "How to Ski, How to tell a Joke, How to Make Pumpkin Bread, Ant collecting for Newbie's, How to draw just about everything! by R. Aaron... and more. Martin watched closer. He was sure he had seen... something. A cat? Well, they are not green! He tried to make sure he was okay? How does one do that when they are not? Well.. .they don't. That is the point of friends, or so Martin would find out.

Then abruptly, the animal came right out, flashed by quickly on a dead run around another chair and back toward the back. Somewhere deeper into the shop, vanishing like a figment of imagination. A moment later, a crash was heard. Not anger, but laughter followed. "Sam, get out of here!" The echo of more laughter.

Suddenly the young woman was again in the room. "Sorry about that. I hope that Samson did not bother you." She smiled. In her hands she was holding a tray of hot steam and warm things, from the toaster oven. Martin found he was both incredibly thirsty, as a man who had just walked from the desert, and so hungry he was considering eating the smaller green intruder. Because of it's size, it could have passed for a chicken. Samson? What a funny name for a feathered pet?

Then she continued as if excited about the news of the day. "Samson, is just visiting. His owner just got married. What a blessing! They needed somewhere to let Sam stay, while they were on their honeymoon. He is a Kakapo, an owl parrot. He goes home in a few days. I will miss him. He has been so fun."

A huge crash followed, like dishes perhaps an entire tray full, hit the carpet, but only clattered and did not shatter. A anxious look, but a cheerful knowing one too, graced her features. "Yes, he has been fun. Samson is very headstrong."

The friendly shop keeper put the tray she had been holding; down on the small table next to the chair. Gently she picked up the vintage floral pot resting on it and chose one of the two containers on the tray, to use. She then poured a cup of steaming liquid into the one she had picked up. It was a fine porcelain cup on a matching saucer... small pink roses on both, with ivy vines... Then she carefully handed it to Martin. He was a little unsure of himself, but took it anyway. The cup jiggled slightly on the plate as he drew it near to himself, enough so to consume at leisure, but it did not tip or spill. An onlooker might notice that the vines that were painted on the cup, specifically matched the ones on the bottom, and after his acceptance, they were no longer aligned.

She then ever so carefully filled her own cup and sat the pot back; on the tray, on the table, beside the big earth-brown chair, that held Mr. Martin Cleaver. She went right over to the opposing chair and plopped down. Her cup not porcelain, but a mug... with the picture of a flamingo painted, and it's head molded... gracefully down and across the actual

223

handle; bent over drinking with it's wings wrapped around the liquid inside, as if loving and sharing it with the drinker.

"Tell me friend? It is a cold day. How come you have come my way?" The young woman smiled pleasantly. "I did not expect anyone, well... perhaps that is not true. I was hoping for... you." Her face satisfying to look at, even amusing..., but something else made him feel safe... Like a kid that had been found and waiting for their parent to come and get them. All the time entertained by a police officer, or teacher, or kind heart, "he made the connection". Being lost and being safe were two sides of the same coin. One, a coin that is, that he had carried in his pocket for luck? Maybe not physically, but powerfully... emotionally. It had not brought him any.

Lost; since the first moment Martin found he was still alive and so many others had died. Right next to him. Inches away... He had done all that he could and served well. He had even received metals for his valor and bravery, earned in sacrifice. It was just the remaining, echoing question... Why? Why me, to be alive... to have a chance to breath another day. At first the exhalation of life filled his heart then the grief of guilt, split it into thousands of mismatched parts. How was I better? Luck?

Then Martin went home to his wife, to his beloved Dorothy. She was ever kind and waiting for him to lead. Years of patience... Yet, Martin no longer wanted to show the way. All things had changed. The dreams and fanciful ideas they cared about together... before he left, now gone. Never returned... just gone. All he longed to do was be at home, and left alone. From that day until the day he left her at the hospital, he had stopped living. Then she died, and he died with her, but found he still walked anyway? How could that be?

Martin just wanted to go back and be where "he was". Flat on his back among the others, waiting for? It had been a big open field full of bodies, that were more like a puzzle with pieces missing on a giant's table, than REAL! Yet it was the place, Martin lived many nights. Martin somehow wanted to make sure it was okay, that he lived while others did not? How could he ever answer that? How could he ever believe his value more than the next guy? Death was forever, and darkness. He had been spared for a time, but it was all gray. Martin just never knew sunshine again after that one horrific moment, ages ago. Now today, all he could remember or long to see was Dorothy's bright smile.

Safe; That was never a feeling Martin allowed himself. "They" were coming for him. He just knew it. At times he could hear them far away. Since Dorothy died, they were closer. That is why he never left the house. Maybe even this day had been a mistake? But then, had it? Martin took a sip of tea and contemplated. He was free. Somehow the bank woman had told the bank man, that his loan was paid off. Insurance?! Martin did not even know they had any. What else? ... cancer...

Martin had so many questions to ask, that it was going to take a while to sort them out. He would need a pad and paper, and a bit of time. Glimpses of things nearly forgotten, and parts of conversation, whispered into nothingness, marched around in a band, no one else could see or hear. He tried to calm his pulse. He drank another sip of tea. It helped. How odd?

"Yes, we carry journals. They are great for writing things down. I like them so much better than just "dairies". I guess each have merits. I always draw outside the lines myself, which is more conducive to a journal." She smiled warmly. We have both, lined and unlined, but I believe you are the first, I mean a lined kind of guy. Someone who believes in facts, once they are presented clearly."

Martin did not really remember asking for anything. A journal? That actually sounded peaceful. Like being able to speak to Dorothy, more tangibly... No not to the dust! No... to her, well maybe indirectly. The one in his heart. The one still very much alive. Perhaps he could write down all the things he remembered, so he would not lose even one to age or time. It would be a pleasure to keep the good, and throw away all the bad. Yes, there was bad. It was ever waiting on the edges of his waking hours. He knew that. He just did not want anyone else to know it as well.

She was beside him holding a book out, before he could consider his reply. How had she moved from her chair, and retrieved the item so quickly, he had not noticed or considered. Martin felt wonderfully... tranquil. He sipped his tea again. Then he drained the cup to the last drop. Martin set the cup and saucer carefully, on the solid silver tray with tiny engraved roses, on the small table next to his chair. Until this moment, he had not closely seen the beauty of everything. Even the table itself... funny, Martin noticed it was in the shape of a French horn on its side. The table I mean. It was as if the designer had used the flat horn part as the table top, and then the long complicated, yet beautiful pipes below as the base. How unique? Then, he accepted the bound papers from her. Martin took the book as if it were a treasure. It was not breakable, yet it felt fragile.

"It is just plain... white?" Martin held it out as he looked at it more carefully. "It does not even have a picture on front? None in the inside. The front and back are just white too?" He felt like a new question was at the edge of his awareness, but could not bring it to the front and form the words, he long to ask...

She did not leave him long in the darkness, but spoke right up. "The cover is always last. You have to work it out. Same really for the back, as that changes too. You need to write things down. The idea is to search for words unseen and emotions so important, as to be priceless. Then capture them, here. She pointed to the bound paper. "To refer back to, when you forget. You need to fill it out first; the inside, all the way to the outside. From that point you will be able to find for yourself, what belongs... what to put on the cover, both front and back... the beginning and the end. It, or in this case you... can not start backwards or even in the middle."

Martin thought her words were a little too poetic maybe, but her heart was very like Dorothy's, he could tell.

Safe. Like in the very presence of angels,
his mother had told him.
How funny, he would remember that now.
Martin could not recall the last time
he ever thought of his childhood.

"It," pointing to the empty book. "It can also be useful for dreaming more about life. Some write wishes, or regrets, while others find something else, better to dwell on, daily. Then maybe plans. Real goals. After you allow yesterday to sweep by, and let go, live today, and maybe just maybe plan for tomorrow. Praying, writing your thoughts to God might be of value." The last part, she let stand there all by itself. Out there in the air, like the very Spirit of the Lord perceptibly filling the room, to full. The limits of the walls... the very boundaries, tested... like every heart and soul, knowing the truth, and yet afraid. Martin wanted to write to God. He wanted to speak to him. He wanted... In one breath he hated Him, and in the next he could not deny the ever lasting presence beside him and around him, even as he tried too.

The word was, is and always will be real!

Martin needed to keep moving. It is what Dorothy use to tell him all the time. He had taken it to heart and since her death, it had kept him composed, especially in times of turmoil. Little did he know that "moving forward" was echoed, in the very pages of the bible again and again. The equivalent definition was the basis of hope, and the truth of Our everlasting Lord.

"What do I owe you for everything?" Martin remembered the time quite suddenly. He felt like he had overstayed, well not really. He felt so welcome, it was only that he had planned to be at the market by now. Lisa must be done with her errands, and if he did not hurry on... she would head toward the bank. Martin Cleaver never wanted to go back their again. And that was his plan.

"Today. It is free. Call it luck if you like, but I would prefer to use the term blessing. As I do not believe in chance at all." The woman smiled. "There is no such thing." She replied solidly. "Besides with the unpredictable weather of late, I will close after you leave. Not to push you out, we have time. There is not a lot of foot traffic anyway this time of year. Regardless I like to be here when I am needed. Consider it a grateful gift from a local shopkeeper." Her winning smile an assurance of truth. "Oh, bring someone back, or refer someone. That always helps. Like ripples in a pound, we help each other. Drops in the ocean, we all rise." Lovely words trailed away.

Martin tried to look closely at her. It was hard to understand, but she seemed to have... just plain features. Not too sharp or soft, just kind and reassuring. Her eyes were bright and sharp, yet made you want to consider the nature of flowers that only come once a year, but return... like clockwork. Her hair was long, shoulder length and held back in a leather tie. The color of it was soft auburn, like the tiny flowers in fall, outside Dorothy's kitchen window. She wore a simple dark sweater, of wool. It smelled funny, like real natural fibers of wool, a sort of homey sent. She also had on simple blue jeans and boots that appeared to be Indian made, maybe? Lovely crafted leather anyway.

"You have been my first and perhaps my only customer of the day at this point." She chimed not unhappily. "One is always better than none, and one is so very precious, never to be considered less, than many." She continued smiling.

Martin stood up from the chair. "Can I at least pay for the tea?" He mumbled humbly. Placing the book inside his jacket, inner breast pocket. Somehow he had just accepted. He would never have done that before. He would not have liked to be indebted. But this did not feel that way at all. The book, it lay close to his heart. Martin felt better in all kinds of ways. He was like a lamb that had been lost, found by the Sheppard and brought back to the path. He had been protected, and told he had value, in ways he had never known before. He had somehow, in some way, been claimed. Even now his right hand wandered to the book, below his jacket's surface, resting safe. then he dropped it again to his side.

The shop owner smiled. "All who thirst are given the chance for eternal life." Brightly she looked into his eyes. "No charge Martin Cleaver. All was paid for long ago..." She gently took his arm, in much the same way she brought him in... Then led him to the front. At the door, she released him.

Together they stood for a moment side by side. They looked out between the letters painted on the front. Flashes filled the sky in the distance. Wow, it had come up fast. Martin felt a sudden urgency to go. He had not stayed too long, as God's timing was perfect. Only, now... he needed to move.

"You will be my last customer today Mr. Cleaver. I think that I will close up. The sky tells me it is time. You were lucky I guess to have caught me." Her face was very bright, full of assurances... hope. "but I would rather say...blessed..."

Martin Cleaver mumbled words of thanks. He impulsively raised his hand in farewell. It felt awkward, but good to have done it. Martin opened the exit, and the small bell rang again. He stepped out. The door closed. The cold was immediate. The temperature must have dropped five degrees. Behind him, he heard the bolt go into place, the door lock tight, and the little screen pulled down, as to show the shop closed. A few heart beats later the lights, what few their were, turned off. The sky was far more threatening than before. Martin's disposition was better however, so the effect was not as pronounced.

Martin took his bearings like any military man and turned toward the market. He went right from the bank and turned left. It was funny, the outside air had become kind of hard to breath. It felt different then when he went in. He walked a little father. The market was only down the street.

Overhead there were burst of lightening here and there. They were sporadic warnings of more to come. Not close, but very intense. Growing. That was not good. The mountains that way, north... usually foretold double what would hit the town. The reason... well known, the weather had no other natural barrier from the mountains base, across the plain to the community.

A funny electrical, static-like energy made Martin's bones hurt. One trepid search of the horizon... the upcoming event, told Martin he better step it up. How come no one said anything on the news channel earlier? That man, "they" had on there was nearly always... completely... wrong. Martin vowed to change channels no matter what, after today. He was glad to leave bad luck, and poorly informed weather men behind in favor of real information. His prolonged loyalty to a wrong idea, very clear. It would be worth a try. Maybe that was not the only change he was going to make. Maybe he would make a whole list and write them down to keep them straight. Questions, concerns and things... in his new white journal.

  Up ahead the light flashed green... in both directions. A bad noise somewhere echoed... heartbeat... heartbeat... heart.. ... ... wham! Crash, splitting wood and shearing metal, torn my force and twisted by unnatural intrusions into the lives of the innocent. Rubber burned and burning and the strong smell of gas... a storm of a different kind, hit, struck and battered, human and machine alike. It was not slow or fast, but a long drawn out wail, of chaos singing true, in defiance of all that was or is or will be... holy.

chirp!

(20)
All Plans Need a "B"

Hours seemed to slide away. Time was on a mission to race by. The sky above had decided that winter had not in fact moved on, but had returned to claim the day with a vengeance. The black clouds that lingered at the edges of the valley, gathered closer, trying to block out the sun and create a thriving environment for shadow, to walk among the living... easily.

Alison, watched as the customers lined up behind the roped markers. It was very unusual for this time of the month. Also, she was supposed to go to lunch, but there was just her and the other girl, running the show. So that would just have to be put off. The best thing that happened all morning was Mr. Cleaver. He had sure left in a hurry. She was really happy for him. He had been through so much. She had come to know Dorothy over the years. She knew the bare bones of things, the military stuff and all the rest. They had even had lunch a couple of times together. Helping each other be better caretakers. Alison was responsible for her father. He had had a stroke. So after work that was her second life.

Together, the both of them... friends had planned an "in case". In case... this day ever happened.

What she did not expect was Mr. Seedtree's response. It was crazy. It was like he had wanted the property, for something else. After Martin Cleaver left, Mr. Seedtree had come out of his office. He had gruffly said something about leaving early and promptly left. That was really okay with both her and her co-worker, as he made the job harder. Nothing was ever good enough. Nothing was acceptable, even if you did things exactly as told. She wanted to leave, but she had been with the bank so long, it was hard. She was suppose to be the manager by now, but somehow they had given the job to the new man. He had only been there a short while, and already many were taking their account else where. The only way to say it, Mr. Seedtree, knew how to make people want to fly away, to escape at the earliest opportunity.

Alison focused on the moment. Regardless if the manager was on hand or not, she would make sure everything ran right and everyone was treated fairly and with respect.

Outside, the front door, Mr. Seedtree headed for his car. Tucked under his left arm were several files. In his right, he grasped the wagon that carried his portable oxygen. It was like carrying a monkey on your back, he hated it so much. When he had enough money, he would not have to carry it anywhere. He would be well taken care of instead. That made him feel better all the way around, well not physically. That was ... well.. that was just...

He stood beside the door of his four door SUV for several minutes. He wrestled with the files, which refused to stay stacked, and tried relentlessly to escape... as if truly alive and acting like captured animals, instead of simple wood pulp and ink. Finally, he got his key in the lock and the door open. Angrily he shoved everything in. The files across the front seat, some falling off and hitting the floor. Then he turned and lifted the small tank into the back seat. Pulled the lever to place his own seat back into position and climbed in.

The sky above was already dark, but the energy that was building gave fair warning of a possible tornado. Hard to know, how or why, but the air... it was still and it was not.

Mr. Seedtree turned the ignition over and through the vehicle into reverse. A few moments later he was leaving the lot.

(21)
The Ride to Heaven

Jack heard more than saw the medical team show up. The approaching alarms were like a song on the old radio. You know a hard rock noise on a soft rock station turned up too loud, before breakfast time even. It was painful to hear... like someone standing next to you... yelling and yelling and yelling into your ear, only a hand's space away. You just want them to stop, but they don't hear you, they are busy... yelling!

There had been an angel. A beautiful crazy seraph, behind the wheel of an old vintage bug? Jack loved antique cars. How could that not be a hallucination? They must be giving him something really wonderful. Jack smiled. It was kind of a solemn expression to anyone watching as he was right and the mediation was kicking right in. Were they here? They must be... The sounds had changed, or were still changing. Where were they? Again... by they, the room felt full and empty.

In the cold space,
between the ceiling and the rafters,
angels drift like butterflies,
ever answering the calls,
of both hope and sorrow!

A mother's song,
a fathers whisper.
A loved one lost, and one born.
Close to heaven and ever nearer to hell.

The flames had eyes. There were animals or maybe things... in the fire. Many were all over him. Consuming his skin like hungry beetles. Then there was a man. No... bigger... and grander, larger than life. He was not alone. There was a small stranger with him. He was yelling! Not the hero, but the little guy. The whole scene was hard to explain. Regardless, "He" was lit up like Christmas, His visage so bright. He blew out the evil candles and saved Jack from more... Nothing burned the Man, nothing hurt Him. He was so bright that He cast no shadow in any direction... dwarfing even the brilliance of the yellow and red hell all around. The little stranger next to him, still yelling the whole time.

Then both the small stranger from no where..., and the "super man", the someone else... in white... along with the wild woman that came in from the sky, the loveliest woman ever... unreal... all of it. Hard to make right in his head. Together, somehow... they, one, two all of them?; had picked him up. It was like Jack was nothing. A feather. A boy or small child maybe? And then they easily walked him right out of the oven. All the time the hissing snakes kept yelling. A voice, a sound, a whisper, a scream, he would never stop hearing it or... himself! Then there was also... a chorus of hecklers, gleefully basking in his pain. Jack felt, burned a..li..ve...!

The last remembrance of things he could not take from his head, was his agreement to fix Mrs. Wix's caddy. Not the right way, but the wrong way; "fix" in the slang term. It had not been an easy decision, but from the time he had the red truck in the bay, until he had returned her car to her that same day, at her house, his life had shifted. He had grown to hate her. It was not like something she had exactly done to him. In fact she had been fair, in all her dealings, paid on time and was a good customer. It was more the way she had looked at him that day. All full of concern...? But instead of making him feel good, it had made him crazy. He just hated that look. By the time he went home that night, all he could think about was getting back at her. Yet he still could not figure out for what, no matter how he tried to think it through. He simply had no specific reason. Well, at least none that made any sense.

She would just find herself moving forward. Jack pictured in his head. Well that is what she use to say right? Or some such stupid thing. She would be driving along and then, she would just be done. That was the plan. She was old anyway so what difference? An odd jolt of guilt or pain struck his heart harder than he thought possible. What would happen to his mom? What had he done? ... He was always hurting people. It happened. He hated it, but...

Then he remembered his conversation with the bank man. He had been a little behind on the property. It was his business, times were slow. It was important to him. The business and his mom, that was his whole life. Mary died. Truth was about that, he had been careless, and reckless and whatever "less..." was left for descriptions, it would be... right. That is if it reflected his stupidity. Since that picture showed up, the truck and all the rest, Jack Lindel had been obsessed, with the past and afraid of the future. For himself and his mother, but mostly... at this time, this moment... just for himself. The rest was now far beyond his ability to care.

Why was he so mad again? By the time he got back from that delivery, it had been too late to call the Cleaver's house. The red truck had been nearly 24 hours in his bay before he got around to it again. Then Mr. Cleaver had laughed at him nearly, when he told him how bad. His truck was a mess! Jack Lindel was a lot of things, but he was no liar. Cleaver could come and check if he liked. He did not want it on his premises anyway. The truck would never run again, it would never drive down the road again, unless you were willing to re-buy just about everything and replace it! Stupid old man. What did he think? That Jack, the owner... did not know how to run a shop?

Every day after until today, Jack Lindel had called the stupid man. Not Mr. Cleaver, but the other stupid man. The insurance man. Jack Lindel was a good guy. Well mostly and he was trying to help out. Sheldon had come by once or twice and that was nice. He had asked about things, but nothing else. What could he say to Sheldon? Sheldon was helping his neighbor in a hard time, even Sheldon's daughter was helping Mr. Cleaver at the house with things. Both were nearly living over there as well, most of the time. That Mr. Cleaver had a lot of friends. That made Jack a little mad. How come he did not have friends?

Then he found his mind wandered again for a while. What were they putting in the small tube that went in the needle in his hand, up past his wrist and elbow and shoulder and, and, and... ? The funny look on the medical lady's face should have alarmed him, but it just didn't. Instead Jack wondered if he would get to see the angel again? The bright bird that flew in from no where, and leaped into the fire. She was a Phoenix. A colorful creature that had mythical aspects. She seemed impervious to the flames all around, and at peace as if at home in that horrific, hellish environment. Nothing made her afraid. It was grand, and miraculous, to have seen at all.

What? Fire? Jack was on fire? No... He had been on fire. The pain was getting worse again. Someone was screaming. It was Jack!

Pastor Joseph was waiting outside the emergency room. He was praying. Actually he had not stopped praying basically since he got within the town limits. He drove right in and found himself pressed to heroism. The young man had not hesitated. His heart belonged to the almighty. Beside him, standing in the hall was Tedra. Not for the first time not for the last, she was on the third floor of the building. This basically was her second home. Mostly because of her father and his connections. But also, being the social worker and working at the white building was convenient, in all kinds of ways. Truthfully, Tedra was glad, she had chosen her field, It gave her a chance to work directly with those that needed help, and sometimes could not even ask for it.

Dr. Macsen was gone for the day. So Doctor Smith was in charge. It was bad for Jack Lindel. He had severe burns over most of his body. If he lived it was going to be a long process to come back to anything resembling normal. He was alive at least for now. That was directly because of the quick thinking and resourcefulness of strangers, risking their own lives.

In the hospital room, Jack tried to answer questions, as he thought they were talking to him. Mostly they were talking to each other, the doctor and the nurse. His voice... more like a mumble, barely below the hearing level of normal folk. The others... they were speaking as to his life expectancy. There were two of them, the doctor and the nurse. Most of what they said, he really did not want to hear in the first place. Finally, Doctor Smith wrote some words and numbers down on Jack's chart at the end of the bed and left the room. The nurse adjusted the drip that was going into his arm. She looked down quickly, tried to smile and then left the room also.

Did he see the mirror of death? The eyes, the truth and window to the soul... reveling what sometimes can not be stated out loud, as to prevent the very appearance of hope, by casting a shadow... that has no source.

Now he was just left, the beeping machine marking off the moments of his life. How long? He felt pretty okay about it. Well, that might be because the drip was going a bit fast. That was okay with him for sure. If he had his way, he would reach right up and crank it over. But for some reason he just did not have the energy to do so. He could not move his arms. He could not move... anything.

The moaning sounds he made were alarming. But Tedra knew they were not going to be better or different for a while, if at all. She stepped back a moment as Doctor Smith walked by and then was followed by the nurse. They all knew Tedra, and never bothered to ask about the preacher. If he was with her, then he was obviously in the right place.

Then Tedra touched the preachers shoulder as he glanced through the door way into the cold room, where Jack lay. "You did a great job." Her voice calm and reassuring. "Your new here? We did not get to say much in the ride over... My name is Tedra Macsen. It was a unique way to meet at the station," her voice as positive about things as she could be... which was not a lot. "I am the on-site worker for the hospital here." The genuine smile she beamed... disarming. Made the whole world a bit nicer as it was all real. Nothing hidden. Even covered in dirt, oil, soot and worse, her faced dirty and smudged, her pretty hair singed in places, she was lovely.

"I am..." Joseph took a moment to slowly intake his breath. Some part of him, remembering the verses about the words...

"I am Joseph Lamb. Pastor Lamb. I am the new pastor for the Grace 1st Church in town. I have not even been there yet. I have not been out to the farm. I have not been to pick up the keys. I have..." His voice trailed off as he kept his eyes on Jack. "This has been a big day." His words were very solemn. As even he was aware the man in the inner room was close to death.

Tedra let her hand drop away. "It is not our success, but the heart of our effort, that God sees." She whispered. "You did great back there, remember, I was there. We were not alone. You know that. There is always a reason." Her voice even lower.

The response was not from the pastor, but the dead man, still breathing in the bed. "Can you hear me." The words were far away. A chocked sound. "I know you are there." Jack's voice was weak. It was muffled, hidden, muffled and disrupted by the air mask. Yet... clear. Desperate. "Please..."

Pastor Lamb stepped into the room. He did not pay attention to Tedra. He was physically drawn, by the soul, crying out. He walked to the side of Jack Lindel's hospital bed. The man was bad off. The machine was beeping away, droning on. It would stop when the patients heart stopped. That was clear. Then it would be used some where else. But this one person, this one... would then be gone forever.

At the side of the bed, Joseph reached out and grasped Jack's damaged hand. Lightly, he touched him as to not cause pain, but give the touch, that was necessary, to know... beyond any doubt, the man near darkness was not alone. He was connected to the living.

"Please. I am so sorry. I am so unworthy of anything. I can not carry it any longer. Please, take it away." Jack started hacking. His lungs damaged by smoke and heat. It was hard to gain air. Even with the help of the mask and tanks and machines. Jack felt like he was drowning, and there was no water. He was thirsty and needed a drink. He was in the desert, lost and desperate for the news of hope. The very thing he felt was not his to have, not his to feel, and his worthless life, a response to all of those feelings.

"I killed her. I was stupid and I murdered... Mary." The word, the last one, he spoke with heartbroken love. Like the very essence of the name encompassed all his dreams of a future, family, laughter, and life. The kind of love that never gets a chance to grow and live and be. The kind that you just touch for an instant and are cheated of its intensity and longevity by fate and chance and ultimately the design of the darkness.

"I saw Him. He is here now." Jack continued. The coughing better, even subdued. "The Savior. He was beside you in the fire. I have seen clearly that means... you are the right one. Please, how can I be forgiven?"

Joseph prayed below hearing of anyone, "Lord, your healing, your comfort, this man... please." He bowed his head. So many things racing, ideas, questions and more. But the focus of God, ever a calm on his own heart, allowed him to give peace, as he could to Jack.

"We are all sinners. We must repent and ask for forgiveness to him directly. Only through Jesus, are we saved. His birth, his life, his death and his resurrection... the gift to all mankind." The answer was sturdy and strong.

"Murders are sinners. I am a sinner." Jack cried. It made it harder to breathe. Then he tried to pull himself together. Time was too short. It had truly run out, and the gift of the moments to follow would mean much, perhaps to a few, or maybe to many?
"Mrs. Wix." The words stronger than before. "I did not want to do it. But I did not want to lose the station. The bank man told me it would help. It would be easy." Jack openly mocked the idea. "Nothing is easy and the cost... far more than money. Please... help Mrs. Wix." The last words falling off and away, like dead leaves on a tree.

The little man became very still. He did not want to interfere with the next moments. Mrs. Wix... Mrs. Wix was exactly why he was here. Why Joseph Malachi Lamb was in town. How he got the job, a place to live and everything else, was connected to her. She was a good friend of his Pastor back home, and specifically invited him. She recommended him to the position to replace the retiring Pastor. Her and the others at the church, had written a letter, and the kind current Pastor's own hand was in the signature line. "We need you."

"Her car is not going to work right. It is going to break in a bad way. It is going to move forward when it should not. No brakes, and the accelerator has been tampered with." Jack fell silent and the machine stopped. Alarms blared and the sound of people running this way, was deafening. Joseph prayed. Then he let the man's hand lay back on the bed, resting beside the vacant body.

Joseph turned like a man, set off on an important race at a dead run, however he had no idea were to journey to. At the door he was nearly overrun as he tried to get out of the way and back into the hall. The hospital staff were in emergency mode, but the out come was already clear. Maybe even merciful, as Jack was terribly burned. Joseph stepped through the door way and then out and around as he could. In the hallway, Tedra was waiting.

(22)
The Point of Friends

***

Up ahead the light flashed green... in both directions. A bad noise somewhere echoed... heartbeat... heartbeat... heart.. ... ... wham! Crash, splitting wood and shearing metal, torn by force and twisted by unnatural intrusions into the lives of the innocent. Rubber burned and burning and the strong smell of gas... a storm of a different kind, hit, struck and battered, human and machine alike. It was not slow or fast, but a long drawn out wail, of chaos singing true, in defiance of all that was or is or will be... holy.

Chirp! Not a bird but a cricket. A black one.

***

Martin came up as fast as he could. Lisa's car now upside down. Kind of a pretzel around the pole. It had been struck not once but twice. How could that be possible? The old man had seen black shadows fly in broad day light. That was the only way he could describe it and no one to tell. No one would believe him anyway. He would be just claimed as crazy. There was a white Caddy, and an SUV, both in the wrong place, going to the same place at the same time from different paths. Then Lisa... or what was left of her, and her car...

He came up and first thing, he could see her trapped upside down, hanging from the belt. He smelled the gas, and knew what was coming. Martin stepped to the door, and tried as he could... Nothing moved. He pummeled the door with his fists, but it was not going to budge. Looking around, there was nothing, nothing to use. That is... except his shoes. Steel towed, ugly tennis shoes. He drew back like he was punting for the giants, back in high school. The power would have sent the pig skin threw the poles squarely and on to Nebraska. The window cracked, like a spider, safety glass... preparing to shatter into a thousand smaller blocks. He repeated the process, with measured movement. The goal to knock it lose and free his friend.

Finally, through, he bent down and wrangled his way into the cab. Martin released the belt and Lisa fell forward on to him. With effort he moved himself and her back to freedom... outside. Exhausted, winded and full of adrenalin, Martin grabbed her wrist and pulled her back along the ground, away from the vehicle.

Heart beat... heart beat... heart ... The explosion was huge. The gas caught and the backend lifted off the ground a full foot. When it came back down the flames had engulfed the car completely.

Lisa had been pulled clear, only a moment ahead of the lethal blast. But she had not escaped. Only gained a few more moments, here on this earth. Martin rose up as the force had knocked him down. He crawled over to where her body lay quiet. He knelt down beside her. She appeared fine. Not even hurt at all. That is except for the cut that ran across her brow. Well that is all that Martin could see. He took off his jacket and put it over her body, trying to keep her warm on the cold ground. Trying to prevent her from shock. He hated having to have moved her, he might have made things worse? But the alternative left no options. The smell, the evil gas smell, it told him all he needed to know. He had been warned before in the military. Trained. Smells, meant things. It was good to pay attention.

Martin bent over slowly, and gently used his right hand; brushed the hair from her face. Then he peered into the very young... angel's visage directly. Like looking at something so beautiful, you dare not look away. As it was fleeting and you knew in the pit of your stomach it was miraculous, and momentary, and shocking and solemn. Lisa was crushed. Some how she had been trampled by the giants of both force and speed. How many broken bones? How much damage to her insides? Worse still, how much pain...?

"Don't worry Mr. Cleaver." She spoke. "Like she did every day to him. Just before breakfast. Her tone level and friendly. It was gentle, and soft, like a breeze, welcomed in summer by everyone."

"Shhh..." he whispered, but it sounded like yelling in his head. "Help is coming!" He forced the words out to be clear. Martin glanced up for a second. The white car, the big one was upside down also. It was a couple of dozen yards away. The SUV, appeared to be okay, at least it was on all four tires. But the driver's side front was certainly going to cost a load to repair and replace as needed. Sirens were already going off. Were they close or far? Martin had no idea. He could not tell. Everything was moving in slow motion, and speeding up and then warping together...? He just wanted them to hurry. He wanted them to be here already.

"You will be all right." Lisa smiled. "Tell father that mother is okay, and that we will be waiting." there was a pause... "for you too." The girls eyes closed ever so slowly. Like windows to heaven shut away from bad on-lookers... that may follow or more precisely, try.

Don't worry? Be alright? Martin was never going to be alright. What ever chance he had, was in his arms, right now. She, this young flower... was slipping away, and he was trying to catch wisps of mist, and breathes of life jewels sparkling in the very air, so incredibly precious...

246

and so intangible to the touch. At least to Martin's hands... What did she mean about her mother? Lisa could see her mother? Her pretty face was so blissful, and completely unchanged from the first time he saw her, the night he was saved. Even now, he had no idea, that he was "saved". Well not until... just... now.

   The wind left Martin's chest. Like a giant creature had punched him in the middle forcing him to expel all that he had inside. All that was still in doubt. His very will to continue rivaling his heart and soul, the desire to kill himself. The hope and faith to live, just one more day. Martin hesitated on the intake of his next breath. A new inhalation of a magnificent scent. It was never going to be the same as it was before.

   That bad... "it" had grown, like a small monkey fed daily and kept close. Riding him into the dirt. Always telling Martin... he was nothing. That he should have died. Convinced of all that ugliness, insecurity and guilt... he had, only taken Dorothy with him, year after year. A joint death they came to share. She would garden and leave flowers all over, and Martin never noticed. She was tending their grave. Putting, pretty petals on their remains. Not a life at all, and not an after life either.

   Lisa, beautiful, bright, sunshine... flower... dying. Right there on the ground.

   Martin looked back across the space between himself and the curb. The white book lay there in the street. The one that the bookshop owner had given him, only a short while ago. He must have dropped it, as he ran to help Lisa. It was no longer white. It was stained. Blood stained! He wanted to cry, a grown man... Right there on the hard black road, covered in ice and debris. The car upside down in flames. Other cars and wrecks near by... People coming and things happening all at the same time. But the clearest thing... Lisa... there before him. Passing away.

The opposing metal bullets weighing thousands of pounds; far more than Lisa's vehicle, had done their job well. None had escaped... the wrath of darkness, let lose by foul deeds.

Air, ice cold, sharp and stabbing... filled Martin's lungs. Released from the stupor, the shock of the moment. he moved. Even as little dots appeared at the edges of his sight, he proceeded. Some part of the man was fighting, to put perspective back into his world. To find a foundation to stand on that "threat" would not, no... could not move. Could not tear down. Would be solid for him, forever.

Martin Cleaver, the man. The sad, lonely empty man; bowed his head. He took Lisa's hand in his. "God..." The word came out in a croak. But it would soon grow, like a single drop in the wind before a mighty storm. It would gather strength from the depths of his losses, to the pits of his personal hells... and then back across his heart, where dreams and Dorothy still dwelt... together.

"Please. You know me, I know you do." a quiet that lasted no time at all. "Please... I believe! You are the almighty. I am so much less than anything worth your time. But... please..." The rest was too munched together between sobs and tears, that left Martin blind.

Prayer, came to him. His heart so low, lifted, healed. Not measured, but accepted. How come he had denied for so long? The clarity now, so piercing. Not because he did not want to believe. He was so sure his soul was just too damaged to be of consequence, even to Jesus.

(23)
The Flight of Angels

Joseph knew now for sure... there was a reason he was here. It was worse than he had dared believe. The blood left his face, his heart skipped a beat... he turned and ran out the entrance of Jack's room. He stopped only for a moment, as if like a man... checking the air before launching an aircraft, no a rocket had taken his place. Power, and might, his very being for existence. The pastor was going to be measured early. How? By trial... of faith.

Tedra was right behind him. Whatever was going on, she wanted to help. At the elevator Joseph slowed down, only long enough to punch the button with force. Down. They had to go "down", to the first floor. Once she caught up and caught a glimpse of his serious features, she held her tongue. Wherever he was going, she was going right along. Whatever plan he had, she had. Tedra could feel the electricity in the air, and it was not from the storm. Well not the one that was brewing outside in the heavens naturally. This was different. Like feeling you forgot something, and finding out that you had. Like feeling lost, and then picked up by your mother. Like being yelled at for something you did not do, but taking the blame for a friend, to keep them from being beaten. The list was long and flashing like a light, memories and currents of force, all around... Like being in their on car accident, their own dangerous plight in flight, in motion... the instances seemed to slow and then go by fast and then randomly repeat. It was unsettling to both, but they did not let "it" win.

Attentive to the new arrivals,
the angels sang softly,
to help those with the worst pains,
know "He" was and is with them.

The first bright soldier fell... purposefully from the ceiling and landed upright and straight on the floor. Truly not touching anything, but ready to do damage to everything. Folded wings, then still as a statue... listening. The black crickets had come. They were not alone. They were in the lobby and coming through the emergency entrance. They had come to infest the white building with their evil. Their lies and their half truths, that make men weak, and stupid. Even those that are schooled, can lose the war, while trying to win a single victory. Beware. Be... careful. It was going to be a terrible day, and wonderful day, a momentous day, to be written down... and given to the song writers... in better times. If any returned, as prayer was needed.

A second soldier dropped from the same place, and stood ready also. They could hear the small legs, so many, cross floors, running over mats, finding holes in things, baseboards, cracks and small spaces, crevices to explore, conquer and keep.

A pungent scent of burned toast and old macaroni left in the skillet two days, came out of the AC/Heater unit. The nurse at the front, Nurse Barns. She was on duty. She was manning her usual desk, watching the garden entrance. Jack had come in earlier. Her heart was still racing. It had been a shock to see him, like that. And, Nancy had only ... a glance. She prayed he would be okay. Nancy had tried to catch Tedra's attention, but there was just no way. Too many people at the same time, and too much going on, so they all rushed together, upstairs, like a squall. Nancy had just been left. She was manning the desk, like a lighthouse man. Her importance and position chained her in place. But her heart, followed the rest, ... everyone... upstairs. Along with her prayers, that kept going that way even now.

The hospital was a big place, but news would come. She already knew there had been a bad explosion at the station. The hospital was in direct connection to the emergency system. So that was clear. The rest was guess work. That included... as to how bad Jack Lindel himself was at this time; hard to say. That was a moment to moment question whose answer was already written. It was just not out there among the ones that would soon know, "hurt". Nancy wanted to run upstairs and help, or at least check on him herself, but she could not. All the time she worked, she tried not to watch the clock. The smell was getting worse.

Finally, Nancy punched the intercom to the other station. Out of no where, Nancy complained. That was not like her at all. She spoke slowly into the receiver to the other woman manning the back area, in charge of maintenance. Then she hung up the phone abruptly feeling sick to her stomach. Nancy had only asked for her to call the maintenance men, as something must have crawled into the ducts and died. She still felt like she might have been very sharp with her coworker. Oddly, she could not figure out why? It was no ones fault? About the dead thing(s) in places...Nancy Barnes, was very closely right, but not.

The time on the big standing clock in the main lobby, was two minutes to 5:00 pm. The perfect time for lots of people as they get off work. They can go home to their real lives and forget all that they do just to keep them. While others do not even understand the concept of time. They no longer work or never worked. They were unable. They were cheated out of the possibility. But in its place, they were given a different path. The importance here was that everyone born from the first to the last... belongs to Him.

When the door opened to level one the sight before them was horrific. It caused Tedra to stifle and unwanted scream. It was a huge effort and a show of surprising courage not to give into the impulse. There were bugs... all kinds of bugs. All over the floors. They were moving... the tiles. Everywhere she looked. Roaches, crickets; not field ones but black,..., odd spiders with misshapen heads, and eyes that did not blink. She dared not stare. The shock of the moment passed, and "they" seemed to fade back within the darker shadows of the counters, the reflections off tables and chairs from the ceiling lamps and surfaces. Had she seen, everything? Had she viewed the truth, raw and caught... off guard. How? By the pastor? Were there steps somehow muffled, by a greater force? He never slowed, not even for a breath. Joseph stepped right out of the small box, the elevator car, and onto the linoleum and the cold, pulled away. As if evil aware that his very touch, would wither them... all of them, like autumn leaves. The little man was covered head to foot by the armor of God. He had a shield and sword. All ran before him, as he was not alone, HE was with him.

A greater presence filled the room, like warm water. Vapor, a sweet perfume. It seeped into the cracks, through the walls, and in all things. Small popping sounds followed. Tedra did not want to know what it was, she just wanted to keep moving forward. Pastor Lamb bounded across the lobby, passed Nancy, gasping in half spoken pleas for information about Jack Lindel, and out the double doors. The ice on the step nearly knocked him down, but instead of falling, he seemed to glide to a corrected safe spot and continue his trek.

Joseph noted an ambulance just coming in. A large fat man was on the gurney. He was hooked up to a air hose from his nose, to a machine. He also wore a mask, to help keep him alive. There was a needle in his hand and fluids being pumped in... life fluids... water...

The man left Joseph with a bad gut ache. The sight of him. He needed to hurry. Time... was no longer moving oddly or in sections, but running faster, linear progression. They were on a set path and he knew it. Now it was only a matter of faith and trust.

The pastor walked on by. He did not even look to see if the heavyset man needed comfort. He did not pray for the man. That was maybe a mistake, but no one was perfect, except Jesus. Joseph felt like part of him was suffocating. He did not have time to figure out why, all he could think was to keep going. He rummaged in his pocket, pulled out his key and jumped in the front seat. There he put the key in the ignition and turned it over. The old vehicle roared to life, like a brand new model. Tedra still on his heals ran around to the other side. Her first try to get in the vehicle beside him failed miserably. The door just would not open. Frustrated she went to the back one and it gave immediately. She jumped in too and he just barely waited for her to close the door. Then he shifted the gear into reverse. Pulled quickly out of the spot, jammed the transmission into drive and floored it.

Tedra was praying under her breath. Already at a loss and having no idea as to how this was going to go, or where? It was the best course of action she could think to do. In this instance, she was just on for the ride. In what ever direction it led, she would do her best to be ready. That was the one thing she was good at, just about everything, "a little". Enough to be dangerous.

Not far was the answer.

Joseph went to exit and pulled out of the drive to the right. Just down the street, past the bank, and the bookshop, before the market, at the light... everything unveiled. There was a fire truck, two police cars and one ambulance on sight. There were a few barriers and the men in blue were trying to make sure the traffic went around, and did not gawk too much. Pastor pressed the brakes has hard as he dared as not to cause panic, or get a ticket. No need in making anyone too mad, before a real fight? Better to see what is going on first.

He stopped the car, badly parked and got out. Without any preemptive thought or prior plan, the man broke out into a run. Joseph felt he could almost hear the angels singing. The sound drew him like a beacon. It was as if a direct note, like a horn blown, long and low before a battle, or perhaps sadly after... that God was not only close, "He" was here, and "He" was taking someone... home. An officer moved to slow Joseph down, but he hailed to him as if he had seen a movie. A science fiction... "look away" and Joseph smiled. The other man did just that. Joseph kept going. He had no special power, only prayer. But his intense expression said much. That and the sash he wore. It was same one many men of the cloth took on, before giving last rights. Or at least it was very similar.

Again, even that was a facade. Joseph knew all the tricks to get into where he needed to be. He had printed passes and I.D.'s for: News Journalist, Inspector for just about everything, Representative for more companies and important agencies then were known, a handful of useful Government badges... oh and just about every other form of I.D. necessary to fight "bad". It came in lots of forms and Joseph Malachi Lamb was a true believer of the word from cover to cover. His faith stronger with each battle and his heart more resilient in its tenacity. So he was ready and expected the worst.

Tedra caught up to him and stood quiet. Waiting for instruction. "Take the other car." Joseph pointed to Lisa's roasting wreck. Martin was on the ground only a few feet away. The heat from the vehicle had made puddles of water, where the ice from the weather had been left by the prior storm. The sky above was working up a brand new batch even now to add to everyone's evening. The temperature had dropped several degrees already. It was going to be a very cold night.

      Martin felt like screaming there, kneeling next to Lisa on cold hard ground, but his voice would not give him the power he wanted, or in this case needed... on his own. Part of his heart began to beg. Every important detail was highlighted and the lesser things seemed more important than ever. A man had tried to take Lisa away. He said she was dead. The whole idea inflamed Martin's soul, to the point of burning him alive in the icy weather. That man! The stranger... Who was he? No one! This was not the garden at the hospital full of pretty flowers, and sadness. There was hope there hidden among the tiny greenery. Martin Cleaver was sure of that now. It had clung to him like a sweet perfume. Now all around him, more powerful than ever. Stronger... the scent intoxicating. No this was not the garden, there was only the might and glory that was real, to those that carried the garden in their hearts.

      Then from nowhere... this woman appeared. She was so beautiful. Only all alight, the glow like dancing fire of a different kind. At first he could not hear her, but knew she spoke. Did she talk to him? No! She was yelling, yes... At the ambulance man at the medic Martin could see. Then she looked down at him... only a few paces away. He could nearly each out and touch her if he liked. But he did not. He did not want to take his attention away from the flower, dying in his hands. He wanted to stop it. He wanted to stop the sand from sliding through the hour glass, if he had to give his own in its place.

      Martin looked back at the woman... "Please. He can save her. I know He can. I don't know how to ask him. I know it because Dorothy told me. She never lied and I believe. I believe! He needs to hear me... I believe!" The man's tone grew weaker and stronger. More desperate and yet even more calm. The plea not just of faith, hope and true belief, but of begging petition. True and honest, deeply felt... empathetic intercessory prayer. Pleading more for another one's well being, more than self, more than one's on life. Martin had no idea the energy building all around. The driver and medic were very still. A quiet seemed to lay over everything. It muted the sirens and seemed to steady even the flashing lights to a beat..., a beat..., a heart beat.

Tedra looked down at Martin Cleaver, a soul lost and found. So open and ready, and so ultimately sad. There was no if or maybe, No test for the Lord. It was a profound request. Martin knew that God, Jesus Christ and the Holy Spirit were real, yesterday, today right now, and all the days of his life from this day to the last, and then forever.

"Martin..." Tedra began quietly stepping closer. "Do you believe?"

"He is real. I have seen Him more than once, but tried to refuse it all. He was there when I was lost, all along. He helped me be strong for my family and country. He was beside me in the fire. He gave me Dorothy. My sweet, sweet... ever patient Dorothy, was a gift. She gave me the knowledge, I just lacked the wisdom. Or that is what I thought. I had to earn it. I had to be good enough, or not at all." Words tumbled out. " I lacked everything. I was stupid and stubborn. I was unworthy..." His voice trailed away a moment. "I killed people Tedra. Then I survived when others did not. I thought it was punishment to make me live and remember. But no, again... it was not. I took out my hate and anger on my wife, and she loved me anyway." Then tears in waves came down his face freely.

Time felt like it stood completely still. Martin could see his breath come out in a mist. The cold was here, all around, but the man did not feel it. Tedra's breath too came in a fine mist. She kept silent.

Martin turned away from the beautiful woman. He gazed back down at Lisa's sweet face. Then he spoke very strongly, loudly, and yet... humbly. "Please...God... I am, Martin Cleaver. I believe in you with my whole heart, my whole being, my whole soul and my eternity. I know now that you came here, born as a man from a virgin, to die for my sins. They were so many, I thought..." he mumbled again... Then he returned stronger in might. "I believe you were crucified, the perfect lamb. I believe you rose from the grave and ascended to heaven. You did not leave us alone here, but gave us your Holy Spirit. Even now I ask, please... accept me. Know my name. And... Thank you... thank you... blessed Lord."

The stillness of the air was full of static electricity. Snow was drifting down lightly, with more to come. Electrical bursts of random light, distant lightening in the background, now circled the little town and could be viewed easily in every direction.

"Lord Jesus, I am small. I am nothing. But, I am yours." Martin fought to control his voice. "Dorothy said all I had to do was ask. So, I am asking. I am begging. I am pleading. Mercy, healing, your hand please. Please, don't let Lisa die. Let her be okay. Not for me, but for so many others that still need her. As if it were for me... I could only add that I know it is your will, and I will accept... what you want of me. I will also accept that of my sweet wife and all that has gone before. I accept you, in every way. Thankful for your blessed sacrifice." He bowed his head and the world felt more cold than ever. "Your will be done Lord. Your will I accept. Wholly and completely I accept in all things." ... "Amen."...

Lisa, nearly gray... was still. Quiet and non moving. A small, then another, so small hardly worth notice... mist, a reaction to the cold, came from her lips... Not quickly, but slowly... gathering strength. It was not even noticed for several beats of her heart, then it was "all to unmistakable". Lisa opened her eyes ever so slowly. She looked up at

Martin, his head bowed in earnest prayer, his body on the ground beside her kneeling. Martin was humble and repentant before the Lord God Almighty!

"Grandpa!" The small barely whispered word, hung there in the icy air, melting all the last vestiges of Martin Cleavers walls.

The man smiled. Not a casual grin, but one lit up by God himself. "Yeah..." Martin mumbled back. "Grandpa." having been claimed. The memory Lisa was not referring too, was a statement she had made. Martin was trying to do as he was told. He was giving her a hard time. She had looked him square in the face, a frying pan held at arms length, full of eggs and such... unconsciously like a weapon... and peacefully stated; From now on you will come out of that room when I tell you breakfast is ready. You will not be late again. You will do as I said, as that is what I would expect from my own grandfather.

After that Martin had basically complied as he had truly made her... not made, but feel less than valued and he knew it. Her tone and stance, were not angry but defensive and protective. Announcing Martin, at first sight by name, "Grandpa." Was a simple affirmation of real affection. The older man was floored, and thrilled and overcome and quiet, even at peace...

(24)
It was getting later...
and the fight had just started!

All around the snow was getting deeper. The two men left near by, waiting to do their jobs, to pick up Lisa's body, to take her over to the hospital. The slow waltz, the easy ride as she was dead.

Then the old man had shown up and that was that. He was not letting anyone get close for any reason. They could force him, but that would look real bad in the papers. Joe Spense, the news man, would send someone over. They would be here soon enough. This was probably big news. The biggest around here for a while. Old Lady Wix's vehicle sure did a number on the other car. Then there was that funny SUV in the center. It had rolled obviously, but landed exactly where it should be. As if it had not been moved. If not for the front end caved in, it appeared untouched. Exactly in the right lane, going the right way. The other crew were handling it. There was a big fat man in that vehicle too, going in. He might be having a heart attack? That was way more important than a dead girl and old man on the ground... this had to be handled, right.

That is when every thing changed. Marvin Ledger the ambulance driver quit smoking on the spot. In fact, he was so scared he went to church every Sunday after until he died at 96 years old. No one could say if he was saved or not, but the fruits of his spirit were many according to rumor, after that night. A real change in his life, by just being there. Waiting to pick up a "load"; a deceased person, whose life was taken by an accident.

Then there was the other man. He was the medic. He was kind of new on the job. On the lazy side, as he had not even bothered to take out his case, as she was cold when they had showed up. To him there did not seem to be any reason to waste good supplies. That was money poured down the drain. A loss the agency could do without. Things were tight these days. Then later, he found his own doubts starring at him in the face. Perhaps he should have made sure. Then there would be solid facts instead of whatever else it was...

The driver, Marvin, crossed his chest and spoke low under his breath. He had been more than sure the girl was dead himself. The younger man had only complied and held off picking her up, as the old man appeared ready to fight it out. That was not part of his job... putting old people on the ground. His mother would have screamed at him and his father would have taken him to the woodshed when he got home; as a kid. The lesson still fresh. "do the right thing." The echo of a strict but loving childhood felt comforting. Not always easy or soft, but real.

The driver not really a practicing Christian at all, watched on as the old man spoke to... God? The driver was not raised in a good home, or taught the right thing(s). His air felt like it matched Lisa Farman on the ground. Cut off and stopped, in the moment of holiness to the point little dark spots filled his vision. He wondered if he had drank more coffee then he should have... or worked too many hours? It was far beyond that. He was awed, and comforted. He felt gently, sweetly... sleepy. He wanted to pay close attention suddenly, but it was a passing desire. The rest of his heart felt... peaceful. He leaned in and his soul stepped closer.

A Savior, able to forgive all? A life unburdened by darkness and full of Light. He saw right there the moment all things made sense. He accepted. "I believe!" Marvin Ledger a nobody, became a somebody to someone that was all important. He accepted God! Jesus His Son, and the

Mighty Holy Spirit... All of it. And he was still a good ten or even fifteen feet away.

The other man the medic, Mark Lostriff. He would be asked later, what he had seen, and found he could not say. Only that he felt very good and had a great day at work, even though it had been snowing and cold the whole time. However, he had no desire to step closer... He was only quiet and waiting, as there was no need to hurry. He got paid by the hour anyway, not the victim. If it were not the case, he might be tempted, but that was a fleeting, funny thought... that blew by, like snowflakes that did not want to melt...but had no choice. So he just watched everything, and never really cared... one way or the other. Busy in his head, as to how he could beat his brother up over a stupid argument. Something about using his truck without asking. Nothing important. Just things... Like if he was going to get a date, with the girl he met, last week? He left a message, but she never called back. Did that mean anything?

Martin, the aged man beside Lisa on the ground. Her life returned, restored and renewed by God. "The are going to take you... there." Martin spoke with confidence. "The..." the word hospital was heavy. It had so many bad meanings. But he knew now, that was going to be okay also.

"Are you coming?" Lisa mumbled back. Speaking just for Martin to hear alone. The volume no more than a whisper.

There was no hesitation is his direct answer. "I will be right along. Not far behind at all. I have to go and find your father. Then we will be at your side." His response like saying goodnight not goodbye at all.

"I will be waiting." She smiled.

"Yes. I know." Martin's answer felt as if the world had grown big and small, at the same time. He had found that there were those beyond his wife, that loved and cared for him. Strangers turned to friends, now family. He had been claimed and it felt... good. Like new shoes. It made him glance down at his funny steel toed green tennis shoes from what must have been a crazy rummage sale... and laugh. Not loudly but mostly to himself, deeply. Dorothy would have loved that he found use of them after all. They had made short work of the glass, and allowed miracles to take place... at least the first ones. The real one, the combined grace of life and forgiveness... the acceptance of the true and only Savior Jesus Christ the Son of God.

Martin touched her cheek, cupped it in his hand lightly. "Be there soon..." Then he let go. With his other hand he motioned for the workers to come right over. As if breaking the funny spell, the men moved immediately to do their jobs. Like butterflies caught in a net on a spring day and then released... unexpectedly, they recovered quickly. The two were a great team and Lisa was going to get the best... as she was in good hands. Both were competent at their positions.

The old man stood up and moved away slowly, with purpose. His eyes still on the young woman the whole time. Judging everything they did, not because it was wrong, but it was the anxiousness of the moment. Trying to give all your best feelings to someone, to tell them, your prayers surround them... Angels go with them. Jesus beside them! But you just stand there trying to be quiet as to not show... what is raging in your heart! The broken flower... was going to need the best of everything and Martin was going to make sure she got it.

God had heard him. His prayer and been listened to, and answered. The man was humbly grateful. He was profoundly unsettled, in ways he still prayed would never ever return to what was, so that he could claim and keep what is and will be. Jesus Christ was his Savior. Life had new meaning. Martin Cleaver was alive!

Tedra standing close, had witnessed a miracle. That was absolutely without doubt. Joyously, not the first time she had been privileged to have seen the working hand of God. It was never the same, and she was sure it happened even more often than she perceived. It was just the big announcements... the ones that brought trumpets to your soul... those were monumental for small humans. But the reality they were all equal. From the smallest blade of grass the giant moons of Jupiter... the grandeur was measureless. Just sometimes more spectacularly seen or expressed in a way to touch our very lives directly.

Tedra stepped forward. she put her arm around Martin's shoulders'. "Let's go find Sheldon."

Martin came awake. Aware now that she was even there at all. How had she just appeared? Grateful however for her very presence as if she had been sent for this purpose. He needed a ride and he had a mission. He recognized her as the Doctor's daughter. Wow, she always seemed to be in the right place?!. He did not like her in the beginning, but so far, he found, he did not like a lot of things, that turned out very good for him. Dorothy would have had a great laugh on that one. Martin Cleaver smiled.

Across a short distance, between the vehicles collided and damaged now worthless hulls. That is except the SUV in the center. Poof. It was just there... Seemingly untouched, but part of the cause, as to all witness reports. Those however would disappear, as would the car. Not right away. Soon.

"Margaret..." The young pastor was beside Mrs. Margaret Wix on the ground. She had been thrown, maybe forty or fifty feet. Her body was twisted and mangled. It was hard to measure the distance of her flight... as the snow was falling and the weather was doing its best to gain attention. The police were here, two cars had been sent out. But they were busy with other people, milling out on the sidewalks, or directing traffic. It was near the 5:00 o'clock hour. So many people coming and going all in a hurry. The accident was like a giant rock thrown in a small pound creating ripples of waves in every direction. No one was getting home on time this night. But that was the least of the issues that would come up.

Mrs. Wix, was considered... dead. A sheet had been placed over her head. Joseph and known it would be her. Long before he pulled the cloth back. He had been sent. He had come has fast as he could. As he pulled back the drape, he felt like retching. He held back his insides. He bowed his head and prayed...

Softly the Pastor spoke, "Margaret, it's Joseph. I am here." He waited. He wanted to comfort and console. He wanted to take her pain away. But that had already happened. She was gone.

A silence, a moment in time that stops...
Margaret... made a small noise. Joseph's heart beat like he had run a race in one minute. "Call out, get help!" It screamed. But instead, he was ever so quiet. Her sweet face, hard to see clearly... so mashed. Teeth missing. Her breath, now only barely seen in the cold... and halted, on its way to the end. Cheating whatever darkness had tried to take, by the full acceptance of all things in His name. Knowing that the purpose of the moment, is ever within and part of... His grand plan. Pastor was fully aware there was no reason to call out. She was dead... or nearly so. "Margaret..." He leaned in and spoke as to a child.

"I... her you." moments hung... stopped... and instance held... tipped back and forth on the point of an imaginary needle, sharp and dangerous. "God has answered me. I I knew you would come. You are needed." The plea in her tone was so strong, spoken so distantly. "Things found a way, and must be beaten back." She coughed and blood spilt out over her lips. "They are at the church. I know... help him..." Her beautiful gray blue eyes went vacant. But they did not reflect the storm above, but the sea of peace in her loving heart. Her last goodbye to this world in a hideous storm, the welcome miracle of the next, indescribable.

There was no time for grief. No time for anything. He was late. Joseph prayed for minutes... even... moments... that would make a difference. Joseph prayed for God's perfect timing.

Evil fire flies whirled erratically.
They danced at the edge of the darkness.
They were gathering both, because of the weather,
and the passing of the hour!
Reflections, mirrors of the true embers,
the fire from the car.
Lives lost... damage done, the effort worthwhile.

Pastor Joseph slowly pulled the sheet back over Mrs. Wix. She was dead, yes. But the body was to be treated with respect. Now the living must be attended to. He got up. Knowing... he was not alone. The angels that had pushed him for the last eighty plus miles, had been busy at the hospital. But now returned to his need. They had fought the blackness out of the walls in the white building... until air again passed through the vents and now/ ready for more, were at his side. The ripples of fire-light tracing patterns across their beings, not here and not there but exactly where God wanted them to be.

Joseph took no noticed as he believed without proof. In his life... all the time the face of the great Savior was everywhere. The best he hoped was that the countenance that he perceived looking back at himself in the mirror each morning was not just Joseph, but the Lord's useful and loving servant. No, Joseph was far from perfect and embraced all of his shortcomings. The reality, the fact... all of his fears, were diminished and then removed by the loving hand of Jesus.

Now Joseph was sure he had been called. As surely as if his Lord was to drive the car himself here. Not away but toward the evil garden... the Garden of Gethsemane... metaphorically represented now, before the pastor.

You can not run or hide...
The enemy is within the walls.
Ugly eyes at the edges,
and corners of every surface.
They knowing "His" name,
can not say it
They are afraid...!
Prayer stronger than all things,
with legs that skitter in the night.

Tedra took Mr. Cleaver to the car. The pastors old car that is. She was facing the passenger side, full well knowing the front door would not open. Suddenly for what seemed like no apparent reason, Tedra pictured kicking the ball in 6th grade. Then her mind centered on the style, brand and model of the car. "Bang" Her boot hit the spot.

...no dent...

Tedra reached over and opened the front broken door. It complied easily. She then stuffed Martin in before he could say a thing and closed him in, then waited... She had taken full notice of Joseph running their way. Her thought; "Wherever he... Joseph Lamb, the new pastor in town, was going... Tedra Macsen was going too. Martin cleaver would just have to go along for the ride. They could find and pick up Sheldon at the same time. But the look on Joseph's face said; "That was not first!" as he approached the car at a dead run.

The young pastor went around and got in to the car. He noted Tedra was already ready and waiting and did not bother to ask anything at all about Martin. He just jumped in. She jumped in also. Not behind Joseph, but behind Martin and kind of in the center. So she could lien over the front seat and get a good view of what was next. Or at least try to catch whatever she could, to be updated on the "plan".

Joseph started the car right up. He pulled from his parked position, having basically already been in the street, from before. The man, the young pastor had been here to this place as a kid. But that was from a child's perspective. He turned right in error. Tedra immediately started navigating. She was like the other side of the coin that Joseph needed now badly. She was glad to be useful at all. Somehow, instinctively she had also gathered... enough clues; Mrs. Wix Caddy, and the appearance of Light, had to be connected to the church. If anything was still traveling or running or worse attacking, it was logical.

The sky above was dark. It might has well have been much later, as by all accounts, time was wonky and disconnected from the normal flow. Like jet lag, no plane involved, just the landing of angels, all around, ready to hold back and or due battle as needed and commanded... Ready for the King, prayer more important than ever. The light gathered like candles lit, one by one, a giant brightness that can not be contained... seen by even those that have no reason to look, but hope. Finding it to be the only explanation worth living for.

All across town, lights were going on.
No one knew why?
Well, some did not know,
but others fell to their knees.
They were sure.
They were the prayer warriors!

The snow that had barely inconvenienced anyone hours ago, was growing in its ability to slow the world down even further. That was the wrong direction for Joseph and his makeshift hero squad. Pastor Joseph Lamb, a new man on the job, tested his first day to the limits of all his worth. Tedra Macsen, a crazy pretender, an earth bound heavily heart that found life curiously easier when living and loving people for God.

Lastly, Martin Cleaver, the young Christian. Barely out of the box, set free from a cage, released from the chains of sin by his gracious and mighty Savior. Even now Martin was sending up more prayers from the front seat. He had no idea what was happening, but when life puts you on a boat, that is leaving the dock, with friends aboard, needing you... you go!

(25)
A Promotion, A Raise, Hope

Surame checked the chart at the end of the bed. Like any other person coming and going. Only she usually was the going individual. The one that retrieved the bodies and took them downstairs, below ground level. Not always, sometimes orderlies would do it also, but mostly she did her own, especially of late. The Morg-Tech had taken to reading the charts quite carefully, as part of her ultimate professional position. It was her job. She was to finish up, and "package" or ship... bodies, remains, loved ones, or a combination thereof. Surame would make sure they all went to the right destinations... in the end!

Random Entry: *Where I come from, a lesson was learned. It may be a little poetic when the translation is completed, but just the same. The emotion will survive.*

It is; you are exactly who you are, which is either for or against, no one is really in the middle. They are just hanging out for the free food and fun at the open house and fair events, but in the end, they will jump. Into the fire, or try to reach the stars. But by then... there just will not be any stars left. They will have melted away. But then that is just kind of... "How do you say that phrase?... a metaphorical story."

Surame had recently been to the bookshop downtown and started a journal. She liked the idea. It had helped her to be... a bit more prophetic. That also made her smile, which she had not done since leaving her brother behind.

Mr. Seedtree was very groggy. He had suffered a small amount of stress in the accident, and felt overwhelmed by the lack of service to his needs. This hospital would hear from him later, when he was up and around. At the moment, he was busy counting the tiles on the ceiling. They were far more interesting then they should be. He had never found them that great in design before now, as he had been here before. Not sick, but... making deals. He had made "house calls" or that is how he thought of it. He was a doctor for the sick, but liked to make people sicker. The reality he was just a banker and finances were creepy. They could be good or bad. He loved the bad.

The drip in the bag, that ran methodically, not randomly... down the tube, to the little prick; the needle in his hand, was helping the world focus in colors of gray, green and tiny bits of red. The machines were too loud. They had placed him on a breather.

Mr. Seedtree thought to himself, "They had better take good care of him. They had better get it together around here. He knew most of their weaknesses. He had great access at the bank to information, about just about everyone in town. That is anyone that had ever cashed a check, made a deposit or opened a Christmas Club account. He had already made full use of much of it. Bending people in ways, they would benefit his pocket and his plans. There was so much more to be done." He thought very well of himself. Although at the moment, he could barely remember if he had put on shoes that day, before going to work? Bleary and bashed from the wreck, life was whirling in all kinds of ways and directions for the big, extremely overweight, greedy... man.

A part of him tried to be alert. The woman in the room, was not a nice person. How had he not seen her even come in? How did he know she was not nice? How come he felt like screaming and she had done nothing. Then the little bag that led from the prick point in his hand... at the wrist, up the tube to the bag hanging in space, stopped dripping. She had taken it down and laid it on the bed next to his huge body. It was up next to his head... as he was now flat on the rolling hospital bed. She then did something with his air tube. Disengaging it from the wall fixture to a mini tank.

"Where are you taking me?" He wanted to ask. Then he wanted to loudly yell. Then he wanted to scream. But found he had no voice at all. She pulled up both the front and rear brakes on the bed. She went to the side, in full view. Seedtree could see her, and then not and then again. A bad metal taste filled his mouth. She pulled up the sheet. Right over his head!?!...

Terror filled his being... like the kind that takes you to another place. The one that makes you wet yourself, in public and you don't even care. You never think about it. All you can consider is... are you going to be; eaten, drowned, strangled, suffocated, pulled apart, burned or buried alive? That was just the beginning of the list. Mr. Seedtree had in some ways helped others meet these fates, but that was of course an entirely different story. This was him. Nadler Frederick Seedtree. He was a big man and a rich man. Sure he had stolen most of it along the way, but it was still his fair and square... as they say.

The last man standing was always the one that got everything. That was the rule. Too bad about his plans for the Cleaver place, but their were others. He had done pretty well, since he had come to this town, this bank. It had only taken a little bit of conniving and bribing the right parties, and he was in full control. How he had ended up here in the hospital was not in the plan A or B. In fact it was not in any plan of his on any level. It was that crazy Mrs. Wix. He had told Lindel to get rid of her and he would see what he could do on his gas station property. It had been easy. The station owner had lots of weaknesses. Not hard at all to exploit. The leverage of the "mom" thing would have been enough, but then the added picture, and the found connection about yet another tragic "accident" at the bridge... well that put everything right over the top.

The old woman's car should not have been there today at all, much less right downtown. Mrs. Wix's vehicle should have been floating in the dirty river. She should have been already gone, handled. Not barreling down Main Street at 5:00 pm? Fool. Stupid fool.

Mr. Seedtree tried to think clearly. The chemicals in his veins working hard to help with pain, ... and what else... he had no idea? In fact he was not altogether sure about the first part.

Surame went to the head end of the bed and pushed it away from the wall. She took her place behind it in order to proceed properly, and then gave a shove. The man was not light by any account on any scale. While he was in here, if he lived, Surame thought he should have his stomach stabled. Someone had already removed his heart, she was sure of it. She had found out the truth, and wanted to make sure she had all she needed to end it.

The Morg-Tech passed two sets of nurses. No one said a word. That made her smile. Why were people so afraid of death. God was forever, and we were all just passing through. She saw now, the wisdom of faith and the divine calm it brought. Not for the last time, she quietly thanked the man or woman that left the bible in the desk down stairs. The one she found. The one she read. That first night and every night since then. It, the living word had been a treasure found, she could not stopped savoring.

The doors to the elevator opened. Mr. Seedtree made a small sound. A man stepped out and looked over at Surame. She beamed him a smile, and quickly said, "The food in the cafeteria is a bit spicy today. Yet, I really enjoyed it."

The man smiled back and kept walking on down the hall. Satisfied that the lovely lady was busy and there was nothing usual to see. That is except the lovely lady.
No one else came or went. She pushed the big man on the moving bed, straight into the waiting... gapping elevator entrance. Then she hit the lower level... morgue button, as if it were second nature. She started humming low to herself. "Amazing grace... how sweet..." The little chimes went off counting the floors as the car moved down.

The little portable oxygen tank was near the red line. Surame was not in a hurry. She was in fact extremely calm. Maybe there was another one in her office. She doubted it, because most of the time, no one needed one in her area. Well, maybe there would still be no one that needed one?

The double doors to the world of the deceased, ten feet away from the elevator. It was a huge space. Many never crossed it at all, afraid to try. They, the entrance doors to Surame's world; were white, cold and metal like everything else. But they were usually a last stop. An end that few could see passed. She pushed the big rolling bed out, of the elevator, kept up the momentum of movement... "once in motion... kept in motion", straight across the tiles, the temporary barrier, between the living and the dead. The next room was not only sterile and hospital clean, it was empty. Well... that is of any one "living" but Surame and Mr. Seedtree.

The room was like a bus stop, that did not allow baggage. You got on, but you only brought yourself. Well you had what you were wearing, sometimes. Other times someone brought the deceased something to wear. But that did not happen every time. Hospital gowns for the rest. Just another cold thought, about death.

Across the room; bodies... six. They were lined up, bagged and tagged, waiting for pick up. Two to go to the cremator, who did a good job, a fair job and was respectable. And, four to the little funeral home, Surame had never visited. That was okay, she did her part... and that was enough.

They the lucky ones... were further prepared for coffin style burials or celebrations of life. Their loved ones sometimes spending a small fortune to say goodbye. Yet the truth; better to spend it on them, those that were here and gone... when they were breathing, or that was Surame's point of view. It amazed her how lost ones became more valuable to some, then when they were alive? Seemed a little creepy to celebrate the dead. It should be to remember them and celebrate the living each and every time. All that they lived for. All that they did. These were far more important memories to keep.

The woman moved to the drawers. These were kind of a holding station for the undecided. A cool refrigerator to make sure time was slowed and rot kept at bay. Surame pulled a big handle on one with no name marker at the front, and the container glided out. It went the whole way. Made of steel, and rollers, to hold an elephant if necessary. The new system worked great. Even the big man would be easy. Surame lined up the man's bed accordingly. His feet would be far inside, his head of course... easy to view. That is if anyone cared to come and claim him. She hit the red button above on the panel, and Seedtree felt himself moving. He wanted to reach up and lift the sheet away, but he could not. For some reason, he was numb, all over.

His breathing had become more shallow. He was fighting the need to gasp. No matter what he did, he could not move. Seedtree wanted to say something. He wanted to yell something. He wanted to scream. He thought he was... He could hear himself. But no one was listening.

The machine finished. Mr. Seedtree was in place. Like all the rest. Surame moved the empty rolling bed away. She hit the blue button and closed the drawer. The man felt himself moving inward. Not down or up. Just...

Surame then pushed the regular mobile bed away. It was so much lighter now, and easy to handle. She turned and walked it upstairs. Singing just under her breath. Life was full of surprises. Things just went right... sometimes.

The Morg-Tech had received a notice earlier today. She had been promoted. Why? Because the position was open. Her manager had had an accident. How sad? He was not a good man. She had found out his dirty little secret, about the selling of bodies. The mismarked COD (Certificate of Death) certificates, written in, for personal gain.

The woman had not made the connection, until Mrs. Wix's death had occurred. It had come over the wire, the emergency scanner. She had one in her office, and often listened, as to know when to be... available, for retrieving and accepting upstairs acquisitions. It was the same name, the one on the letter that got her the job. It was also the same one on the letter that had promoted her to the position of Morg-Supervisor, and Manager.

Peaceful Saints Hospital
Downtown, Near Where You Live
Here to serve... the public!
***

Dear Surame Kelly,

In recognition of your fine work, You have been promoted both in title and duties as the new manager of your very important department here at the hospital. I know that you will be up to the task. You have shown great professionalism in all your duties. Your repeated thoughtfulness, and kindness toward the victims and survivors of and in; the most delicate area of need, has been duly noted.

We know here, of your superior work efforts and stand behind you one hundred percent, in all your tasks. May your days be as blessed to you, as you have been to us, or will be.

Now and forever.

Signed,
Mrs. Margaret Wix,
Supervisor
Head Chair Member
Peaceful Saints Hospital

It is important to note there was no date on the letter at all.

Surame knew exactly who Mr. Seedtree was and what he had done. Cheating old people out of their land for profit. Putting them away before their time. Leaving them cut off as they would be from others... at their weakest. How had she found out? Well besides the crumbs found here and there, left by careless... half-hazard individuals in their logs and tracking; on the sheets in charts, or the number of supplies used and not used. It only took some one with decent math skills to know everything about everything. It all added up to an answer of "bad math". Lies become very visible, when they are painted outside the lines with such fury. Money and more money... makes everyone lackadaisical at some point. That is true especially as concerns those eaten up by its temptation.

Her own boss, well the old one. Before she had received the cool letter. He had well, been... both "slapdash and slipshod". Jacob Blane. That was his name, or had been. Until recently they had never had much to do with each other at all. Each did their job the way they should and that was enough. Mr. Blane, just liked to do the extras, his way. Surame learned, she could do that too. Even now he was cooling in the drawer next to Seedtree. She had only asked him a few questions, but he caved without effort. Now he was dead. Well all the way, not in limbo. His choices having been made by him or for him, it was hard to figure. Again, bad math.

Some men, have no backbone at all. Surame thought him a coward, a leach that sucked on others. Now no longer a problem for anyone. Surame had found he really loved energy drinks. He had... one too many. His heart had raced too fast... and he just died. Funny that. Not quickly as he to had made an early trip to the land of "Surame". She had lit up like a nova in the sky, when she connected not only him, but his accomplice(s). Now she just needed, well, she did not have to have, but it would have been better too... an admission of guilt.

Inside the drawer. Sound was absent. Well, except for the labored breathing of Mr. Seedtree. Finally, he could feel just a little of his face. Like life returning to flesh too long left cold. Then his cheeks and eyes, his ears and head. Then his neck, so he slowly moved it to change the position. Even in the dark, he could see. Just barely. Just sadly, clearly enough to be sure. Jacob Blane was looking right at him. Dead!

A cold mist left his mouth. He wanted it to be a scream. So loud and so strong they would here him in both heaven and hell. But instead, it was just a whisper... Not of prayer, but of hate, anger, rage and defiance.

No answer was returned.

(26)
A Bridge too Far

Sheldon had been out to the Braxly farm all day. He had helped with their prized mare. She was giving birth, and somehow breach had forced a call to the vet early. He had drove out quickly and been there all day. Now, he was covered in dirt and muck. Most of it from the stalls inside the barn. There had been a baby. A new baby, that was in good shape. An all white colt. A male. A huge shock considering the non-descript, and non-planned nature of the breeding parents. The Braxly's were overwhelmed. Their son was overseas at the moment, serving the country. It was going to be his horse, as a surprise, when he came back. How they were going to keep that secret, was hard to say.

Mrs. Braxly had cried. She said it was a sign. That was the answer she needed. God had sent her hope, when she was worried about her first born. No, not a superstitious woman, just taking it as a visible answer and affirmation of her constantly begged, prayer. The woman was so thankful that she hugged Sheldon unexpectedly, long and hard. She whispered inside his ear, "You are a gift..." Then she released him.

The weather outside had turned from okay, or even nice to down right bad. The storms from the mountains to the north had come again. The weather man had said they were all done, but he seldom got it right. Looking up had made Sheldon fill with concern. For no reason at all, he found he felt, he had stayed too long. Something was wrong. Something bad was coming, or worse already here.

He had quickly gathered up his supplies and tools, closed his bag and wished both Mr. and Mrs. Braxly a good night. Mr. Braxly could barely stop shaking his hand. He just wanted to believe every word he heard his wife speak. The concerns he had for his own son were not the same. Mr. Braxly knew that if his son died, it would be the will of God. He was protected. He was loved and cared for, every day, from the first day, he had laid eyes upon him, to the next time, he was sure to see him again. Mr. Braxly firmly believed that children were a gift to raise, but not to keep. They were a blessing to enjoy and cherish.

Sheldon tried hard not to be impolite. They wanted him to stay for dinner. They wanted to feed him. They wanted to thank him a thousand times before he left, beyond the monetary cheapness of dollars alone. They paid, they always paid well. They even paid more, as they knew Lisa was saving for school.

Sheldon had saved the mare. The mother was doing great. Because of prayer and faith, the little, tiny... perfect colt was also doing well. "He" had used Sheldon. Both mother and baby, were doing fine, and were growing stronger by the moment. Finally Sheldon disengaged himself from the good intentioned couple and headed for his truck. He did not bother to open the back or stow his gear, he just opened the front and tossed it across to the empty seat. He rummaged in his pocket and pulled out the key. Got in and brought it to life... like magic.

The lightening in the distance flashed, warning it was going to be more than a causal storm. It was going to be a whopper.

Sheldon pulled out the long drive and headed for the highway. He had a choice. He could go straight to the bridge, and right to town, or the long way. That would take an hour. The vet hated the bridge more than his own daughter did. It had been there he had lost his parents. It had been there he had lost his loving wife. But the road crews had long since certified it "safe". The truck sat idle for several moments. The decision was unconscious. It also was undeniably tangible and real. The ripples of a battle were very real, going on all around. Here, where he was, and in town... and where else... remained to be seen.

A giant fire ball went up in the sky. It was in the direction of town It was a cloud of death. It lingered and then grudgingly dispersed as if torn apart quickly not to allow others to see. Too late. Sheldon had viewed everything. He threw the truck into gear and turned toward the bridge. He floored the vehicle. It responded sluggishly at first, not being the usual response from the driver, but then complied. Sheldon felt a strong sense of God's presence. He began praying for all that he was worth. For what? He had no idea. The man just knew... everything was falling apart!

At the crossing that had taken numerous lives not all connected by;
paper files, pictures taken poorly, forms mistakenly written,
or trails of tears by those affected,
heat was rising.
In the bitter cold of an ice storm,
the door was opening,
a rip in the fabric...

A small being stood a few paces from the structure.
Just this side of the line.
There would be a toll required,
but it was not going to be collected.
The angel, the navigator.
This time he did not hold a map.
Instead...
he prepared.

Hissing sounds and the noise of crickets...
not field ones, but black like tiny dots of emptiness,
echoing and surrounding all things they could reach from the pit.
All things close, near by; and still living were in terrible danger. .

Something... shadowy and unformed molded and shifted
in and out of the growing night air.
It was expanding... larger and ever more threatening by the moment.
It appeared to try to move away from the metal,
somehow alive;
and reach out,
to touch the arrogant intruder,
challenger to it's power.

Not one thing(s), but many...
each jeering and laughing,
then and yet
afraid of being the first,
to receive what was coming!

The moment before,
that heralds all that will follow...

A stillness... the sound deadened, not gone at all, but muffled. A louder, stronger, much more violent resonance... shook the entire span of the metal structure.. All of it from one end to the other, as if a giant hand had punched from below. The water, swollen from the storm, rushed passed faster, filled with the abundance of rainfall further north, drenching the land, washed southward, even and ever trying to take the bridge out. Nature violently taking a role in the real world, echoing that of the hidden one. The goal, take the man's soul one way or the other... with it. Knowing that the town fathers could be bought and the evil span would be replaced. It had happened before. It would happen again.

Evil had held this place far longer than before the structure had come to rest, here. It had lain quiet as it possibly, and ate what was available. Then...the pylons for the metal structure were placed. It was all wrong. "They" should have been more carefully. The beams were not set correctly. Instead they were installed not on the solid rock below; but in favor of the unpredictable shifting mud. Giant posts set to rest in the sands of faith without works. False hope, and love embraced with lies.. It all made no sense, except in dreams or poetry, yet undreamt and unwritten. It like a parasite... somehow attached not to the truth, but the shifting earth. Most assuredly sounding mythic, but alive, and holding on like a real monster, a venomous spider of gigantic proportion at the end of a web, for flies, trapped.

The small figure pulled a sword. Not any sword, but the one containing wrath. This place had long held "bad" and it was time to change all of that. Sheldon, the man was on his way. While the evil considered it's luck to be good, it wavered as to the definition, realizing that a challenge had been made. Someone had dared to stand right there, in the road. They or it or whatever... was and is, or at least to be as it was felt... different. Scarier than a Mac Truck running full force. Yet, it... whatever... it was.. was small.

David and Goliath was not just a story for small children. David was God's champion. He tor down the giant, not of himself, but of and for God. This small angel, the solider, warrior of God was ready. This thing, this darkness would claim no more. Not even one. The wings on his back spread... not open all the way, but ready for flight. This would be, a battle on all levels. In the air, on land, in water, in fire and flood, this world and the next all at the same time. His brother, his sister else where... however... he was still not afraid. God was always with him. Jesus was and is forever King!

"You... it is time." The words clearly spoken out loud. the ever so soft breeze in answer ruffling his pristine white feathers, as if the Spirit of the Lord passed by, and around, giving strength and sureness to the moment. Evil was not welcome here, that was clear. It was past time to clear, clean and wash the road.

The unseen and the seen, the black and the white, the alive and the dead, the past and the present and the yet to be collided. The metal danced in black fire, while the sword of light, cast shadows on all things not of God. Each crack of blade to blade, whips to reality, left the sky reeling in lightening and thunder rolling out... in all directions across the atmosphere and some on the ground. The storm, heavier all around. Causing sight to be difficult threw the turmoil. Glimpses of hell and heaven, coupled into a mighty mix of thrashing fire and icy darkness.

Time. How long? Maybe minutes, probably hours, but more likely eons, and never ending, just moving forward until the time the Lord returns.

Sheldon drove up to the bridge. The snow was coming down hard and the river looked bad. It was very swollen. His heart told him, he was even now... perhaps too late. So he swallowed hard, threw caution to the wind and went on across. About half way, the whole structure seemed to lift a foot or so and then slam back down. The truck did not stop. Sheldon just tried harder to force the accelerator closer to the floor, even though it was already sitting on it.

Then... he was clear... of the bridge. Sheldon drove on, to town.

Behind him, the metal buckled. The bridge itself seemed to shrink in... like the reaction of a black hole...or even closer to a nova sun, smaller and smaller in all directions to a point of nothing; then it exploded outward in a thousand metal shards... none bigger than a foot or less. They all, and I mean all of them... fell into the fast moving river. It was as if the bridge had never been built at all.

Sheldon did not look back. Instead he powered on. He had no idea what had blown up or what had happened, will happen or was happening, but the urgency had remained.

(27)
Passing the Flame

The church was lit up like the strip in Las Vegas. Only it was all coming from and inside of the one building. There was no fire at all. It was just wide open. The front lights, the back lights, the light to the parking area all of them, on. The small office and rooms up stairs, and the ones behind the main building were on. All of it, again on. Lit up bright. The bell room and the chamber for prayer near there, off to the side, not much larger than a clothes closet, was also lit up. Nothing was left off, that could be used to drive back the "black".

The pitched-ness, the cloud above... a gathering of darkness, evil of every kind, from lies to deceit, and even murder. The building of God, built and used for His worship... , was being degraded and fouled, by evil. At least, "it" was trying to do just that. Then the black formed into beings, separate and together, waiting... and mocking... acting brave. "They" knew and had always known what was coming. Laughing, believing "it" had grown to the point so strong that it, or they or him... were unstoppable. The design above in the vapors... ugly and ancient. A blasphemy to the cross on the steeple. A sacrilege that would not go unpunished. The angels were ready. They only awaited "His" presence as always. God's mighty Light to shine!

The songs of heaven,
can only hope to chorus the music of His coming,
heard by all who know His love.

Pastor Joseph turned into the parking lot, crossed it without slowing; jumped the next garden curb as if in an Olympic race was in full process and roared in as if a cargo plane had landed; precisely and perfectly at the bottom of the old fitted tight stone, rather small, three step stairway... to the double door entry. The great oak doors completely open and the weather; welcome... or not... taking full advantage.

Seen by some or many, but only the few as is needed to witness. The same special beings, having pushed the car still on empty the whole way... the angels of glory... flew forward and on. Met in the air by black holes.

They went forward, flying like mighty eagles released into the wild, after too long held in a cage. They went passed the pastor's car moving at random, but truly in a pattern. Still steadily flying on ...forward... at the Lord's command.

    The young pastor threw open his door. Jumped out in one motion, gathered his balance and headed for the stair. One, two, three, the top step; the landing before the entrance. The one to the main double doors... was iced. Ready to knock down the unsuspecting. to slow down help from arrival.

Chirps...
Small snapping sounds...
popping everywhere!
Laughter, excitement...
hopeful pain.

*   Up above, in the heavens the light of God flashed and the lightening that followed was the very hand of the Lord, seen in our world... and the next, one in the same. Swords of fire, white hot, searing back the blackness of nameless evil, not content to wait for the right time... written in the Lord's word. Testing the waters, to see if "it" or even "they" could establish a foot hold among the lost.*

The ice, the black ice failed. Joseph was too much in a hurry. He was called by God and there was no time to waste. He leaped in one bound. One, two, three steps and then; Joseph landed. He had catapulted his whole body in his zest to comply with the need. He was all in. God, the Holy Spirit filled him, and Joseph was humbled, ready and prepared to serve.

The old pastor was here. Joseph could feel him, somehow. The very tangible presence of God, standing beside him, guiding his steps. Protecting and keeping him from evil all around, trying to get in. Trying to win. Joseph could never understand all of it and had no desire to even know. Not now. The moment was all about trust, doing all that he could do the best that he could do it. He was content that his Lord had not now or had ever given him a spirit of fear.

The old man, the pastor... had served fifty years and was going to retire. That is what brought Joseph to this town this church this day at this time. He had received a letter. He had come as he was asked. Oddly, several things had come up to keep Joseph from being on time, back in the big city, but each time... failed. Then since the new pastor had arrived, he had already been thrown fire balls, snow balls, and the evil of silent daggers. Only barely being missed each time, interference from the "other" side, no doubt. Just less conspicuous then the blatant attacks led by evil.

Tedra leaped out of the back of the Pastor's car. She quickly stepped forward to the front. Then she opened Martin's door. The door handle complied, the mechanism within functioned perfectly. Just exactly as she knew it would. Somehow, someway, not broken or stuck at all. There was also no dent, as if it would have been noticed anyway. The car not being exactly in the greatest of shapes to begin with. Then she motioned Martin to wait. Or at least let her go first. Martin Cleaver should not probably be here, but there was no way he was going to be left. That argument would have been a bad vine that had no fruit... ever. Martin Cleaver was on fire, and things were not settled. Martin wasn't stupid. He had seen miracles real ones... that he personally had asked for and come to reality right before his eyes. His bones told him a feeling more sure than his guts as his friend in the military would tease; *of this night, all should not be rushed over or thought out too quickly...* then he... Pete... was finished and passed to the next world. There in the pit of hell, next to Martin who had lived... his friend had been lifted by the spirit of God all around.

Martin now remembered so clearly, what had been blocked out before. He had gained his past, and felt all of the same emotions... before. Laying next to Pete Wilson in the trench, years ago. Him, Pete that is..., all the time talking about God, and Martin just hoping to die. Now he was very much alive, more than ever and he was doing what God had planned. The man, Martin..., was more than sure of it. He felt like singing, but held back. That would come later. Crazy yes, but not insane. Just so happy for the first time in so long, and now pressed to serious confrontation with all things ugly and evil. No time to run and read the bible. Only to have what Dorothy had given him, pieces and discussions. Now all of it, ready to hand, as if it had been recorded and waiting to be played out loud by his voice and his heart.

Seconds meaning everything, and passing quickly, they both turned toward the small church and worked their way around the car and up the stair. Careful of the black ice still waiting for a victim.

Already far inside... Joseph had passed through the foyer. Flyers from the prior week's service were scattered all over the floor. The big coffee pot was smashed to the ground. Coffee grounds everywhere. Empty prayer requests and leaflets, pamphlets about Jesus and all the services the church provided to the community for "free" of charge, also among the debris.

Someone, (or maybe thing...? Not a safe thought at all...) had torn up, or rather messed up the place. No severe damage was readily apparent. Just things bad kids would do, that needed to be here for class, instead of being board and mischievous.

Joseph kept moving, slowly, cautiously... aware, more was coming.

The main sanctuary was empty. Everything was very bright. Joseph felt compelled, ever forward. Behind the stage there was a song room and a bell room. He remembered as clear as yesterday, when he had been allowed back there. Once. It had been a special occasion and all the kids got to see, the "bell" room. There was a story about the bells, the old preacher told him. Well, he had told it to all the kids. He said the bells ring to bring the people, but only the late ones. As the "others" have already arrived. But it is good to sing to the lost, so they can be found."

Joseph was pulled that way.

At the door, that led to the bells, Joseph grabbed the handled and pulled. Not slow but quick and with great force. Their in front of him, a man dressed in torn blue jeans, a red sweater with a logo, Joseph did not recognize, and a bar. A metal bar in his hand. Maybe it was a wrench? It did not matter. It was a weapon. He... it... had already struck the old man grasped by the collar laying partially... bodily... on the floor. The intruder had just reared back to do it again. The young pastor flew, as if he had been carried by an angel and sped by the use of heavenly wings, a bullet forward to the mark... "Bam!" The bodies tangled and rolled. After that Joseph got to his feet and promptly forgot the fact he was a peaceful man.

The rage that followed unleashed, was mirrored in the beings above, fighting the black.

The man looked wild-eyed at Joseph, on drugs? Probably. More than likely at this point. But the reason for all of this, did not have to be a sane one. It was just ugly, evil and without proper words to define, only one instance. By that the world was full of things gone wrong. This one just happened to have found a place, here in this town, among these people.

Joseph saw for the first time, the bat wings. A shift in the very air around everything. One moment an angry man was before the pastor, the next something completely different. Otherworldly, disturbing in ways that were hard to define in either place. At the first occurrence, when Joseph had been struck, it hit him hard on the side of his face. It took a moment for Joseph to come back from the reeling shock. But then, power surged even greater. The truth revealed to the man, Joseph... and "it" repulsed his soul. The pastor cried out, "GOD!"

The resulting strike of incredible strength was felt by all around. The strange man, the being... was barely clear of Joseph but only just... The sky above flashed daylight for a single instance... a bolt of energy, came directly from the heavens... Power released from the sky... penetrated the bell tower, melting the metal of its structure into place, the ringer tight against the side; and never slowed. It shot like a mighty piercing arrow --- straight across the distance, passed Joseph Malachi Lamb, by a breath and for a single moment..., the beat of pure man's heart... it, the authority and force... seared the evil, bright hot. Burnt flesh, the smell, a mixed perfume; charcoaled meat and charred bone, . Death...

Tedra had already moved to the old pastor's side. Marcus Pinwheel, Sr. was not a normal man you would image doing well in any fight. He was only about five foot two, and slightly plump. But somehow Tedra had a new respect. Her thoughts concerning size and worth had changed much in just the last few hours. As he lay there on the floor, just near the prayer closest, where he had been sending up all his best, it was clear he had fought with his whole heart. Somehow he had gathered strength, from all that he had, then relied on the wide shoulder's of the Lord.

The flash of light still seared slightly across her vision, like looking at the sun a moment too long. It would pass. Pastor Pinwheel must have know "it" was coming. The lights... on all over the Church. That said a lot. Evil is afraid of the Light... and for good reason. Nothing was normal about any of this.

When the lightening struck she had seen "it" and never would forget it. Everyone one had. That is... both herself and Joseph. The exception had been Martin. He had been out in the main sanctuary. He had been wondering what to do next, and having found no ready at hand person to throttle, he had fallen to his knees. Martin had been praying... the whole time. It did not take a veteran Christian to know that the world was battling here, in the other rooms, outside and all around. And that there were very real victories and even sometimes defeats... the passing of life..., but in the end only Jesus, was, is and always will be King. Dorothy repeatedly told him that if you can do nothing else, pray. He used to smirk when she said it, or even discount it. Now he felt alive, and grateful for her ever vigilant heart. She had loved him more than he ever knew. And now that he had found God, he understood.

Joseph was quiet. Everything was okay. He knew it. Well, at least for this moment. The next, well that seemed to be an ongoing crazy "E" ride ticket. His faith had not been shaken, but strengthened.

The man, the young man... Joseph... ran back to the old man's side, knowing that the thief, or whatever he or "it" was, was dead. The most important thing now. His friend, the Pastor. "Sir," He began. "Pastor Pinwheel?" Josephs visage the full emotion of concern revealed. Joseph knelt down on the floor. He grasped the elder's hand and prayed.

Tedra was beside him. She leaned down and touched Joseph's shoulder. "I hear the ambulance. They will be here soon." She spoke with calm empathy. Then she stood... back up... and stepped back.

Joseph took a long breath, it had been a hard day. It was not even done. The young man looked up, right into the old man's face. He was not sure how long was still left, but did not believe it to be much.

Marcus Pinwheel spoke low. "I knew you were coming. I just had to wait." He kind of mumbled, but Joseph understood. The large lump on the side of the man's head was swelling fast. The pastor glanced slowly at Tedra. And then he looked across at Martin, who had just walked into the bell room. "I see you brought help. You are going to need it as it is not over, until the King returns." A sweet look touched his features.

"They will be here soon." Joseph tried to be comforting." I am sorry I was late."

"No. You were not late. You came in God's time. Now I get to go home. Do not be sad. I am happy. Thank you." He smiled... and then he faded, his very spirit slipped away... and then his body was still. The pleasant look on his bruised features did not match the pain that should have been felt and reflected. It was not. It was bliss.

(28)
Divide and Conquer

Sheldon found he was not alone in the cab. The map was on seat next to him. The map Lisa always used to get them to those new apartments across town, where they had all the cats. So many cats..! The funny landlord just did not care for dogs. Sheldon was an equal time, kind of guy. Did not matter what breed, only that it had paws or hooves. Back to the moment, the map. It was out, usually kept neatly folded away in the glove box. The city had put in a few changes to the main route and some of the streets were still under construction. Why? The map? It was not there before. It had just appeared. It only made Martin press the accelerator down harder. The truck was not fast, but it was complying. The weather worsening as if unnaturally fed.

The small angel, having caught up with the truck,
was in the right place once again...
the navigator smiled.

One block, two, the church would come up first and then Main street. That felt like miles away, no matter how Sheldon ate up the space. The explosion, had been that direction. At the last moment a driver turned down the one way, his way. Right at him, head on. Where did they come from? What was happening?

Sheldon prepared, and tried to plan out his path ahead. At the last second the stirring wheel whirled left and right and the oncoming vehicle sped by, never slowing. If he had seen, the driver, which he had not... He would not have known... the man. The fact would become apparent later to the right people at the right time. But for now, it was generally informative to know, the man was file 643, drunk again. Heading home. His lovely wife would be there still, waiting as before. Seriously too stupid to know that evil only dwells where it is kept and fed. Shine a light and everything shows true. Good or evil, it is better never to be blind or to live that way.

The church, it was all bright. Sheldon slammed on the breaks. His momentum making his old truck slide for fifty feet. First side ways one way and then another, not seeing the angels and black empty holes... dart around, battering against the vehicle, like a toy in a game.

The ambulance coming the other way, skidded just as hard from the other direction. Like a funny dance they circled, in the middle giving each partner a chance to wave to the other. It was like they had all day and it was just a ride at the carnival to be enjoyed. Then everything came to a stop. The men in uniforms and medical gear leaped out and headed for the church doorway. They had maneuvered around the pastors car... but it was not a big problem. Then carefully they stepped around the obvious trap of black ice at the top. Then they went inside.

Silly darkness, it would take more than ice of any kind to slow heroes.

Sheldon jumped from the cab of his own truck and ran across the front lawn area, buried in a half foot of fresh snow. Part of him wanted to rush on, downtown or to the hospital, the other part was torn wondering if he could help here? There was no sign of an explosion, but the sirens gave a clear definition of emergency none the less. Not really able to figure out which place he was supposed to be. Only knowing that he was guided, pulled and pushed forward. The man was ever alert to "action" in either direction.

Standing next to the white car, the pastor's vehicle, Sheldon did not know if he should go right in or wait? Police sirens were wailing.

Clearly what ever was happening, was still in motion to some degree. Risking making someone mad, and not really caring, he bounded on up the stair. One, two, three... He hit the very top and his right foot touched the ice. "It" had waited and waited, and never given up. Finally!

Sheldon flew forward, his feet one way his body the next. It was a nightmare ballet, which had no music, except the wild sounds of a man, lost in a clumsy rescue attempt, to be of help to others. If it were not such a sad night, it would have been funny. He ended up sitting on his butt, which would end up hurting for a month. He also had a sprained right foot. That would take longer to heal as he was never good at following the direction of medical advice.

A police officer pulled up in a car, lights flashing. An officer got out and proceeded toward the church. He stopped in his tracks, as he caught sight of something high in the air. The flashing of lights, not lightening. He was transfixed by the beauty and power, like a small child watching fireworks for the first time.

The ambulance having somehow trailed the pastor, arrived earlier on. Now, everyone was crossing paths. The body of the late pastor was on the gurney and being wheeled out as they found Sheldon still sitting at the front. They, were careful not to fall, and got the rolling bed across fairly easily. There was a bit of stifled... half... laughter... here and there. Sheldon was in a bad way. The one man said he would come right back to help, and Sheldon just motioned him on. He could make it to the doctor... he mumbled a reply he did not even care to make. He was feeling anxious about everything, and was still wasn't any closer to finding out what had happened.

Moment before...inside, the bell room, Joseph watched over the pastor's body like it had been his own father's, as it was carefully loaded onto the rolling gurney. Joseph felt only slightly unsure of himself. The man before him had served fifty years here within these walls. It was a big responsibility to care for the flock. It was a matter of life and death, this world and the next, in ways rarely seen by most. Joseph was to be the new pastor, immediately. There would be no ceremony or celebration. There would be healing. That is what would be needed. Joseph Malachi Lamb, Pastor, of the First Main Church. True it was a small town, but that had nothing to do with its importance to God. It was a huge title, for any man, fully aware he could never carry the load, without Jesus his personal savior and King. Joseph was going to have to hit the road running, so to speak. Well, he had not fallen yet, so surely God was with him. That made everything possible.

What would Sunday be like? He had only been here in town less than twenty-four hours. Wow, Joseph was ready for at least a long quiet Saturday, to sleep for a while. But that was for later, and a few loose ends had to be worked out.

Joseph turned to Tedra. It was the first time he had allowed himself to exhale. She was magnificent. Her hair dark and mysterious, but he remembered she had been on fire. He had seen it... when? He could not be sure. Not the kind of flame that consumed, but the one that surrounded and embraced... God. The one that let her walk, or at least drive through fire, and help rescue a trapped preacher and a station man. The fruits of her spirit so colorful, and bright as to shine in the darkness even to a blind man.

"Your bea ...u .. ti.ful!" He gawked. "Will you marry me?"

Tedra flushed. Her hair was a rats nest, she had not had time to look in a mirror for at least eighteen hours, other than washing her hands from time to time. Her clothes had soot marks and a few burned areas. But she herself,... untouched. Not one singe. Well... maybe a hair or two. But that was not to say she had any true damage at all. Tedra was ready to go another round. Bring it! If God and his army of angels were near, then there was cause to rise. There was a need to pray, but not desperately... or sadly... but cheerfully and with power. His mighty hand so close to the earth this night, Tedra wanted to shout. She wanted to dance like David in the streets. The snow falling softly now outside, would simply be a child's treat... a chance for leaving snow angels... on every park lawn..., for God to see and laugh and smile at his children's true worship.

Then she looked right at the man. He was a little shorter than she was used to for a date. They were eye to eye, not tall and "handsome". Kind of a plain man, but yet... there was a look that said volumes, ready to read. But for a husband? Well, as she considered her values and the losers she had left in a wake of destruction to herself, nearly every time, maybe God had a plan? Joseph was short true, compared to some but he had proven in one day, that he was taller than every man she had ever met, other than her own father. That was a tall order to fill. Tedra brushed her hands through her hair, unconsciously, wishing she had brushed it in the car. "Thank you..." Then she smiled. she had replied to the first part, but felt overcome by the second. Even speechless for a moment, which was highly new to Tedra. The night was dark, but even if it were broad day light, the shine would have still been brighter. Her face was lovely.

Joseph felt suddenly clumsy. He felt out of place and his words had just gotten ahead of his head. He could not take them back and really did not want to either. He just had not planned to say them quite that way... right out there. "uh... Can you get a ride? I am going to clean up here a little," His voiced trailed a bit. "Well, I mean... Close the doors and windows, and pick up the coffee pot." He looked a little gray from lack of eating and exhaustion. His spirit however, shiny bright, that nothing would stop him still. Should the darkness care to go another round, he was ready. Or at least he believed he was... "and then... I am going home."

What a funny thought. Joseph Malachi Lamb had been given a house by Marci Samuels. When she died, she had passed it to him directly. He barely remembered the old woman from when he was a kid. But she remembered him always. How that happened was just another miracle. That she would give him a place, a home. Then there was something about letters and the bank, and a Mr. Seedtree? That was some man that was very insistent on buying him out. Joseph had only been there a few times as a kid, with his mom, that is Mrs. Samuel's home. He had been very young. He did not remember much at all, but the answer was and would be the same. No. Joseph was not a seller. He had never been given such a gift. He had plans. Besides being the new pastor here in town, would be the right job. He wanted to open a children's home. Maybe one for unwed young mothers. Young mother's... that needed help, like his own, long ago. She had gone to the clinic to abort Joseph Lamb, and Dorothy Cleaver, and Mrs. Wix had pleaded... no. His mother had been saved. Joseph had been saved.

The proof... if his mother had no options, he would never have come here this day. God's will was mighty his plan perfect. His timing, flawless. It was still going on the real war against evil and Joseph knew that from the first day he was told of Jesus. According to the paperwork he received, which was still in the trunk of the old white car; there was at least forty acres that went with the place. Oh, and a note that there was also some chickens and cows... He was to ask Sheldon Farman about that. He would be handling their care, until Joseph's arrival.

Tedra looked at the man kind of funny. "Can I get a ride?" She laughed lightly, the sound like running water, to a thirsty man. "Like you do this everyday?" She seemed a little dumfounded. Explosions, flying bat men, shooting electricity, mighty arrows from heaven, dancing fire monsters... and... It was all drifting together, like logs in a river at the mouth of a canyon.

Joseph smiled softly. "Yep. Well, maybe not every day. Only... most days. God is always with us. <u>That</u> is everyday!" His only sadness, Joseph had no time with his friend, Pastor Marcus Pinwheel. He had known him as a kid, but that was ... long... ago. He had lost so much, and he had not even considered any of it closely. Here before his eyes, Pastor Marcus Pinwheel died. Earlier it had been Mrs. Margaret Wix. Before both of those it was Marci Samuels. All angels that had done their best to serve. He had much to pray and be thankful for... but little time of late to do it. His relationship had been one on one and immediate and showed no signs of being any different soon. Kneeling and showing true worship, that was to follow. Joseph would be doing that, until his dying days. Happily.

"I would love to take you out to coffee, breakfast, lunch.... dinner... you eat... right?" His voice trailed off again... a little. He was trying to say something more, but and then..."to thank you properly for your craziness. You are truly the angel of madness. I mean that in all the nicest ways." Trying to be friendly. Tripping over his pleasant words, a clumsy poet without a rhyming stanza anywhere. Feeling so very awkward. He did better in elementary school talking to girls than he was doing right now. What a failure, he kept hearing in his head. Yet, he was pushed to continue. "We have a lot to talk about. Not the least is to find out how bad your car got wrecked. I always liked VW's." Then he smiled warmly, and truly. His eyes sharp clear and piercing blue, like the sky in high summer.

Martin looked from one to the next. He wanted to ask, a question. It was just their in the air like smoke, drifting about. He wanted to say, "Why don't you just kiss her???" but did not.

Several empty moments hung...

Then... Martin had to go to the bathroom. He had to speak up. He did not want to, but life moved on, regardless. "Can I get a ride?".

(29)
Another Bad Penny

Surame worked when she liked now. She set her own hours. Her new position, her promotion in full affect, that is as of earlier this morning. She noticed that the hospital staff, treated her better. They had all been informed. Not that they were mean before, but when the other man was "alive", they seemed fearful. Like seriously afraid of the morgue. Surame did not like that. Her boss had died. Even now he was in the cooler. Funny that? She did not sign off on his certificate. She did not even bother to find out if it were correct, as she did the others. Knowing now that he was selling the bodies of old people, oh... and the young also... to the "market", made her angry. Not the kind of upset you get when you are cheated or misled on a small scale, we are talking off the charts. Richter Scale 12... Earth shattering.

The man had been disrespectful to the dead. True they were all just dust and Surame was strong in her faith. No issue there. But that did not give him the right to make money on the bodies. Dealings in the dark, were always unworthy, and seen as foul and ugly as they truly are... when brought to the surface of plain view.

The woman gave a funny smile, like a cat that had more mice caught than it could eat. How pleasant not to have to live between the lines, and that she could be open. No longer stepping on egg shells, as she found the truth. It was not the hospital... it was not death... it was the living monsters that turned all of it into hell here, among the living. That was changing. She could tell, from the events of this night... so far. She was not going home... She was staying... Nothing was going to drag her out of here.

The emergency sirens again came barreling to stop quickly at the double door entrance. The two men got out and opened the back. Between them they did exactly as they always do... dropped the legs of the gurney first to the ground and then pulled out the rolling bed. When it got to the end, the second set collapsed and the bed hit the ground with a bang. The man on the bed, made a noise, but not much of one. He was so drunk he did not care. He just wanted another drink and he was really mad he had been cut off. When he got back to the house his wife had better have bought some beer. If she had not, his plan was clear. He would make an example. She was worthless, She had better do better. Or else!

Then he seemed to close his eyes, and rest. The medics grabbed both sides of the bed and picked it up. They managed to get the wheels down and held into place, sufficient enough to wheel the patient forward again, into the white house.

The doors swung back and the bed rolled through. A thousand, patients had come this way over the years. In fact way more than that. All had a right to fair and adequate service. But not all patients deserved fair or adequate. Some demanded compliance greater than servitude. Then believed themselves larger than life and worth more than the next guy by twice. Roger Morris, was one of "those".

The nurses took all his vitals. They set him right up and released the medics. The patient had moved into the next position, along the chain. They put a mask over his face and gave him oxygen. The woman looked down as she did and wondered if he had left any liquor for the other customers. He reeked of beer, and hard stuff. None of it a good smell the first round, but only more foul coming up the second time. Which was now. Even his body, had odor. The man was not a big bather... Then evil itself had a certain smell, it clung to some more than others. In some cases it embraced and was embraced back. While more than less felt a constant annoyance to them, like hay fever... but only seasonal.

Kurt Barber was an intern here. He watched the whole thing. The man being brought in on a chariot. Treated well. The word was he had wrapped his vehicle around a pole. That was just the ending part. Before he did that, there had been several close calls, a few minor accidents, and one dead. One man was dead. The radio said they were bringing that one in shortly. So Kurt realized this new patient, Roger Morris, was a killer. He had murdered in favor of drink. He had taken parting to a level that would haunt him forever. Kurt was not terribly sorry for him. He had lost his brother a few years back, to just such a man. If no one was around, he would strangle the stranger himself. He felt so connected by his inner rage.

Surame bumped Kurt by accident. "Oh, I am sorry." She had come up from the lower level, to get a look at what was happening. The electricity here at the hospital was flickering... The lights. She had noticed the irregularity... but had not complained. It seemed to match, every time she was to expect... guests. She caught his eyes. They tell everything to everyone, if you are not careful. The Morg-Tech was dead on. She could have read his mind, out loud, as if holding a book and standing in front of an audience.
"Not worth it my friend. He is less than you think, not worth all that you will be." Then she walked on.

Kurt felt like he had be doused with warm water. Not cold and hostile, but comforting. The anger dissipated. He, the drunk... was not the same man that had taken the younger man's own brother. It was just another idiot. Kurt shrugged his shoulders and went on about his other chores. Surame walked on into the patient's room.

She went to the bag that was hanging high on the pole to the side. The liquid they were giving him, was just the usual. They were trying to restore his fluids. That really was not necessary, Surame thought. As he would be a lot less needy soon.

"Who are you?" He gruffly asked. His belligerent mood only more intense, as he was coming out of things. He wanted more of the dog that bit him. He wanted to stay drunk. He liked it that way best. Everything went his way when he was drunk. It should anyway. As he was important. The only one that was not clear on that was his wife. And she was going to be clear on that one way or the other. He would keep telling her until she got it. Sometimes she would not listen right away, so he had to hit her a couple of times... then she would comply.

"I am here to take you on down now." Surame softly answered.

"Down? Down wear?" He seemed to catch the idea that this was not a good thing. That he was not ... Safe!

"You will be okay." She smiled. She took the small syringe out of her pocket and calmly stuck him in the arm. Not as you would usually expect, but kind of suddenly and on purpose. He wanted to say something else, but found... he could not. He just felt like floating.

Surame then finished her task. Released the bed brakes and pushed him on out the door. She waived at Kurt as she went by. She even smiled. He waved back. He felt better. He had never seen her except in passing. But he found, he would not have minded being friends. Perhaps he would make more effort when he got the chance next. At the moment he just went on about his business.

Surame went to the big elevator, pushed the bed inside and hit the button. Just like clock work she was below in no time at all. No one about, few ever were. She went straight on into her new office. Really it was her old office, only she was new. Promoted. She stepped to the big drawers and hit the button again. The long metal slide, rolled out. She lined up the Roger Morris's bed and made the transfer. Roger watched her the whole time. As he could, when she was in his vision's range as otherwise... He could not move. He could not scream. Then he felt the drawer moving and he was being sealed in. He was going to hell. he was screaming.. maybe not out loud as to be heard by the living. But he was screaming loud enough to be heard by the dead.

Mr. Seedtree came awake. He had dozed off. It had been heaven, a reprieve from... *"Oh my god"*... he was still here. He was still captive in a hole, by an insane person. she was all nice, but not. She was all smiles, but evil. He found he could barely move his head. His eyes opened again, and his partner... was still starring at him. Eyes open, right back at him... and blank. It appeared he had tried to get out... maybe as he was not laying flat as a body should be. The sides of each drawer... a glass or plexi-glass. Why? Why would anyone build this file cabinet for bodies, with clear inside walls? As for Seedtree, he could hardly move. His own body stuffed the cavity to the limits. He could barely breathe. He was doing that all on his own badly. The tank... was on empty. It was a labor, but he would not give up. Hate, never gives up!

With a huge effort of will he moved his head again. Slowly... the muscles complained but complied. The scene to the drawer on the other side. The dim interior well lit for his view. He had long since adjusted to the near darkness. A wild man was screaming, not loudly, but obviously he was trying. It was more like air passing out his mouth and nose, randomly rushing in and out. Seedtree knew, because he had done the same. Stupid man, no one is listening. That lady out there... she is deaf. Or at least that is what Seedtree wanted to spout out. No words came. None at all.

Seedtree felt less lonely somehow, there in the near complete dark. The saying was true. Misery really does love company. Some part of his soul quaked in fear, a tiny piece. The rest raging against the tangible walls of his prison, the physical one and the mental one as well.

(30)
Someone Call the Police?

The sparks were less and less. The show was coming to a close. The officer felt peaceful. The snow drifted down all around, making everything feel quiet and right. He shook his head, and made a small comment to himself about changing back to regular coffee. Decaf was just not okay.

The ambulance was leaving with the old pastor's body... not in a hurry. There was no reason to be. The officer waived. They all waved back. It felt funny. He walked on across the lawn, and around the white car. Sheldon was sitting right there.

"I was driving in. I was heading over, and then... saw the lights." Timothy Strepper spoke with humble caution. Afraid of the answer, but unwilling to turn away from the facts. Everyone knew him has Officer Tim. The kids loved him. He loved them back. This was his church. He had not been directly called, but had found his way... The main force of the small town still handling the major accident, blocks north.

Sheldon started to ask his own questions, but was cut off. Martin Cleaver was on the steps of the church. Dorothy would have been so proud. He had come so far, and was moving still toward the full knowledge of God. His hunger just now growing in the pit of his stomach, and his thirst strong, willing to accept the life spring of Jesus. "Just who I needed when I needed him." Martin nearly sang. "Tedra, Sheldon's right here!" He turned and yelled back over his shoulder. He had left the silly young people to their awkward goodbyes and future plans. But this was important. He needed to get Sheldon to Lisa.

Tedra walked out. She stood beside Martin a moment, then put her hand on his arm. We all need to get moving. She glanced down. "What happened to you?"

Embarrassed, Sheldon replied. I was trying to rush in and forgot this stupid stoop. Come this spring I am going to fix this somehow. I am not the first, and I know I will not be the last, unless I do something about it." he tried to sound positive. He was freezing, his butt ached and he was wondering if he could still walk.

Joseph, the pastor of the First Church on main, came out next. He walked a little taller than before. He had been promoted, and given a job, a position of importance. He would do his very best to show he was worthy. But it would not be his works that won him a place at the foot of God. But his belief alone in his holy savior, his King. But in the mean time, doing all that he could do for his King here in this place, was a blessing. "I heard your name... Sheldon." Joseph grinned. I think I need to talk to you about some chickens and cows?"

Martin turned all serious. First we need to get him to his daughter. His features were a mixture of sadness, happy thoughts and concern well quelled by the peace of God.

"Lisa!?!" Sheldon turned serious as well.

Tedra answered. "She is going to be okay. I know." Her words having a calming affect on the man. Seeing the ambulance drive off, she realized that they were going to need transport.

"My truck is right over there." Sheldon pointed back the way he had come. Which was also exactly where the police officer was still standing. He seemed... entranced.

"Perfect. I will take you over to the hospital." Tedra was on it.

Joseph looked at her, then looked on at the police officer. "I will stay and speak with him. Then I can take Martin home."

Martin was okay with all of it. Going home sounded like heaven. He really did not want to go back to the hospital. He would have gone, no doubt. He loved Lisa, like his own grandkid. That made Sheldon his son. That was okay with him also. Both had done more and been more to him, then any one else, other than his own wife. Yet Martin was tired. Bone tired, and his bed would be so welcome at this point, he decided to just be quiet.

All things decided by all concerned... Tedra got Sheldon's keys and brought the truck a bit closer. Then Joseph and Tedra helped him gain his feet and get to the cab. She popped into the driver's seat, waved in a friendly manner to Joseph... oh yeah and Martin. Mostly to Joseph. He had smitten her heart, like no one ever had.

She put the truck into gear and headed for the big white building. All the time Sheldon demanding every detail of the preceding hours. It would not be for days that the news of the bridge being out went all over town. What happened to it was hard to say. It just fell into the water. The road crews could not figure out why or how. Only that it had happened. Barriers were put into place, and there was talk about simply not putting it back. That all happened months later, at the meeting. The one they had every month about what was happening and how to keep their little town safe and a great place for families. The mayor, and a few others, were always working at things.

Joseph, poor Joseph. Too many things to do in one day, and not enough time. He walked right over to the officer, who seemed a bit spaced. "Hello, my name is Joseph Malachi Lamb. Please come on in." Officer Tim complied like a lost sheep to a Sheppard. All the time he mumbled about having to make a report, or gather information.

Joseph just guided the uniformed man around his own white car, up the steps, one, two, three and steadily across the ice. Then to the open doors. Officer Tim finally coming out of a kind of shock. "Can you tell me, Pastor Sir, what happened?"

Martin followed the other two men. While he was inside the front foyer, he picked up the coffee pot and set up upright on the counter. It was going to take a lot of effort to put this all back together, before Sunday. How was that going to happen, was just too much to think about. Martin walked further inside again and sat down in a chair. He bowed his head in prayer, and in ... sleep...

Not long at all, Officer Strepper was done. He had been given enough to report, an intruder had made a mess at the church. Somehow he was gone. No one could say how he got out. He had killed the pastor. That was horrific. Yet. the officer felt oddly accepting of the details. Then he was in his car, then he was driving away. Then Joseph, touched Martin gently on the arm. "Sir... let's take you home."

Martin smiled.

312

(31)Dorothy, a fragrance... a perfume.

The porch light was off. The house was dark. He was not surprised as they had been gone all day. They had not planned to be, but that is just what happens some times. Life is a constantly changing possibility.

Love for today...
tomorrow is not promised!

Joseph looked over at his passenger. "See you on Sunday?"

Martin grinned. "Yes." Then he opened the door to the old car, which was still by the way running on E, and got out. He closed it and stepped back. Joseph put the car into gear and left out the drive. He was going home. He was going to his new home... which would soon be a home for many... that had none.

The sky above was quieter. The snow was softly falling now. The storm having hit harder than expected, was causing trouble all over, but here. It was not. It was peaceful, and inviting. Martin felt like a kid that had gone to the county fair, and ridden every ride not once but twice. Some even maybe four or five times. His heart was happy and overcome. He was reborn... He was... born again.

Martin Cleaver turned and faced the dark house. It would not be dark for long. It was even now only a few minutes before the sun would rise. It would change everything. Starting fresh with a new day. He walked up the stone path, to the steps. then slowly, to the top. He looked back in time to see Josephs small car, disappear in the distance. Not forever, but at least until God's day, Sunday. Then they would meet again. He had so many questions, and so much he wanted to know and learn. But at the moment, it was cold and he was tired.

He moved to the front door and touched the handle. How many time he had done this, with anger, with bad feelings with... a lost soul. Now he was home. Martin was a little sad as his wife had always faced, whatever he dished out with a smile. How she did that was clearly because of God. He saw that now. However, this was different. He did not feel that way any more and never wanted to be that way again, ever. Once found he could not fathom the idea of ever being wayward again.

Martin grasped the handle and turned the knob. He opened the door. He stepped into the living room. He took off his heavy jacket, which had helped keep him warm all day. A book fell to the ground. It was plain and white. Their were stains on it, from all that had happened. But it was still in tact. It made him stop, remember and smile. How had he still had it on him? Martin would have thought it lost, at some point or other. But no. It was right there at his feet.

He bent down and picked up the bound paper. It felt good to hold. Then he turned and hit the light switch on the wall. The room came to life all around. But that was just the beginning. The front window curtains had been drawn and left open, so that when the sun hit them, it met no resistance. The world lit up. Sunrise! Flowers of every color, every where. Nearly every surface from the couch, the curtains, the wallpaper, even the candy dish on the side table. All of it. Roses, carnations, daisy's and sunflowers, but more, and others... Martin stood, tears filling his eyes.

There were also books. They lined all the shelves all around. Not one but many. They were the exact same size and shape as the one he had in his own hand. But these... they had covers. They had stories in side about life... about Dorothy's life. She had been writing for years. It had been her way of getting through the rough parts. Martin had not lost his wife, he had a chance to know her more deeply than he realized. All the moments lost to depression and sadness would at least be gained again, in the happiness of her thoughts, her dreams, her desires.

That funny lady at the bookshop had made it clear. That the cover always came later. That is why Martin had never noticed until now. All Dorothy's books had covers. It was his that was still being written. This gave him a huge sense of belonging, something he had long been without.

Sleep disappeared. He sat his own white journal down on the coffee table. He grabbed the nearest one of Dorothy's he could reach. He cautiously, gently opened its binder... her words... right there. Heaven may not be on earth, but God knew how to restore his soul. He had given him "Hope". Left all around him, waiting for him to see it, for exactly what it was!

(32)
What you bring with you...
Is all that you take.

Surame spent most of the few hours reading from her bible. She was not a cruel woman. Not by nature anyway. It was more a physical response to being repulsed by minions that had no empathy. Everyone living or not, deserved a chance to be respected, loved and cared for. They deserved to be safe, or at least feel safe.

That was a major component to Surame Kelly's life. Safe. It was a simple word that had meaning so deep, it was hard to gauge. The very effort to calculate would have exhausted even the finest mathematician. Surame had no real idea herself.

A new body was coming in. Surame had received a short call, from upstairs. They let her know it was coming straight in, as there was nothing to do, other than process the body. Another dead person. Only this was the victim of the drunk driver. The very same driver that she had tucked away in the drawer, safely. Considering his options and his alternatives... he and his god had a lot to talk about before he left here. That made her feel a bit more, okay with things. Everyone should be given a chance.

She had a special place she had already put him, the drunk driver man. Right next to her other guests. It was only fair they understood each other and had time to talk, and be friendly. Well, that is if they weren't dead. Which of course they were. That is what the paperwork said. Seedtree had her boss changing it all the time. To fit Seedtree's or his own, Mr. Blane's needs; ultimately to fit both their bulging pocket books. Then

Mr. Lindel died upstairs. That had been real bad. She felt sorry for that nurse, Nancy Barns. She had been attached... or so it seemed. She was crying in the garden. All by herself, after the news was distributed to staff. Surame had thought to say something to her, but did not. What could she say...? She did not really know Nancy Barns and she did not know Mr. Lindel. But the fact that he had something to do with Seedtree, well, that said a lot. All by itself it was bad news. How did she make the connection? Very sharp hearing. The one thing about working with the dead, everyone sort of avoided you. They acted like you simply did not exist. So they did not have to acknowledge their own mortality.

That nice cremator man, Edward Dego would be due in later in the morning. He was going to come for the pick up. Perhaps he would run into Nancy? Surame had heard him mention her name once or twice in passing. But it had a ring to it every time. One that let people know, he was ... daydreaming... or wishfully... thinking... Nancy could probably use some positives right now. Then there was the other lady. The one at the church. She would probably be around also. She was like Dorothy Cleaver... a roving angel. What was her name again? Oh yeah... Colleen Hines.

The door opened to her main department area and a man pushed a body into the room. It was Kurt this time. The orderly from earlier. He was in a pretty good mood. Time to get off and go home. Well, he had pulled a long duty and deserved to go home. The sun would be out maybe. The storm was moving south for now. Everyone was in a better mood, just to see it go. Surame jumped right up and walked right over. "Thanks." She said. Then stepped right up to the body and took control. "I got this from here." She smiled.

"Your still working. Wow. You have long hours too." He replied. "Thanks. I am heading home. Have a great night, or in this case...

day." and then he turned and left. Back out the double doors, across the small foyer area and right to the elevator. He hit the button and moments later he was gone.

      Surame lingered for a moment. They were all better. The mood of everything had changed. Why or how was not very clear, but it was tangible. Then she looked down. The blanket, the decency disguise. It hid death from the every day passers by, as if by hiding the corpse, it would not ever touch them. They could push the bed, and leave it and be done... Always looking back over their shoulder for the shadow, the blackness of the unknown that came, for all. But that was all wrong thinking from the root. A silly notion, by fearful people, that don't know God, or don't know him well. She took her right hand and pulled it back. A sharp intake of breath followed. Masaro was right there. Her brother. How had be made it out? How had he made it here??? She was shocked and speechless and filled with pain. He was here and he was dead?

      Her vision blurred. She wanted to scream, but had trained her "self" too long to be passive and quiet. So her second emotion took right over. She ran her hand down the side of the bed to the hanging chart. Surame wanted to make sure their was no mistake. The report was right there. Hit and run driver. Killed on site.

      Surame's thoughts raced. Somehow this fit and did not. How had Masaro gotten to be here? No idea. The why was becoming all too apparent. Hit and run driver, by a known drunk, is very convenient. Oddly, her boss had passed this day, no connection there...? or none she could figure out. Then there was the Seedtree man. Well that was going a stretch, more like roach. He was not happy surely. Surame had found out about the bodies, the sales and the cancer thing. She must not have been the only one. Tedra also knew. Maybe that is why she had asked for all that information a while back. Then there was the burned up Mr. Lindel?

He had told that preacher things, before he, the preacher that is... ran out the door. She had noticed as the pastor left... his eyes. They were piercing and intense. The kind of thing you see where life and death are concerned. Her world was caving in and exploding. The anguish of years missing him, the guilt of surviving, the prayers for this moment. But not this moment, a different one. One where they were united and life was renewed. This was far from that... This was horrific.

Quietly, calmly she turned to the drawers. Mr. Lindel, waiting for pick up. Then, her boss... or was her boss, Mr. Blane. Cause of death, strangely... suicide. He seemed like a fairly level headed man for a thief and a creep, but what else, was anyone's guess. That was funny, because it only fit if he was scared. Going to jail for selling bodies that was one thing. But killing himself... seemed extreme? Better to wait to the last word as to how things went, he might even beat the rap in the system these day. After all that... if things were still all wrong; then he could always off himself, as a last resort. So many times the guilty were set free on minor details. Then there was the fat man's drawer. It had put quite the strain on the apparatus that moves the gliding beds, just to get him in. He was still alive. Surame would have known otherwise. She just would have. The fact she had not made a decision on things, was a testament to her reserve. Now, however things were changed.

The last drawer was the new man. Yeah he was still alive. What had pushed her to go and get him? Alison Handsa, the lady from the bank had passed her in the hall upstairs. She had been looking for Seedtree. When the drunk came in on a gurney, Alison was standing nearby. She made a comment off handedly, in concern maybe. "That's the same man that was in Mr. Seedtree's office earlier today?"... no one was really listening. Surame was really no one after all. That is until she received her promotion. That just happened... Today! That bit of nothing, led her to take action. Even now Mr. Rogers... the pitiful drunk, should be awake, if not able to move. Hope he was enjoying the quiet as it was not going to last.

Surame looked at her watch. She should have been gone already, but there was no one coming in to replace her. Eventually, they would probably get some one to take the night shift, but maybe she would keep it. After all it was really the best time for reading the bible and being... quiet.

The New... Morg-Supervisor moved to the big drawer and hit the button. The drawer slid out two feet. The terrified, very sober, Mr. Roger's peered straight ahead, his eyes wide open. Surame moved into view. "Hello." She smiled. You seemed to be here by mistake. That happens around here. No one will care... no one will notice. I just want that to be clear from the start. So that when we finish you will understand that I mean... exactly what I say. Do you understand?" Surame waited. Nothing. "Blink once for yes, and twice for no." She waited again.

Two blinks followed.

"You were at the bank today? No don't answer, I don't have a lot of time, and I am a good guesser. So let me continue, and you think about it as I go. In fact, we... will consider everything together. First I want to tell you a story. You like stories right?" She waited.

Two blinks. Sweat forming at the man's brow and trickling into his eyes, burning them ever so slightly.

"Well, the man over there;" and Surame pointed to the first drawer in the row. Mr. Roger's had no way of seeing what she was pointing at even if he wanted too, but he did not want to make things worse. He just waited. "He could not make his payments. He made bad deals, with bad people. Now he is dead. His station is burned to the ground, and he is a tater tot." The last part was not funny at all. "Now let's talk about why you might have went to see Mr. Seedtree. Oh and just so you know. He is right there, this time pointing to the drawer next to Mr. Rogers. It was not comforting, none of it. "Did he set you up to kill someone today? The rest fills in the blanks all by itself... as soon as you confirm all that I already believe. There will be plenty to convict you of murder. No doubt, but that would be a long process. Here, we can just... be done." Surame felt cold, and empty.

"I am sorry, I did not bring my special gift. I had prepared a present earlier for Mr. Seedtree, but you can have his. Then I will make him another one." She turned and walked back to her desk. The man could hear her soft steps on the hard icy floor. She pulled the top right drawer of the desk open. The one that contained both the syringe she had prepared... earlier....and the Lord's book. Sadly it was there... right next to the vial of death... the Holy Bible. Not letting herself take time to think or consider forgiveness, much less fill in the blanks... like how did Masaro even get here? Or what else she did or did not know, she turned back to the big file cabinet. There Mr. Roger's was sticking out of a drawer waiting for what ever was going to happen. He could not scream, he could not run. He could not do anything! She crossed the space slowly and with purpose.

"Surame. I am so glad I caught you before you went home. I am beat." Tedra Macsen came out of no where. Surame had not heard the elevator. She always heard it? But not this time. Tedra was not driving a crazy VW this time, but changing the parameters of the instance, like switching on an electric light in the dark. " am so glad you found him. Must have been yet one more mistake. There has sure been a lot of those lately." Tedra pushed the rolling bed right in. Tedra continued right over to the tray where Mr. Rogers was fearfully waiting, breathing his last breath, and wondering if he had time enough for regret? But doubting it.

She hit the button and the drawer continued all the way out. Then she hit the following secondary switch to shift the dead body back onto a hospital gurney. It was a rolling bed, but not a very comfortable one. It was one of the ones they used often in the emergency area. Just for moving people, they were not sure were staying. No pillow, no extras, just bare bones of what was needed.

Tedra leaned over so the man could see her clearly. He started blinking his eyes. Was he trying to say something or even more afraid than before. It was hard to say. Surame would have rationally thought it was all about her and all that had happened in the last few hours. Here in the dark where secrets are kept, things became very clear. But that was not probably accurate. Something told Mr. Rogers that he had not been rescued at all. The feeling to the room, was more like two predators deciding how to divide up a kill.

Rogers was suddenly fully confronted by Tedra's lovely face. "Hello file 643. I am so glad I found you. The officer is looking for you right upstairs. Now be nice, and quiet. We will just head right up." She grinned. This man had been more than a thorn in her side for a very long time. She had wanted him to be dealt with... but until now had no success. He was going to go away. He was going to be charged with murder. That would also free up his wife and kids to have a chance at a real life. That worked out just fine the way Tedra Macsen liked things. A family on the right path with the father was better, but since that was not in the cards... Tedra was very flexible. She could find other ways, while he was gone to help his wife and kids. At least they would be safe...

The Morg-Supervisor started to say something. Anything. But was not sure what? Nothing came out.

Tedra stood back up and looked over to Surame. She could not help but see the needle in her hand waiting to be used, but seemed to just dismiss it. She smiled again, a very friendly, compelling calming and restoring look. Then she moved to the end of the table with Mr. Roger's in place. She pushed the rolling bed toward the exit. Tedra stopped at the double doors, before going out into the entry area, before the elevators. She looked back with a mischievous all knowing smile. "Thank you for all your hard work. Because of you, this one is going down for murder. This time she was not talking to the "living corpse" but to the family of the victim. Her own heart was twisted in knots. How would she feel if it had been her only brother? Or any brother? Or any sister, mother, father or other kin or simple friend? Drunk was a terrible sin. Murder, just an addition to the other problems too many to count.

Tedra tried to do her best to convey the point. "I know it is not enough. It will never be enough. I am so sorry." Tedra had been one of the people that had arranged for her brother to come to America. Mrs. Wix had been in on it. Even Dorothy Cleaver had had a hand. But in the end, all they had done, was kill him. Maybe not directly, but still.

"You need to understand. Your boss, well he was not a happy man. He killed himself." Tedra spoke low and direct. She felt that Surame needed to know everything. It would not bring back her kin, but it might help her in some small way. "Blain was going to be put away for raping a young woman. She is having a baby, and it is his. She told me, finally. Then, I told him... and well." Tedra shrugged. By that, what could be concluded? Did Tedra help Blain? She did not say so exactly, but it was a question still... in the air... between the two women. Then she continued, "He decided that bad people that hurt young girls going to jail was a scary possibility. Even thugs have standards I guess? How is killing yourself better? I don't understand. But I am glad to not be able too, understand I mean. No one should." Tedra turned back and pushed the gurney a little further.

Then she stopped again. "One more thing; the big man. You know... The fat guy. Well, they are looking for him too. This place is crazy tonight. The shift chain, the major one, for the main staff upstairs... as you know is in about fifteen minutes. Or should I say this morning then, I guess. I am so glad Mrs. Wix put you in charge down here." Her face became all serious. "Again, let me say with my soul... I am very sorry for your loss. I did not know it was him. I did not know it was your brother... I only just found out." Her heart clearly breaking for Surame. "I just want to tell you how much I wish I could take your pain, but you are supported. You have friends here. You are claimed." Tedra's eyes grew bright.

Surame wanted to say something. She of course was not a big talker... But a word out of her face, out of her mouth; would have been a step in the right direction. She just stood there with the syringe, knowing full well without reserve that she would have gladly used it. The man was a murderer and deserved to die. He really deserved to die badly. That was torture and Surame had not completely lost her mind. She was not going to do that. But removing him from life, that felt right.

"Upstairs. They are looking, because they are going to charge him with attempted murder. It seems he has had something to do with the motivation behind Mr. Roger's erratic escapades. The ones resulting in our being here. There are also other charges, theft, the selling of dead bodies, blackmail, fraud, and more. It is a long list. He will never be able to hurt anyone again. Ask yourself, what would "He" want of you now? "Obviously referring to her own brother.

Surame wanted to cry. She did not. She wanted to scream. She did not. Instead she touched the button above the empty sliding drawer and it closed. Then she simply walked over to the wall and put the needle in the disposal container. Then she turned and faced Tedra. "A fat man like him would make a pretty toy in prison." Her voice much stronger than she thought it would be, once found. "I will see what I can do to locate Mr. Seedtree. Things are very busy around here too, and unsettled." She gave a funny, awkward smile.

Tedra brightened and smiled back. "Great. See yah upstairs." Then she turned and continued to the elevator, hit the button and waited. The doors opened nearly immediately and she shoved the gurney inside.

Surame went to retrieve another rolling table. She felt strangely relieved and yet cheated. It took her no time at all to find what she needed. Returning to the giant file cabinet she hit the button. The drawer slowly came out. Mr. Seedtree's eyes wide with fear. "There you are. Silly man." She nearly laughed out loud. "Your not dead yet, but you could be, anytime. I just wanted you to know that in my country, I am a doctor. Well, really I am a scientist. Kind of like on the same level as a surgeon here in America. We will not go into all that now. But let us say, I am just as good as any upstairs. Maybe even better than a few. I have implanted a capsule that will slowly dissolve. You will never find it, you will waste your time to try. But you will die, and it will not be quick. No one will ever believe you. They will just write; cancer on your death cert." She grinned. " If you say nothing of our time together, and say the truth only, accepting your guilt and punishment, I will save you. But if not, I have no reason at all to consider it, now or ever. Okay?" She did not really expect a reply. "Lets get upstairs. We would not want to disappoint Tedra Macsen, from being a super hero and saving you. But you see, I know evil, I have seen its face. You have that look." She moved to the head of the cart, now having transferred him again and shoved him toward the door. "You Mr. Seedtree... are the very visage of ugly."

Mr. Seedtree was still basically paralyzed. He wondered if or when he would not be... ever also?

(33)
Grateful Hearts and Ever Friends

Tedra wheeled the gurney right out of the elevator to confront Officer Tim... "Just the man I am looking for." Tedra brightened. "I found your drunk. Silly thing, I don't understand. They thought he was dead, and not the victim?" Perhaps not a good joke, but saying the truth, so close to the moment, let suspicion find no home to rest.

Tim liked the way she smiled. She was saying something about something, but he really, and quite suddenly, lost all thought as to what, or why or even who? Then he came back to the ground. "Wow, it is busy up here tonight." was his only reply. His only quiet thought... how beautiful she was...!

Tedra continued forward back to the right room. She set him right up. All the time, Mr. Roger's blinking like he was having a spasm attack. He felt frozen, and vulnerable, and oddly thankful, to be still alive. Tedra even put the needle back in his arm. The sack was waiting with fluid. So someone was helping beyond the doctor's daughter, with everything that was going on, just further than the front line... scenes, that all others concerned themselves with. Tedra had not been licensed, but could do basically all things she saw someone else do... if only once. It was a gift. The officer never even thought to say anything. He had no idea if that was usual or not... as he knew she worked here. Or maybe, he could not clearly remember.?!. She was the doctor's daughter. He had never gotten this close before, to say more than "hi" in passing. Wow, she smelled like wild lilac, or maybe lavender. That scent his mom used to wear. He could not remember which name for which flower. But Tedra smelled like flowers regardless, a whole field of them.

Cheerfully she spoke. "Okay then. You can wait with him if you like. I think they gave your criminal something but it will not last too much longer. There might be after affects. Like hallucinations and such, he was after all, in an accident and drinking. Hard to tell what else he did to himself, or what might be a consequence from... without basic tests being returned. I don't think any of that is likely to come back soon. They are over worked downstairs." Tedra was chatty like a chicken. A brief reference to Marci Samuels came to mind. Tedra had grown to appreciate the small creatures in her visits to the old lady, as friendly beings. They were useful to learn every day tasks, like being "busy". When active and moving, time seems to do funny things. It makes moments pass, or at least parts of them... disappear from view. Like camouflage in the air, words twisting and looks holding questions not spoken tightly tied and then forgotten.

Tim just heard her song. Right there she was moving her lips and sweet sounds were coming out. Music was playing also. He had no idea from where. Something about hallucinations... He preferred the word "dreams".

"I will catch you soon. I have to check back in on Sheldon. You heard he fell on his butt?" She laughed... everyone knew Sheldon. He was a good guy. It was maybe an assumption that Tim knew him, but everyone knew Tim the same way. They were kind of the "same", their personalities anyway.

"I will wait here. My partner will be up shortly and we can arrange transportation. I don't want to take my eyes off the man. Seems he is really slippery." He tried to come back to himself and be a bit more professional. Then he waved, but she had already gone... missing probably all or most of what he had mumbled.

Tedra went back now to the intensive care. That is where she had left Sheldon. Next to his sweet daughter. Lisa had been fully awake and talking a mile a minute. She could not explain everything, but she wanted too. She was making a wonderful, best effort. "There were angels, and fire, and lightening, and..." Lisa would not stop.

The doctors were nothing less than amazed. Yes, she had bruises everywhere, and her right leg, was broke. Not bad, according to the pediatric doc on staff. Even now they had put a cast on it already, and made her very comfortable. Compared to the possibilities of being burned alive and who knows what else, had happened, the current diagnosis, was incredible. Tedra smiled wider... as she knew Lisa had died. She had watched. She had seen. She believed. It was grand!

Tedra stood a few steps outside the smaller area. Her father came up behind her and put his hand on her shoulder. "Hello my little girl. I see it has been a busy night. You did not come home? But I think I know why..." His tone was comforting. Tedra had missed the very sound of his voice. It felt like she had been gone, somewhere "else" for a time. And now had returned home.

She turned and hugged him. Not for a moment, but for many. Tedra was so thankful, he was safe and there, where he belonged; in her world. Exactly as she expected him to be. Helping others every day, like the good man that he was and is and will always be. She was full of things to talk about herself, and wanted to share them with her father, the one here in the hospital, her arms around him, and the Holy One, that she knew kept her and all the others in his hand close during the storm. Tears came to her eyes. They would not be held back. She was so happy about so much, and sad about the rest.

(34)
Insurance pays and life returns to normal.

"It is good to see you Mr. Cleaver." Joseph Lamb smiled. At the unexpected yet welcome crossing of paths. They were in the bank of all places. Martin swore up and down to himself he would never come back here again. Especially after the last time. But today was different in all kinds of ways. He was even in a good mood.

The young pastor had come to the bank to finish up the paperwork to the house. His house. His dream was in full motion. It was going to be a home, for those that had none. Particularly for young moms in trouble and their children. Just like his mom, was once. He was all settled in at the church. Many of the ladies with lovely pretty, pink pins, had come to help with that. Turned out, the pink roses had nothing to do with cancer. They had to do with the sisters of the First Church on Main Street. It was just a friendly symbol, like a badge of honor as an usher, serving each other and all those around.

Marci Samuels was a good woman. No she was a great woman. She had helped out at the church, until she was no longer able. Then she came home and stayed home. Dorothy would come by, until she too got sick. Then it was only the angel... Tedra and her father toward the end. But Marci had died truly happy. Her faith in the Lord ever her constant companion.

The day He came to take her home... to heaven, was not a surprise. She had known it was only a matter of time. That evil Mr. Seedtree had contacted her more than once. Even that other man, that Blane guy, had come by... once... the mule bit him and he did not return. That made her laugh... all day. Alison, the other lady, she had made calls also. Marci liked the young woman and believed everything she said. God was smiling on that young woman. Marci was very sure. Because she listened. She heard all the stories of how Marci herself had wanted children, and never had any. Giving the property to the church, or in this case to the pastor was the perfect idea.

"Thanks. Glad to run into you, as I won't be in church next Sunday." Martin meekly stated ."But it is for a good reason." A spirited good natured look came to his features. That made Joseph very attentive. "I, have made a plan. I am taking the box with the ashes to New York. Dorothy's box. I am going to take her to the park she never got to go to." He rushed it all out quickly. A little louder than he meant it to be.

"I found her diary. Well, I guess she was quite the writer. I found a lot of books, she wrote in. All over the house, once I saw the first one. It was like tomatoes worms in her garden." He smiled. Knowing that once spotted, just one, the rest were magically revealed. "They have... her thoughts." There he paused and drew closer to the younger man. Confidentially continuing as if confession of sorts, "Things about her hopes and dreams, I had not listened to." His eyes grew misty. There were a few people in the lobby, but no one really paid attention. So Martin continued.

Joseph wanted to tell him, she was already gone. She was in heaven. But instead, he was silent.

As if he had heard, clearly; Martin continued. "I know, she is not in the box. Don't look that way at me. I know it is just dust. But it is the best representation of loving her I got left." The last part was a bit solemn. Martin still felt an incredible hole in his life where his wife was concerned. Yes, he wrote to her. His journal was full the first night. Then followed again by several more in the days and weeks that followed since.

He would probably continue until his last breath. He had returned for more journals more than once to the little bookshop, but requested only the white covered ones specifically now. He had come a long way.

"Where?" Joseph grinned. Clearly understanding this was a pilgrimage to honor a memory.

"The Liberty Island. I want to take her to the statue of liberty. She had a thing about the place, I only recently found out about the whole thing. So, I know it is not her, but still, I can go. And I can take the memory of her with me. When I see her again, in God's court, I will hug her and tell her all about it also. A tear traced down his cheek. A little embarrassed, but in a sweet way, a vulnerable once in a life time, emotional way.

"Are you going by yourself?" Joseph had a sudden concern. He had seen this man in action. Maybe he should be concerned for New York, his heart filled with the warm sense of God. He had prayed and miracles had been performed. Joseph never doubted before, but this was like reading a book, seeing the movie and loving both, then being allowed to go to the live action performance brought it all to a different level. The highest clouds in the sky... a view of heaven.

The old man smiled wider than before. Sheldon is going with me. He is still on crutches, but he agreed. I am taking my new blue truck. I decided I liked the color blue better than red. I only found out recently it was Dorothy's very favorite color as well. Besides Sheldon is driving Lisa crazy, pushing her all the time in therapy. Between the two of them they are driving the hospital staff insane. At least in the physical therapy department that is."

Alison walked up. She approached as a professional, as not to interrupt right away. A pleasant smile for both on her face. "Hello gentleman. So glad you have come this morning. Mr., I mean Pastor... I have the paperwork ready. Everything is in order and the transfer is complete. Insurance cleared all debt, and the property is yours." The woman loved this kind of news. She had been waiting all morning for him to come. She had talked with the insurance department at the head office, and everything was now in order.

Turning to Mr. Cleaver she smiled again. "Mr. Cleaver. I once again apologize for your previous visit to our establishment. I only asked you to come by this morning, as your property has also been cleared. It seems the same agent was selling life insurance down that whole block, eighteen houses, in all. It was like a minor miracle, that for one reason or another, they are all caught up on payments, or doing much better." Alison grinned. "Oh, and Mr. Cleaver; in future always ask for me for all your needs. I am the new bank manager. Mr. Seedtree, well he is not working here anymore."

Martin was beaming. He was so happy, for Joseph, for himself, and even for Alison. She was a good woman. It was not her fault that Mr. Seedtree had hurt so many. It seemed like things were going the right way now.

"Okay then, I am on my way." Martin Cleaver held out his hand. Joseph Lamb shook it firmly. "You are ever surrounded by angels..." and then he released the younger man. He turned and awkwardly shook Alison's hand. "Thank you for doing a fine job." Then he was done. None to soon in his book. "Catch you next Sunday pastor!" He finished and headed out.

Joseph waved and felt honored. He had found he was not alone in a strange town, or at least one that he had not come to since he was a child. He had simply come home. It was all around. Everyone either knew him, or was glad to see him, or was thrilled he had come. Joseph was walking on air.

(35)
It's not a waltz!
✻✻✻

Martin was driving and Sheldon was shotgun. No one noticed the angels, hanging off the tailgate. They just went along for the ride. They liked the new truck. Blue was such a lovely color, like the sky. The traffic was not even bad, if there was such a thing as good, in the City of New York. Both men had never been here, and the map was hard to understand, but the truck just seemed to go the right way. Martin just felt right about the day.

The navigator, sitting on top, the wind ruffling his wings. This was the right thing. This was God's will. Letting go of dust was a mission of importance. The symbolic love between a husband and wife, was nothing less than beautiful. God's blessing and union a give and take, a learning to get a long, a loving without bounds, then a peace. That comes from knowing you have finally accepted, there is a heaven. Dorothy was already there, and Martin would be there... some day. Just not today.

The small box sat between Martin and Sheldon. It was like having her right there, in his heart. The whole trip. He dared not speak crazy, to her directly. Sheldon would believe he had lost his mind maybe? So he just did it with his heart. Telling her how sorry he was they had not gone together... before now. Sheldon was a pour substitute for his love. But a good friend, a son he never had, was more than he could ever have hoped for, and knew it was a gift. Nothing less would or could describe it.

They found it. Right where it was supposed to be. As if it could be some where else? How silly! The weather was really nice, a break from the winter. Spring ever at the edges and ready to take over. Martin pulled into the lot. It was the one that led to the boats. The boats that would take them both over to the island. Martin did not know exactly what he planned to do... once he was out there. But he was at least going to take her all over the place. He was going to circle the statue and look out ever viewing area. He was going to take his time and make it a memory. One that he could cherish in a special way, and take with him... to her. Although he knew now that heaven was ever more incredible, and more astounding than anything left here behind. But... it was for both... Dorothy and himself. He believed that Dorothy was watching... somehow... and would approve.

Martin stopped the truck. He put into park. Then he looked at Sheldon. "Let's pray!" Never in a million years would he have said that to anyone before. Now, it was like, second nature. This was important to him. He had come a long way, and the pull was strong. He had no idea why, but he was trying to fix the remaining pieces of his personal puzzle, that was still shifting and changing. Maybe he would not live long enough to ever see it make sense, or form a clear picture? But at least he will have lived, truly lived from this day to the end.

Sheldon smiled. Sounds like the best idea ever. Looking around with very big eyes. Yes, he had served in the military, but that was a long while back. And he had never, no NEVER been to New York. That alone was an "eye opener". In ways he was not altogether sure he was comfortable with.

They, the two men bowed their heads.

"Amen." Martin voiced. It was like a song, right at the end... that you catch on the radio, sad, that you missed the beginning. Martin let go of Sheldon's hand. "I will get your crutches out of the back." Sheldon having not only landed on his butt, but had also done a nice number on his ankle. It was still injured some and giving him a bit of trouble even now. So, crutches, were still recommended. He was just a bit of a cripple. Doctor Macsen was an excellent doctor. If he said do something, you just did it. That way you got better way faster.

Sheldon waited. He also watched the people coming and going. All kinds. Some tourists, workers, every day sorts, back and forth to work and play. He was so glad, they had come and would even be happier when they were leaving.

A van followed them in. It was a an early model non descript kind of thing. It had been hit a few times in the side and rear, but that had not damaged it's drivability. The man behind the wheel was just a little high. Well, the real stuff had not kicked in yet. He wanted to come down and pick Neta up and take her back. She would have some dough by now. That way they could party. He was looking forward to that. She partied real good, once he motivated her a bit.

He did not slow down and powered on by Martin, as he had the back end open of the camper. The angel... tugged Martin closer. He thought he lost his balance and concern crossed his features. Then it quickly left. While the van continued on... searching for a spot in the crowed place. It was almost 4:00. The place, the tourist stop would close before too long. So Selah had to be on the last boat, or one of the last ones.

Martin grabbed the crutches and walked to the passenger side of the truck. He opened the door and helped Sheldon get out. Then he let Sheldon go on passed him, to the back of the truck, as that was the right direction for heading to the boats. It was later than they wanted. They had been slowed by traffic once they got to the city. Like that was unexpected? Not! But now they just had enough time to catch one of the last boats out. Sheldon did not think they would be over long. But he was willing to stay as long as needed. He would even get a hotel room and come back if it were necessary. He had lost his own wife, and coming to terms with that... was not a thing that quickly happened. It was a stepping stone process the whole way. He was again, ever thankful that he had Jesus the whole time. If not, he could not imagine the loss. As it was truly great, with even the shared burden... mostly carried by God... and just loved on by Sheldon.

Martin Andrew Cleaver looked into the cab. The box, containing the sweet remains of his wife's body was there. It was blue with flowers. Lovely flowers. The strange handle that he hated all along and felt out of place, was perfect now. As if they were "holding hands". Maybe that was not easy for everyone to get, but those that miss the touch of their sweet love now gone, truly comprehend the depth of that pain.

He tenderly reached across and grasped the handle. Then drew it out as if he had opened the door for his wife. He smiled. Then he stepped back and closed the truck door. Turned to where Sheldon was already waiting on the sidewalk and headed his direction. Once standing beside him they silently, reverently continued together toward the gate. People were still coming and going, fast and furious to get where they needed to be. Even on vacation or spending time out, they moved, with a hurried tempo.

Neta had been caught off guard. She had finished heaving up whatever she had ate for the last week. Well maybe not that far back, but it really felt like it. She was just going to get back in the line and go. All her thoughts of a good days hall, disappearing slowly. She would be thrilled just to get to the main land. She wiped her mouth off the best she could with her sleeve. The taste was terrible, and she was really thirsty, but no where to get a drink. The water fountain for the public was on the far side, not near the docs here. She straightened her clothes and her appearance the best she could and got back in line. She had just missed the previous boat. Thankfully... the last boat... they always waited...

On shore, Sheldon and Martin bought tickets. The man at the counter repeatedly called "last out". Meaning if you wanted to go before close, this was the one and only chance. Sheldon was more than willing to rush forward. If they could do it today, now, then they would be able to go home. That was a wonderful idea. They would not have to wait, spend the night and come back tomorrow. He thought more and more of it, as the night was coming. He just appreciated home so much, since he left.

The ride out was great. The sea in the harbor was like a giant rocker, lulling the occupants to sleep, or to at least be in a pleasant frame of mind. That is all except the one. The man that had followed them into the parking lot. He had parked the white, piece of crap and pushed his way through the lines to the boat. He yelled and made them even hold the gate... there was a bit of a scene. Martin and Sheldon had stayed clear. He looked like trouble on several levels. Martin kept his eye on things, and held onto the handle of the box a bit tighter. He also kept Sheldon in clear view, at arms length. The voyage took a little while, so they found seats. The crutches were slowing Sheldon down, but he really could not do with out them as yet.

Finally, in the distance, from his position... peering out; Martin let himself look. There she was. Lady Liberty. It was a few moments of silent appreciation, as he took in the wonder of things. A lovely tribute to this grand country, this land of the free. Some part of him wanted to kick himself for not coming sooner. But he fought back the sadness that would come with that train of thought. This was a good thing. This was a check mark on the final list of turning his life around.

They did not say much. Together, Martin and Sheldon just looked out. It was worth the trip. Martin felt the tenseness he had carried fall away. He felt all the bad memoires wash overboard. He felt... he had made the right move. This was a good thing.

At the other end, they opened the gate and let down the ramp. The people filed off. There was a speaker man in the tourist box; telling people they only had forty-five minutes. Then there would be a boat leaving again. It would be considered the last boat of the day. Anything else would be staff only and maintenance. It was a warning. That was maybe not long enough. But maybe it was. Martin did not care, he was here. He had made it. They walked off the small vessel together, and then down the ramp. The old man helped the young man all the way. They set off at the bottom to go on into the main park. Then Martin realized, he had left Dorothy behind. How could that have happened? He was furious with himself.

Their were still a lot of people, most leaving on the very same boat, they just got off; that was now going right back to the main land. As that is how they moved the people, shuttling them over the water, all day long.

Neta was glad the boat had docked. She stepped closer to the line to get on. Then... the big bruiser guy stopped her. "Hey kid? I know you. Are you supposed to be back here?" She felt her heart sink. Yeah he was right, but she had dressed different and came anyway. This was the best place to make a dollar, or at least that she could find. The alternative to bring in the amount Morgan wanted, would have been on her back. It made her crazy to think about. That is what happened to her at home. Leaving should have been better! Running away! But it was not. It was worse. Well, most of the time. At least she could get away better here dealing with Morgan, then at home. There was no escape at all there.

Morgan spotted Neta from his vantage. She was just getting on the boat to return. His prize was right there. How convenient. He could just wait right here, and go back with her. She would come to him. He did not even have to get off the boat at all. He simply had to ride back. Not wanting to be seen too soon and scare her, he stepped away from the rail... for now. This would be great. She will be so stunned, Morgan grinned. The drugs he shot up earlier, just now really having an effect. Every color was so very bright and perfect. Morgan could see the small grains in the wooden chairs, the tourist used. The benches were bolted down... but seemed to float a little. Kind of like the ocean all around. Well in his head anyway. Morgan worked his way up the stair, to the second level, observation deck. He could get a great view of everything from there. Morgan waited, like seagull... going to follow with his eyes, and eat the chum leavings of whatever was available. Then... he could take her on home..., to the apartment.

Back at the gate; another man came up beside the gorilla, "Let the girl go." She had never seen this guy before. He must be new, not to know her on sight. For some reason, she prayed under her breath, "God please get me out of this." and the message went up... the plea, the bleating sound of a lamb. The Sheppard heard. He always does. The world was about to know exactly what that meant first hand.

The first man let her go. Neta did not wait around. She would have liked to say thank you, but fear pushed her forward. All she had to do was get across the puddle and go back. To what? ... Whatever... At least she was not spending another night in the hall. That was a really bad place. Morgan took his time last on the last occasion pulling her out. He was punishing her then and if he had to do it again? Well it would be worse without a doubt. . He knew how much she was afraid and took full advantage every chance. But... he had taken her in. She owed him. He made that clear.

Now, Neta seized the opportunity presented. She nearly ran up the ramp. Quickly the girl was lost among all the other passengers. the runaway, turned thief among other "things" to survive, was back to business. She causally viewed all the seats. There were always left behinds. People in a hurry and today was no different. She spotted the pretty box with the handle. Casually, Neta made a path that direction and picked it up off the bench like it had always been part of her on hand. No one noticed, probably no one cared to look. They were busy coming and going. It was kind of a strange box, and not all that light. Not heavy either. Neta glanced about again... the thought that someone would return and look for it very strong in her thoughts. She decided to go up the stair to the second level. If anything bad happened she could just drop it over the side. Maybe she would get a chance to at least look inside before that, then take the stuff and dump the box anyway. Sadly she would hate to do that, somehow it made her feel... cheerless. Silly! But it was kind of obvious, so "it", the container would be easy to spot.

Martin rushed out one gate and up the next. He kind of made a couple of people a little mad, but he kept saying, "my wife, my wife..." so they let him pass. Right behind him, hobbling, and bobbling the whole way was Sheldon. This was crazy. How had they left the box?

The big guy at the top, the one that let people on or off, was seriously going to be a problem. Hard to say why Sheldon could tell, other than he had seen his kind before, while in the military. He was a stay in line and wait your turn kind of man. Emergencies never set well with those type. They rather follow the rules and sort it out later, if there was a later.

Martin had military experience too. He knew the look, maybe even better than Sheldon. He got real close then bolted by. It was amazing, as if Martin had been picked up and thrown onto the ship. It was already moving away... leaving the doc. The big ape sized man turned, in an effort to do his best to stop Mr. Cleaver. Sheldon being right behind very close, was still moving in a seriously crazy and erratic fashion. He had learned to work the crutches in the last five minutes to a somewhat better degree, thankfully. Panic does that to you. The gate man now between Martin, and himself; Sheldon, found a whole new issue he had to deal with. Sheldon had used speed and motion to leverage... no catapult himself into the air. The goal to jump the small curb and take off like superman. He was not going to be left behind.

To his shock and miscalculation Sheldon missed his final target by an inch. He cleared the man in uniform... barely short of his goal however. One lousy inch, might as well have been a mile. The ocean, right up to the dock hungry for the clumsy hero. But no! Somehow, someway, the deck was right there. His hand clung to something and then nothing... and then Martin. The old man, pulled him aboard. Both winded they turned to search. Not even missing a beat. It was not like she was alive, but it was like losing her all over again. Symbolically failing in even this small task. Martin was beside himself, but holding it together. He would succeed. Every fiber of his being told him that. He was assured by the Holy Spirit...
<u>Back at the doc...</u>

The sure footed giant, with more strength the brains, turned jus in time to reach for air. Just air! Having missed the old man by nearly nothing he became unbalanced. He fell right over the rail instead. The commotion on the doc that followed was a combination of laughter and professional rescue by those in authority.

<u>Our heroes keep moving...</u>

First they both checked the seat they had been in and then divided the task of the rest of the ship. Sheldon went one way and Martin the other. Sheldon was not near as fast, as he was now down to hobbling. His crazy stunt had left his crutches on the docs, tangled in "gorilla". That would be funny any other day, and maybe it would be later, but he kept to the task at hand. Someone probably would find her and turn her in. They would not know what the ashes were maybe? Or, then... how would he feel if he found a box, with flowers... Sheldon kept looking. He asked around as well, describing the box. Soon... lots of nice people were all looking... there were helpful words, like "Hope you find it, and no not over here... " coming from all over. That is all over the bottom level.

Martin went up the big stair in the middle to the upper deck. It was a great place to see the incredible skyline of New York. The Lady Liberty was retreating behind them. He stopped at the very top step and glanced around. There were only a couple of older tourists up on top near the front. But in the back... there was a man. It was that vulgar ugly man that had driven passed him in the parking lot. He was hitting this girl. HE WAS HITTING HER!!! RIGHT THERE... IN FRONT OF WITNESSES AND NO ONE WAS DOING A THING!

He felt angry. Not a little, but a lot. The kind of thing you hold onto way too long. Martin had no idea it was even there. But it was. Then he saw Dorothy's flower box. It was on the deck between him and the two strangers. There was maybe a space of ten feet or perhaps twelve to where havoc was taking place. Snap!, not like a tiny twig but a log, jammed in a canyon, finally let loose. Martin barreled forward. In a crazy motion a young man would have a hard time following; he grabbed up his wife. The box with the handle, ready. It fit well in his hand. Funny, like it had been ordered that way on purpose.

Step, step... ste. ! Martin Andrew Cleaver pulled back his arm and swung with all his might. "Bang!" Perfect hit. The big man stumbled and let go of the girl. She fell to the deck. At the same time; the old couple that had been looking out over the ocean, now were aware of the scuffle. They quietly went toward the exit and back downstairs, not wanting to be any part of anything crazy.

Sheldon had tried everywhere else. He was now making his way one step at a time to the top, the second level viewing deck. His ankle still giving him a lot of trouble, but he was intent on working hard to help. At the top, he came up just in time to see, both the beginning of Martin's Olympic run and then his incredible warrior attack. It made him smile... here he was thinking that Martin needed him. He was doing pretty good on his own. Whatever had set the old man off, Sheldon was sure it was a good reason. Then he realized who the thug was. The evil man in the parking lot that had almost hit Martin.

On the ground at the feet of both Martin and the man was a young girl. She was a little younger than Lisa maybe. His own hero instincts pulled him forward. Obviously the girl was part of everything. He went forward as fast as he could. The whole time the scene before him was like a dark play. In the process of using the box, the lovely box, that Sheldon had sent for, to hold Dorothy, it had opened. The contents spilled into the ocean breeze. Accepted into the night, an embrace... a testament to the beautiful words... dust to dust. Then Morgan recovered angry and pulled the gun. He had considered robbing a store earlier and carried it. Suddenly it was in his hand. It was pointed... It was...

Dust filled his eyes. Drifted back... brought back... it was back... Like an angel holding a shield up in front of the old man. Protecting him and making sure... he was safe. Martin pulled back, and hit him again, even harder with the empty box. Morgan flew backward over the rail. No one noticed below.

Morgan found himself floating, mentally and physically. He was angry and the night was consuming the land. The last rays of sun, vanishing in the distance. Cold the water was so cold... The evil man found he did not really care. The drugs taking over. Funny, the new stuff was really strong. He liked it that way. The stronger the better.

Martin immediately yelled out man overboard. But they were very close to the port, only fifty or maybe a hundred yards out. They went into emergency mode, once they heard, but they still parked the big boat. The captain called the coast guard and the search was on.

"My name is Martin Cleaver. I am going home. Do you have somewhere to go?" He waited the girl said nothing. "Do you have a home?" He went over to where the girl was sitting, now on the hard bench.

"Thank you, Sir." She chocked out. There were no tears in her eyes. "I know what that was now. I am so sorry. I thought..." She wanted to cry, but no tears would come. What was going to happen next? People were screaming everywhere. The police were called, the coast guard. There would be questions.

"We are going home. Now!" Martin looked at Sheldon. He had hobbled closer as to hear the conversation. The younger man nodded. They were done here. They had done the right thing. They had report the man overboard. They were just not willing to report the rest. Martin looked on the deck near the rail. The pretty box was on its side. He walked over, as the gates were opening down below, letting people out; and dropped it overboard. It was just a container. Everything of importance had been cherished and set free.

Martin turned and motioned to Sheldon. They went down the stair together. The girl, stunned, and sick, soar and scared... followed. No one really took any notice of them as they went through the crowds, everyone in a hurry to get home. Some looking for the man, some asking questions, no one really knowing what was happening. Behind in the harbor boats already scanning the surface. Their small group, kept moving forward.

Out in the parking lot they went straight to the truck. Martin opened the door for Sheldon to get right in. Sheldon complied without a word. Then he went to the back of the truck where Neta was standing. Just standing there.

"Are you okay?" Martin asked.

"No." The girl's meek voice replied in earnest. Then, "I prayed to go home, but I don't have one. Then you showed up. You and that woman." awe was in her tone. "And that funny man..." referring to Sheldon. His klutzy maneuvers not missed by her... ever sharp eyes. Dorothy? An angel? Dust in the wind of imagination?

"I prayed and He answered. Maybe I am the answer now to your prayer. I don't know. But I would never be here any other time for any other reason." He smiled warmly. "Get in... Let's go home."

Fearful at first and then more assured, the presence of God so powerful... she hopped in and slid to the center. Martin climbed in after and started the truck. He put it in reverse and headed out. An ambulance was coming in, so they had to wait to take their turn. It appeared that Morgan had been found after all. Dead or alive? Well, the gun said a lot about what could have happened, as compared to what did.

Martin waited... waited... and then... softly pressed the accelerator. The angels took up positions in the back and the navigator landed on the roof. Home sounded pretty great! The two at the back pushed the vehicle a little faster, as home was ever a yearning of all the occupants. The navigator, thrilled to retrace the route to a better tomorrow.

Joseph Malachi Lamb, Pastor of the First Main Church and his sweet wife to be Tedra Lamb-Macsen were about to have one more saved MOM, and child... for their new unwed mother's home. She could join the other young lady already there. The one that Bane had hurt. She was recovering and doing well. They could help each other and become stronger. What a blessing all around. The trip to New York had been worth it after all. Martin was going to have to stop by the book store and get another blank book. Life was moving forward fast and he liked keeping track.

The Forever Dance

The musician tunes his instrument,
　　preparing for the dance.
The tall young man is ready,
　　you can see it in his stance.
Suddenly he spies his lovely lady,
　　entering through the door.
His heart begins to pound,
　　as he crosses the ballroom floor.
Bowing low in greeting,
　　he offers her his hand.
Her eyes return a smile,
　　and the crowd begins to stand.

Many years from now, when the day is done,
　　All will be quiet, and the night begun.
On the fresh night air, if you'll but listen,
　　You will hear the musician.
He plays this special song for you,
　　Because you're in love and that is true.
Together clasp each others hands,
　　and in your memories the crowd still stands.
"The Dance!" the singer calls aloud,
　　Is sung for each new married vow.
No one knows just why or how,
　　but it will continue years from now.

Notes and Acknowledgements

New and Upcoming Books
Author Information

Hope and Holidays
Available Now in Print

Redneck Mustard Seeds
Available Now in Print

Award Winning International Poet

https://www.poetrysoup.com/me/AnnFoster

A. Foster
aka Ann Foster
Annette Foster

Jesus loves YOU!

So what's next?
Looking for another book…
I am now working on a western. It is my first ever. I love trying new things. The desert is were I live, and I truly love it. I plan to take trips to do research in all areas of the western Untied States. The goal is to bring realism and life to the pages I present.

Thank you again for your kind readership and support.
Please like me, follow me, review me, and pass my name along.

Finest regards,

Ann

More Books!

If you received this from a friend, please check back to www.booksbyafoster.com.
All rights reserved, copyright by A. Foster aka Annette Foster
All pictures reserved copyright by CAP

A friend in the Woods by A. Foster
A man crashes in the forest. The friends that come to help him out, may eat him instead? Well, the fact is the animals are Shifters. They are human scientists with genetically altered and upgraded DNA. The alterations allow them to become other forms. They are hiding out to stop the Company from using their Science to create Forever Soldiers. Slaves! But they may get more then they bargained for!
ISBN 9780463330166

Take a chance "Romance" by A. Foster
An evening out, never to forget!
Karen, returns home after over ten years, to the family farm. It was all due to the death of her brother. Tim. She finds herself working through hard emotions from loss and regret to hope and maybe even love? The little town of Last Stop is not very friendly at first, but acceptance of Karen into their lives is quickly evident.
On Valentine's Day, Will the Postman for Last Stop delivers her an invitation, to take a chance. She just can not seem to decline it, no matter how she tries.
ISBN 9781370690107

Babbit the Rabbit by A. Foster
Babbit works for The Boss. He is a klutzy, left-footed, messenger and errand runner, nicknamed "The Rabbit". He accidentally loses the "Protection Book" at the Metro Library while there, with his nephew. The Metro happens to be the "Titanic" of all libraries. The "Book" could put The Boss away for life! In an effort to find the book, Babbit and The

Boss's son Joseph, rope the whole crazy gang into going to the Library to find it, before Officer Maren or anyone else, lay their hands on it.
The adventures that follow are a recipe for havoc, chaos, and disaster.
ISBN 9781370799404

Don't forget to pass this along. Tell a friend.
Free books...
www.booksbyAFoster.com
Freedom to read!

God Bless America!
Keep her strong
and safe
forever.

In Jesus Holy Name.
Amen.

Made in the USA
Columbia, SC
03 April 2023